The Underland Tarot

XIII: Stories of Transformation
XVIII: Stories of Mischief & Mayhem

Underland Arcana Deck One
Underland Arcana Deck Two

UNDERLAND ARCANA DECK TWO

This book is published by Underland Press, which is part of Firebird Creative, LLC (Clackamas, OR).

Second, the Querent lays out the cards . . .

Edited by Mark Teppo
Book Design and Layout by Firebird Creative
Cover art by artbalitskiy/stock.adobe.com

This Underland Press trade edition of the second year of *Underland Arcana* has been released in conjunction with the Hunter's Moon.

Underland Press
www.underlandpress.com

DECK TWO

To H, eternally twined in thorns.

Willoughbuoy

~ *Hermester Barrington*

I suppose the phrase "imaginary friend" will work as well as other. My uncertainty arises because he's not imaginary to *me*—but if you look over my left shoulder, close one eye and squint the other, you might be able to see him, or think that you do.

People have seen a lot of strange things when they do that—a thin tall figure with long fingers in a pale jumpsuit and bat's wings, a girl with rabbit ears in a frock, Dame Helen Mirren, my favorite actress— but most of them see a man in his thirties to fifties at a desk, leaning over a keyboard, scanning through books, scribbling notes, frowning all the while. He stands next to a window through which one can see the tops of trees—pines, most people say—on a golf course. He often supports himself with one hand on a desk—a Craftsman, I think, like my own, but not as well cared for. The light comes in as in a Vermeer painting, at an angle, and, reflected from the papers scattered on his desk, illuminating his face from beneath. Based on descriptions by those who have seen him over the years, he has aged since first he was spotted.

Mind, he's not exactly anyone I would have imagined as my imaginary friend—I would have expected some version of Prometheus, or Coyote, or that girl at the supermarket who shyly flirts with me, but we don't always get to pick our friends, do we? At least not imaginary ones.

He has only appeared directly to me once. At 3:12 AM, precisely—I don't know how I know that, because we don't have any clocks in the house—he opened the door to the bedchamber, and, frowning, stood at the end of the bed and recited that Robert Frost poem about a cord of maple logs burning slowly in the swamp. While I was figuring out how to respond, he knocked over a glass of water on the bedstand and disappeared. Getting out of bed to clean it up, I glanced out the window, and saw the lawn and the lake littered with loose pages, on which I had been writing my poetry, and which I had left on the deck . . . I went out and fetched them, the ones on the lawn I mean. When I looked up, Willoughbuoy was standing in the window, looking down at me, but he was gone by the time I got back upstairs.

I've also seen him in dreams late in the morning, when my bladder awakens me. As I debate whether I want to arise, I recall him before the memory fades—it's 5 AM, but he's already at work on his book, on ideas of progress in the Atlantic world in the 19th century, before he goes off to his day job (he's an archivist at a law firm). He mutters to himself in any number of European languages as he searches through the pages of a book, sometimes more than one at a time. He takes a sip of some soft drink, some knock off version of a much more popular heavily caffeinated citrus soda, the original being my own preferred beverage—and winces as it hits a bad tooth. I sometimes get back to sleep afterwards, but never dream of him again, if I do.

Sometimes he is writing fiction, viewers say, a novel shaped like a Klein bottle about an amateur protozoologist/haiku poet. I've heard this from people who don't know that this description fits me pretty nicely, so perhaps there's something to it.

I first learned about him some thirty years ago. My wife Fayaway and her friend, Mistress Dionaea, were discussing the best way to use magnets, a Leyden jar, and a gyroscope to figure out the exact shape of the earth, when Dionaea stopped, stared past me, and said, "Hermester, there's someone standing behind you, over your left shoulder." Our questions to Dionaea elicited the following information: he was tall and slender, with a full head of thin chestnut hair, a t shirt and jeans, and Birkenstocks. He was holding a chapbook edition of "Bartleby the Scrivener," with illustrations by Barry Moser—our copy, as it turned out, which was missing the next time I looked for it. He was standing in front of a window—the window, in fact, that I have already described. "He wants to tell you that his name is 'Willoughbuoy,'" Dionaea said then, and spelled it out and told me how to pronounce it, which brought to my mind the image of a tall slender lad bending in a breeze I could not feel. Somebody's car alarm went off then, and the vision or whatever it was disappeared.

He has borrowed or stolen a number of our books since then—usually works that would interest him, I suppose. Occasionally I find works on our bookshelves that no one remembers acquiring—*Alice in Wonderland* in the language of the Voynich manuscript; a dismembered copy of *Hopscotch* with the "chapters arranged," a handwritten note reads, "for ease of reading;" a rough draft of *The Da Vinci Code* autographed by Michael Baigent and Richard Leigh. If he is trying to tell me something by stealing my books, or leaving others, I'm not sure what it is.

I've thought about writing his book, tentatively titled *The Millennium is on the Horizon*, for him—he seems to rewrite the same chapters over and over—but maybe a book about time and fugitive progress should be impossible to finish. Someone once said that in order to be happy, you should find a project that you enjoy and which is too big to complete in your lifetime. That being said, it doesn't seem to be working for him.

I can only imagine why he might have been appearing to me over the years. Is he the dross of my realized desires? A reminder of the decades in which I lived a life of drudgery, moving through my life as if befogged? Might he be a sort of *memento mori*, or an admonition to be true to my own self? I had hoped that by writing about him, I would exorcise him, but I having drafted and revised this piece for three nights in a row, he has nonetheless appeared in my dreams on the past three mornings, and has been the focus of my mind's eye as I stumble out of bed and fumble my slippers onto my feet. As has been the case in the past, his image remained in my thoughts until I turned my hand to my pursuits—my haiku, my protozoology, my ficciones—and then, at about the same time that the dew evaporated from the leaves of the sycamores outside the windows, my memory of him faded as I turned to greet the morning sun.

Why Don't We Add a Cozy Little Cabin?

~ Mike Robinson

Finally, after two years and just over a hundred thousand YouTube subscribers, Oliver Young felt comfortable enough to tell people what he really did. Although, when pitched the question in public, he rarely beat Angela to the swing.

"He's today's Bob Ross," she would say, usually leaning with one arm on his shoulder. "He's a one-man art school. Everyone digs his paintings."

Well, that was of course a lie, as heartening for her support as it was grating for its untruth. Like Bob Ross, he did landscapes on his channel—as indicated by the name, *Youngscapes*—though he aimed to add more dynamic variety, even a touch of the surreal. One of his more popular was the Atlantean ruins canvas, with a smoldering Pompeii-style volcano looming in the background. "Deviant" pieces, he sometimes called them. For the most part, his repertoire was forests and streams—quick mental escapes into Mother Nature.

Of course, a wider dragnet catches the delectable and detestable, and the trolls rode in parasitically on the backs of his fans. *Rip-off*, said some of the milder ones. *When you gonna paint some tits or something cmon it aint PBS.* Or those from the art world, so claimed, who with haughty diplomacy weighed in that he was another paint-by-numbers kind of guy—in short, a hack.

But it was no troll or critic that pushed him to the brink, that stripped over twenty pounds from him and reunited him with cigarettes and forced a wedge between him and Angela and remains responsible for his last upload being over six months ago.

It had actually been a fan. A fan who, as Oliver still claims, no less than saved his life.

For now.

☉

As far as Oliver could tell, there was no other reason for it to have started during that episode, his 37th. Or why "it" (and who knew what "it" referred to) chose that canvas.

He'd been tired the night before and that morning and, even with two espressos in him, hadn't prep-sketched anything particularly interesting. Thus, the episode, already a day late for the weekly upload schedule set by his producer (also Angela), was going to be generic filler. Or, as they called it among themselves, a hand-warmer.

"Every once in a while it's good to recalibrate a little," he told the camera at the beginning of the episode. "To brush up on basics, and to appreciate the so-called 'normal' beauty of Nature." Palette in one hand, with the other he emphatically dabbed his brush toward the viewer. "And remember, as always, at the end I'll take a few calls for Q and A."

By then, the ending Q&A segments had grown from occasional to regular, a must for when he did live shows, which he'd been doing more of as viewership grew.

The scene he had in mind was simple: a forested riverbank with lordly Grand Teton-like mountains sawtoothed across the horizon. Snowcapped, of course. Maybe with bulbous clouds sliding over the summits. Like Ross, there was unabashed romance in his subjects, and in the way he approached them. Some used words like sappy or sentimental. 'Borderline schmaltzy' was one that had made him grin. He never thought twice about it, especially as he got older. If art gave you a sense of wonder or nostalgia, or even just that warm-cider-in-your-belly feeling, it was slowly, infinitesimally, diluting the poisons of the world.

For the first twenty-one minutes of his thirty-three-minute episode, nothing unusual happened. He had knifed in most of the evergreens, dabbed in the river and the riverbank and was about two-thirds of the way through the majestic visual sentence of the background mountains.

"You know what," he said. "I like this area. I might want a place to live here. So . . ." He moved down toward a clearing near the riverbank. "Why don't we add a cozy little cabin?"

To anyone watching (except that one fan, of course) the late idea to paint in a cabin appeared just as he intended it: a fun afterthought, a rustic punctuation mark of human habitation that temporarily fulfilled just another of Oliver's regular Thoreau fantasies.

Truth was, he'd no idea why the idea had felt so urgent, why the impulse to add his cozy little cabin had dizzied through him so primally, as if he'd been walking and, glancing down for the first time, realized he was mere feet from a cliff's edge and had to pull back.

Standing behind the lights and the camera, Angela looked concerned. He felt paler.

And though not really indicated by the close-up shot, his hand quivered that much more when laying down the roof and the wood panels and the highlights of the cabin. More detailed work always brought to his fingers the apprehensive tremble of his perfectionism—something which, privately, he hoped his live shows would subdue—but this was a colder, graver tremble.

He painted no doors or windows.

"Okay, there we go," he said, flashing a smile at the camera, then adding his own episode-ending catchphrase: "The world is now that much bigger."

Yes, one painting bigger. One vision bigger. One unit of beauty bigger.

The Q&A segment began. Callers ringing in from all over, so often lifting his spirit with every accent or strange new name, with the knowledge that he was making his mark, defying all borders and merging something of his spirit and imagination with so many others'.

He fielded three calls before taking hers. One concerned paintbrush sizes, another easel brands, another from London asked why it was that he couldn't get the snow right on his own "infernal mountains"?

Then came her call. A Joanne Bell. From Twilight Falls, California.

"Hi Ollie," she said. He noticed Angela's eyes widen at this unexpected show of familiarity. Only certain family members called him Ollie. "I don't have much time, really. But I wanted to make sure I got to you quick and clear—"

"Okay." His brow furrowed.

"I'm very glad you put a cabin in the painting," said this Joanne Bell from California. "And I'll bet you're glad, too."

Coldness rimmed his organs. He swallowed, his eyes narrowed a little and he maintained his smile. In later reviewing the footage, Oliver thought he actually looked pretty composed.

"I always like putting in those details," he said. There was no way he could keep the confusion from his voice, which seemed perfectly reasonable—who wouldn't be confused by the oddball statement?

"The problem is," Joanne continued, "you need to put a cabin in each of your pieces from now on."

"Pardon?"

"I'm a big fan and I don't want to scare you . . ." Joanne's voice seemed to volley between wise, middle-aged throatiness and a flightier youthfulness. There was a faint echo on her end. "But the cabin needs to be there. That's the only thing it'll recognize."

"Joanne, I'm n—"

"Oliver," she said, more forcefully. "It tried to come through you. But you contained it. And it *will* be contained. As long as the cabin is there."

"And what is it, exactly?"

No response, only dull electric click. Oliver shook violently now, a condition only worsened by efforts to suppress it. Some alarming, ambiguous truth rampaged within. His outer demeanor remained puzzled yet polite, no more than a twitchy dance of eyebrows and half-grins.

"Thank you, Joanne of California, for the ring," said Oliver. "I'm so glad you enjoy the show. Let's go to one more caller here . . ."

The last question came from Texas, an older man annoyed that "my palm trees never come out as good as yers." With a chuckle, the caller added, "They always look like dead spiders."

There was no saying when he awoke that night, because he never really fell asleep. Sleep had deserted him, leaving Oliver only with its mocking shadow, that loose dream-state that was more a brief dimming awareness, lit with the flashes of delirious little movies assembled by his tired, thought-wrung mind.

By two AM, Oliver found himself reanimating a motion he'd successfully stifled for almost a decade, but which right then felt eminently natural. He rose, dressed and left his house for the 7-11, on a tunnel-visioned task to buy a pack of Native Spirits.

He smoked one on the way back.

Only when he saw the porch light of his house again did something of his more conscious self, the Oliver of Today, break through the relapsed automaton and realize that he'd forgotten his phone, that even in her sleep Angela had probably sensed the half-empty bed and woken up and flipped out (a little) and would even smell the smoke on him. Not that she was one to talk, having quit her "only do it with the girls" phase less than two years ago.

But the house remained dark and still. From the living room, he heard Angela grunt in her sleep. The darkness was like overgrowth, swallowing an old, abandoned building.

Second unlit cigarette between his lips, Oliver grabbed his sketchbook and pencils and stepped out onto the back patio, where he hunkered down on the couch swing and stared at the night and, with the click of the lighter, blew smoke at it.

His pencil hovered over the blank page. A muscle twitched in his forearm. Here he was alone, at home, surrounded by night shadow yet Oliver felt transported back to those childhood moments of drawing in public, when the act itself exerted its own gravity, pulling in those passing curious eyes eager to glimpse some unfinished creation.

Something now huddled over him.

With his third cigarette, the automaton took over again, and Oliver began sketching. He hadn't done faces in a while, and for good reason—they were never his strong suit. Nevermind portraits of actual people. But a good challenging hand-warmer always kept the dust from accumulating.

He drew Angela, best as he could. Or started to, anyway. Like the cigarette run, the choice had not been totally conscious, but the tug of a familiar current to which he found himself surrendering. Almost too easily.

He'd sketched in the basic framework—the spheres, the rough measuring lines—and had begun the features when some dull click in his brain made him pause, brought him to attention that whatever was coming through him or the pencil was not Angela but a thing with larger eyes and a larger mouth that, like an even more odious version of the impish kid who would pry into his drawing sessions to judge or direct, suggested itself in his every movement.

His trembling increased. His arm had become a wind tunnel amidst a hastening gale.

The cabin.

He wrenched his hand to the lower righthand corner of the page, where he quickly sketched the cabin: same height, some angle, no doors or windows. He couldn't tell if it was exact, of course, and his heart raced thinking that maybe he needed the same materials, the oils, the palette knife, the exact same strokes of the exact same measurements . . .

But, with the cabin crudely finished, all shaded and erect, Oliver's tremble weakened.

The cork in place.

Ash from the burning cigarette in his lips crumbled onto the page and slid off onto his lap. He shut the sketchbook, removed the cigarette and breathed.

Angela stared at him from across the kitchen island, over the steam of her morning coffee. Perched on his stool, Oliver's gaze was mostly sunk in his bowl of soggy cornflakes.

"You believe that weird caller?" she asked.

"It's not about believing. It's . . . feeling. You saw me." He shoved a dripping spoonful into his mouth. "You told me I looked pale toward the end and I told you why."

"Ollie." Angela snorted. "Part of you never crawled out from under the bed. Mostly I find that endearing and I even love that about you. But—"

"Something took hold of me. Even before she called. I've never had a panic attack, I don't think, but I imagine it was on that scale. It was like a voiceless voice and it said, *Stop it it's coming stop it's coming stop—*"

"I know. I get it." Angela set down her coffee and crossed her arms. "All right, now I'm about to sound a little out there, but— what if she put those thoughts in your head? Before calling?"

Oliver studied her. "You mean, like telepathy?"

"Maybe. Or something more, I don't know, technical. Aren't there ways to focus sounds at people now? Like those Americans in Cuba that got sick that weird sound no one else heard."

Oliver shrugged, munched his cereal though he had no appetite. "Nothing about this feels technical. I feel cursed. In some . . . medieval way. And I don't know why. Or what."

Angela leaned forward on the counter. He saw in her eyes a certain caution he realized he'd not seen since their first date. "And what's the deal from here on out?" she said. Her tone bothered him. It was cool, a little exasperated. The tone of a metal-boned businesswoman annoyed that the assembly worker's severed arm might *dare* delay the product. "Do you just paint woodland scenes with cabins? They didn't have cabins in Atlantis. And you can't exactly put cabins in your coral reef pieces. Or . . ." She leaned up, crossed her arms again. With a crack of humanity in her voice again, she said, "You stop the show, and stop painting?"

He bussed his half-finished bowl to the kitchen sink.

"No," he said. "I don't want that."

That afternoon, Oliver shut himself in his studio. He mounted a blank canvas and stared at it. Just days ago, the blankness would thrill and terrify him, in that exalted, sublime way he imagined skiers felt when gazing down an unblemished alpine run. Now the terror had crashed to earth, become a primordial thing that oozed and crawled.

And yet, the urge to paint, to draw, to reproduce himself artistically, had not diminished. It almost seemed to have grown, gaining heat in its own springtime fever. A heightened lust to engage and to spread.

In the righthand corner, he painted a cabin. Same size, same angle. He inhaled.

Exhaled.

In regarding the rest of the canvas, Oliver felt lightened. The unholy terror had lifted away once more to the realm of that sublime thrill-terror. The blankness was his again. And so, brush in hand, he began skating and skipping and swirling across it, becoming both watcher and doer.

He made a costal landscape, pine trees arrayed along a rocky beach, weathered cliffs sloping away into curling, crashing waves. The cabin was clearly not an organic part of it. But—had it freed him? Could he pass it off, in time, as just a quirky signature?

Oliver resented that he was even standing here doing and thinking all this. Why?

What had he done?

Biting his lower lip, he stared at the cabin. Something . . . bulged there, but not physically. There was a stirring that he could almost feel on a distinct, vibrational level.

With a mix of anger, curiosity and a burst of perhaps undue confidence, Oliver grabbed his palette knife, scraped up a sliver of yellow and leaned into the outer wall of the cabin—where, after a brief pause, he added a small, glowing window.

He recoiled a little. Watched. What breath he was holding he released in small, hiccupping sputters. Testing. Yes. Cautious. Reserving some in case—

—what?

Oliver wasn't sure how long he looked at his yellow dab of a window. The edge of his vision clouded over, some timeless fog encroaching on his senses, his seconds.

Eventually, he turned to wipe off the knife and wash the brushes. He almost didn't want to look again. But he did.

A tiny silhouette stared from the window. He could see nothing but the circular head and shoulders. He felt its gaze.

Shaking, he grabbed the palette knife, cut a line of brown and scraped out the window.

Then he hurried out the studio.

That she came from a small city—or large town, as it were—Oliver considered a hopeful sign. She was easy to find. There was only one Joanne Bell in Twilight Falls, California.

It had been a week since he'd set foot in his studio, the days a sludgy tide of Netflix and YouTube binging, solo hikes and smoking (about which Angela said nothing, as if long resigned to the habit's return), all blurred at the edges by a buildup of harried thoughts, willed distractions to outrun deeper thoughts, and the growing itch to paint.

Across social media, Angela made the announcement that *Youngscapes* would be going on hiatus. It was Oliver's idea to make a video of himself saying the same thing, to assuage any concerns he might be sick.

Though he did feel ill.

Less than ten minutes into Google and he had Bell's phone number, the one listed, anyway. He spent several more whiskey-smeared minutes following her name into Facebook, where, again, the Twilight Falls signifier made for an easy trail.

As expected, she was an older woman, maybe early sixties, with gray curls and a melancholic smile. Oliver recognized her banner image as a version of a tropical waterfall grotto he'd presented on Youngscsapes maybe eight months ago. By the looks of it, she was pretty good. A little heavy-handed, but lightness came with practice.

She hadn't updated in over a month, and the top posts all appeared to be from other people.

. . . praying for you . . .

. . . in my thoughts every night . . .

. . . so wrong and so weird . . .

. . . ♥♥♥ *. . .*

He made his way down and found a post from a Diana Bell, blonde and visibly younger: *Thank you for all the support re: Mom. She's still in stable condition. I visit every other day and read to her as the docs think that helps (have heard that too). I think it does but may just be convincing myself. Doug and the kids come w/ me as much as they can. Trevor plays his flute for her.*

Scrolling further, Oliver came across a link to a GoFundMe campaign for "Joanne Bell's Medical Expenses." A foreboding gathered around his mind which he tried to ignore. Diana Bell, presumably her daughter, had also posted a batch of Joanne's paintings—all landscapes, some direct copies or deviations of *Youngscapes* canvases, others more original. Multiple people had "liked" and "loved" and commented on the pictures.

. . . She loved her art. Was getting so good, too! . . .

. . . I remember during a picnic how she had to stop eating and sketch . . .

. . . Hopefully she'll be able to paint again . . .

One comment asked: *She has more recent stuff, right?*

To which Diana had replied: *She does. But I've decided not to post them. She became weirdly obsessed with doing cottages. Kept polluting her pictures with them and I wouldn't be able to say why. That was the first weird thing I noticed (though I didn't realize how crazy it had gotten) and I'm positive it had something to do with her current condition but we're all clueless. MRI and stuff were clean.*

Heart pounding, Oliver scrolled down and saw a post from Diana Bell from just over a month ago.

All friends and family: my mom Joanne is in the hospital. She is in a coma. Hard for me to even type those words. No one is sure what happened. It's a mystery because I know some of you were concerned since she kind of stopped posting here (she always loved posting her art) and truth be told I noticed odd behavior leading up to this but so far doctors aren't sure what caused her coma. They are thinking of transferring her to UCSF.

Only when it reached a certain threshold of bloodletting pain did Oliver realize he was biting his lower lip, and that a thousand muscles in his body were aching and taut. He kept scrolling.

He was both heartened and horrified to stumble across his own face, smiling back at him from what turned out to be the last thing Joanne herself had shared—the 24th episode of *Youngscapes.*

Smoking and pacing his backyard, Oliver waited four rings before she picked up.

"Mr. Young?"

"Call me Oliver," he said. "Or Ollie."

"Okay." Diana Bell sounded curt, guarded. Understandable. He was used to this demeanor now. Angela had affected it every day since they'd pre-empted the show.

"I appreciate you talking to me," he said.

"It's not big deal. You were one of Mom's favorite artists. Or channels, I guess. Thank you again for the kind words."

"Sure." The meat of the discussion, the very reason why they were on the phone together, grew thick and smoky and vortex-like between them. "So, I'm assuming you watched the episode I sent you?"

"I did." There was a shudder-breathed pause. "I don't know what to tell you. It certainly sounds exactly like my mom. Even though . . ."

Even though, Oliver's brain finished, she was in a coma by then.

"Something was wrong with her, leading up to it all," said Diana. "I feel cheated of closure, of any kind of explanation. What particularly disturbed me about what . . . 'she' said, I guess, to you was that she herself had started painting—"

"Cottages, right?"

"Uh huh. She was sort of a closet Thomas Kinkade fan. She liked nature, but also her quaint comforts. She even talked of retiring to some nice mountain cottage around here, near the redwoods somewhere. So she loved to paint her fantasy." Diana signed, a long sigh that contained the last few weeks. "And I thought she was getting obsessed with it. She would always have a cottage in her art, even if it didn't make sense. And she started adding more. Two, three. I didn't really understand at the time how crazy it got."

Flicking ash from his cigarette, Oliver watched the embers spark out and fade in the wet grass. "What do you mean, 'crazy'?"

Another pause. Oliver thought he could hear the hum of her hesitation.

"It'd be easier if I just showed you," Diana said. "Mind if I send you a few photos?"

His stomach tightened. "No, go ahead."

He put the phone on speaker and watched the screen, waiting, dragging long and slow on the cigarette, the smoke obscuring his vision and he thought how that might be good and that he ought to just hang up and even turn off the phone and put it away for now and then forever.

A text arrived. Then another.

And another.

He drew in a mouthful of smoke and held it as he opened the first text. It contained a picture of a canvas leaning against a wall—high cliffs, distant snowy peaks, pine trees.

And three identical cottages, in a row.

The second picture: a marshland piece, with six cottages arrayed across the bank.

Third picture: three open sketchbooks, littered with the same cottage, some in pencil, others ink, one in charcoal.

Fourth picture: no canvas, no sketchbook. Just a shot of a bedroom, its partially empty bookshelves, a dresser and a lone mattress and a glowing lamp throwing light on—

The walls. Where the cottage was everywhere. Manic wallpaper put up one repeating image at a time. The room felt like a braiding of determination and despair, the sweat-stride of prey running from pursuing jaws but deep down knowing the inevitable. It had the futility of someone trying to plug up every pore on their body, lest something get in.

But there were too many pores.

The weeks became months. Oliver increasingly felt like he was holding back a train. The desire to paint, to sketch, to doodle, to release something, anything, thickened in his veins, emotional plaque that even seemed to assimilate other more bodily desires—to the point that all of him became just a vessel for the passage of breath and the swelling press of this drive.

Though they had a decent amount of money in the bank, Angela insisted they both get "at least part-time jobs, if you want to piss away all we've built." By the third month, the fight had drained from Oliver, and he no longer responded to such comments.

He actually came to appreciate the distraction of looking for work. Though he took walks a couple times a day, which became multiple times a day, he had begun to feel useless and imprisoned. Funny, too, since, by the metric of sheer hours, he'd spent more time in his home when doing *Youngscapes*. But he had escapes then: magic brush rides into beautiful, fantastical Elsewheres that fulfilled him. Regular liaisons with his muse.

Surprisingly, he and Angela had more frequent sex. It was release, some kind, anyway, but the mood was different—disconnected and temperamental.

It was normally sometime in the post-coital hour, with the sweat cooling and aches subsiding, that Angela brought up nostalgia for *Youngscapes* and her desire to bring it back. "I still go through the socials," she said. "You got lots of fans waiting for you."

Oliver landed a part-time job at Hartmann's Market, two districts over. Mildly concerned about being recognized, even though it had only happened once, he considered asking that they not put him on cashier duty, yet he kept quiet.

A little over a week into the new job, Oliver burst from bed, consumed with the dream that had visited him. He'd been painting, as free and unencumbered as he'd been since that first time in his parents' garage when he was five. The endeavor had seemed wildly, dangerously unhinged, creations run amuck, world after vivid world.

"The cabin," he muttered half-consciously. He had to tame all the creation, otherwise it might slip through. Spill out.

He had managed to stumble down most of the hallway when the first bit of awareness struck him.

Where are you going?

By the time he'd woken up, he found himself poised over the kitchen island, elbows on the cold tile and pencil in his hand, quivering above a blank notepad. It took another few lugubrious seconds to convince himself he'd not actually drawn or painted anything. At that point, he'd done nothing in nearly half a year.

The clock read 3:36 AM. He didn't sleep that night, and called in sick to work the next day.

That afternoon, he received a call from Hartmann's manager, a pockmarked guy named Blake who Oliver wasn't sure was younger than he, and didn't want to find out.

"Hey Oliver," Blake said. "Sorry, I know you're under the weather, but I just found out about your YouTube channel. Holy cow! Amazin'!"

He frowned, tried to keep his voice lighthearted. "Who spilled the beans?"

"A customer. Regular. She recognized you, asked if it was you."

"It's me. I guess."

"Amazin'! Listen, I won't bother you further, but given this new info, how would you like to do some in-store murals for us? Same pay. But it would be your main focus. No stocking, no cash registers, nothing. For as long as it takes."

Oliver bit his lower lip. "Could I do what I wanted?"

"Well, within reason, sure. Why don't you and I chat about it tomorrow, during lunch?"

Closing his eyes, Oliver said, "Yeah. Um, sure."

"Amazin'!" said Blake. "See you then."

He dreaded sleep that night, but was pleasantly surprised to be granted five hours' worth. Few dreams came to him, at least those he remembered, though on waking around dawn Oliver had the vague impression of light flares in darkness, like muzzle-flashes across some deeper trench in his mind, and some thunderous thing strengthening.

Approaching.

"There's our resident arteest!" Blake said, arms outspread as he leaned back almost dangerously in his desk chair. Oliver stood in the doorway of the man's office. "Sit down. Let's rap."

Oliver sat on the edge of the office's only other chair.

"First things first," said Blake. Grinning with awareness of his own goofy positivity, he pushed a blank paper and pen over to Oliver. "I'm sorry to be like this, but you gotta give me a little sketch, and sign it. So I can retire well-off."

Taking the pen in hand, Oliver felt the swell of six months of pent-up expression, every urge that had come to him but had not left, forced into slumber but now stirring awake in his bones at this smallest and silliest of requests.

"Doodle whatever you want," Blake said. "So long as you sign it."

"Okay." Oliver touched pen to paper. "How about, um, a little cabin?"

Blake blinked. "Like in the woods? Sure. Whatever."

Oliver drew the cabin. Though rusty, his muscles had not forgotten their motion. Some small pressure lifted, but it was like a passage in fog, quick to be swallowed once more. His hand hovered over the paper.

Blake glanced over. "Did you sign it?"

His hand trembled. "I will."

"The world is that much bigger now," Blake said. "That's what you always say, right?"

Oliver hesitated.

"You okay, man? You look kinda pale. Still sick?"

With the best grin he could muster, Oliver said, "Let me add one more."

The Witches' Parliament

~ *Jordan Taylor*

"England is governed not by logic but by parliament."
~ Benjamin Disraeli

In a dark, secret wood stood a dark, secret house. The house was made of wood shingles and good English stone, with many rounded towers and cupolas and dull silver windows, and a wide, wrap-around porch on which no one would ever take lemonade. There was no garden, no drive, nor even a narrow path, its stone foundations rising from the dirt and the moss and the twisted roots as if it were a mushroom grown from the forest floor. On the peeling front door hung a knocker in the shape of an owl with dull citrine eyes, holding a twisted branch in its hooked beak.

The knotted trunks of oak and ash and thorn trees pressed close round the house on all sides, their branches overhanging the peaked eaves. No bit of sky showed its face in that wood. A chill wind rattled the branches and sent brown leaves dancing across the wide, bare porch. In England it was May. In the wood, it was whatever month the witches felt it should be.

A candle flared to life in the window of an upper story.

Owls swooped in and out of the house's rounded attic windows, circling the towers and perching on branches to await their turn to enter: small tawny owls and little gray owls with ruffled feathers, great horned owls with fierce hooked beaks, and even a few snowy owls with dark markings on their chests and wings, like the curling paper bark of a birch tree.

The owls disappeared into the dark, secret house in an endless stream, a great flock of owls, which is not called a flock at all, but a *parliament.*

In the downstairs of the house, a great many lights were lit all at once.

The inside of the house was full of light, now, and of witches, and owls. As each owl alighted on the upper landing of the grand, sweeping staircase it shivered into the form of witch—a woman young, or old, or somewhere in-between; beautiful, or ugly, or plain; fat or slim, dark or fair, sweet-tempered or passionate—so many women it seemed impossible that such a house, filled as it already was with patterned wallpaper and rich carpets and carved mantlepieces and over-stuffed furniture and candles and teacups and trinkets, could hold them all. Perhaps the house was larger inside than out, or perhaps the women-who-were-owls and the owls-who-were-women were actually very small, no bigger than the owls they'd been.

In any case, all were gathered in the front parlor now, talking over one another and shouting across their raised cups of tea. A fire crackled merrily in the hearth. A few younger witches shoved one another in a corner over who should get the last comfortable seat. The Lady Zenobia arched her white eyebrows and tapped her silver teaspoon against her bone china cup.

The room went quite as a grave.

"My sisters," the Lady Zenobia said, "You all know why our Parliament has gathered. We have been tracking this development for the better part of a year. I will open the debate." She paused to draw in a breath. "Should we interfere yet again?"

In most parliaments, speeches are punctuated by the warm and rousing call of "My brothers!" In the witches' parliament, one said "My sisters!" instead.

The Lady Zenobia raised her teacup to her lips as the room erupted into chaos around her. Though her long, thick hair was as white as bleached bone, her face was firm and unlined, her body beneath her rustling silk dress still that of a strong young woman.

"How dare he!"

"These *men*!"

"They think they can just take, and take, that their ambitions count for everything and ours for nothing—"

"After all our work! Wives made barren!"

"Princesses and uncles killed!"

"And one assassination diverted already!"

"She is *ours*!" a fierce witch proclaimed, and the cry was taken up round the room. "Ours, ours!"

"And so we will interfere on her behalf again," a decisive young witch spoke up. Her dark eyes flashed. "Or set our kind back another hundred years!"

"No more! This has gone far enough!" an old crone shrieked from the back. "We have broken our first rule! The first vow that we swore! *Do. Not. Interfere!*"

The Lady Zenobia cleared her throat.

The din subsided.

"Do not interfere' is our *second* vow, Lady Anne," a round, middle-aged witch said tartly in the ensuing silence. "The first is 'Do no evil."

Lady Anne snorted and waved her hand in front of her face.

"We will take a vote, then," the Lady Zenobia said when the two had finished. "Those who would go back to the old ways, those who would watch, and wait?"

"And those opposed?"

"Then we will need to be closer than this." The Lady Zenobia waved her hand. "Green Park, I think."

In the depths of night, when even the theaters were closed, when the only traffic in London's streets were the most well-heeled gentlemen and ladies passing through on their way home from parties, and the most down-at-the-heels men and women passing through on their way to a penny-worth of coffee and bread from a stall before the workday began, Young England gathered in Simpson's cigar divan.

Simpson's was a typical lounge for wealthy gentlemen—a comfortable drawing room all of leather couches and polished wood and green-shaded gas lamps, above the cigar shop of the same name, on the Strand. Pop your head in on this night, and you'd be forgiven for thinking that Young England was a being made of cigar smoke and fog.

But there were three beings moving within that obscuring smoke, that secret fog, three beings in impeccable eveningwear with their hats set on their knees, cigars held languidly in their long fingers, cups of coffee on tables and trays. They had been through many cups of coffee, and their cigars had almost burnt down to stubs.

On a low, round table, in the center of the room, lay a brace of pistols, their barrels and stocks chased with silver scrolls. They shone wickedly in the light of the flickering fire in the hearth. None of the beings looked at them.

The pistols had been procured from a pawnbroker and money-lender in Covent Garden. This was meant to make them untraceable. None of the fashionable beings had thought to choose a more utilitarian pair.

"What England needs is a hero," the being with the mustache was saying. He stubbed his cigar out on the nearest tabletop, a horrid display of bad manners. "A King Arthur, to guide us through this Industrial mess, to lead and inspire the populace. Instead we're given a weak puppet, first of that philandering Whig," grunts heard round the room, "And then of a blasted German!"

"Yes," a dark being in the corner drawled from the depths of a leather armchair. His eyes flared from the midst of the cloud of cigar smoke which obscured his face. "Because the last Arthur we had did so well. After his disastrous run as Prime Minister, Lord Wellington is still cowering behind iron curtains in the depths of Apsley House." He slurped at his coffee with disgust.

"Peace, John, Dizzy," an elegant being with dark muttonchops spoke. "We are all in agreement here. Though I beg you, Dizzy, before you go any further, to remember the first attempt."

Had the beings not been gentlemen, they might have shuddered. The first man to attempt what they now spoke of had not only mysteriously failed, but been sent to Bedlam in perpetuity.

"Good god, George, must you bring that up again? The first attempt failed, so what?" the being called John blustered. "We are better men." He raised his eyebrows meaningfully.

Dizzy rolled his eyes as he puffed on his cigar. He was young, with the piercing eyes of a satirist. "I have told you both: I have seen the future that awaits England if we do not act. It is of this that I am afraid, not of our task. That I will gladly shoulder on my own, and leave the two of you out of it."

The other men waited as Dizzy took a small notebook out of his breast pocket to scribble the lines down: *I have seen the future . . . That I will gladly shoulder . . .*

"Seriously, Dizzy," George flung down his coffee cup in exasperation as the notebook and pencil were replaced, "No one knows what you mean when you speak like that—"

But John pounded his fist on the table, drowning George out. "Well said! If a man wants a thing done properly, then he must do it himself."

"I never heard you volunteer," Dizzy drawled, though his eyes were hard. He wrinkled his nose and gave a droll curl of his lip. "I suppose the action will necessitate some sort of uncouth *disguise*. I will have to visit Petticoat Lane tomorrow. What an *adventure*." He flicked a speck of ash from his trouser leg, rearranged the fabric so that the seam was a perfect straight line down his calf.

George gave him a stricken look. "I beg of you, for the last time, reconsider. Let John and I draw upon our fathers' funds, or use some of Mary Anne's—your debts are considerable, I know, but surely with her income you needn't do this yourself—"

"No," Dizzy's eyes flared. "I will not have her—or you—involved." John folded his hands and said nothing.

"Think of your place in Parliament," George pleaded, the delicate lines of his face drawn tight. "You are the greatest influence we have. If caught, you will be arrested and tried. You will ruin your reputation, your ambitions, your dreams..."

Dizzy laughed, a quick bark of a sound. "My reputation is ruined already. And as for my dreams –"

"When you see the future," George tried, "Do you see no role for yourself?"

Dizzy rose from his chair, his face set. He stubbed out his cigar in a glass ashtray and flipped his silk hat onto his head before shrugging on his overcoat. He picked the pistols up from the table, testing their weight, and suddenly the two other beings could not look at him.

"*Ambition's debt must be paid*," he said, and he plunged the pistols deep into his overcoat pockets.

In the bright, secret house in the dark, secret wood, somewhere in Green Park, a witch turned over a card. She wore black velvet, tightly corseted, and a diamond brooch sparkled on her right shoulder. Curls of dark hair, touched with gray, spilled over the left. She was called Lady Grace.

Her lace cuffs trailed across the tarot spread, her long fingernails tapping the densely patterned backs of the cards. She sat at the head of the house's enormous dining table, the Lady Zenobia at her side. The other witches crowded around wherever they could fit, leaning into the heat of the candelabras which lined the polished tabletop. This was made easier by the fact that a small number of them were now missing.

"Seven of swords," Lady Grace said solemnly.

"Secrets," the witches all murmured. "Occult knowledge?"

"No, no," one scoffed. "It's the weapons in his pockets."

Lady Grace set the card aside with a flick of her wrist, and turned over the one which had been hidden behind it. The witches all gasped.

"Death."

Dizzy walked out of Simpson's and into the London night, his head still swimming with cigar smoke and dreams. Though it was early May, there was a damp chill to the air, and the fog clung to the cobbled streets. The air stank of factory smoke and sewage and the sea, even here. He passed down the brightly-lit Strand and through vast, empty Trafalgar Square, his feet unconsciously directing him towards home and Mayfair.

His plan had been set for weeks; he'd only been waiting for John to procure the pistols and shot. Tomorrow afternoon, during her weekly Sunday drive along Pall-Mall in her open carriage, he would be waiting in the crowd, in disguise. As she passed him, he would step forward, and then—

He shook his head, dodging across the intersection with Haymarket Street. Then all he had foreseen would be averted.

It had been Dizzy's grandfather, for whom he was named, whom had introduced him to the Kabbalah. Though Dizzy's own father had baptized his entire family when Dizzy was twelve—had gone so far as to change their last name—his grandfather had wished to ensure that some wisdom, some traditions of their ancestors, survived.

Often Dizzy wished he had chosen someone else.

Unbidden came the image of his laughing Mary Anne: her chestnut curls, her pert mouth, her mirth-filled eyes.

But no, there was no reason for him to hesitate, none at all; his dreams had come to naught—his novels read by the masses but discounted by the critics and upper classes, his first speech to Parliament disastrous. Even Mary Anne—she well knew that his reasons in marrying her were mercenary. How, then, could she love him now?

The pistols in his pockets seemed to weigh more than they should, and he shuffled to a stop in the center of the street, his hands pressed to his eyes. Carriages and carts clattered around him. Drivers called out.

He would remain on the Back Bench his entire life, until he died, a creature of contempt.

"*Hath not a Jew eyes?*" he murmured to himself.

In the bright, secret house, the witches whispered amongst themselves, eyeing the overturned card.

"It is reversed," the Lady Zenobia said, unperturbed, and the fearful whispers changed to surprise.

"Rebirth?

Lady Grace turned over the next card, and this time the witches nodded. "There he is."

"The Hierophant. The high priest."

"Also reversed," one pointed out.

"Under different circumstances . . ." Lady Grace tapped the card.

"From what we have learned, he could be useful, no doubt," Lady Anne said.

In the witch's deck, the Hierophant was represented by a raven captured mid-flight, a rod held in his beak.

The young witch who'd been so set on their interference, who was called Lady Flora, reached out to touch the image on the card with one finger. "I've always wondered what the rod is meant to be," she laughed. "Lately it's looked almost like a nib pen!"

"*Shush*," Lady Anne said, and Lady Grace turned over the next card in her spread.

"The Queen of Wands." The witches exchanged knowing looks.

And, "The Two of Swords."

"Opposing forces."

"A clash between two great powers," the Lady Zenobia said.

Dizzy stood on the gently-lit path through Green Park, gulping breaths of the fresher cool air. He could not quite remember how he had gotten there—the park was not technically on his way home—though he did remember a wish to delay his homecoming, to clear his mind. A gentle breeze sent flower petals and leaves and scraps of rubbish dancing towards him.

His friends had spoken in terms of party affiliation, of puppets and leaders of men; while in his head churned the factories that splintered England's landscape and dined on the peasantry, the flies swarming the silent huts of India, the rooms of drugged sleepers in China.

And crouching at the center of England's destruction, like a dark, squat spider: the widow queen, her clinging web ensnaring the world.

He slipped his hands into his overcoat pockets, curled his fingers around the triggers of his pistols.

Soon he was stumbling in the darkness beneath the park's eaves, cursing the Select Committee for Urban Planning. Somewhere on the path behind him the widely-spaced gas lamps had run out, but he was no longer exactly sure where.

The path, too, had dwindled under his feet, to no more than a dirt foot-path. He could recall nowhere like this in Green Park.

A rush of air, past his left ear. He turned, drawing a gun and swinging it round. A glint of moonlight caught the silver-chased barrel, reflected from a pair of round, glowing eyes in the branches above him.

Coo hoooo.

Dizzy lowered his arm, his body trembling.

It was only an owl.

"The Nine of Swords," Lady Grace said. The light of the candela-bras flickered over her still face.

"Dark dreams. Fear."

"The Two of Wands."

"He thinks he has made up his mind." The witches laughed.

"The Eight of Swords." Lady Grace smiled. "At last."

"He's entered our wood."

Dizzy crashed through piles of dead leaves, dodged around the ancient trunks of oak and ash and thorn trees, tripping over their twisted roots. The path through the dark wood—for Green Park this no longer was, could not be—had long since run out.

It should be May, he knew it was May, and yet the branches of the trees were all bare, a cold autumn wind shaking them. Owls swooped through the spaces between them, their eyes points of fire in the night, their calls climbing up his spine.

There was some magic at work here, the feeling of it set his teeth on edge—a magic that was not his.

An owl dived at him, knocking his hat from his head.

Panting, he ran on.

In the witches' House of Parliament, Lady Grace turned over the ninth card.

A Grecian woman, a blindfold around her eyes, held a pair of scales in one hand. Lady Grace's face lit with triumph. She reached for the final card in her spread.

"Shhh!" the Lady Zenobia hissed. "Did you hear that?"

The witches froze, Lady Grace's fingers hovering over the last unturned card.

Three loud raps, from the owl-shaped knocker on their house's front door.

The dining room was full of women.

After Dizzy's mad dash through the woods, it was brilliantly lit and suffocatingly hot, the walls papered in an absurdly feminine rose chintz. There were cards scattered across the vast tabletop, candelabras dripping wax, chairs crowded into every spare space. A needlepoint sampler hung on one wall.

"Pay Your Debts," it read, in an intricate gothic script.

Dizzy lingered in the doorway, his heart pounding under what seemed to be one hundred frank and unwavering gazes. He could feel his perfectly starched linen shirt sticking to his skin with sweat. The Lady Zenobia smiled at him as she swept through the maze of chairs to the head of the table.

It had been she whom had responded to his pounding fist on the front door. Three owls had swept into the impossible house behind him, carried on a gust of wind and a flurry of dead leaves. They'd alighted on the parquet floor, preening their ruffled feathers with tiny hooked beaks, while Dizzy struggled to catch his breath.

There had been acorns and insects and spiders' webs in his tousled hair and overcoat. Mud caked his buffed shoes and trouser cuffs. He looked up as the Lady Zenobia shut the door, running his hands through his hair and shaking out his clothes, and his grunt of disgust caught in his throat.

Where the three owls had been stood three young women, their hands folded demurely in front of their skirts.

"Welcome, Mr. D'Israeli," the Lady Zenobia said. She was dressed as a wealthy gentlewoman, and yet, as she turned towards him, her long hair swung loose behind her back like a child's.

Dizzy winced at the mispronunciation. "Disraeli," Dizzy had corrected her, "Please. Mr. Benjamin Disraeli, madam."

"I beg your pardon," he'd called as she led him from the hall, "But how do you know me? Why have you brought me here? And who— Where—" He'd faltered, and she'd paused before the set of glass doors which led to the dining room and turned back to him with a smile, the sort of smile a man could break himself on.

"We have been watching you, Mr. Benjamin Disraeli," she'd said. "We know all about you. Your family history, your deepest desires, your motives . . ."

Dizzy's breath hitched, and the two pistols pressed into his ribcage. "My motives?" he asked. And, in a hoarse gasp: "You work for Her Majesty?" His head spun with the implications.

The woman laughed at him, a deep sound like a funeral bell. "Of course not, Mr. Disraeli. We work for ourselves. I am called the Lady Zenobia," she turned and shoved open the pair of glass doors, "And this is my Parliament."

It was then that he had frozen under the intent gaze of a hundred pairs of eyes.

Her voice, from behind him, was teasing. "We are witches, Mr. Disraeli."

The Lady Zenobia's seat at the head of the table was like a throne, higher than those around her, the back carved into three spiraling points. As she sat, Dizzy's perception of the room shifted subtly to reflect a judge and jury, with himself standing in the place of the accused. He reached for his hat, found it gone, and stuffed his hands into his overcoat pockets.

"I hope I am not expected to make a speech," he quipped. "If this parliament has any concourse with mine, you'll know that I am hopeless in that regard." The room remained stonily silent, save for the collective breathing of one hundred or more women.

The Lady Zenobia arched her eyebrows. "Turn out your pockets, Mr. Disraeli."

Dizzy squared his shoulders, his dark eyes flashing defiantly. He laid the pair of pistols on the table, amongst the cards, where they gleamed smugly in the brilliant light. His skin went cold as he took note of the image of blind Justice, her scales held high in one hand. The women exchanged glances, murmuring and shifting in their seats.

"Benjamin Disraeli," the Lady Zenobia said, her eyes hard, "You stand accused of plotting to commit high treason to kill the queen, Alexandrina Victoria I, God save her. How do you plead?"

"You have not seen what I have seen!" Dizzy thundered, and his anguished face swept back and forth across the room. "Swaths of dead—here, round the world—the loss of England's very way of life!"

The Lady Zenobia's eyes glinted. "And for this you would commit murder? The murder of your queen?"

Dizzy paused. The fire swept from his eyes, so that he seemed to shrink before the women's faces. "No," he admitted, pressing his palms to his eyes. "From the moment I took up the pistols, I've known that I could not." He shook his bowed head. "The thought of it was driving me mad."

"A convenient end," the Lady Zenobia mused, "Saving England from its fate," and Dizzy looked up at her in surprise.

She shook her head. "You say that England's way of life will be lost." Her voice rose, and she spread her arms wide. "I say, let England lose it! The world of men is passing—let it pass!" The women surrounding her shouted out in agreement.

"You say that you can see the future," the witch who sat at the Lady Zenobia's side spoke up. "Have you seen this?" She leaned towards him, over the table, and a diamond flashed on her shoulder. "Two decades from now, when her husband dies, Victoria will mourn for the better part of a century, but she will never marry again. Do you understand? She will reign solo for the rest of her life!"

"The widow queen." Dizzy stared at her. "But she will plunge the world into darkness."

"In all darkness," the Lady Zenobia said, "Is a glimmer of light." She seemed to have grown taller, her eyes sharp and bright as jewels, her voice filling the room, and Dizzy took a surprised step back, hitting the cooler glass of the door.

A young witch with dark eyes stood up. "A decade from now, a woman will write that women have been excluded from every aspect of government but the highest, the regal, at which Victoria succeeds."

Women around the room murmured in agreement. "She is the starting point, the lynch-pin," their voices echoed. "You would take that away from us?"

Dizzy stretched his hands out to them. "If you have seen all this, then you must understand! The Kabbalah has shown me these things for a reason—a great war which will cover the world in yellow clouds of gas." The witches were shaking their heads, "Trenches that split the countryside like arteries of black blood." He stepped forward, trembling, willing them to understand. "And all because of her! I see it constantly, awake and in my dreams. If I am not strong enough to stop it, you must be!"

"And all because of her," the Lady Zenobia repeated thoughtfully. She shook her head, and Dizzy's heart sank. "We will not be silenced. We will not give her up. But she will make mistakes, yes. Bad decisions. War. Mankind will tear itself apart," her eyes glittered. "That is what mankind does."

"She will need to be balanced," the witch in the diamond brooch said.

"A Prime Minister from the opposing party, perhaps?" the young witch spoke up. "A man."

"Her opposite," another said, "Creative and empathetic, with a quick wit."

"Someone far-seeing." The Lady Zenobia smiled wryly.

"Someone to check her."

"As she will check him."

Dizzy clutched the edge of the tabletop, a howling wind sweeping through his mind. He must have missed something. Surely, they could not mean . . .Would such a solution even work?

The Lady Zenobia stood up from her place at the head of the table and came towards him. "We will not let you wriggle out of your destiny so easily, you see?" She held out her hand, and one of the younger girls put a branch of willow in her palm.

"You will leave the pistols here," she said, as she paused to stand before him. "If you agree to this, I must take the memories and the knowledge from you as well. And from your friends." She raised the willow wand, her long fingers loose. "The Kabbalah may show you other things, but it will never again show you this."

Dizzy looked into her eyes, a blue as cold and remote as the stars. He suddenly felt wrung out, exhausted, his horror and his anguish gone. Impossibly, hope was rising in his breast. This was what he had dreamt of, a dream kept secret from all, even Mary Anne.

No middle-class Jew had ever been made Prime Minister.

The Lady Zenobia smiled as if reading his thoughts. "It will be no small task. But you will not shoulder it alone. We can promise you that." The witches nodded behind her.

"Yes," Dizzy said, and he bowed his head and knelt.

"*You will find friends in life,*" the Lady Zenobia spoke, and her voice once again filled the room as she tapped each of his shoulders with the willow wand. "*And they will be women.*"

Behind them, from her seat at the table, Lady Flora nudged the pair of pistols aside to surreptitiously turn over the final tarot card.

It was The Empress.

Dizzy stood in the middle of the Queen's Walk beneath the eaves of Green Park's rustling trees. The gas lamps shown around him, and overhead, the night sky was lightening to gray. He thrust his hands into his overcoat pockets against the chill in the wind, and for a moment he was surprised to find them empty.

He was sure he'd been carrying something—something heavy—but what?

He riffled through his other pockets, pulling out his notebook. He flipped to the latest page.

"It is not the task itself I fear, for I will not shoulder it alone," he read.

Where had he heard that? He shrugged and replaced the notebook.

There was no hat on his head. He must have misplaced it some-where in the course of the night, but where?

Where had he been?

The only thing he could remember was a brass doorknocker, shaped like an owl, a willow branch held in its beak. Which of his friends' houses could that be?

He shook his head in confusion. He must have been very, very drunk.

He pushed his hands deeper into his pockets and set out for Mayfair, whistling one of his favorite drinking songs. Perhaps it was not too early to come across a flower seller in the streets. Mary Anne would be waiting for him, and she would be worried.

The Brief Aeronauts

~ Charles Wilkinson

The haunted lawn: not be photographed; its full condition only half-glimpsed, even by the imagination; a hint of mist; what rises from the bone-broth; a ghost in the ground; some things eat the grass.

At the end of a dirt track, always muddy, except for three days at the height of summer, it's the house you see first; gray stucco over pale red brickwork that shows through in patches: grazed flesh and sickening skin. A wooden door pillaged four centuries ago from a slighted castle three miles up the road. The curved arch over the lintel, a later addition, and a pitched roof, slates missing, the worst holes patched with blue tarpaulin. Diamond-paned windows, a few smashed. On the far side, the lawn stretching out beneath the hill is frayed. Hogweed and ferns thrive in the flowerbeds.

All who live in the parish know the house is Hexter Hall, the name too grandiose for a yeoman's cottage hiding beneath a late Victorian facade. You will not be invited inside, and neither will I. So let's enter with the fumes from the log fire. A tall thin man who comes from a long line of tall thin men lies on a sofa. He is coughing, possibly because of the smoke that hangs across the room like lace; but his chest is congenitally weak. Conceivably he was wheezing and spluttering before the match was lit.

On the far side of the room, next to the only window, not so dirty as to exclude rather than admit light, a middle-aged man in a blue blazer sits on a Windsor chair. He brings with him a whiff of sea salt and polished brass. A member of a yacht club, this is what you imagine. I'm unconvinced, for Hexter Hall is far from the coast. The man opens a brown leather briefcase and produces two glossy magazines devoted to aviation and aeronautical matters.

"With our compliments," says the man, whose name you are now told is Justin Buckey. "We're so grateful you've agreed to be interviewed. In addition to your fee you'll be given three complimentary copies of the issue in which our conversation appears."

As he moves to place the magazines on a low table next to the sofa, something invisible touches his face. A soft irritation over the eyes. A spider's web? He brushes it away; then looks at his hand. No silk on the palm.

"You'll stay the night, of course," replies Ned Hexter, not reaching out for a magazine "We're very quiet here as a rule. Imogen will be delighted to have company at supper. Our son's coming back from London. But not till tomorrow."

Hexter is dressed in a dung-beetle-brown corduroy suit and a moleskin waistcoat. His sandals, worn over thick green socks, are propped on the armrest at the far end of the sofa. His head is supported by a threadbare velvet cushion; his long thin face, crowned by white hair that might once have been red, is pale and dominated by the kind of straight nose seen in paintings of medieval monarchs. The mouth beneath: pale rose pink and pursed. I wonder if you've met anyone like Hexter? Justin Buckey has not.

It's humid outside. How many degrees warmer than Hexter Hall, which has no central heating? Not an inkling this afternoon that the lawn is inhabited. We cannot hear the worms underneath or the moan of the trapped ghost. The hedge at the bottom of the garden is rust-brown; killed three years ago by frost. I have a good view of the back of Hexter Hall, one I'm willing to share with you. Most of the stucco has long since fallen off, exposing shoddy brickwork and beams that no one has bothered to paint black. On the ground floor, there is a sash window with several clean panes. The roof tiles are no longer visible beneath the moss. An unstable chimney stack is pointed with nothing stronger than grass. You ask when we can make our way over the weed-riddled lawn and then peer through the window. If we can no longer listen in, at least we can watch them. You follow me as I drift over to the window. The dark brown furniture is too large for the room; the pictures in sumptuously carved and gilded frames must once have hung on far higher walls. They have the merit of concealing the damp. Ned Hexter has risen from the sofa and is warming the back of his long legs by the log fire, which has ceased smoking. Justin Buckey still sits in the Windsor chair. He has been writing in a notebook. What are they talking about? you ask. It is time to inveigle ourselves through a crack in the glass.

Ned Hexter has been speaking mainly of his family history and helicopters, I reply; I thought to spare you the former; much of it is tedious. Now we will hear them plainly.

"I dream of it every night, falling out of the sky in flames," says Hexter.

"There were no survivors."

How could there have been? On impact, it crumpled like an insect. Anyone who hadn't already been asphyxiated or burnt to death would have died as soon as it hit the ground."

"And the helicopter's design?" Buckey begins carefully. "Do you feel . . . well, later some your ideas were adapted with great success."

For a long time, Hexter stares straight ahead. Is he thinking of the men who died or his failure to take out a patent? It is hard to tell, but from our position just inside the room all we can see is the harrowing grief that has condensed his flesh till the skin is taut across his bones. He nods and replies so softly as to be barely audible: "It was a beautiful machine. Beautiful things are often dangerous." He moves away from the fire. "But you must be hungry. I eat very little these days. But there is cake . . . or something . . . in the kitchen. You'll take a cup of tea, at the very least?"

"Yes, tea will be welcome. And whatever else is most convenient."

"I'm afraid that Imogen won't be able to join us. I still have hopes that she may be up to a little supper."

"Your wife. Is she ill?"

Hexter pauses for a moment, as if considering a fine point of law. "Let us say she has changed greatly during these past few months."

"Nor herself?"

"Quite! Now if you'll excuse me."

What you cannot know, and neither Ned nor Justin could be aware of, is that Adrian Hexter, heir to Hexter Hall, its damp rooms, the half-dead lawn and colony of spiders, is at this moment making his way along the road. It will be minutes before he reaches the dirt track. There is no interest in seeing Ned search the cupboards for a cake tin or watching him brew tea in a chipped brown pot; neither is observing Buckey turning the pages of his leather- bound note-book of any significance. From a window over the porch we will witness Adrian's approach.

What should we discuss while we wait? You wish to learn more about Ned Hexter. Why is he living in a ruinous house with no cen-tral heating? First, you must understand that none of the Hexters last for long. Note their portraits on the staircase; the line of lin-eage-proud, short-lived men ascending to the second floor, com-plete with pictures of their willowy, swan-faced wives. A Hexter would never marry anyone who was not thin and tall. Throughout history most Hexters have, on reaching the age of majority, started well, but few survived long enough to consolidate their achieve-ments. During the infancy and childhood of every succeeding heir, ground was lost: socially, financially - and often literally. The estate has dwindled to the Hall, with its legacy of a haunted lawn.

Ned Hexter talks mostly of helicopters. His family history is a subsidiary interest; he is the longest lived of all the Hexters. He trained as an aeronautical engineer. His ambition, fulfilled with fateful consequences, was to create the most elegant machine ever to take to the air. Whilst capable of carrying a sufficient comple-ment of men to make it a commercial and military proposition, it proved slender, no ungainly pot-bellied troop carrier. Its blades were narrow; almost invisible once airborne. It was perhaps the most silent of helicopters ever designed, rising without undue dis-turbance, though its thrust and lift were evident as a flattening of grass. I have a photograph of one here. The early model was paint-ed sky blue. Hexter hoped that once sufficient height was gained they would be imperceptible; even on cloudy days seeming no more than a patch of the blue breaking through. He saw them as combin-ing grace, stealth and resilience, as secret as anything made of metal could be in the sky.

But now Adrian Hexter is at the end of the dirt track. Though it is drier than usual, it is still sticky beneath the overhanging beech trees. He moves fluently and at great speed, as if there were not a ridge of dried mud or a pothole beneath him; his progress is pre-ternaturally linear. Like his forebears, he is long-limbed. Is he taller than any of them? This is surely not unlikely. You say he seems less substantial. He is wearing a transparent overcoat, somewhat shimmering. An odd way to dress on a balmy afternoon.

We must go downstairs now. The tea has brewed. Ned has found a walnut cake; it sits igneous and dangerously brown in the center of the table. Will the knife be sharp enough to cut it?

The first cup has been poured when the front door is opened and then banged shut. Ned stands heron-like, tea pot in hand. No visitors are expected.

"Who can that be? We are so seldom disturbed at the Hall."

"You mentioned your son . . . earlier," Justin reminds him.

"Not expected until tomorrow. It would be most unlike . . .'"

Then Adrian is in the living-room: a rush of thrashing arms and legs. He's taller than seems strictly conceivably and appears confused. After striking his head on a beam, he sinks into an armchair. His upper body is clad in some kind of waterproof, although the arms are covered by a different material, almost translucent and made of a delicate fabric.

"Well, this is unexpected," Ned remarks. "I'm sure you'd like to see your mother. Unfortunately she's indisposed. We had hopes she would join us for supper, but I suspect that will not now be the case."

"Sorry . . . I'm early. I need to change. That's the problem," said Adrian. His voice is high-pitched yet dry; almost nothing more than a faint squeaking and scraping at a window pane.

"There is nothing to prevent you from changing upstairs. But first I should introduce Justin Buckey. From *Aviation and Aeronautical News*. He's interviewing me."

"Really? I expect to fly soon."

The expression on Buckey's face is one of comprehensive perplexity. He is at a loss to know who or what is addressing him: in English to be sure and the content ordinary enough. But he has never been spoken to in such unfamiliar tones. Finally he manages: "Where to?"

But Adrian has already lost interest. Now it's the orange glow of a lampshade that attracts him.

"Cake, Adrian?" asks Ned. If he is in any way discomfited by his son's appearance and manner, he is disguising it.

"No, thank you, Father. I'm . . . hardly eating at the moment."

"Very well. Perhaps it would be best if you change now. I hope you'll manage a little something for supper."

Adrian has risen unsteadily to his feet; his thin legs look as if they are on the verge of crumpling beneath him. For a moment, he is unsure where to go next. He seems incapable of anything more than imbecilic arm-fluttering. Then he regains control of his body and flickers across the room to the foot of the staircase.

"Now you were asking about the Hexter A6 Helicopter."

"Ah yes," says Buckey, floundering.

"You'll have heard it said that it was a flimsy machine. But the problems were less to do with the design than the materials. The crash was most regrettable, of course."

When Buckey next looks towards the staircase, there's no sign of Adrian. The sounds from above seem almost indefinable, although they could be the old beams settling or a disturbance in the water pipes.

You've seen the photographs and the footage, the machine slowing for a few seconds, suddenly losing height, clipping the top of the canopy on the way down. Then from a different camera, some way off: a view of open fields, the wood in the middle distance. The gray-black smoke rising. Afterwards, the spidery wreckage: the blades twisted, the rest a blackened abdomen. Of course, Hexter refused to accept the blame, although that didn't prevent recriminations and the court case.

In his study, you'll see the designs for the Hexter A6 framed on the wall. And here's an oil painting he commissioned of the A7, flying over the Oxfordshire countryside: as close to being airborne as a machine that never got off the drawing board can be. Hexter believes that his plans were stolen. These box files contain letters from solicitors and counsel. The case went against him. Some thought him unlucky. There hasn't been much to spend on the Hall since then. Lawsuits alleging his intellectual property had been stolen added to the debt. He had to sell what little farmland there was on the estate. He was left with the house and the lawn.

Here's his desk and on the top of it a photograph of Imogen, taken at an air show in the years before the crash. It must have been a cold day for her to wrap up like that. It's only her face that tells you how thin she was. See how the wind has caught her long yellow hair; for a moment, a bright flare on a gray lusterless day. She's in her room now and Adrian's asleep in his. If you listen carefully you can hear Ned cooking supper in the kitchen below. Now it is evening the house is colder. In the living room, Buckey is pacing up and down, plotting tomorrow's early departure. When we slip downstairs, I'm sure that, with Ned out of the room, we'll see him place another log on the fire.

Ned's serving some anonymous meat and thick gray gravy from an orange casserole dish. There's bread in a basket in the middle of the table. Buckey must wonder whether it's warmer in the kitchen. Then he starts. Something small, a moth perhaps, is nibbling at the nape of his neck.

"I'm afraid Imogen is indisposed," says Ned, once he's sitting down. He offers Justin a glass of water. "A pity. She was such an enchanting conversationalist and a great deal better informed about helicopters than one might imagine."

"And your son. What is he reading at university?"

"Aeronautical engineering. Now you may think that is perfectly predictable. But it's become clear that in important respects he takes after his mother."

"Oh!"

"He's started to lose his appetite. I do think it's so important to eat something, don't you agree?"

"Yes," Justin replies, pushing the meat to one side of his plate and toying with the gravy.

"Of course, these days Imogen eats practically nothing. A little honey perhaps."

"What does her doctor say?" asks Justin, as he examines a bread roll.

"Nothing. She hasn't got one."

"Mightn't it be a good idea to . . ."

"No, they're hopeless when it comes to people with Imogen's condition. I've done what I can. Made certain modifications."

"To help her get around the room."

"Yes, I suppose you could say that. She lost a leg the other day."

Hexter speaks of helicopters till late in the evening. Justin is tired by the time they climb the staircase. His host stops to listen at Imogen's door, but there is no sound apart from a noise that might be two of the softest, most fragile things in the world being rubbed together.

From his bed Justin cannot hear Alex in the next room, alighting for a moment on objects, knocking against the walls and then pressing his face to the window pane; for now it is dark, his only desire is to reach the moon.

It's past seven in the morning when Justin makes his way down the staircase. The house is silent. Every piece of furniture seems less itself, as if hiding the potential for use: the table not designed for anything to rest on it, flowers in a vase or a book, but simply an object constructed from wood. He imagines he's first to get up; then through the one good window he spots Ned Hexter on the lawn. He goes out of the back door to join him. It's a fine day, all the more to be valued for being in late summer. The blue above them has the high gloss of a finished product.

A stretch of lawn closest to the pavement is rife with wild flowers and weeds: yarrow, sheep's sorrel, speedwell and coltsfoot. Further on it's studded with plantains smothering the grass. Hexter's standing towards the back, where little flourishes. In spite of the recent rain there are dry, yellowish-brown patches.

"I'll be off soon," says Justin. "I might beat the worst of the rush hour in town."

"Have you seen Adrian?"

"No, not since last night."

"I hope he's up soon. That boy needs to mate."

"Well . . . I think I'd better . . ."

"You're not going yet . . . surely. There's a lot to tell you. After the crash, I went abroad for a year. One of the mothers kept on coming round here. She was quite mad. Making all kinds of accusations. When I returned, the people in the village told me that she'd buried her son's bones right here in the lawn. I've never found them. He was the pilot."

"Do you think he's here . . . beneath us?"

"Not directly. They'll rise soon, but the pilot's ghost won't be with them Although there are days when I know there has been some kind of . . . anyway, you must meet Imogen before you go."

"That's very good of you, but if you don't mind . . ."

"Come on, she'll be most upset if you leave without saying a word."

Hexter's shepherding him back into the house, past the suitcase, which is packed and waiting in the living-room, and up the staircase.

"I'll give Adrian a call first if you don't mind. The window of opportunity is limited. They don't live for very long, the original species." Ned raps on his son's door three times: no reply. "It could happen any time soon. You don't want to miss it." Then turning to Justin: "Incredible! The lassitude of late adolescence."

"Yes, I've one of my own."

Hexter moves on down the corridor and without knocking enters Imogen's room.

"She doesn't seem at her best this morning," he says, signaling to his guest to come in. It takes Justin more than a moment to comprehend precisely what is in front him. The room is empty, apart from a life form he is initially unable to identify. Later he will attribute this to the fact that even the most commonplace creature will be difficult to recognize if magnified perhaps a million times or more. It is evidently an insect of some sort. It has six long legs that appear pencil-line thin in comparison to the mass of the segmented abdomen. The head has compound eyes and antennae, but also a mop of what looks like yellowish-gray human hair. The lips, supple and feminine, are larger than expected, still capable of kissing. The wings are intricate and translucent.

"She lost two of her legs recently. I've replaced them with very fine steel prosthetics. The slightly shinier ones. Do you see? They seem to be holding up well, but one of her own might break off at any minute. So very fragile, alas!"

"I'd better . . . or I'll miss . . ."

"Hold on! Imogen, this is a Mr Buckey. He's something of an authority on helicopters."

The dry sound of a wing brushing against the wall; a metal leg flexing; a pink tongue protrudes—a response?

"Simply must dash. It's been wonderful to . . ."

Then down the stairs and into the living-room. As Justin picks up his suitcase and makes for the front door, he spots Adrian bumping softly against a window pane. Although his waterproof has turned into two wings, his face, refined by inbreeding, is still recognizable. His hair has gone. A full transition appears imminent.

As Justin runs down the drive, his suitcase swinging beside him, a crane fly, its movements marvelously co-ordinated, is swimming through the liquid gleam of late summer air; not clumsy, as it would be inside, but an athlete of the insect world. Within seconds, another has passed him, and then a third. The aeronauts are out to play. Rapturous and long-legged, the crane flies have risen from the lawn. Look how they make love on the wing!

Black eggs in the soil. I have been Hexter, Buckey, Adrian, Imogen, the table, a staircase, a teapot and more besides. I thank you for your time. Let's not wait for winter under the lawn: the pilot's ghost, the leatherjackets feeding on roots. In a dark corner of a room, a ten-day- old crane fly will die, withered by the quest for light, its last flight ending away from the beautiful, dangerous sun.

The Time Traveler's Assistant Discovers What Could Have Been

~ *Scott Edelman*

The Time Traveler's Assistant, understanding that whether the Time Traveler himself spent many months or mere moments in the past correlated not at all to the speed with which the world moved forward in this present, this future, expected the universe to instantaneously change by the time the blinding flash signaling the world's first successful human transmission faded.

The control room's barely functional equipment, with lights which often threw off sparks as they blinked data updates; the log book going back decades, tracking the far too many deaths caused by their experiments; the off-putting portrait fading with the years as it hung askew on one wall, keeping the target of their project constantly in their minds; even the flavor of the air, not yet fully recovered from all the wars between then and now, and perhaps never to do so without their intervention . . . each of these things and many more should have altered. But they had not.

To their great frustration, the Time Traveler's Assistant noted—alone now in a room where moments before there had been two—everything was as it had been.

Did that mean the mission had failed?

Perhaps. But perhaps it had succeeded.

Or perhaps both. That was one way the time streams could be perceived, at least according to certain of the physicists.

But the Time Traveler's Assistant believed in the actual, not the theoretical, such was their training, and so, as minutes passed, with nothing in the room having transformed, they knew—someone would have to follow.

And looking at the dials beneath their fingers they then knew—*they* would have to follow. And not years from now. But *now* now.

The Time Traveler's Assistant had not anticipated this.

The Time Traveler's Assistant did not want this.

But unexpectedly, enough energy remained pulsing through the interconnected machinery which filled the squalid warehouse to allow for one more trip. The group—impatient as only those attempting time travel could be—would not have to wait years for a second attempt.

And there was no time to tell the others, because it needed to happen before the power faded, or else this precious opportunity to possibly prevent yesterday's catastrophe would be lost. They flipped the switches once more, exactly as they had mere moments before, only this time, as the small, dark room began to echo with a hum which grew into an urgent crackle, the Time Traveler's Assistant without hesitation stepped from behind the control board and into the blindingly bright chamber.

So brilliant was the room they could barely make out the nearby door fly open, and so loud they could not decipher the shouts. But it did not matter. There was no time to explain their sudden need to disappear.

And then the blaze of white nothing vanished, and as the eyes of the Time Traveler's Assistant adjusted, they could see the walls which had surrounded them had vanished as well, and they were standing in only rubble and ash, bent rebar and broken bricks, without a sense of having travelled. It was almost as if the room which had been about them had abruptly collapsed. But not quite . . . for not even the footprint of their former boundaries was there any longer.

They were now . . . elsewhere.

They had done it after all. They had gone back. But . . . to where?

The coordinates the team had carefully calculated should not have taken the Time Traveler who'd preceded them to a place of such devastation, and the Time Traveler's Assistant—who briefly thought they perhaps no longer needed to think of themselves as merely an Assistant, for they were now a Time Traveler as well— knew they shouldn't have arrived in the midst of such destruction either, for the sealed fate they were hoping to avert still waited in the (now) future place between their own (left behind) future and this (present) past.

They stood ankle deep in red ash, beside a brick wall which had collapsed just enough to create a ledge low enough to peer over.

The air was both fouler and purer than what they exhaled from their own time in the moments after their arrival, a paradox they set aside to contemplate later. But for now . . . where was now? Were they inside of what was once a building? Or outside? There was no clear way to tell. But they could hear voices, and until they were able to determine whether those belonged to people who might try to stop them from accomplishing their mission, it was best to stay hidden, even though . . .

What was their mission anyway? The Time Traveler had one, and had the training to see it through, but that was then and this was now—or maybe it was also then, for time was a confusing thing—and there was no way, based on their environment, that the same task as previously devised could possibly cure the ills they'd inherited.

They looked over the barrier and saw the identical red dust in which they stood stretched all the way to the horizon, punctuated by rubble, and as well as dozens of people who were walking about, apparently aimlessly, leaving trails of mist rising in their wakes. Remarkably for all the stirring up of the grit of what had been lost, the air did not smell of destruction—which they continued to find surprising. It was a better scent than that of the world left behind, and with its unfamiliar tang, almost pleasant.

Someone coughed to their side, far too close for comfort in this or any age. They took a sudden step away and fell back over a brick, a cloud of dust rising to swallow not only them but also the one who had approached.

As the particles settled around them, the Time Traveler's Assistant looked up at what presented as a woman according to their memories of the signifiers of this time. They were glad for the dust which had coated their garb, for it would perhaps mean they would not seem as out of place as they felt. After all, there had been no way to prepare for a journey the way the Time Traveler had. And the cougher's hard-worn clothing was years old, as was their own, but unlike their own, her multi-layered clothing was ragged and filthy. She made no notice of that distinction between them, though, seemed concerned only with a photograph in her outstretched hand.

"I'm sorry," she said, with a cracked voice which spoke of an age even greater than she seemed under the grime. "Please forgive me.

I didn't mean to startle you. But have you seen my husband? They took him away. They—"

Her voice cracked, and she lowered her head, pushing the photograph closer.

The Time Traveler's Assistant thought the photo so blurry, the image could have been of anyone, perhaps even the Time Traveler himself—was that why the machine had brought them back to this time and place?—because there was a fix which required them to both take action at once?—but then blinked to clear the tears and grit from their eyes, and saw . . . no. So they shook their head, to which the woman said no more, only backed slowly away, mumbling, then turned to vanish around the other side of the wall.

The Time Traveler's Assistant got back to their feet and peered carefully around the wall's edge, watching as the woman hobbled into the distance. But as she vanished, they rose fully, for what was the point in hiding? The team hadn't been working to wash away the centuries only to waste the moments which were then revealed.

Dozens of people milled about in what could have been mistaken for a vast desert, if not for the wreckage scattered about. Perhaps one of them might be made to reveal information which would explain what had pulled them to this date and time. But whom to approach first?

They came out from behind their hiding place, entered the orbit of bodies, and moved slowly about within them. Some seemed familiar with the path they trod, and cloaked in regret, while others picked their way slowly forward as if all was new to them. Surveying the faces of these long dead, they struggled to remember the lessons of this time, such as how to greet in a non-threatening way, how to ask without seeming overly inquisitive, how to move one's body without giving offense, all lessons the original Time Traveler had so well memorized—until they came upon what at first appeared to be a mound of discarded cloth.

They paused for a moment, for such scraps seemed odd to be abandoned in that way, considering the threadbare condition of those who moved nearby, to whom such shreds would surely be precious—and to their great surprise realized . . . no. There was movement beneath the rags. There was . . . a body.

They knelt and folded back a patchwork of rough cloth to find . . . a child.

It had been a long while since the Time Traveler's Assistant had seen anybody so young, one of the many crises the Time Traveler's trip back was meant to solve, and yet, but a symptom of the true crisis.

"Are you all right, child?" they asked. "Is anyone taking care of you?"

It was a question the Time Traveler's Assistant almost did not bother asking, for so self-absorbed were each of those around them it was an answer in itself. Whatever this place once might have been, it was no longer a community. It had been shattered. Shattered by the one they would centuries hence band together to stop.

The child curled up more deeply within its cloth, and frantically backed away, heels etching ruts into the red dust beneath.

"No," they continued. "Don't be afraid. I'm not here to harm you. There's no need to be afraid of me."

"It's not you he's afraid of. It's all of us. It's everyone."

The Time Traveler's Assistant turned to see a young man, or what appeared to be a young man. This moment demanded judgement which they, up in their own era, did not have to make. Why did things in the past have to be so complicated? A slash of cloth across his face obscured one eye.

In response to their obvious gaze, he pointed toward his face, then held his arms wide to encompass everything about him.

"That was what came from trying to prevent this," he said.

"Are you . . . ?" They were afraid to say the words, for fear they could be true. What could he have meant by prevention? Could he be yet another time traveler, a later follower who leapt back years after them, once the team regrouped and was able to make a further attempt to change what the Time Traveler had not, and what they themselves had not yet changed, would not change?

"Yes," he said, though the words which followed proved his answer to what was in their thoughts was actually no. "I am. And I'm not the only protester nearly killed by a supposedly non-lethal pellet. Non-lethal? What's that supposed to mean? There's nothing that isn't lethal, not when used by people like *them*. I'm lucky an eye was all I lost. It could have been worse. Much worse. At least my cracked skull healed."

He rapped the top of his head with his knuckles and smiled.

The Time Traveler's Assistant swallowed, not ready for this world, not knowing what they were being called on to do, if in fact anything could be done.

"And the child?"

They looked over at the mound beneath where the wriggling had stopped ever since the Time Traveler's Assistant had ceased addressing it.

"I've never heard him speak," answered the man. "At least—not words. All I know is, he was once taken from his parents and caged, because of . . ."

He voice trailed off, and he pressed his lips tightly together. Instead of continuing, he merely shrugged, as if to say—there was, of course, no *need* to say. Was there?

"Ever since then, those of us who are able, watch out for him as best we can, give him food, offer shelter when the storms come. He doesn't always accept it. He's broken."

"That is kind of you."

"Well," he said, shrugging again, and looking at the invisible child. "We're all broken. So tell me—where have you come from?"

Before the Time Traveler's Assistant could answer, could even begin to think of how to answer—because though the Time Traveler had rehearsed believable identities, plausible histories, they had done no such thing—another voice behind joined the questioning, only this one was loud and angry.

"Yes, where do you come from? I haven't seen you here before. Why are you here?"

The Time Traveler's Assistant turned and froze at the sight of the large man, never having been questioned in such a manner. He tugged at his grimy red cap, so shredded there was barely enough band left to the thing to hold the brim in place, and spat at their feet.

"We don't get strangers around here often, and when we do, we don't like them. And not just that—what religion are you? Huh? What's wrong with you? Why aren't you saying anything? Come on, tell me—where do you come from?"

Before they could give any answer at all, not a word, not even a syllable, her assailant moved even closer, and shouted.

"Forget it! Don't bother answering! I don't give a damn. It doesn't matter. Wherever it was, why don't you go back where you came from?"

The Time Traveler's Assistant surprised themselves by emitting a sob which vibrated their entire body so deeply their knees almost buckled, because the question brought home what they already knew, but had been trying to keep the recognition of at a distance. Go back where they came from? They could not. They could never return to where they'd been mere minutes before. This was a one-way trip, just as it had been for the Time Traveler who'd preceded them. And not just because no such mechanism to boomerang home existed—but because the loss of home was the entire point of such a trip. Where they came from, if all was successful, should no longer exist.

"Back off," said the one-eyed man to the hate-filled newcomer, interposing himself between them. "Your old wars have no place here. Leave the visitor alone."

"Why don't you mind your own business?" came the reply, along with a push, and then the two of them were rolling in the dust. The Time Traveler's Assistant could barely make them out beneath the rising red mist.

They took that moment, after one last look at the pile of cloth beneath which hid a broken child, to move on. But there seemed to be nowhere to move on *to*, no possible point of purpose. All that was around were the ruins of what once was—distressing evidence of what the initial Time Traveler had been sent to the past to prevent. Yes, they supposed a society of sorts had grown out of the wreckage between the past and their present, now future, but the centuries of pain between those two points seemed insurmountable. So much had been lost, so much seemed beyond recovery.

Faced with the reality of what once had been theoretical, it was impossible to deny that The Time Traveler had failed. And because of the endless dust and ash which stretched far into the distance, masking any horizon, the Time Traveler's Assistant knew they would not succeed. But neither would they fail. They hadn't even been given a chance to try.

They were too late. What had happened had already happened, and it would be up to another to fix what was for them clearly unfixable.

They walked away, trying to ignore the shouting of the men behind, and the whimpering of the child as well. Each brought on a great despair at being able to communicate with anyone here. Perhaps this meant communication outside one's own time wasn't possible. Shuffling ahead, though, they knew they had to try.

In the middle distance, they could make out a waist-high rectangular block built of bricks and wood, behind which sat a man. Or what seemed at first glance to be a man, for the true details of the figure were masked beneath a conglomeration of strange artifacts with which he'd adorned himself.

His face had been smeared with what appeared to be clay, and atop his head were twigs woven together to form a helmet of sorts, almost as if what once was hair had solidified. As the Time Traveler's Assistant drew closer, they understood the construction before the man to be a crude desk he had made for himself. He pushed papers across the surface, occasionally slashing at one with the point of a small, broken stick, appearing to act out some type of signing ritual.

There was something far too familiar about the man, impossibly familiar, and as the Time Traveler's Assistant approached even nearer, a fading portrait popped into their memory, one seen so often as to have become little more than the background noise of their former life. They froze. Their feet became lead, and after a beat, they almost backed away.

Almost.

As they quivered in that moment of indecision, the man looked up, noticing them. He smiled, his teeth bizarrely white against that discolored face, and waved them over with fingers too small for the hand which bore them.

The Time Traveler's Assistant stood before the makeshift desk, trying to see this man as he had been before, stripping him of mud, and twigs, and the immeasurable weight of crushed history. And seeing what was revealed, they thought. . .this cannot be. They must be mistaken. They could not have been randomly brought to this here, this now, this . . . this man.

And then he flung open his arms, taking in the ground on which they stood, and all the horrors which ringed them, and said, "I alone can fix this."

Only then was the Time Travelers's Assistant certain that . . . yes. *Yes,* they thought. Yes. *But*—

"No," they said. "No, you can't. It's far too late for that."

"What did you say?" asked the man, anger in his voice. They could tell he was unused to being contradicted. They *knew* he was unused to being contradicted, one of the reasons time travel was the only way to repair the future.

It was too late to fix what had been broken, perhaps. But not too late for justice. The Time Traveler's Assistant reached across the mockery of a desk, and by the overly long strip of cloth which hung from his neck, grabbed the man, the one whose incompetence, arrogance, ignorance, and greed had caused all this. That he had survived what he had wrought was an abomination. They began to pull him across the top of the structure he had built. They would take care of this man, and then dismantle the replica of a desk he never deserved to have.

"Hey!" he shouted, as his helmet flew off and vanished into the dust. "Hey, hey, hey! You can't do that."

The man's voice changed then with his protestations, in tone, in timber, no longer embodying the bluster of before, and as the Time Traveler's Assistant pulled him along, toward the wall behind which they had first manifested, he started to shout nonsense words, seeming to speak not just to them, but to the universe. They could not understand the man's meaning, but assumed the words would have made sense if they'd shared the same time of birth. No matter— once they were out of sight of the others, the two of them would talk, and the Time Traveler's Assistant would make him understand what he had done. If he was capable of understanding, that is.

But before they had gone more than a few meters, the Time Traveler's Assistant was tackled and separated from their captive. They were surprised to see their assailants were the two men who'd earlier been fighting—each now held one of their arms, no longer appearing to be enemies—and even the comatose child, suddenly energetic, had joined the group, pushing at their back.

A few more joined them to make sure the Time Traveler's Assistant had no choice but to walk where they pulled, and as others rushed forward to hold electronic devices in their direction, they were dragged toward what at first seemed a far distant horizon, but once through a wall of smoke and fog, was revealed to be something more, a flaw in their previous perception. The land did not continue on the other side, for there was only a wall, one painted to resemble a dwindling continuation of what had been left behind. Then a door opened, and they moved through it to a room bare of destruction.

The Time Traveler's Assistant was startled to see people there with crisp clothes and clean faces, and machinery, too, not so very different in appearance from what had sent them from far in the future, and numerous small screens on which could be seen the land of red dust they'd just left behind. So many questions filled their mind, but before they could utter any of them, they were hustled through another door, one which brought them outside again, only this outside, a true outside, was nothing like the former outside—a false outside, the Time Traveler's Assistant now understood—from which they'd been banished.

Before they could take it all in, they were spun about. Only one other remained with them. It was her defender, the one missing an eye, who removed the cloth from across his face to reveal—that was another illusion. Unlike his earlier welcoming demeanor, he was angry now, and no longer willing to take their side.

"I don't know what that was all about, but you're out of here. I don't even know how you got in. Everybody on the list is accounted for, and you're not one of them. You didn't have a ticket."

The Time Traveler's Assistant said nothing, far more disoriented by the journey they'd taken over the past minute than they'd been by the one which had encompassed centuries.

"Why would you want to sneak in?" he continued. "Why would you want to ruin everything for everybody? Keep moving, and we won't have to get the police involved."

He waited for an answer, then frowned, and turned, and went back through the doors from which they'd both come.

As he vanished, they gawked at the building in front of them, and at the sign above the door through which they'd just been pushed. A marquee read:

WHAT COULD HAVE BEEN

And beneath that, in slightly smaller letters:

AN IMMERSIVE EXPERIENCE
OF A FUTURE THAT NEVER WAS

Below those large letters, between two doors which led to the mock world from which they'd been evicted, was a poster illustrated with a grotesque drawing of the man the Time Traveler had previously gone back to prevent from being born, and wrapping round that image a barely decipherable—to their eyes—script which told them of the lie they'd just been living:

> *Experience the tomorrow which was almost ours in a fully interactive experience. Freely wander the world from which we were rescued, and be grateful. Six performances only.*

The Time Traveler's Assistant understood now. They'd arrived at a where and when unattached to any change point they could manipulate to save their future, and the man they thought deserved punishment was not at all that man, only some sort of actor. But if that were so, then . . . where was now? They'd felt lost earlier attempting to unravel the meaning of the world of red dust, the world which proved to be an illusion, but felt no less lost now that a truth had been revealed. Was this what the Time Traveler himself had experienced on his failed mission? Had he become lost as well, first in time, and then to despair?

They dropped to the curb, devoid of a desire to go on, and took several gulps of the fresh air—fresher than the remembered world of the future left behind, and fresher by far than the false future from which they'd just been evicted—hoping to clear their mind. They slapped red dust off their jacket, and when the flecks settled, took another deep breath, and for the first time, truly looked at this outer world into which they'd been thrust.

The structures around them stood tall, nothing like the false future in the building behind, or the middle future which waited between the past as the Time Traveler's Assistant understood it and the future they'd left behind. The casualness of those who wandered nearby was almost infuriating, for they felt the people who walked down the street should be celebrating. Shouldn't they? How could they be oblivious to the absence of the horrible days ahead which had somehow been lifted from them?

Or would it have been their present? There was no way of knowing. For this time was most definitely not the time it was supposed to be, and instead one in which the destruction caused by a madman had been transmuted from reality into a theatrical performance, so perhaps the Time Traveler who proceeded them had caused a change after all. But if so, then why was the world the Time Traveler's Assistant had left behind unchanged? Why had they needed to follow into that blazing chamber?

A hum arose from behind as if in answer to their questions, and when they turned toward the all-too-familiar sound, they saw the theater which had fooled them was gone, and in its place, a flickering circle, close enough and large enough so the world behind was subsumed in a crackling of energy which grew into a wall of lightning struggling to coalesce into something more. They instinctively recoiled, throwing an arm over their eyes.

Once the brightness dimmed and they could bear to look again, they saw the coruscating sparks had become a shimmering window, and on the other side stood those with whom the Time Traveler's Assistant had until that afternoon worked, only . . . older. *Much* older.

The room her friends occupied was an unfamiliar one, too, with equipment even more complicated than that which had propelled them there. They recognized the woman at the center of the group as someone who had once been her peer, though based on her position in the room, and the deferential glances of the others, was now the leader. Her eyes widened on seeing them, but though she moved her lips, no sound came.

The Time Traveler's Assistant shook their head, and spoke, to which their old friend—now truly old—also shook her head, then frowned. She twisted a screen to face out through the portal, then looked down and began typing.

"It is good to see you again after all these years," scrolled the words.

"It is good to see you as well," said the Time Traveler's Assistant, then fell silent, not merely because they knew they could not be heard, but due to the sight of their friend's tears rolling down through what the years had made of her. They thought of how their own brief moment had turned into their comrade's decades, and how the gaps each had experienced could not possibly be compared.

"We have good news," the scrolling went on. "We located a message the first traveler had left behind for us, etched into metal plates and buried where he knew we would find them, which meant that once we finally perfected the technology, we were able to pinpoint that time of fracture between when you and your predecessor landed, and thus able to complete the original mission. Actually, no. Not quite the original mission, but one close enough so the things which were meant to happen did not. The world he was sent back to prevent was never born. The path you followed in hopes of changing no longer needs to be changed. We have taken a step sideways, breaking free of that time stream. And you have shuffled sideways as well."

Their friend looked up from the keyboard then, a radiant expression evident on her face. But that faded as soon as their eyes met, and she returned to her typing.

"Oh, how I wish you could see it. How I wish we could bring you back to learn what we have become. But . . . we haven't perfected the means of return, and don't know if we ever will. We wanted you to know, though . . . to know we have done as we hoped. We have to go now. There isn't enough power to continue this transmission. We are sorry."

The Time Traveler's Assistant's friend looked up one final time, and nodded. They nodded, too. Silently, they tried in every physical way they knew how to make sure those left behind understood they were accepting of their fate.

They would have to be.

The portal shrunk away until, with a final pop and a metallic smell, it vanished, revealing the building behind and the theater's front door. The Time Traveler's Assistant stepped inside, and behind a counter saw one of the men who'd only watched as they'd been dragged by before being tossed out.

"I am sorry," they said to him. "May I go back? I promise I won't cause any more trouble. I . . . I understand now."

He looked at them for a few moments, expression blank, and the Time Traveler's Assistant was about to continue their pleading when he nodded, then led them to a doorway. Once opened, the Time Traveler's Assistant looked through on the future which never happened, populated with actors who only pretended to suffer the fates the election of a madman would cause, and in the distance, the actor who pretended to be that man himself.

"What could have been," they whispered.

"Yes," said man beside them. "That's the name of the show. Are you going in?"

The Time Traveler's Assistant stood silently for one further moment, looking at the past they in a small way had helped prevent, and then stepped through, joyfully kicking up the dust of a future which never was.

Nickel Hill

~ Wade Peterson

Thomas Rusk gave his insulated tumbler a quick shake and frowned. He'd gone through his morning coffee without realizing it, half listening to Pastor Wigfall's sunrise service. He'd been busy setting up his smoker on the concrete slab on the park's south side and must have lost track of time while arranging hickory and post oak in the hot box because when he looked up, the service was over and a dozen people had taken his place, doing yoga with faces to the sun.

It was the sandalwood and sage perfuming the air that had made him look up and take notice. It seemed out of place in Nickel Hill, another Californiacation of his hometown, transplants trading their gridlock and earthquakes for the affordable housing and tornadoes of west Texas. Fortunately, there was a give and take when it came to traditions like carnival day and the newcomers were willing to add to the event rather than remodel it. It was a subtle but important distinction that everyone accepted for the good of the town. A little yoga was fine, so long as nobody forced him to join in.

And even if Thomas had minded the incense, hardwood smoke and sizzling fat would soon overpower it.

Distant thunder rumbled, shaking Thomas from his thoughts. A storm front boiled to the south, pushing darkened anvil heads along its boundary. The weatherman said it should stay below Nickel Hill and give them clear skies by the afternoon, but you could never be sure with Texas weather. Thomas tried taking another swig from his tumbler before remembering it was empty and set it down so he didn't further embarrass himself. He spared a glance at the other pit masters on their pads scattered around the park, tinkering with their rigs and taking inventory of their meats. He reckoned it wouldn't hurt for him to make another pass, either.

Thomas checked the bubble levels on the rig's legs, made sure the vent covers turned free, and used a compass to ensure he was cardinally aligned with the hotbox's fresh air intake pointing due south. The yoga enthusiasts wrapped up and passed him with mats rolled under their arms and slung over shoulders, wishing him well.

"Thomas!" His buddy Pick Henderson bellowed and broke away from the group. He grabbed a popsicle from Thomas's cooler and plopped himself in a folding chair.

"I didn't know you had taken up yoga, Pick," Thomas said.

"The man on the tee-vee says it's good for ya. Helps the circulation."

"Does it? Sure Peggy Whitlow has nothing to do with it?"

"I had noticed her in the front row, matter of fact. A pure coincidence, I assure you." Pick peeled the white paper wrapper from the popsicle and upon discovering it was orange, wrinkled his nose. He half-rose towards the cooler for another, but sat back down at Thomas's raised eyebrow.

"I swear you put the oranges on top just to spite me."

"Not my fault you don't pay attention, Pick," Thomas said.

A microphone turned on with a thump and squeal of feedback. Pastor Wigfall stood in the central gazebo, red-faced. "Sorry about that, folks. Electrical gadgets just don't like me, I guess.

Welcome to carnival day! If it's y'all's first time here, you're in for a treat. It can be a bit much to take in at first, especially for the little ones, but by the end of the day, you'll all understand what makes Nickel Hill so special, and it's not just because of the brisket." The crowd chuckled and Pick hoisted his popsicle in salute.

The pastor pointed to a ring of pink granite stones arranged around a tall obelisk at the park's very center, the shadows cast by the morning sun creeping along tracks etched into the obelisk's surface. "Looks like we have a minute or so before things kick off, so I just wanted to remind y'all that after the 5K run/walk, there'll be a community sing-along with the Wind Riddlers behind me here, face painting over yonder, the art show on the square, and junior rodeo out at the stockyards. Don't forget to head on back here in at sundown for the barbecue, elotes, and deep-fried Oreos."

A tinny horn beeped several times behind Wigfall who turned and shaded his eyes. "Is that? It sure is! This year's lottery winner Clem Haberstroh!" Wigfall waved at a man being paraded around the 5K's starting line in a side-by-side ATV, accepting drinks and handshakes from runners and spectators alike with a forced smile on his face.

"Be sure to say hi to Clem before the day's done, y'all. Well, it's almost time, folks," Pastor Wigfall said and turned to those gathered at the northwest corner of the town square. "Runners ready?" The starter raised a green flag. How about you youngins at the maypole?" Kids no older than eight shouted and waved their ribbons while their parents sitting on hay bales a few feet away brought up their phones, ready to record. "Pit masters?" Thomas gave a thumbs-up with the others. Wigfall looked over his shoulder at the band. "Ready, fellas?" Wigfall took off his Stetson and held it in the air as he counted down, the shadows creeping ever closer to a particular mark on the obelisk. When they touched the mark, Wigfall dropped his hat.

A starting pistol barked. The Wind Riddlers launched into the carnival's official song "Joan's Fiery Carnation," and a troupe of women dressed in colorful skirts danced with men wearing black jackets with silver stitching. Thomas didn't envy them. The song always sounded more like a church hymn than something festive, but the dancers made it work. They always did.

Thomas checked the wood one last time. He'd stacked the hardwood starters like a jungle gym with bits of sage and mesquite twigs snaking between layers, the optimal balance between order and chaos a young fire needed. He struck a match and held it to a packet wrapped in red butcher's paper at the stack's center. The packet caught at once and Thomas jumped back, though he had been expecting it.

"Wigfall makes his starters potent," Pick said.

"He does that."

A group of teens mumbled past his rig, heads together, clothes rumpled, and bleary-eyed from lack of sleep due to last night's bonfire. Several had that surprised look Thomas remembered from a night-before-carnival bonfire in his younger days when he and Peggy Whitlow had been sweethearts. Sometimes the more evangelical folk talked about shutting down the pre-carnival bonfire, like they had in Worthington, but when clouds like today's started gathering and the thunder rumbled, such talk quieted down.

"Fire's snuffed," Pick said.

Thomas snorted. "That's not funny, Pick."

"If I'm lyin' I'm dyin', Tom."

Sure enough, the starter was out, paper singed only a little and the wood not at all. Wigfall's wax seal hadn't even melted. Thomas stuck another match and held the flame against one of the starter's unburnt corners. It flared a little, then died. He struck another match, then another, with no luck.

"Maybe it got wet," Pick said

"It's bone dry."

"You got the vents closed or something?" Pick asked.

He knew they weren't, but he checked again. "Airflow's fine." Thunder rumbled. The distant clouds had taken on an undulation he didn't like. Those were clouds fixing to spew lemon-sized hailstones, or worse. Time to stop messing around.

Thomas went to the tool chest in the back of his pickup and brought out an acetylene torch. He sparked it to life and held the tip of the white-blue flame to the starter, which began to glow and smolder.

Pick bit through the last of his popsicle and tossed the stick aside. "Hells yeah, that's how you do it, Tom."

"It's not catching. As soon as I take it away, it dies."

"Should I go find some newspaper or something?" Pick asked with a shaky voice. "Hell, you could just light the wood direct, you hold that torch on it long enough."

Thomas waved the torch's flame over the hickory and oak for several minutes, but not even the splinters would catch. "It's no good, Pick."

Pick's head swiveled over the field. "Everyone else is lit up, Tom."

"I'm aware."

"They're fixin' to put the briskets in soon."

"That's how you barbecue."

"Maybe I could run my LP rig over here. There's nowhere that says we can't use gas."

"Someone in Worthington used gas once in their carnival. Once."

"Right. Okay." Pick bounced from foot to foot." There ain't gonna be enough if you don't do your share, all I'm saying."

Thomas counted to three in his head before responding. "Tellin' me the obvious helps me not at all, Pick. How about you go get the pastor?"

Pick nodded and said, "Yeah, that's a good idea," before taking off at a run.

Thomas unloaded the firebox and checked the wood over. Each log was quarter-split with bone-dry faces. On a hunch, he waved the torch over a piece of hickory. The grain darkened and smoldered, splinters glowed, and a hint of sweet smoke tickled his nose. Nothing wrong with the wood.

He turned at the side-by-side's four-stroke chuffing as it pulled up. Pastor Wigfall slid from the passenger seat. "Morning, Thomas," he said with a nod.

Thomas nodded back. "Pastor. Maxey." The ATV shook as Maxey Harmelink nodded back from behind the wheel. He was a big boy, was Maxey, junior rodeo champ and all-state defensive tackle in his day. Could have played college ball at UT, but Maxey never felt the need to leave town.

"Pick said your grill won't light?"

Thomas led the pastor through the morning's attempts. Wigfall's frown lines deepened as the story wrapped up. The pastor glanced south before heading for the ATV and returning with a forked stick from the storage box. Fine copper wire coiled along the stick's length, ending in a thin strand that Wigfall wrapped around his wrist. He closed his eyes and murmured to himself as he passed the stick along Thomas's barbeque rig. A tremor began along Wigfall's arm as he crossed to the other side and he lunged forward suddenly, going to one knee and yelping as his knee barked on the concrete. The pastor opened his eyes and clucked his tongue.

"It's not your wood, or your setup, it's the rig itself." He reached under the rig's angle iron frame and came away with a tiny idol wrapped in silver cloth.

"Mesquite covered with Nomex," Wigfall said.

"Sumbitch," Thomas said.

Wigfall set the idol across the forked stick and slowly turned in a circle. The stick began twitching and Wigfall began passing it back and forth in smaller and smaller arcs until the stick vibrated constantly. The pastor sighted along its length before removing the idol and untangling himself from the divining rod's copper wire.

"Maxey, why don't you ask the gentleman wearing runner bib 349 for a private word?"

Maxey started the ATV up and glanced over his shoulder. "The guy with the orange bandana? Doesn't look local." Wigfall nodded. "That's the one." Maxey fiddled with a walkie-talkie and began speaking into it with clipped tones. As he spun the ATV around Wigfall called out, "Alive, mind!"

"How much you want to bet he's from Worthington?" Wigfall said.

Thomas turned his head and spat. "No bet. Damn fools."

"There comes a time when FEMA just can't help you anymore." Wigfall cut a piece of kitchen string from Thomas's BBQ kit and tied the idol to Pick's popsicle stick. The Nomex covering went into the trash. "Here's your new starter."

Thomas built a hickory and oak cage around the idol and lit a match. The idol smoldered with an oily flame for a few seconds before erupting and setting the kindling alight. Something like a car's backfire cracked and he turned in time to see the runner in the orange headband stumble and fall. The man pushed himself up and ran off the course, only to be taken down with another shot from Maxey's bean bag gun, followed by a tackle. Maxey had the the man with the orange headband hog-tied and loaded on the the ATV's rack within moments.

"You got the offering from here, Tom?" Wigfall said.

"Reckon so."

The pastor clapped him on the shoulder and smiled. "I'll leave you to it. I'm off to find Clem."

Later that day, with the briskets casting their siren's call on the breeze, Clem stopped by. He pumped Thomas and Pick's hands with gusto and inquired after the briskets. Would they be ready on time? When Thomas assured him they would, he broke into a grin too crooked to be fake. They talked football over a beer, though Clem's gaze kept drifting to a group of cheerful overtired teens stacking hay bales against the maypole and its criss-crossed ribbons.

Tom frowned at his beer and gave it a shake. Empty. The foam coozy had fooled him into thinking he had a sip left. His phone chirped, and he dug it from his pocket. "Weather service says the county's due for large hail, flash flood warning, possible rain-wrapped twisters."

Pick sat up straighter. "Heading our way?"

"Nah, more down Worthington area, then up to Bowie."

Clem tapped at his nearly empty beer and glanced back at the maypole. "You ever think about moving?" Clem asked.

Pick and Thomas shifted in their chairs and shared a glance. "Move where?" asked Pick.

Clem waved his hand. "I don't know. Somewhere a guy doesn't have to worry about tornados, hail, and such."

Thomas rose and fished out a couple of cold ones from the cooler. "If such a place exists, it sure ain't in Texas." He cracked a can and handed it to Clem.

Clem sipped at the foam and scooted his chair to face away from the preparations. "Yeah, I expect you're right." He gave them a weak smile. "You hear out in Carolina they use mustard and vinegar on their barbecue?"

Pick shook his head slowly. "That ain't right."

"Blasphemy," Thomas agreed.

These Waters

~ *M. Shedric Simpson*

The hands that drew me up were not the hands that had pushed me down. "It's okay," she said. Her eyes were brown, and her skin was dark, and her fingers wrapped tight around my wrists. "I've got you." She pulled, and I fell onto the rocky shore beside her.

A dull and listless light accosted me, and I squeezed my eyes shut. Anything seemed searingly bright after those silt-clouded depths.

"I'm Asha," the girl said. "Can you talk?"

I drew a breath and forced out the word. "Yes," I said, surprised to find it was true. I still felt the memory of water flooding my lungs, like a clenched fist inside my breast. "I think so." I looked up and she smiled at me.

It was a warm smile, but sad too. It was the smile I'd seen on my mother's face when she was reminiscing. "Do you remember how you got here?"

A beer bottle skating across the ground. The bright stab of pain on the back of my skull. The world spun before I even understood it was the bottle that had struck me. "I was walking by the river," I said. "But something happened."

Hey! Fucker! The words rang in my head. The pickup truck skidded to a halt, and four boys piled out of the bed in the back. A boot crashed into my ribs, and my body curled up like a pillbug's. *Go back to where you came from!*

"It's okay if you don't remember," Asha said. She tucked a twist of unruly brown hair behind her ear. "A lot of people don't."

But I remembered it too well. The flurry of words and blows that rained down. *Shit, look at him bleed!* the boy said, but I couldn't see it, all I could see was the muddy brown sky. *I ain't going to jail for no chink. You better finish what you started.*

I felt my hands twisting, and I looked away from Asha, not wanting her to see what was written on my face. Humiliation, rage, and hate formed a knot inside my heart; their threads cut through me like burning steel. "I drowned," I told her.

"We all did."

I tried to struggle when they dragged me into the river. I was still fighting when the blonde boy pushed my head beneath the water. But I was too weak. I'd always been smaller than the other boys. Whorls of silt blotted out the sky, and I couldn't hold my breath any longer.

"All?" I glanced around. We weren't alone on the shore. Other figures huddled beneath the murky sky. Children, all of them. A few were barely more than infants.

"About a hundred of us, now. There weren't so many when I came here." She placed her hand over mine. "If you're ready, I'll show you around."

"I'd like that," I said. Anything was better than reliving those moments over and over again. I pulled off my right shoe and placed it on the rock. I'd lost the other in the river, and I didn't think I'd see it again.

I shoved my socks into my pockets as Asha led me away from the shore. The soil was warm beneath my bare feet, as if heated by the sun, though I couldn't tell if it was night or day. A persistent breeze swept in from the water, cold and metallic and tasting of stone.

"Let's go up the hill," she said. "There's a fire, and you can get a view of the whole island."

I looked beyond her shoulder at the landscape above. Figures nestled amidst the pale grass that covered the slope. Some slept, curled into tight balls, while others stared out across the water in some long and silent vigil. Few seemed to notice our passage.

The grass was waist-deep and silken to the touch. I found myself yearning to lie down in it as well, but I followed Asha up the well-worn footpath instead. We passed a dwarf tree, leafless and skeletal. Dark bulbous fruit hung from its branches.

Asha grasped one. The tree shivered in protest, but relented. She pressed the fruit into my hand. "You can eat these," she said. "Actually, there isn't much else to eat. I tried catching fish once, but they smelled wrong."

"Wrong?"

She shrugged. "Like they'd died days ago, even though they were still moving. So I just let them go."

I nodded and held onto the fruit as she turned back to the trail. It felt warm in my hand. "What's wrong with the children? Why aren't they playing, or doing anything?"

"They're waiting," she said. "Some leave as soon as they get here, but for others . . . It's been a long time."

"How long have you been here?"

She glanced down at her feet. I couldn't see the look on her face, but her voice was ragged when she answered. "I don't really know anymore."

I didn't push her any further. We turned at the switchback and headed up along the ridge. The view opened up around us. The island was made of three low hills, all dressed in the same pale fields, and fringed with jagged black rocks. Across the water to my left and right lay the distant banks of the great river, though I could see nothing of what waited there. Faint points of light drifted across the span between them, crossing always toward my left, against the course of the wind.

The trail cut away from the ridge and into a small hollow near the top of the hill. A group of children huddled around a campfire there. Asha caught my hand and drew me towards them. A boy in a faded tank top stared at me with bright blue eyes. His skin was white and his hair was the color of dust.

"You're new," he said.

"My name's Lee." My father had spelled my name with the hanzi, but I always pictured it the way my mother had written it.

"I'm Toby," he said. He looked up at Asha. "One of them is leaving."

"Where?"

He stood and pointed down the slope. "Over there. He just started walking. Should we do anything?"

"It's his time," Asha said. "He has to go."

She let go of my hand and moved beside Toby. I stepped next to her and gazed down the hill until I saw it too. A boy walking through the waxen field below. He might have been twelve at most; the grass came up halfway up his chest. None of the other children moved to stop him as he walked toward the shore.

"Where is he going?"

"Out there," Asha said. "One of those boats."

When she said it, I could see them for what they were. The tiny drifting lights were lanterns, hung from the prows of boats that crossed between the two banks. A lone figure sat in each. "They're crossing over," I said. "The souls of the dead."

"I think so."

It didn't surprise me the way I thought it should have. I had died. It stood to reason that the others here had died as well. Some part of me had known it ever since I'd climbed back out of the water. "What about the boy?"

"Watch."

The boy pulled off his shirt as he reached the shoreline, then waded waist-deep into the water. He dropped the shirt, and the current pulled it downstream. His shoulders trembled, and then he dove. The river devoured him with barely a ripple. A few seconds later it was as if he'd never existed.

"I see him," Toby said.

I strained against the uneasy light. A flicker of movement pierced the surface—an iridescent shimmer where there should have been a boy. It slid further out into the depths. A jagged fin. The serpentine twist of a coiling tail. Out, and deeper, until I could no longer track it.

We stood in silence for a long minute. The wind that wrapped around the island sent waves through the fields beneath us and painted whitecaps on the water. Toby sucked in a deep breath, and I felt myself do the same, tensing in anticipation.

One of the drifting lights flickered out. The silhouette of the boat vanished.

"He made it," Toby said. His voice was sad.

"Of course he did," Asha answered. "You will too, one day. I promise."

"Mmhmm."

Asha turned back to the fire, and I did too. We sat down on rocks. The other three children never glanced up, only stared into the flames with the ruminative gaze of ancient pyromancers.

"What happened out there?" I asked. "What was that boat?"

"He found the person who'd drowned him," Asha said. "And carried them to the depths, so now they'll never cross over. He'll feast on their flesh for eternity."

My chest tightened. "Is that all we're here for? Just waiting—just waiting for that?"

"To set things right. To punish the ones who murdered us," she said. "That's what we're waiting for."

I still held the fruit in my hands, and I tore it open to focus on something else. The flesh inside was white, and filled with pockets of glistening black seeds. Like a pomegranate in monochrome. I slid one of the seeds past my lips and held it between my tongue and the roof of my mouth until it disintegrated. It was sweet, almost too sweet at first, but it drew my mind away from the taut wires inside my breast.

"Can I get some wood for the fire?" I asked Asha at last.

"It just burns," she said. "It always has. I think it's not really a fire. Just—the memory of a fire."

I nodded, though I didn't understand. I itched for something to do. I was like my father in that way. His hands had never been idle. I still remembered the grass stains on his fingers when he'd grabbed me and lifted me up to the sky.

My father had come with the factory, but when the factory moved away, he'd stayed for me and my mother. There were no jobs for a foreign engineer in town, so he took what work he could find. He trimmed hedges and fixed motors. He made sure there was always food on the table and new shirts in my closet. If there was ever any despair inside his heart, he channeled it into his work and never let it show. Not even on the day he died. I still remember Mrs. Siegel shouting at him from her porch when he collapsed in the middle of her yard. He kept trying to stand up and push the mower, even after his heart had stopped.

I swallowed another pomegranate seed and looked at Asha. "So there's nothing to do? No work?"

Her eyes burned. "This is our work. Keeping watch. Waiting for our time."

"Who are you waiting for, then?"

Her mouth twisted. "I don't know. I don't remember much of what came before this. Just glimpses here and there. Flames and darkness. Water, like ice inside my lungs. Someone calling my name."

I shook my head. "If you don't know who you're waiting for, how will you know when they cross?"

"Everyone knows. They always do," she said. "Whoever did this—" She pulled the collar of her dress to the side, and I saw the puckered scar beneath her clavicle. "I'll know when they come."

I knew I was asking the wrong questions, but it was too late to stop. "If you don't even know who it was, then why not let it go? Just walk away?"

"Don't you think people have tried? We can't just leave." She glared at me. "There's a reason that we're here."

I opened my mouth to protest, but she stood up and turned away. "I'm going for a walk."

"I'm sorry," I called after her, but she didn't respond. There was only the faint rustling as her figure parted the pale grasses, and then the cold wind stole even that.

"It's okay," Toby said. "She'll be back."

The flames whirled. I held out my hands and caught a whisper of warmth, or maybe it was only the memory of warmth.

"I think she's been here a long time," he said. "I think it's hard for her to keep waiting."

He didn't look more than six, but I wondered how long he'd lingered here. "I shouldn't have pushed her."

Toby wrapped his arms around his knees and shivered. "It's not really you that she's mad at. It's me."

"Why would she be mad at you?"

He frowned. "Because I'm leaving soon, and she'll still be here."

I saw the way his legs shook, just like the shoulders of the boy who'd walked into the river. I saw his eyes, wide and darting. "You can feel it," I said.

"But I don't want to."

"It's nothing to be scared of. Asha said it's what we're here for."

"But she didn't mean to do it. I know she didn't. She was just upset."

"What do you mean?"

"My mom. She would have come back for me, if the car hadn't fallen in the river. I know she would have." He looked up at me with eyes that shone desperately. "I don't want to hurt her."

"Then don't," I said. "Don't go." I felt sick to my stomach.

"But you said it too. It's why we're here. We have to go."

"I was wrong. Go somewhere else. Anywhere but here."

He shook his head. "I can feel it pulling me already."

"I'm sorry." The words weren't enough, but they were all I had.

"It's okay," he said. "It's just what happens, right? Maybe I don't have to hurt her. Maybe I can just hold her, like I used to before the river." He turned his eyes back to the flames. "She was always nice to me, even when she was sad."

My hands curled into fists and my thoughts twisted against each other. I didn't know who I hated more. The mother who'd drowned him in the river, or the world that had cast him up on these shores just to torture her. I saw the face of the blonde boy, shoving me beneath the water. The ripples distorted his face. My jaw ached from clenching, or maybe it was just the memory of pain. I forced myself to eat another pomegranate seed, chewing it mechanically. "I'm sure she loved you," I said.

The flames were silent, without any of the crackle and roar of the school bonfire last month. The quiet made the sky above us feel enormous and heavy. I leaned closer to the fire, watching the embers spiral skyward. I don't know if I dreamt, or even if I slept, but I know that time passed in that timeless place, and it was only Toby's restless stirring that brought me back to myself.

His face was taut with worry. I wished I could believe the story he'd told himself, but I knew Asha was right. All of us here had been murdered. There was a reason we were here. "Can't sleep?" I asked.

"No," he answered. "You?"

I shook my head.

"The fruit helps sometimes. Make it easier to rest." He glanced over his shoulder at the river. "But Asha won't eat it anymore."

"I don't think I need it either." I understood her anger; I was wrong to have denied it to her. I wanted to let mine burn, but I hated the feeling that I was being used by this place.

"I wanted to wait until she came back," Toby said. He hugged his legs against his chest. "Will you come with me instead?"

"Is it time?"

His breaths were quick and shallow. He nodded.

I stood and took his hand. He climbed shakily to his feet. "I'm scared."

"Everything's going to be okay," I said. My mother had told me the same thing, with sad dark eyes, before my father's funeral. But when we'd gotten home, she'd held me when I cried for hours.

We followed the winding path through the fields of pale grass, until we came to the river's edge. Toby stepped onto the bare rock and looked up at me. "I don't want to go."

I knelt, so that we were eye to eye. "Then stay," I told him.

He shivered and pulled away from me, but I caught his other hand and held him. He craned his head to look over his shoulder. "It won't let me." Panic tugged at his voice. "Help me. Please."

I pulled him close and wrapped my arms around him. "Of course." I didn't have any choice. My mother would have done the same in a heartbeat.

Every muscle in his body pulled taut, and he froze like a panicked deer, until his body erupted in tremors. His flesh turned to ice, so cold that it burned my arms. He uttered a choked sob. "Don't let me go. Please. Don't let go."

"I won't," I said. "I promise."

I kept hold of him, but the trembling didn't pass. He cried out, and his skin peeled away. Glittering scales rippled along his shoulder. Bones twisted unnaturally beneath his tank top. I clutched him against my chest, desperate to stop the change. Spined fins erupted from his shoulder blades. I gasped as they tore through my arms, but I didn't let go. There were no fins. I felt no pain. It was just the memory of pain.

There were no words to his cries, just a plaintive whimper that went on and on. The uneasy sky whirled overhead. The pale shoulder beneath my cheek was sometimes skin, sometimes scales, and sometimes both at once. His tears soaked the back of my shirt.

I pulled him against me, rocking gently. His breath came in ragged gulps. Slits flared along his neck, then sealed shut again. My mother would have sung to him, but I had my father's voice, so I just held him until the shaking stopped.

The scales crumbled into shimmering dust, and the wind carried them away. The boy sucked in a lungful of air, then let it out slowly. "She's gone," he said. "She's gone."

I released him, and he took a timid step back. "She's gonna be okay," I said. "You are too."

Toby slipped his hand inside mine as I stood back up, and we stood and watched the boats crossing in silence. I knew that one of them would call to me, one day. My flesh would writhe, and I would go out to meet the boy that had pressed me under the water. But I remembered my father too, lifting me up as if he were returning a constellation to the sky.

"You shouldn't have done that." Asha's voice rang out behind me.

I realized that my hand was empty. I turned, but there was no sign of Toby. I hoped that wherever he'd gone was somewhere better than what this place had meant for him. "It was what he wanted," I said.

Asha stood at the edge of the field, her mouth drawn into an angry slash. There were other children too. Some looked on with horror, others wide-eyed with wonder.

She shook her head. "That wasn't right."

I took a deep breath. I held the air inside of me, dark and metallic and tasting of stone. "Maybe that's for each of us to decide." I peeled off my shirt and dropped it on the black rocks. The cold wind wrapped around my body. "Maybe there's a reason we're here, but I have to believe that there's something more." I turned away, feeling Asha's accusing eyes upon me. "I don't know what's waiting over there, but I'm going to find out."

I waded out into the river. Gravel shifted beneath my feet, and I fought for balance. Waves crashed around my waist, pushing me toward the shore. For every step I took, the river only cast me further back. There was a weight inside of me—a knot that hung like an anchor from my heart. The image of the boy who'd held me under. Like a sickly jewel, it gleamed in my mind. Full of hate and heavier than anything. But I didn't need it anymore. It belonged to this place, and I did not. I cut the threads that bound it one at a time, all the shame and hurt and bitterness, until the current carried it away.

I felt my father's hands lifting me up. My mother's hands wrapped around me. Those were the hands that mattered. Boats drifted like fireflies in the distance, drawn always toward that distant shore. Like the promise of daybreak, I would reach it too.

The water embraced me, and I swam.

Holy Viper of the Old Greek Diner

~ Marilee Dahlman

Stupid and nasty, his enemies called him. Nico tried to ignore the sting of such insults. After all, at the crumbling Demeter Diner in downtown Chicago, who was in charge? Him. The remarkable Nico, newly elected leader of a great society. The beauty of it! Dark serpents hissing and snapping as they writhe over peeling linoleum, twisting through the rhythms of daily life, cycles of hunt and sleep, attack and dormancy. Violent creatures, but also civilized, still following ancient Greek traditions—gymnastics and track races, leisurely steam baths, and seasonal festivals honoring the goddess of rebirth, Demeter. She hadn't appeared in six thousand years and blight had ravaged the world for the last five hundred. On the diner's eastern wall, a fresco of the goddess stood faded but watchful. She wore black robes and held a basket of wilting poppies, the bright red a symbol of resurrection, as all molting serpents well-knew.

Nico turned his attention away from the goddess and back to the assembly. He slid his tongue across his fangs and cleared his throat. Ah, democracy. It was a splendid thing. "We must restore the values of past generations," he said, emphasizing every s with a long hiss. He'd assumed his favorite perch atop the host stand. The assembly packed the diner's floor, broad heads arched high and tails vibrating.

Zander, his old nemesis, reclined on the cracked table of the corner booth. Gray-scaled and well-oiled members of the old guard surrounded him, all comfortable on the plush leather seats. Zander slowly coiled and uncoiled his long, heavy body, waiting for silence. Nico's venom glands contracted. These old males with their soft bellies and milky pupils. They lived in luxury, nothing but fancy degrees and lineage justifying their power. And Nico remembered well his first day serving in assembly when Zander had called him a "small-snouted distraction," and the rest of the old guard snickered.

Today, they wouldn't laugh.

Zander raised his head to speak. "We are overcrowded. Food is scarce and you—"

"Treasonous elites!" Nico's hissed mutter provoked the thud of tails against the floor. Wind shook the diner's roof. The day darkened and earth groaned with another eruption of the new volcano on Lake Shore Drive. "Rumors of apocalypse are greatly exaggerated," Nico went on. "I will tell you the true threat! Do you know what it is? Barbarians! They approach from all sides! The solution?"

The assembly began chanting. They all knew the answer.

"Gates!" Nico roared. "We shall build gates of gold. Beautiful gates. Gates like you've never seen before."

Maria, his chief ally and serpent-in-charge of stores, met his gaze. Red scales circled her throat like a ruby necklace. Colonels stood at attention, medals from the wolf-war gleaming. The assembly screamed chants. Nico nodded, and Maria and the colonels slithered toward Zander. The ruling old guard unceremoniously slunk away, leaving Zander alone to face the mob. Over his forked tongue, even at this distance, Nico could smell the old snake's fear.

"Gates won't stop the permanent setting of the sun." Zander's words were soft. Maria and the colonels, trailed by the assembly, crawled closer. The chanting stopped.

"This elite has failed us. Now—prove your heroic virtues!" Nico's final word ended in a screaming hiss.

The assembly followed his order. Fresh meat was indeed scarce these days, but that night they feasted well on Zander-fleshed gyros.

The next few months unraveled in glorious fashion. The weather worsened but that was nothing new. With Zander finished, Nico wielded extraordinary power, aided by allies who believed in strength above all else. The old diner seethed, a boiling pit of carnivorous back-biting and treachery among his own supporters and subversion by Zander loyalists and gray-scaled philosophers. But Nico reigned popular. He dispatched soldiers to canvas the city, find prey and fetch it back to the diner, usually mice or rats and once a small deer. He ordered it hung bloody on stakes and organized savage wrestling competitions awarding prey as the prize. Citizens needed entertainment to fill the dim days of existence, and the violence helped solve the chronic over-population issues.

"The solution is to be tough," Nico raged triumphantly from his pedestal. As a young serpent, he'd been a strong contender in track contests and once placed first in the all-age high-jump. As an adult, he couldn't count the number of times he'd smashed the head of an adversary, sunk his fangs deep into prey, and ingested still-throbbing red flesh all for himself. Others could get tough, or they could eat worms.

Then, one day, he lost.

A young soldier named Albert was toying with a wiggling lizard just outside the diner's kitchen. Nico smelled the morsel and his head darted toward it, saliva already filling his mouth. Albert, instinctively and quite stupidly, whipped his tail and struck Nico with a stunning blow. "*Waste* him," Nico hissed, head swimming. A colonel promptly complied, and seconds later Albert's body was being dragged to the kitchen. Nico trailed after and began to consume Albert whole.

The next day, another warning sign.

Nico lay on the kitchen tile, blood cool, mind drifting, still digesting large hunks of Albert. Reeling from his loss, his head and ego bruised, Nico had gorged and retreated to the crawlspace under the ovens for a long day of digestion. He didn't especially love the diner's kitchen, and rarely hung out there, a windowless place of utter darkness. He preferred to lounge on the cold asphalt of the cracked parking lot and gaze up at the stars, wonder what it would be like to fly, serve as a winged serpent pulling Demeter's chariot, starlight reflecting from his orange-flecked scales for all to see.

His numb mind barely registered Maria's voice. It oozed low, somewhere near the back pantry with its empty bottles of olive oil and crackling parchment paper.

"He's *lost* it."

Nico tensed. He swallowed and forced down a juicy burp.

Voices murmured low.

Maria's voice again: "He says he saw ghosts."

Nico's jaw tightened. He'd mentioned that in confidence during an ouzo-drenched evening last week. He had simply mentioned that now and then, in his moments of glory on the host stand, he'd experienced some spiritual moments. Flashes, of a sort. He had witnessed ghosts of humans at the tables, servers striding down the aisles with moussaka, the aroma of spiced lamb filling the air. Ephemeral traces of the past, perhaps. Or maybe—in this world of endless molt and rebirth, existence at the mercy of the goddess of food and famine—some hint of the future.

"The assembly will support me." Maria's voice again. Not argumentative. *Authoritative.* The conniving reptile!

Snatches of words: *Poison. Slice. Smother.*

Albert's clogging remains sent darts of heartburn up Nico's throat. Smothering. Of all the ways to die, it would be the worst. The ignominy of it. To die smashed to the ground, night sky hidden by crawling, angry bodies above him. A plot! His own allies! The rest of the night he couldn't sleep. He stayed alert, frozen in his hiding place, listening to the plotters crunch and suck on the rest of Albert's remains. By morning, Nico had a plan.

He summoned the assembly.

In the main corridor unfurling from the entrance, booths to one side and counter on the other, the serpentine governing class spread before him: traitorous Maria, hard-scaled colonels, stretching and sanguine athletes, smirking poets and philosophers, a few silent and glaring Zander loyalists in the cheap seats near the back patio, and—his real source of power—all the rank-and-file who represented the common snake. True believers, who understood that viper society needed to be strong and secure, above all else.

From atop the host stand, Nico reared back and bellowed. "The golden gates—"

Gates, gates, gates! The answering chant erupted before he could finish. The enthusiasm! Back-stabbing Maria, the smug colonels— he'd show them. He eyed the philosophers, wondered what sort of false and twisted stories they would spin about him next. There was Bertrand, black-tailed and weathered, Cinder with a red triangular scale below his eye like a bloody teardrop. Devious creatures, these philosophers and their writings. At least they had the sense to wince and cower, silver-edged backs pressed against the Demeter fresco.

The chanting finally quieted enough for Nico to speak again.

"I have an important announcement." He paused for effect. "I shall embark on an odyssey."

Heads cocked all over the restaurant. His words weren't part of the usual script.

"A brief journey, but important."

He caught Maria's gaze. Her vertical pupils darkened and painted red lips twitched.

"I shall find the strategically correct location to construct the first gate. A shining golden gate, which shall strike fear and wonder in the hearts of all. I shall mark that place with my commanding scent, and loyal workers will begin to build." Nico drew a long breath. "And I shall brave the primitive barbarians to do it!"

Nico bared his fangs. The crowd screamed and drummed tails in support of their leader.

Nico set forth on his odyssey after an appropriate amount of scale-to-scale tail contact and speeches. He selected several bodyguards and a poet to accompany him, all of them young and hungry. The poet Pieter would compose an epic and recite it upon their return. This would add incomparably to Nico's overall mystique. Maria and the colonels would stay at the diner. In his absence, they could take the heat for limited fresh food. Nico departed in glory, with chants and applause following in his wake long after the diner fell out of sight.

"We'll return with fresh kills, while we're at it," Nico said. "A promotion to captain to whoever spots a deer!" The three young guards flicked their tails in pleasure. They fanned out in protection formation.

"May Demeter protect the *lives* of this brave *five*," said Pieter.

Nico grunted. Not the best poet, but it was impossible to find a decent poet or philosopher who wasn't a secret Zander loyalist. Why didn't the elites understand that the gates were a symbol? Golden gates represented superiority, virtue, the prowess of their society compared to all others.

They slithered through a city smashed by wind and earthquake. Caved in, crumbling buildings, streets steepled by tectonic grinds, glass everywhere. Nico didn't mind the journey. The cool air, days short and dim, the stars always shining. Snakes hadn't caused this destruction. It was the humans, of course, and they hadn't been spotted in years. Deadly carnivorous cousins, but unlike serpents, humans were not gifted with the ability to regenerate.

"You'd better write something good," Nico said to Pieter. "I want a glorious vibe. Lots of action."

Pieter would have to get creative. They'd encountered nothing living yet, aside from a few insects, and who cared about those? The desolation disturbed Nico but didn't surprise him. He'd been a young serpent once, out scrounging for all he could find. Life was supposed to be a cycle, but the whole world seemed in permanent decline. All the more reason to grab what power he could, however he could. His mind wandered to next steps, once he'd deposed of Maria and a few colonels and squeezed the entire ruling class into gasping prey under his complete control.

When he returned to the diner, he would phase in new rites of violence. That's why their serpentine ecosystem was so successful. Resources were limited, and would only become more so. Fierce competition—fangs snapping, tails lashing, beautiful snake-on-snake blood games—they weeded the population down to size. Survival of the fittest. And, at the moment, he—Nico—was fittest of all. Maybe they could wage another pointless war against wolves. He'd carve society down so that the best cuts of meat went straight to him on a silver platter.

Their little band kept slithering.

"Ah, darkness upon darkness . . ." said Pieter. "Has our wrathful goddess provided grain for these creatures?"

Nico twisted his upper body to look up. There—perched on the roof of church—a thousand crows watched their progress. Some flapped wings and paced, others sat still as rain-battered gargoyles. Ugly creatures, but under the feathers beat blood and warm flesh. A thousand meals, tantalizingly within sight and out of striking distance. Nico's belly grumbled. Oh, but to have a god's strength! His cursed form bound always to earth. He had only his cruel wits and fangs to serve his needs.

"We are growing near," Nico said. He could sense the impatience and fatigue of the young guards. The poet trailed behind, always short-of-breath. "All of this territory belongs to us, conquered long ago by our heroic ancestors who came from the old world, Greece." It was true. They all knew it. "It is up to us to secure it for future generations."

Even Nico felt tired now. It was far enough. They should stop here, near this human church. One of the guards claimed he spotted pigs to the east, another said he'd spotted a patch of living cornstalks. Red-tinged vapors oozed up from cracks in the earth, providing a dramatic effect. Nico clicked his tongue against his fangs, considering. It didn't matter what site he selected for the first golden gate. They did not actually have any gold, for one thing. But still, Nico's body kept contracting and stretching, skirting over gravel, every instinct demanding that he keep going.

Soon those instincts proved correct. He sensed something in the distance. They all heard it: a relentless roaring. Like thunder, but softer, more controlled, shouts of a crowd at the last moment of a hundred-yard dash. But if these were united voices, they didn't stop.

"Danger ahead," Nico hissed. "Barbarians."

It could not be actual barbarians. There weren't any. A few prowling coyotes, perhaps, or unauthorized frog colonies squatting in concrete lagoons.

"Work it in," said Nico, with a look back towards Pieter, who'd fallen out-of-sight behind broken rubble. "The sound."

"Yes, composing in my mind," gasped Pieter. "I have lyrics, meter, meaning. Ah—"

A scream from the poet, suddenly cut off. Nico and the guards stopped and stared at each other.

Maria? The colonels? "Close in," Nico ordered.

They did, but too late. As they slithered toward Pieter, tall and hairy creatures grasping spears lunged toward them. Not monkeys, not gods . . .

"Humans," said a guard in a low whisper.

Nico barely heard it. For he was already escaping, every muscle flexing, his head, belly and tail grasping for traction on earth and propelling himself forward, every survival instinct in his body raging—find darkness! Now! Metal clanged on stone inches from his head. Pain burst along his spine before he managed to reach safety of a narrow pipe. The steel compressed his bleeding body, but he was safe for the moment. He winced at the hissing cries and moans behind him.

He slithered on. When the pipe ended, he chose routes offering the most darkness, always moving closer to that roaring sound. It was unfortunate about the others but he'd eventually work his way back to the diner. Lone survivor—he could build a true hero persona. And humans returned! The assembly would feed on that news for a long time.

A strong fishy smell mixed with mud-slick metal slid over Nico's tongue. Without warning, he came upon it, and he drew up short. An ocean lay before him—a place that, he was certain, had once been part of the city. Now, it was towering cliffs battered by swirling black waters, buildings and streets perched along a precipice. Howling winds and smashing earthquakes would send more concrete and glass sliding to a watery burial. To the north, a river spewed water into the ocean, creating a misty, deafening waterfall.

This was a gate. Towering cliffs and endless dark waters. A divine, living gate. Nico sighed—even if they could build golden gates, it would pale in comparison to this. He lifted his gaze to the stars and the lone moon struggling to control the waves. Huge black birds with scaled wings spun in lazy circles above the water. Nico dropped his head to the mud and shut his eyes. How he envied them, the ability to soar, their commanding gaze for miles!

He sensed a close and familiar scent. He whipped around, poised to strike. Serpents surrounded him in a half-circle, cornering him with the cliff to his back.

"Your reign is over, Nico."

Nico stared in dismay. It wasn't Maria or the colonels. The scales of these snakes were weathered, their dark eyes cloudy from years of squinting at texts. Black-tailed Bertrand, Cinder with the bloody teardrop, and three of their weak-spined philosopher pals.

"Elites." Nico snapped his tail and glared. "Zander loyalists! Lying and lazy philosophers! Molt your weak scales and reveal the traitor beneath!" Words that the supporters liked to hear. But these five philosophers just nodded as if expecting the tirade.

The wind strengthened. Nico hugged his body close to the ground and raised his head. "This is assassination." He kept his tone firm and grave.

They answered him with a sharp, unified hiss. Nico backed closer to the cliff's edge.

"I'll enjoy watching you plunge to your death," Bertrand said. "A fatal end to your power-hungry rule. You shall fall!"

Fall, fall, fall, they chanted.

Fear chilled Nico's cold heart to ice. This was indeed a bad way to perish. A long slide into oblivion, drowning by water and pure darkness. Could he fight? His stomach turned. These were creakingly old snakes but he was outnumbered, exhausted from the journey, and his spear wounds still seeped blood. He looked again at the stars. Perhaps there would be an odyssey beyond this one, another life, privilege and power beyond anything he had experienced on lowly earth. He shivered, feeling his scales harden. By the goddess, he was molting from fear.

He hissed with all his strength. "Oh lady of the great cycle of life and death, my queen Demeter—"

The assassins writhed closer, eyes wide, eager for the kill. "You use the name of the holy mother in vain! Across your deceitful lips and putrid fangs!"

Nico spat. Venom harmless without a bite, but the splatter across Bertrand's face felt gratifying. He had the right to invoke the divine. "Goddess of famine—"

"Goddess of *fertility*!"

Nico could scream louder. "Goddess of hunger—*vengeance—RAGE!*"

The assassins replied in joined scream that drowned the roar of wind and waves. "The law-bringer! Our lady of civilized existence!"

"Matron of decay," Nico muttered. He hunched his spine and prepared for stinging blows that would send him hurling over the edge. He breathed in, sensing the reptile scent of his assassins, the fishy waters below . . . and the sweet aroma of poppies in bloom. Nico frowned.

The serpents crawled closer. "Fall, fall—"

The chant was cut off with a collective gasp. The snakes froze, their unblinking eyes targeting something behind Nico. Near his tail, he sensed heat. A beautiful heat of melting gold, the dark heat of a heart burned black over fire. His inner ear vibrated with the sound of a scrape of stone and wretched moan.

He slowly turned.

A female in human form, dripping and wild, wrenched herself over the cliff's edge to safe ground. With dignified speed, she hauled herself upright. Clouds freed the moon to cast its light upon the woman. She wore a rotting black gown and cloak. Her hair hung in thick braids, her skin gleamed as if swept with oil, and the veins in her wrists and hands were dark, like snakes squirmed within her flesh instead of blood. She wielded a goat's horn spilling plump seeds.

Nico stared, cool air sliding over his fangs as he gasped for breath. All this time, living even deeper than he, in some dark cave beneath a cliff, above a sea?

"Demeter," the other snakes murmured, bowing low.

She ignored them and flung seeds that arched high. Nico followed their flight and saw that humans had advanced close to attack again. Now they cowered. The seeds sprung to life as living plants and an instant later dropped their fruit and grains. The humans shrieked with pleasure and gathered them.

Demeter raised her hands to the stars and clapped them in summons. At this, Nico screamed in delight. Streaking down from the heavens was a golden chariot pulled by a team of glowing, winged serpents.

"Take me, take me, take me!" Nico and the elites screamed. This was their queen. She brought destruction—ashes, rising water, darkness. But also, growth and life. The grand cycle. Nico imagined wings sprouting from his scales. He could see it—feel it—gliding through the night sky with the deity on divine missions. "Take me," he whispered. "I will serve you. I will serve you *best.*"

Demeter heard him, she heard them all, the hissing cries of the serpents desperate for attention. Fear ravaged Nico's soul—not of her, not of death, but of being ignored, forgotten, forced to accept the same fate as the lowly others. Demeter gazed down, her braids curling as if each was alive, her flesh glowing. Nico coiled his body, and with all his might, he sprung toward her, the longest, highest jump his body had ever achieved.

Demeter caught Nico and held him like she wanted to hold him. She raised him, far higher above the ground than he'd ever been before.

At her warm touch, Nico shuddered with a vision. An all-consuming sense of his future death and rebirth. Not wings. His cold blood would someday become warm ash. The ash would become sprout and stalk and bloom handsome scarlet, that striking color, that symbol of death and resurrection.

And then it was over.

Demeter gently placed him back into the mud and stepped onto her chariot. The gold flashed as she rose higher and disappeared. The only sign of where she'd gone was the eastern sky, where, for the first time in many years, a sunrise radiated bright yellow.

Nico set off for the diner, the sun warm on his back. The goddess's touch had healed his wounds, and he soon crawled out of his old skin. His new scales, a whole new self, shone bright and black. Nico and the philosophers were quiet on the return journey, reflecting. Tears crept down Nico's face, but he also found that his raw feelings soon faded and the practicalities of life reasserted themselves. Glares from the philosophers disturbed him and he moved quickly, staying out of reach of any strike.

They reached the diner during quiet twilight, snakes waking from afternoon naps on quake-battered asphalt, stretching in preparation for nocturnal hunts. "Nico!" the snakes cried. "Sunlight! New life!"

Indeed, Nico could see green weeds stabbing through concrete cracks, clover reaching over the rim of pots that stood sentry at the diner door. Inside, taking up his speaking position atop the host stand, he spied new spider in a corner and a beetle scurrying across the linoleum.

"The gates?" the assembly inquired. "Barbarians?"

"Forget the gates!" Nico hissed. "And never mind the barbarians." The philosophers slithered in and took up seats near the back patio. Maria and the colonels sat close by. Nico's mind squeezed and churned. His gaze lifted to the faded fresco of the goddess. In front of everyone, more scales shriveled off his body and he heaved with silent tears. The assembly fell silent. Nico gathered himself enough to choke out words.

"We have been chosen. *You* have been chosen." Hundreds of snakes stared back at him. "Our whole community will be remade. We are all woven together, loyal to the divine lady of the cycle of life and death." Nico eyed the philosophers, who slowly nodded agreement. "Our fate is clear. We shall rebuild her altar, and renew the ancient practices of worship. We thank her, she who has given us dry scales, cool blood, the ability to regenerate, to remake ourselves and our lives." Nico paused and cried out: "Oh goddess of fertility and famine, I am your lowly servant, the viper. Hear my hissing prayer for a freshly reborn regime! A *righteous* regime!"

Assembly tails began to pound. He counted quickly. Close to three hundred snakes. Far too many, even if the new light on earth brought many mice and rats. He composed his face to a stern expression and stared down the assembly. "Those who don't shed their old skins and comply with the ideals of the new order will meet the consequences. They shall—"

"Burn!" a philosopher shouted from the back.

Burn, burn, burn, the assembly chanted. The heads of the assembly bobbed up and down. Even Maria and the colonels followed suit. Someone lit incense.

"As your leader," Nico said, "I shall decide who must burn!"

The assembly roared its assent and continued its chant.

Nico demanded garments reflecting his elevated spiritual status, and young snakes quickly fetched him a veiled headdress and beaded vestments, crafted in some past generation that had first settled the diner. They found icons of the goddess and set up the chipped vases and plates and dusty paintings at the wall fresco to create an impressive altar.

Appropriately adorned, Nico kept hissing, fueling the crowd into religious fervor, enjoying his dominance, his brain growing dizzy with power and the sweet scent of myrrh. Night fell. He could no longer see the twisting and snapping assembly. But Nico was the most cold-blooded snake of all, and as the citizens of Demeter Diner writhed in righteous excitement, he could feel their heat.

A Random Aquarium at the Pier

~ *Joshua Flowers*

You stretch your tiny arms past the edge of the pier as an Atlantic wind billows your sundress. Beneath you, waves hit the thick, barnacled pillars of the pier with all their force, yet you feel no shaking. No one atop the busy tourist space seems worried about the sea's casual wrath.

A finger snaps for your attention, but you don't respond fast enough. Your mother yanks your hand into hers, her grip too tight, as she scans over the crowd on tiptoes. Her heavy purse dangles at the crook of her bronze elbow. She wears a white sundress similar to yours, but that is an accident. When she bought it for you months ago, she was too tired to notice she bought you a smaller version of something she already owned.

"Fucking place," she whispers under her breath. You hear the swear but say nothing. Even you, for all your childish faults, can tell your mother needs a moment out of the sour, sweat-soaked air and noisy groupings of tourists. She needs somewhere dark where she can close her eyes, knock her head back, and take a deep shot of breath.

She decides on a destination and drags you. The fingers hooked into your wrist hurt. Not enough to bruise (not yet) but enough to notice. Poor child. You know your mother doesn't mean it, so you're trying hard to just be thankful she is spending her one day-off with you. Instead of sleeping, she's exploring a pier she hates because you once mentioned over diner that you'd like to visit it.

The two of you move towards an uninteresting building laid next to others like a brick laid into a wall. The name escapes you as a pair of women in wide-brim hats obscure the sign above the door. Years later, when you have grown into the shape of your mother, you will tell your story to other girls grown into mothers, and they won't believe you. You won't believe you. That'll drive you a little mad, but that's alright. That's what childhood memories are meant to do.

In the present, your mother lets go inside the dimly lit lobby. You find a seat on a bench bathed in neon as she pays for tickets. Your pink sneakers clash against the blue and black swirls of the carpeted floor. Whatever this place is, they regularly vacuum as it's all too clean for the pier. Mother returns with two tickets: they have ghostly faces stamped above the word "ADMISSION."

"Where are we?"

"Who knows, but it's got air conditioning." Your mother takes a deep breath. The cool lighting is enough to hide her burnt cheeks. She notices your apprehension. "It'll be fun. Come on."

You follow her further in. Truthfully, you would have liked to listen to the waves a little longer, but the money is already spent, so you keep your mouth shut. Besides, following at the heels of mothers is what children do.

Through a large pair of doors (one blue, one black) you find a man in a gaudy suit blocking your way. He greets you both with a deep bow and has the air of a theatre villain. A man of big monologues who is killed at the end by a simple kick.

"Welcome," he says in a deep voice, "To my Aquarium of Horrors!"

First Exhibit—The Phantasmal

Pickled Screams

The tank is bright red and lights you in the color of a blood bath. The guide reads aloud from a notecard he produces from his jacket pocket. "Most screams can be pickled. All you need is the right apparatus, and a tank filled with special soul-absorbing jelly. Screams, being a shed part of the soul, usually dissipate in the air within moments, but the jelly prevents that dull end. If you bring your face close, you can see them bounce from wall to wall."

With a smile, the guide gestures his white hand to the glass. You crane your neck back at your mother. She is near the entrance, raising an eyebrow at the sight. Her eyes lock with yours, and you can tell she wants to say, "It's alright hun. You can get close," but she hesitates. Her phone buzzes, and now that it's in her hand, you know the words won't come. She'll ignore you until she's ready.

The guide gestures again towards the tank. Mustering a little courage, you step up. The red glow is soft on your eyes. Staring inside is like peering into a massive block of strawberry jelly.

A foggy face presses against the glass in front of you with a soft thump. Their eyes are twisted and mouth wide in a scream. The face pulls away. Somewhere you can't see, another thump.

You flinch.

You didn't mean to, but you did. The guide saw.

The Drowned Man

Two spotlights illuminate a phony seafloor of foam. A pale white man is inside, sitting on a cheap fold-out chair. His shirtless body is bloated, and thin weeds of hair float above his mostly bald top.

"Does a drowned man need much explanation?" The guide says with a soft, solitary chuckle.

The drowned man turns towards you, but you can tell he sees nothing. His eyes are foggy white orbs. He's like dad back when he used to live with you, too drunk to see anything more than shapes. You glance at your mother, wondering if she notices too, but she's still on her phone. She hasn't pulled her face up since the screams.

A Prophecy

Lights swirl around the center of the tank, twisting water in a dazzling display that catches your breath. Suddenly this strange trip is worth it.

"Sailors of olde would look for these out at sea. They'd bring their boats beside the churning light and toss a man down. If he came back up, he'd return with a new heading towards glory."

You step closer, wanting to press your face to the glass like the pickled screams. Inside the light, you think you see yourself but older. The glass keeps you too far away to view clearly. There is so much you can't tell. Are you beautiful? Are your father and mother nearby, or are you alone? The light gives you no answers. You want to get closer to it. Enveloped by it. Maybe then you would understand.

"Careful," the guide says. You glance up at him. Something about his over-the-top persona keeps you on edge. "It is easy to get lost in a prophecy of the future. Usually, it's of such amazing quality, one would forget they had to ever trudge through a less elegant past to reach their revelation."

From the corner of your eyes, you see your mother finally put away her phone. She still lingers at the edge of the exhibit with a dull-eyed stare. You suspect she wasn't even listening to the guide. Part of you wants to beg her over, afraid she might miss your dazzling future. Another part of you—the selfish, evil part of you that would wake your poor, overworked, exhausted mother from a nap demanding food and love—says, *Keep this for yourself. She doesn't care.* It is a petty kind of revenge. New to you, but one you'll understand better as you grow older.

When you turn back to the light, you see the specter of yourself walking alone. She is in some kind of large, empty space (for a moment, you think a field), and the moon hangs low in a daylight sky. There is something off about this older you, but the prophecy is too hazy to tell what.

Transfixed, you think about standing in the spot forever, waiting to see the final destination of your future self. Maybe then you'll finally understand why this vision is so important. Why it grips you so strongly.

"What happens if someone stays in the light too long?" you ask, feeling a sting from your dry eyes. You've forgotten to blink.

The guide smiles. "Don't you remember the last display?"

Second Exhibit—The Mawcillious Murderers

Congo Teeth Fish

Lime green lights illuminate the rocky tank. Its floor is decorated with plastic gold and toy skulls. Above the gaudy display, rows of teeth swim back and forth on tiny, red fins. Each tooth is the shape of a porcupine quill curved behind the body of the fish. Ironically, you can't actually see their mouths. The teeth get in the way.

"The Teeth Fish are a rare breed that only exist in one, large lake in the Congo. The locals took great care to preserve the population as they subsist on a very meaty diet. Funnily enough, these hungry fish are not ones for cannibalism. Perhaps they find one another too difficult to chew?" He chuckles then checks his watch. "Look at that. Feeding time."

A worker tosses hunks of cow into the tank. The clear water turns a messy, transparent red. Teeth swarm the meat and tear it apart in a feast so thorough they lick the blood from the water. In a blink, the tank is clean again like nothing happened. Just a tank full of teeth swimming about.

Maine Knife Lobsters

You ask your mother what she thought of the fish.

"It was a little dark," she admitted, "But as long as you're enjoying yourself."

You say nothing. It takes a few more steps before your mother thinks to ask if you are enjoying yourself instead of presuming like she often does. As you answer, the next display greets you with angry smashes against glass.

You hear them before you see them. Their massive claws are as large as your head with white tips that darken into nightshade shells. The color just barely hides the lobster's furious, pearl-shaped eyes. There are four in the tank, and when they see you, they go into a frenzy. Their attack is furious as they stab, as they pinch, as they want desperately to rip you down to the marrow of your bones.

The guide pulls out a notecard and starts to speak, but you can't hear what is said of them over their infuriated drumming. It occurs to you that your mother probably didn't hear your answer either. She says nothing about it, so you do likewise.

Coral Dragons

The name stirs a fantastical hope in you. Dragons? Here? They're real? You feel like the main character of a fantasy book, about to discover the beginnings of a magical adventure.

Your smile fades when you see them. They look like sea horses, but instead of flowery limbs, these dragons have coral spirals shaped like buttercream frosting flowers. The fish don't swim but hop across the sandy floor in spasmodic jerks. They float from one spot to the next as if pretending to swim and failing.

Nothing in this exhibit captivates you. Your mother stands by a corner, rubbing the dried sweat from her face. She closes her eyes like she's trying to beckon a quick moment of sleep. You've never seen anyone sleep while standing up (like you've never seen teeth fish, lobsters, or dragons before today), but if anyone could do it, it's your mother.

This is the first day off she's had in weeks. After this, she goes back to work at the midnight shift. You know it's likely Granma will put you to bed again when you get home, but maybe if you sleep in late, you might wake up with your mother in her bed. You could sneak into her arms. Snuggle beneath them. Pretend she had never left at all.

Third Exhibit—The Horrors

The Dredge

At first, you think it looks like an octopus. A very thin, very sickly-looking octopus. When you count the tentacles, you realize there are too many, then think it resembles more a floating patch of seagrass. In the shaggy, flowing mass, you see something beneath. A boney, withered arm. You blink, and it vanishes in the shuffle of tendrils.

"There are maybe two hundred Dredges in the world. They roam the ocean floor as if searching for something, but no one knows what. In all observation, no one has ever seen them eat, yet they do hunt. A Dredge will grab fish and smash their heads against the nearest rock. They'll let their dead prey float in the water and move on, perpetually continuing their search. Sometimes unlucky explorers will swim too close to them. They often end up like the fish."

As you stare, a boney foot like a burned-up skeleton appears before disappearing again. It takes you too long to realize the creature isn't swimming but walking. In the sand, you can see the marks of the shriveled tentacles dragging behind. There are no footprints.

Your mother steps up behind you. "This one kind of reminds me of your father," she says as a little joke, but you don't laugh. This isn't the one that reminded you of your father. She hadn't been paying attention for that one. Noticing she has a little more peppiness now that you're both somewhere cool, you decide to leave that annoyance behind. This is your favorite version of your mother: the one that has the energy to give you attention.

The two of you stare at the Dredge for a long while (to the irritation of the guide who wishes to move onto his next horror), and each of you guesses a thing it might be looking for. Treasure. Friends. Cigarettes. A drink. The principal's office--you say this one and your mother laughs, remembering the time she needed twenty minutes to find the parent-teacher meeting. Family.

Both your jokes die off from boredom as you realize the Dredge has been simply walking in circles this entire time.

The Discarded Warrior

They look like a knight but not. They're a fish. Kind of? It has a thick tail and two arms, both poking out a round shell. The shape is awkward as if it's hunched inside. You can't tell if it has a human head or fish head beneath. Somehow it sees you then swims to a corner. You hear crying as if someone was sobbing right by your shoulder.

"What you see is a thing from an ancient race that took up war against an even older enemy. Unsurprisingly, they lost. Their war had been needless and futile, ending in a defeat so thoroughly gruesome, each subsequent generation only knew how to cower."

The thing breaks off a sharp shard from a corner of its shell and tries to stab itself through the chest, but the shell blocks the blow. The crying intensifies, and you realize you've never seen something so large cry. Not an adult. Not your mother nor father. After a certain age, you expect people to forget how. This unhealthy notion will be reinforced when your Granma passes and your mother will be too proud to show her tears. That will be hard, but not nearly as hard as when your father swerves into a canal. For that death, your mother will dance with revelry.

At the display, your mother is bothered by the stabbing. You can see her hand twitch to shield your eyes but stop because she knows you've already seen too much. Trying to protect you now would be silly.

Once the shard of shell shatters in the creature's hand, it tumbles over the sand to get to the other corner. It breaks off a new piece and returns to attacking itself.

The guide shakes his head. "It's all for show. If it truly wanted to end things, it would. Even the most pitiful of us can think of at least one way to the grave."

The Visitor

They dance the way only things that swim can. Six fins entwined within one another push the creature up to the top of the tank before it spins above—showing off dazzling, orange scales—then dives down. With a twirl, it stops itself from smashing against the steel floor. They hadn't bothered to put up any flourishes in the tank. No illusions to distract from the fact this is a beautiful thing inside a cage.

The guide tells you he knows nothing of the Visitor, just that they aren't from your world. You think he's lying. The fish appears normal albeit strange. It's like a giant goldfish, a size between you and your mother. The size of an older sibling.

As you move, The Visitor follows, dragging itself against the glass to get closer to you. You put a hand where its body would be, and it spins in delight. Your mother pulls out her phone to get a video, but the guide blocks her. He reminds her that there are no pictures or recordings allowed in his aquarium.

They both look away as The Visitor folds its fins over the glass where your hand touches. You think the fins resemble the ribbons on your school's maypole piled atop the ground. You can see something stir beneath.

It stings your palm through the glass, and you jump back. Neither the guide nor your mother notice, still arguing about the picture policy. You shake out your hand, and the pain vanishes. There is no mark on the glass. Your palm appears fine. The orange thing dances excitedly as you move on. All the while, your mother complains about being unable to capture the memory.

☉

Special Exhibit

The hallway curves as if you've reached the end, yet the guide brings you to one last thing: a rickety, steel plate cage dangling from a chain above a pit. He opens it and gestures inside. "We have a special exhibit under construction, though considering what wonderful guests you've been, I thought you might enjoy a glimpse."

Your mother places both hands on your shoulder as if ready to pick you up and carry you away. The guide sees this but doesn't take it personally. To show you it's safe, he steps inside the cage first then twists around the empty space.

Still unsure, your mother looks to you, lets you decide. Deep inside your soul, something beckons you to see what's next in a language you don't know but think you could pronounce if you tried. A meeting that almost feels like fate. A name half-noticed further down the page by a wandering eye.

You shrug, and your mother takes this as affirmation for one last horror. The two of you step into the cage with the guide. The door shuts on its own, and the cage lurches downward like an elevator. The soft neon that had accompanied you the entire time fades as you sink into a pit of shadows. The cage drops fast enough for you to feel it in your stomach. It's tough to keep your pink sneakers steady.

The cage slows and gently settles atop a bed of sand in a pitch-black room. You can't see the edges of the walls or ceiling. Only dark abyss. The cage opens, and the guide shows you out.

"Don't wander away. We wouldn't want you two getting lost."

Ortro

The guide says nothing more. He stands with his hands behind his back, gazing at the distance. You stare too yet see nothing. A long time passes, and your mother asks if maybe you should leave. You ask for five more minutes. After coming this far, you want to see this last thing.

Six glowing eyes open in the air a great distance away, and you realize you're not in a room. What exists around you is a sky without stars and a horizon that never knew light. The six blue-light eyes, positioned like a spider's, don't illuminate its own body well. The head is like a sea-rotted cube that has eaten off its own corners atop a too-thin neck that disappears into the abyss. The lights face you. Stare back at you. For minutes, you try to decipher the rest of its body through the dark but cannot. In a blink, the eyes inch closer.

"We should go," your mother says, a rattle in her voice. You and her look back. The guide is gone. The opened cage remains.

When you check on the eyes, they are far too close. They loom like a set of blue suns. You still can't see what kind of body the neck leads to. Your mother grabs you by the wrist and drags you back into the cage.

The door shuts.

The cage goes up.

Your mother shifts her hands over yours then squeezes.

As you fly away, the eyes follow. They keep pace. Between the two, you worry the cage is slower even though your guts strain from its momentum. You expect a shadow drenched limb to appear from the darkness to smash you apart.

Despite your fears, you see nothing. Only the eyes.

They don't shrink as if you've outrun them but blink out one by one. You and your mother are in pure, total, heavy darkness for but a moment before the cage pulls itself back up into an aquarium flooded by neon.

You're at the end, and a nice teenager in a booth thanks you for stopping by then points at the gift shop. Inside are some cheap stickers, poorly made stuffed animals, and shirts. On a shelf, you learn the creature with six eyes is called Ortro and priced at nineteen ninety-nine as a black threaded ball with six felt dots stitched into it. The rest of the selection is equally disappointing, but your mother encourages you to pick something out.

"You want to remember today, right?"

You do. After all, it was a day spent with your mother. You pick out a t-shirt with "The Aquarium of Horror" printed on the front. The font choice is dull, and there are no pictures to add visual flair, but it fits over your white dress. A few months later, you'll lose the shirt and forget the name of the place as the memory nestles alongside forgotten dreams.

A few steps, and you're back on the hot pier. The air-conditioning had become so natural that you forgot how sweltering it is outside. To fight against the heat, your mother buys ice cream. The two of you sit on a bench as waves of people pass by. Some chocolate drips onto the shirt, but the dark blue fabric makes it impossible to notice.

The two of you chat about the aquarium, and she asks if you liked it. You said you did, and it's true. Listening, your mother nods. She asks what your favorite display was. You say the prophecy. The swirl of lights and the shadow of your future self still linger in the back of your mind. You hope to dream of it like you sometimes do of when your mother and father got along.

In fact, you will dream again of it. Much, much later, after the prophesized event had already occurred. You'll wake from the dream, covered in sweat as your own child lays nestled beside you. Memories of the aquarium will feel so clear you'd think you've read it in a story. The difference being, you finally understand the prophecy as if submerged in it like a sailor of olde.

The light tried to tell you of a disastrous family diner. Your mother will say something of your then dead father, and you'll explode on her. The first time in years. It will be an awful fight that ends in you fleeing with tears. On the drive back home, you'll think of your childhood because what else has your mother left you to think about? Intrusive thoughts will hit one after the other, and the small space of your car will start to suffocate.

You'll stop beside a random field, get out, and walk through it as if hoping to vanish into the distant tree line. Each step through overgrown grass will bring a new memory, and soon you'll traverse through the long history of quiet moments that made up your life. Not just the bad, but the good too. Like the day your mother took you to a random aquarium on the pier. You'll remember the shirt you lost, and feel a pang in your heart knowing it's gone forever.

In that field, you'll reflect, and it will be one of the most important moments of your life. It'll be when you accept how hard your childhood was for both you and your mother. You'll appreciate how much work your Granma put in to making a home, how tough the long hours had to have been for your mother who surely wanted to spend more days at piers with you, and how despite the massive love for your father, he was never a perfect man. That will also be when you allow yourself to hurt, to recognize the pain of wishing your mother had more to give, and that wishing for attention never made you selfish.

You will stand beneath a ghostly moon lurking in the shifting twilight, and despite the conflicting feelings of love and pain, you'll decide to forgive your mother. In forgiveness, you'll find a new, strange, horrifying, mesmerizing, beautiful peace you'll have never thought possible before.

But that moment is in the future. There is no forgiveness in you now because you're just beginning to recognize the pain.

As you two talk, the heat beats down on you. You watch the energy melt from your mother. You try to ask about her favorite part of the aquarium, but she gives vague answers. Some passersby step on her toes. Her face gets angry and red, blending with the sunburn set into her cheeks. Sweat soaks through the dress, making your new shirt heavy.

Your mother checks the time and accidentally lets out a sigh. You pretend not to notice, but your mother panics. She yanks you by the wrists to haul you to another attraction. Somewhere away from the heat and bitter guilt that swims behind both your heels.

New Caldwell Metropolitan Guard Cold Case Files
On the Disappearance of Oliver Wolsey

~ *John Klima*

Item List

- *Hand-copied pages from Constable Marcus Gurney's journal*
- *Transcriptions of interviews conducted by Metropolitan Guard with various individuals:*
  - *Graham Douglas*
  - *Edgar Shipman*
  - *Roger Blokeman*
  - *[REDACTED]*
  - *Ignatius Howlett*
- *Meeting minutes from New Caldwell Tarot and Magic Guilds wherein discussion of Oliver Wolsey occurred:*
  - *Redhands (Health and Medicine Tarot Guild)*
  - *Speakers for the Decayed (Communication with the Dead Tarot Guild)*
- *Partial tarot deck of mixed provenance*
- *Longshoreman's hook, bloody (stored in paper as per instruction from the Blood Mage branch of the Metropolitan Guard)*

⟩—๑

Health and Medicine Tarot Guild Meeting
Monday, August 3rd, 1874

Members in Attendance
[REDACTED] Chair
[REDACTED] Vice-Chair
[REDACTED] Secretary
[REDACTED] Treasurer
[REDACTED] Chair-Elect
[REDACTED] Past Chair

[REDACTED] Director
[REDACTED] Director
[REDACTED] Director
Members Not in Attendance
[REDACTED] Director
[REDACTED] Director
[REDACTED] Director
[REDACTED] Director
Guests in Attendance
Oliver Wolsey
Staff in Attendance
Nym Vernon
Reynaldo Stafford
Edgar Cromwell

1. Call to Order
Chair called meeting to order at six o'clock in the evening of the third of August, 1874.

2. Approval of Agenda
ON A MOTION MADE by [REDACTED], SECONDED by [REDACTED] and CARRIED, the agenda was approved as circulated.

3. Conflict of Interest
Director [REDACTED] recuses himself from discussion of NEW BUSINESS due to a CONFLICT OF INTEREST.

4. Approval of Previous Minutes
ON A MOTION DULY MADE by [REDACTED]SECONDED by [REDACTED] and CARRIED the draft minutes of the Guild's meeting of the second of July were approved as presented.

5. Old Business
a. Redhands Name
[REDACTED] opened discussion on the colloquial name of the Guild—'Redhands'—which he disdains. [REDACTED] asked the attending board for ideas of how to stop the pernicious name from the public's tongues.

[REDACTED] stated that there was no way to control the public and since 'Redhands' was spoken often under auspices of fear, that the Guild should embrace it.

Followed a moment of shouting by several Guild members including [REDACTED], [REDACTED], and [REDACTED] among others. Chair banged the gavel until the shouting wore down. He declared this business closed.

Chair noted this was the sixteenth consecutive meeting that [REDACTED] had brought this item to the agenda with no solution and no movement towards change. It was declared to be un-agendable in the future.

  b.   Membership

[REDACTED] reported that after reviewing membership files after last meeting there was no need to seek out new members. [REDACTED] apologized for wasting Oliver Wolsey's time as his petition for membership would not be brought to the Guild at this time.

  6.   New Business
  a.   Printing Press

[REDACTED] MADE A MOTION to stop using The Elementary Pot printing house and purchase a printing press for the Guild to create tarot cards in private. The MOTION was SECONDED by [REDACTED] and CARRIED via ROLL CALL VOTE.

  b.   Card Manufacture

[REDACTED] made a subsequent MOTION that [REDACTED], while recused from discussion, be put in charge of purchasing the printing press and then card manufacture given his experience in the field. SECONDED by [REDACTED] and CARRIED via ROLL CALL VOTE.

  7.   Committee Reports
None

  8.   Staff Reports

Nym Vernon reported that the staff had found a solution for the rat problem in the Guild's kitchens, namely obtaining several cats. Vernon also reported that construction had finished on the upstairs residences and after a coat of paint the Guild officers could move in.

Edgar Cromwell reported that their current launderer had switched soaps and was causing their robes to become pink rather than retaining their deep scarlet. The Chair gave permission to seek a new launderer.

9.   Adjournment
ON A MOTION MADE by [REDACTED], SECONDED by [RE-DACTED] and CARRIED, the meeting was adjourned at nine o'clock.

꒰ꔫ

Hand-copied transcript of Constable Marcus Gurney's journal, entry dated August 6th

Thinking back on last night I will endeavor to put my thoughts into a reasonable facsimile of sense and order.

Not long into my beat around the Nine Points a pair of youths caught my attention and brought me down to the nearby docks. The young men directed me to where a crowd gathered near Pier Four. My constable's badge and dragon's ash truncheon opened a path for me to the center of the assembled mass of humanity.

I could immediately see what had transformed their curiosity into general unruliness. A dark-skinned man lay on the pier in a growing pool of blood, a bloody longshoreman's hook on the wooden pier beside him.

The crowd seemed both fearful and disdainful of this man. I recognized him as a soldier under my commend from my days in the Royal Navy and moved in close to see what I could do.

I called him by name, James, and cradled his head in my lap, shocking many in the crowd. My memory was of a good sailor, strong swimmer, and fearless soldier.

James recognized me and grabbed my coat forcibly. He told me I had to find the boy, had to avenge this terrible act of bodily harm. I assured James that I would do everything in my power to bring about justice. There was little that could be done to save his life. The most I could do was make him comfortable.

James said that the scurrilous scamp stole from him. That they had agreed upon a price for the scrimshaw and the young man did not have enough money. The scrimshaw had not been easy to obtain and James wanted true value for his efforts.

James was attacked from behind by the honorless youth and gutted like some bottom feeder. Then the youth took the scrimshaw from him and ran.

James repeated this story several times as the Metropolitan Guard Crime Investigation Squad arrived with their arcane leather portmanteaus to gather evidence and do what they could to solve the crime.

James went still in my arms. He had expired.

Upon seeing James dead, the MGCIS stopped and conferred with each other. Then, they picked up the hook from the pier, stored it in one of their evidence bags, and left the scene.

I found it disgraceful that the MGCIS did nothing more than collect a single piece of evidence and leave without interviewing any of the crowd. All the same, with James expired, the crowd dispersed and went back to their everyday business.

I spent the remainder of my shift finding someone who would take James' body and ensure that it was interred properly. There was little to no hope of finding family but the least I could do was make sure his body wasn't left on the piers for the rats.

Upon returning to the station, my sergeant berated me for a full half hour for wasting time on dark scum when I could have been helping good citizens. I disagreed with the assessment of wasted time, but I kept my mouth shut.

Partial tarot deck of mixed provenance

Major Arcana 0 – The Fool - missing
Major Arcana I - The Magician - missing
Major Arcana II – Fire (Communication with the Dead Tarot Guild)
Major Arcana III – Water (Communication with the Dead Tarot Guild)
Major Arcana IV – Air (Communication with the Dead Tarot Guild)
Major Arcana V – Earth (Communication with the Dead Tarot Guild)

Major Arcana VI – The Lovers - missing
Major Arcana VII – The Chariot - missing
Major Arcana VIII – Equity (Health and Medicine Tarot Guild)
Major Arcana IX – Philosopher (Health and Medicine Tarot Guild)
Major Arcana X – Wheel of Fortune – cast in bronze and image etched deeply into its surface
Major Arcana XI – Strength - missing
Major Arcana XII – The Hanged Man - missing
Major Arcana XIII – Death - missing
Major Arcana XIV – Temperance - missing
Major Arcana XV – Illness (Communication with the Dead Tarot Guild)
Major Arcana XVI – The Tower - missing
Major Arcana XVII – Blood (Health and Medicine Tarot Guild)
Major Arcana XVIII – The Moon - carved from scrimshaw. When held one can hear crashing waves from the ocean.
Major Arcana XIX – Misery (Communication with the Dead Tarot Guild)
Major Arcana XX – Judgment – image tattooed on skin of unknown mammal, perhaps human, attached to card-sized piece of dragon's ash.
Major Arcana XXI – The World – missing

- *Minor Arcana from Communication with the Dead Tarot (Pentacles and Cups; with exceptions noted below, only the Two, Five, Six, and Nine of Pentacles, and the Three, Six, and Eight of Cups were found with this deck)*
- *Minor Arcana from Battle Guild Tarot (Swords; with exceptions noted below, only the Two of Swords was found with the deck)*
- *Minor Arcana from Health and Medicine Guild (Wands; with exceptions noted below, only the Three, Five, and Six of Wands were found with this deck)*

Noted Exceptions:
- *Ace of Pentacles, Ace of Cups, Ace of Swords, and Ace of Wands – cards made of thin marble sheets with mother-of-pearl inlay. The card backs are blank.*

- *Three of Cups, Six of Wands, Nine of Pentacles, and Nine of Swords* – cards made of dried sheets of seaweed with simple ink designs drawn on the front.
- *Knave of Pentacles* – card made of glass with exquisitely painted card front. The card back has repeating designs of pentacles etched into the glass surface.
- *Knave of Cups* – card is made of a delicate, thin piece of black shale; one of its corners is slightly crumbled. The card front looks blank. The card is identifiable due to its back having *der Schurke der Tassen* written on it in chalk.
- *Knave of Swords* – card scorched as if set aflame; front and back damaged to the point where it is unable to determine the image on the front nor the design on the back.
- *Knave of Wands* – card is made of dragon's ash with design burned into the card front. The card back is blank.

⌁

Interview of Graham Douglas, Captain of The Walpole
(conducted by Inspector Chauncey Gibb)
Friday August 7th, 1874

Chauncey Gibb: Can you tell me how you knew James Gough?

Graham Douglas: Guff? Is that how you pronounce it?

CG: *[pause]* I believe so.

GD: Well, I learn something new every day. That's how I stay so young! Always learning!

CG: And how did you know him?

GD: James was a sailor on *The Walpole*. Good sailor. Had Naval experience.

CG: Was it a problem that the man was dark skinned?

GD: Not for me, sir. Now, I don't like what you're implying, that he was mistreated just because of the color of his—

CG: Did his shipmates have issue with his skin color?

GD: No sir. If any did, I'd have them overboard before you can say spit. He was a Navy man! Lots of folks don't have that type of muster but James did. And I'll let you know, if he was good enough for His Majesty's Navy, he's more than good enough for me!

CG: Was it possible that someone on the crew resented his Naval past, maybe a crew member that couldn't pass the Naval exams? *[The record states that Graham Douglas paused before shaking his head.]*
GD: Look, I'm not as much a fool as I appear. I'm sure there were men on the ship that had never worked with someone like James, but I tell you, he worked for me for two, three years. If there was problems with the crew, there's no way he would last that long.
CG: What kind of cargo does *The Walpole* carry?
GD: Nothing unusual. We start up the coast to the north, picking up lumber, whales, furs . . . the type of things you can't get down here. We head south, drop some cargo off, pick some up—textiles, wheat, corn, and the like—and then head further south. At the end we drop off the last of cargo from the north, some from around here, and pick up cotton, sugar, and such. Then we head back up coast making stops along the way. By the time we're back north again *The Walpole* is empty and sitting high in the water.
CG: No slaves or firearms?
GD: No sir. No illegal cargo. There's too much money to make with legitimate work.
CG: What do you know about Oliver Wolsey?
GD: That bastard. Killed one of my best sailors. I'd put a hook to him were he in front of me! Is he a big bloke?
CG: What? No, Wolsey is a youth. Barely over five feet tall.
GD: Huh. James was a big man. Tall for sure, I'm surprised Wolsey got the best of him.
CG: From what we can tell, Wolsey surprised him from behind. So you say you never met Wolsey?
GD: No. I wouldn't know the man if he was you.
CG: Any idea what Gough and he would have in common?
GD: James was a friend to the whalers up north. Did a tidy side business selling carved whale bone . . . scrimshaw? I suspect that bastard wanted some of that and James stood his ground on his price.
CG: You didn't care that one of your employees worked on the side?
GD: I don't allow sailors to do trade on *The Walpole* and they can't be looking to make an extra coin if there's still work to do. If

their work is done, their time is their business. They know my work is good so they'll be back in the morning.

CG: If you think of anything else, please contact us.

GD: I will but don't sit up waiting for me.

꘎

Interview of Edgar Shipman, longshoreman in New Caldwell Seaport, member of The Hive union
(conducted by Inspector Chauncey Gibb)
Friday August 7ᵗʰ, 1874

Chauncey Gibb: Can you tell me how you knew James Gough?

Edgar Shipman: He's that darkskin that got killed the other night?

CG: He was. Yes.

ES: I knew of him. We didn't trade words.

CG: What about scrimshaw?

ES: I wouldn't touch anything from him if it came with a year's supply of golden pussy.

CG: Are you saying you did not like the man?

ES: I'm saying I don't know him. And I have no time for his type. The only way we'd talk is if he was in my way to the pub.

CG: So you wouldn't quarrel with the man?

ES: I don't start stuff. If he came at me, he should be prepared for a fight.

CG: From what I hear, the Hive is barely more than a gang of thugs ready to fight at the merest provocation. You're telling me someone like you who has a severe dislike of darkskinned people and is a proud member of the Hive wouldn't go out of your way to create problems for James Gough?

ES: [silent for a long time] We've been told to leave *The Walpole* and its crew alone. I won't say no more about it and that's more than you should hear.

CG: Did you know Oliver Wolsey?

ES: Agh. That little blighter was under everyone's feet. Always with the questions about the seaport and cargo and how we unload cargo. If you want to know about someone I would go out of my way to fuck with? That Wolsey is one.

CG: Where were you on the night of August 5th?

ES: Don't know. Drinking or fucking. That's all I do at night. Eventually I blackout and someone wakes me to come empty some cargo.

CG: So you weren't in the seaport when Wolsey attacked Gough?

ES: I wasn't on that pier, but I never really leave the seaport. To be honest inspector? I would've been just like the rest of the crowd if I was there. Standing and watching. Not helping. There's no money to be made in being kind to people.

CG: If you think of anything else, please contact us.

ES: Oh, no thank you, inspector.

[The record notes that shipman tore Inspector Gibb's card in half before departing.]

꒰꒱

Interview - David Blokeman, proprietor of The Beautiful Lamp
(conducted by Inspector Chauncey Gibb)
Tuesday August 11th, 1874

David Blokeman: Are you here to help me with my claim of insurance?

Chauncey Gibb: Um, no. I'm with the Metropolitan Guard. Can you tell me how you knew Oliver Wolsey?

DB: Is that the name of the asshole that started a fucking fire and swung a fucking giant sword around? I've got notches in my joist work deep enough that I'm afraid to sleep upstairs!

CG: So you never met Wolsey before he entered your bar the other morning?

DB: No. Never saw the kid before. I thought about not letting him in but he had coin for a drink and coin wins over better judgment I guess.

CG: He hardly seems old enough to drink.

DB: As far as I know inspector there's no limit to how young you can be to taste a pint of ale. I've made the choice to not have kids of my own and then have to worry about bad choices they make, I'm certainly not going to worry about someone else's kids' bad choices.

CG: Did you notice anything unusual about Wolsey?

DB: Like I said, he was young and that always makes me suspicious. Then he kept fiddling with his damn tarot. They always make me nervous. I don't like Guild folk in my tavern and flashing cards around is one way to get the Guilds sniffing about.

CG: Why not ask him to leave?

DB: He had coin and was taking his sweet damn time finishing his beer. Probably the first time he ever tasted it and couldn't understand why everyone loves it so much.

CG: When did Constable Gurney arrive?

DB: Probably a few hours after Wolsey. I don't keep track of everyone but I suspect Gurney comes into The Lamp around eleven every day. He has lunch.

CG: Does he drink on the job?

DB: He has lunch.

CG: Did Gurney mention anything about Wolsey?

DB: Oh aye. We made a deep conversation about the lad. Wondering where his mother was and if we should take him in like a stray cat.

CG: There's no need for cheek my good man.

DB: Probably not, but that's what I have to give. Gurney saw him and asked a question or two about him. Unlike me, Gurney always needs to know why.

CG: When did you notice the Redhands?

DB: To be fair, I didn't. But in a bit, when Gurney heads over to Wolsey's table, he motions for a round of drinks. I see him looking toward the corner of the room, and that's when I saw 'em, but only because I felt like they wanted to be seen. Does that make sense?

CG: Some. What happened next?

DB: You see, my memory is a little fuzzy about that. I'm in back a lot because I'm preparing for the dock workers to come in after the ships are emptied and restocked. I was coming out front when it felt like the whole place is spinning like after the war when we all had too much drink.

CG: The floor was spinning?

DB: Not for real. It just felt like it was. As quickly as I feel it, it stops. I get out front to see what's happening and before I can round the corner of the bar, I hear shouting.

One of the Redhands is partway out the door but he's laying on the ground on fire. Wolsey has a great big sword in his hands.

Gurney has his truncheon out, but he isn't getting too close to that blade. The other Redhands is peeling cards off a deck and speaking quietly.

I think about heading right back into the kitchen when there's a bright flash of light. So bright it near blinded me. I can't really speak to what happened.

I heard Gurney shouting that Wolsey should put down his sword and back up against the wall. Wolsey was shouting something about not letting the Redhands take him alive. There was a lot of other noise but nothing I could make out.

By the time my eyes cleared up, there was just Gurney in the bar talking to some inspectors. The Redhands were gone. Wolsey was gone.

CG: Thank you. You've been very helpful. If you think of anything else, please contact us.

DB: I will. If you see an insurer out and about, send them here.

⌁

Hand-copied transcript of Constable Marcus Gurney's journal, entry dated August 11th

I met Oliver Wolsey yesterday, murderer of former Lance Corporal James Gough, and more importantly, someone I considered a friend. At first, I did not know who he was or I would have worked to apprehend him on the spot.

The Sergeant had shared his name out before the constables were released to their beats. I had a name and the vaguest description. He could have been any number of youths I pass on a daily basis.

As it was, I entered The Beautiful Lamp yesterday midday for my standard meal and pint. I noted a youth sitting a table with a mostly full pint glass playing with an unusual deck of cards. Initially I was not aware that they were tarot.

David, the proprietor, already had my pint on the bar and I knew the food would be coming shortly. I liked to get in before the dock workers finished up unloading and loading ships at the seaport. The Lamp got loud and disorderly and I liked a bit of quiet. It also didn't make sense to spend a lot of time breaking up fights and arguments when it was just men blowing off steam. If I was there as a member of the Metropolitan Guard, it would behoove me to uphold the law which would not endear me to anyone.

I asked James about the young man and he mentioned that the youth was at the front door when he opened up for the day. The youth had coin and the bar was empty. James would chase him out when the dock workers arrived.

I ate my meal—some delicious fried fish and potatoes—but kept an eye on the young man. At that moment it was clear to me that he was working with a tarot deck and not one of the gambling decks James kept behind the bar for the workers.

The young man played a few cards from a Diviners tarot, which was odd as he was not dressed in the Diviners Guild vestments. It varied from guild to guild, but in general the guilds did not like outsiders using their cards.

I went to put more fish in my mouth and almost missed when the next card he placed was from the Battle Tarot Guild. I had never heard of someone blending decks. I decided to have a word with the young man.

I was finishing my pint when he laid out a card carved from scrimshaw. When the card hit the table, it glowed softly. There was no chance that was a coincidence. He fit the description from the Sergeant and the scrimshaw settled it for me: this was my suspect.

I set down my empty glass and readied myself to walk over when he pulled a cream-colored card with a single red handprint on its back and set it into his tableau. What I had taken for a nervous tick of looking towards the door was now clearly the young man keeping an eye on the pair sitting in a dark corner of the tavern.

Their red vestments were so dark I hadn't noticed them at first, but there were two members of the Health and Medicine Tarot Guild watching the young man.

Known as Redhands, the Health and Medicine Tarot Guild definitely did not allow their cards to be handled by anyone outside their guild. How Oliver came to possess such cards was beyond my imagination.

I knew it was imperative to apprehend Oliver, not just to hold him accountable for the murder of James Gough, but to protect him from the Health and Medicine Tarot Guild. If they got their hands on him, James' killer would never see justice.

I moved to Oliver's table and he tried to get me to leave him alone. I appealed to his wellbeing and good judgment to get him out of the tavern safely. Oliver scoffed and said that he could take care of himself.

I took a different tack and said that I didn't want my favorite tavern getting busted up in whatever was going to happen between him and the guild members in the corner.

Oliver didn't answer; he just pulled an over-sized card from his deck whose back was covered in elephants and crocodiles. I wasn't sure which guild those cards were from. Then he smiled at me—the cheek of this youth!—and drew a card that looked like polished bronze and set it in the center of his tableau. A Wheel of Fortune was etched delicately into the card's front.

When he placed it, it appeared that the cards were floating above, beneath, and in the table. As I watched, the table appeared to revolve slowly and I had to grip its sides to keep from falling out of my chair.

I tried to speak, but my mind was busy trying to keep from sliding away. The entire floor felt like it was tipping slowly and that I was certain to crash down into it before too long.

Oliver swept the cards up and shuffled his deck with a giggle and the room stopped moving.

I had to get this situation under control.

I called him kid and Oliver corrected me with his full name. One of the two Redhands stood and left the tavern quickly. I shouted for him to stop but he kept going.

Oliver shuffled the deck rapidly but I could tell his attention was on the remaining Redhands. I looked over and saw the guild member was shuffling his own deck.

He moved rapidly.

He stood and swung his right hand forward in one motion. A huge flash of light nearly blinded me. I could see indistinct shapes, but nothing more.

As my eyes cleared up, I saw Oliver push himself back from the table, put his hands together, and pulled a long glowing sword from somewhere. A smoldering card fell to the table.

The guild member threw another card at Oliver and he blocked it with his sword and rushed the guild member who stood stock still, clearly not expecting Oliver to be able to fight back.

Neither had been trained to fight as I had. I was between them before either knew I was moving. I met Oliver's sword with my truncheon which stopped the sword, but it bit into the wood which should not have been possible.

The Redhands threw another card but this one exploded into a thick cloud of smoke when it struck the floor. I was trying to wrest the sword from Oliver's hands and therefore wasn't able to stop this guild member either. I could smell burning as the smoke did not clear.

Oliver's sword hit my truncheon a second time but turned into mist. Because I was pressing so hard against the sword, when it disappeared I toppled to the floor. Before I could regain my feet, Oliver was over me and out the door.

I worked with Blokeman to get the fire out.

My superior insisted that Oliver must have had the sword on him and that I merely missed it. I agreed that he was correct. But we both knew that magic was a thing that happened in New Caldwell even if the official Metropolitan Guard line was to deny its existence. That was absurd as members of all the Mage Unions worked within the Metropolitan Guard departments.

꒰꒱

Communication with the Dead Tarot Guild Board Meeting
August 13th, 1874

Board Members in Attendance
Ford Xavier (President)
Gregory Fullmore (Vice-President)
Sid Fawns (Secretary)
Roscoe Matson (Treasurer)
Gerald Collins
Ignatius Howlett
Emmet Norman
Richard Purcell
Bryan Potter
Percival Xavier

Board Members Not in Attendance
Elder Cook
Virgil Gleeson
Benedict Smith
Orrin Skidd.

1. Call to Order

Chair called meeting to order at eight o'clock in the evening of the thirteenth of August, 1874.

2. Approval of Agenda

ON A MOTION MADE by Howlett, SECONDED by Potter and CARRIED, the agenda was approved as circulated.

3. Conflict of Interest

None.

4. Approval of Previous Minutes

ON A MOTION DULY MADE by Collins SECONDED by Howlett and CARRIED the draft minutes of the Guild's meeting of the seventeenth of July were approved as presented.

5. Old Business

a. Membership Dues

Treasurer Matson read off a list of members who still needed to pay their dues. He reminded all those present that the Guild could not run itself as a business and be considered a serious Guild if they did not have the funds owed from members. All members of the Guild were vetted prior to being allowed and as such, the Guild knew that everyone could afford the dues.

President Xavier MADE A MOTION that dues needed to be paid before the next meeting or membership would be revoked. MOTION SECONDED by Howlett and CARRIED in a unanimous vote.

b. Vestments

Treasurer Matson reported that new vestments had arrived from the tailor and were available for all fully paid members.

6. New Business

a. Oliver Wolsey

Ignatius Howlett wanted to bring to the Guild's attention that there was a young man going about New Caldwell brazenly using cards from multiple Guilds. Howlett had it on good authority that this Wolsey character held multiple Communication with the Dead Tarot cards and thought the board should launch an investigation into how Wolsey obtained the cards.

Purcell MOVED that the board form an investigatory committee which was SECONDED by Howlett and CARRIED in a unanimous vote.

b. Membership Dues Increase

Treasurer Matson indicated that the board should consider raising dues if it was going to continue its push for new members. The Guildhall was a historical building in a prime area, and those costs were not going to go down in the future.

Additionally, the tarot cards were quite expensive to manufacture and since the board was unwilling to change the materials used in card manufacture, those costs had to be covered somewhere.

President Xavier clarified that board was not going to move the Guildhall to a new location as it was a major reason that attracted new members and members of the public looking for its services. President Xavier further explained that it wasn't just merely being unwilling to change the cards structure, but that they were unable to because changing the materials used to manufacture the cards would render them unusable for the Guild's activities in communicating with the dead.

President Xavier TABLED discussion on this matter for the next meeting.

7. Committee Reports

MEMBERSHIP COMMITTEE reported that they had ten new members ready for vetting. Treasurer Matson questioned if it was sensible to be increasing membership numbers so rapidly.

President Xavier explained that if the Guild wanted to compete with the Prophets of the Unknown, then increasing its numbers was the only way.

Howlett MADE A MOTION to have the potential candidates vetted and invited to the next meeting. MOTION SECONDED by President Xavier and CARRIED unanimously.

No other committees met since the last meeting.

8.   Staff Reports

None.

9.   Adjournment

ON A MOTION MADE by Howlett, SECONDED by Purcell and CARRIED, the meeting was adjourned at nine o'clock.

꒰◦

Interview of [NAME REDACTED], member of Health and Medicine Tarot Guild (Conducted by Inspector Chauncey Gibb) Friday August 14th, 1874

Chauncey Gibb, Inspector: How did the Health and Medicine Tarot Guild become aware of Oliver Wolsey?

[NAME REDACTED]: He was invited to a board meeting by [REDACTED]. I understand he was to petition to become a member.

CG: Does your Guild take on a lot of new members?

[NR]: [REDACTED]

CG: So it was unusual for Wolsey to actually attend a meeting to request becoming a member?

[NR]: Yes, very much so.

CG: Was there ever any serious thought given to listening to his plea?

[NR]: No.

CG: How did Wolsey appear at the meeting? Was he nervous? Excited?

[NR]: [REDACTED]

CG: One could surmise that Wolsey would be disappointed to give up his time to attend a purposeless meeting. He could even reasonably be angry at his treatment.

[NR]: The Health and Medicine Tarot Guild is not a social club. If Wolsey did the research he purported to have done, he would know before attending the meeting that the chance of him successfully becoming a member was essentially zero.

CG: So why bother?

[NR]: You would have to ask him that.

CG: We will.

[NR]: So the Metropolitan Guard has him in custody?

CG: I cannot comment on the status of our investigation. What was the Guild's reaction when you learned that Wolsey was using tarot from your Guild without permission?

[NR]: [REDACTED]

CG: I'm surprised you would admit that to a member of the Metropolitan Guard.

[NR]: [REDACTED]

CG: Sir, I'm confident in our investigation. The Guild should step aside and let the proper authorities handle this matter.

[NR]: [REDACTED]

CG: Thank you sir. You have my card should you need to reach me.

⥼

Interview of Ignatius Howlett, member of Communication with the Dead Tarot Guild
(Conducted by Inspector Chauncey Gibb)
Friday August 14th, 1874

Chauncey Gibb: How did the Communication with the Dead Tarot Guild become aware of Oliver Wolsey?

Ignatius Howlett: Some of our agents, Guild staff you know, reported to us that there was a young man, recently arrived to New Caldwell, that was flashing an unusual tarot deck to anyone who wanted to see. It was Wolsey, and he had cards from our tarot, which isn't allowed.

CG: Does the Guild do anything to enforce who has access to your tarot?

IH: We have very strict ordinances in place to regulate who can enter and exit the facilities where our tarot are made. At least I thought we had strict ordinances in place. We are an exclusive

Guild, not for just any member of society. No, we are made up of the best, the highest members of society. It irks me to no end that this wastrel was able to steal Tarot from us.

CG: So how would Wolsey have gone about obtaining your Tarot?

IH: I honestly have no idea. I suspect some member of our staff feels underpaid or some such nonsense and took money from this ragamuffin for a handful of tarot. You see, to most people I suspect their understanding is so lacking that the tarot appear as nothing more than glorified playing cards, but they are much more than that.

CG: Your staff understands the tarot? Understands the power of the cards?

IH: Under my oversight, staff was fully vetted prior to hiring. Background checks, references, sponsorship by members . . .

But now that my talents are needed elsewhere in the Guild I suspect that all is lacking now and Potter and Xavier—Percival Xavier, not President Xavier—are doing a right shoddy job of hiring staff.

CG: Is it possible that Wolsey stole the cards?

IH: I'd actually prefer to learn that he stole them rather than obtaining them through some malfeasance by staff. We've created an investigatory committee to look into the matter.

CG: Excellent. I'll give you my card so you can provide us with any new information you feel is relevant.

IH: Of course. And here is my card in case you need to ask any more questions. I'm always more than happy to talk about the Guild.

꒙ꕥ

Hand-copied transcript of Constable Marcus Gurney's journal, entry dated Sunday August 16ᵗʰ

The Nine Points is a difficult place to investigate crime. Gang activity makes residents reluctant to talk in the best of times. Now I needed to find someone in the Nine Points who was playing with fire as far as the Tarot Guilds were concerned and I doubted whether I could find anyone willing to talk.

I left word for my typical informants that I was trying to locate Wolsey. Normally they needed a day or two to gather information and that was time I did not have. It was a long shot to ask them for help, but I had to try everything I could.

I wandered in and out of the typical places criminals went to when trying to lay low, but there was no sign of Wolsey and everyone refused to talk to me.

I was too well known and it was too well known what I wanted.

I stood at an empty street corner thinking about my next move. Any other night I would have to watch out for fast-moving carriages, street toughs, magicians, street walkers, and even the occasionally higher-class person looking for something out of the ordinary.

The fact that the streets were empty was a bad sign. I figured my best hope would be to find Wolsey's body.

Something prodded me in the back and a rough voice told me not to turn around. The voice gave me a recent location of Wolsey and encouraged me to hurry.

Wolsey's room at the New Caldwell Youth Association was essentially bare. There were few affects and little in the way of belongings.

Wolsey was gone. I held little hope of getting another tip to his whereabouts. But sometimes luck is on your side.

On a side table was a stack of tarot cards. I picked them up and put them in my pocket. There was a scrap of paper on the table and when I picked it up it was an attempt at forgery for a ticket on a ship heading south.

I headed to the seaport as fast as I could. I doubted I would find Wolsey on the ship scrawled on the fake ticket now in my pocket, but again, I had to follow what leads I had.

When I arrived at the dock in question, the ship was already away from the pier and heading out to sea.

It was too far to be certain, but I would swear an oath that standing at the stern of the boat was Wolsey. He was waving to me. If I squinted, I could imagine a smile on his face.

He had gotten away but he could never return. New Caldwell was now closed to him. If he ever came back, I would likely only learn about it because he was in the morgue.

Proof of Stake

~ *D. T. O'Conaill*

The following represents the most up to date compilation of information available on the clearnet surrounding the token known as $STOKR. The below is not intended to be considered as an exhaustive source of knowledge on this asset, nor are any of the statements contained therein to be considered as an endorsement of the return prospects of investment in this token. Given the fragmentary nature of this collection of documents, reflective of the generally fragmentary nature of knowledge about this token, the author cannot advise any specific action in regards to fund or capital engagement with this asset at present. The below represents due diligence undertaken on behalf of the DeSelby Fund incorporated in Hybrasil and is not intended as advisory to the aforementioned or any other fund, trader or entity.

☉

"StokerLabs, and its premier decentralised financial product $STOKR, represent a new frontier in the world of defi that combines ground-breaking technological development, prosaic insight into the purpose and nature of human consciousness and privacy-tools in order to revolutionise the landscape of blockchain-assisted task scalability. $STOKR as an asset finds the heart of its innovation in its quality of telescopy: it moves from macro to more granular modalities with unprecedented efficiency, bringing together transanglospheric financial footlooseness with a distinctly wry attitude peculiar to our own small north Atlantic island."
—**An excerpt from the $STOKR white paper**

"Wen this thing gonna 10X Ive got a fat sack to build my apocalypse bunker w"
—Transcribed from a screenshot taken in a private telegram channel for $STOKR investors

"Much has been written about just how plagued the emergent world of "decentralised finance" is with scams of all varieties. So called "rug pulls" and the endless proliferation of derisively named "shitcoins" have been one major consequence of this brand new technological space and its minting of overnight millionaires. Just as hyped up scams are predictably endemic to such a new and ever-altering technological space, so too is the rejoinder that every upcoming project hyped into existence promises to bring us something "radically new and never before seen." Whether by the alchemy of jamming together previously existed buzzwords into unusual combinations or plucking neologisms of their own out of thin air each and every new token that blackens the skies of our feeds seems to desperately screech and crow about its own novelty. But $STOKR is the real deal. But if "advanced technology" and the "metaverse" and "quantum blockchains" have become worn cliches coming from crypto developers themselves, then no doubt hard-nosed and breathless declaration of a token's technological "real deal" status are a cliche of crypto-watcher blogs like mine. But this time it's the real thing. For serious guys"
—Excerpt from an archive of the Medium page of an individual using the penname MachineOfLovingGrace

As should be evident from these snippets the problem of understanding the nature of the $STOKR token is besieged not only by its own idiosyncratic nature but also the general "crypto-haze" endemic to its form. Its promoters speak in generalities as jargon filled as they are fantastic and its loud supporters take up detractors' claims of the commodity as a "cult" with great and unironic enthusiasm. While the latter is the case with many in the space of so-called "Decentralised Finance" the holders and boosters of $STOKR embody this mindset in a far more elaborate and theatrical way as they have molded their communities and rituals on a variety of pre-Christian mystery religions of the ancient world. Smaller investors are referred to as "initiates" while more established investors, especially those either directly related to the developers themselves or involved in sub-communities that interpret and catalogue the actions of developers and the token's place in the broader economy, gain the title of "hierophant."

The above extracts involve contributions from, in order, the developers, an initiate and a moderately-well known hierophant. Given the consistency of standard crypto-space jargon across each excerpt we would not ordinarily suggest a stake in this token as an ongoing concern for the fund but further research has suggested to us that the clearnet and mainstream social communications of $STOKR boosters represent a deliberate strategy of occlusion on their part. What follows is more indicative of the substance of the community and the investment opportunity it might represent. Read on at your own risk. Invest carefully. Do not get captured.

> *"My thanks to Hierophant E and Hierophant σ for assisting myself and other new initiates in explicating the nature of the value stored within and represented by our tokens. Each day our understanding grows more full and rich and the true potential of this metatechnological feat becomes less and less opaque. The cult now sees plainly the hidden hands that operate behind the to-ings and fro-ings of this world and sees it fit to seize them with fits. We are but one rung up the ladder of paralysing the Powers That Be. Let us endeavor each day to climb one more higher."*
> —Initiate Foxtrot, who has been linked to the clearnet personality of AdmiralSenzu88, speaking on one of the $STOKR communities on the custom MeshNet.

> *"The following coordinates have encoded our security for this session. 53°38'01.0"N 7°41'09.8"W. 53°40'16.8"N 9°03'49.8"W. 52.222166, -7.760268. This portion of the arcane working is locked into the firmament on the basis of the keys placed in the previously mentioned sites. These sacrifices provide stability to the chain and liquid value to our universe. We thank the brave initiates for the quality of their staking."*

—Hierophant Ж, speaking of vital 'burial keys' at a meeting hosted at a location which we cannot disclose and which does not, in the traditional sense, exist.

"Holy shit are we going to be the official Crypto token of the Bram Stoker Festival in Dublin!! Time for this thing to go to the MOOOOOOOOOOOOOOOOON"
—@KingCong/Moon4Sam, a minor Twitter crypto personality

As should be evident from the above excerpts the nature of the $STOKR token is far more arcane and involved than the usual crypto-space bloviating about advanced technologies and new paradigms of financial technology. Although the space of cryptocurrency and associate technologies contains much of its own in-jargon and feverish, cult-like atmospheres the $STOKR token community truly embraces these elements and takes them to the nth degree. The Bram Stoker Festival, based in Dublin, has denied any connection to and knowledge of the $STOKR crypto token following a number of inquiries. In this regard, as many others in its surface communiques and those portions of its that peak out like iceberg tips from the clearnet, $STOKR resembles other cryptocurrencies that "pump" on the basis of partnership rumours that never come to fruition. However the fact that at least two unidentified bodies have been discovered in the locations marked in the above communication as 'key sites' points to something that stakes out $STOKR as a radically departure from its contemporaries. This makes it a fertile investment opportunity for movers with the mind and the stomach for such growth possibilities.

"We are bonded in wood and blood. These are the oldest measures of values and, according with the circular notion of technological time that has been revealed to us, shall also be the future of our value system. We are staked by flesh and the spooling out of arterial systems like the pulling of a thread to unravel the substance of the world-order. The old flesh is the new technology. The old blood is the new currency. HODL $STOKR"

—Entitled "Summation of $STOKR value set/ White Paper 2.8" this was found on a scrap of paper tucked into an empty jewel case tapped to the back of an iron girder in the unfinished site of the Parkway Valley Shopping Centre Development, Limerick, Ireland

A dispassionate review of the broad range of materials surrounding this token suggests an investment opportunity both risky and compelling. Our due diligence complete on behalf of the DeSelby Fund the authors would like to full-throatedly endorse the fund take up a substantial position in this token. By any means necessary.

Halos

~ *D. Thea Baldrick*

"Every morning the old woman . . . cried,
'Hansel, put out your finger, that I may feel
if you are getting fat.' But Hansel always
stretched out a bone, and the old dame,
whose eyes were dim, could not see it,
thinking always it was Hansel's finger."
—*Hansel and Gretel, 1887*

Deep in the woods, bisected by Route 27, in a house found only by invitation, I have a lab with sixteen avian species and a firebird. One cage on the floor sits empty with the latch undone and the door open. Upstairs I have a room with mice. The aquariums are in the basement.

Gretel came often to sit among the birds and to read or watch. Hansel was too afraid, or too wise, and never returned, but his sister was there on the day I poured agar into petri dishes for the new bacteria. I made hundreds of petri dishes at a time. When they cooled, I put them in the refrigerator. After a few days, I would take them out for inoculation.

"Old woman, old woman, old woman, says I," Gretel said between bites of the apple I had left for her. She was sitting curled up in my armchair, an open book in her lap, "What does this mean? I don't understand."

"Nobody does," I said, "Probably." It was a non-answer, but I was busy.

"But you haven't looked."

"It doesn't matter. The level of understanding remains the same."

"Look," she insisted.

It was the equation that I was always scribbling down, in margins, on the end leaf, in the condensation on the window, or in the ashes in the fire. Once I amused myself by having an orb weaver incorporate it into his web. It took surprisingly little manipulation of the spider's brain. "That means," I told her, "that based on evolutionary theory, what we see is not real and what's more, cannot be real. Reality, as we see it, is an impossibility."

There was a long silence. I went back to work.

Finally, she said, "If that is true, what is reality?"

"That would be the right question."

"And what would be the right answer?"

"I don't know."

Exasperated, she shut the book with a clap. The birds fluttered in their cages, the firebird repositioned herself and Gretel came over to watch me pour.

"Stand back," I said. "It is easy to contaminate this."

She stepped back. "What are you growing this time?"

"*Staphylococcus stravinski.*"

"What is it for?"

"It grows on bird feathers. I am adding two genes that I have designed."

"To the bird feathers?"

"No, no, to the bacteria. It's too difficult to add them to the bird. I would have to wait too long for the results."

"So why are you adding the genes?"

"I am, for obvious reasons, interested in aging. The first gene should make the bacteria live longer. The second gene turns the bacteria gold, so I know which bacteria I have tampered with."

When she left, she had the temerity to hug me, and as she walked through the woods, I could hear her singing, "Old woman, old woman, old woman, says I, oh whither, oh whither, oh wither, so high?"

Silly girl.

The next time she came, she was older, and I was not. She gained on time with a remarkable speed, and yet, I know her own perception was that time passed with an excruciating slowness. I hardly aged at all from one point to another and yet time fled from me at a rate I found breathtaking. That observation has kept me up at night, thinking.

"Old woman," she said as she peered in at the birds, who all had gold feathers, except for the firebird, "Do you think they are happy in the cages?" She was eating another apple. As usual her questions were flavored with apple chunks and saliva. The birds were pecking at their seeds. The aquarium creatures were picking at bloodworms and plankton. The upstairs mice nibbled on pellets. Everything was eating all the time.

"The feathers are infected now with the *Staphylococcus stravinski*," I said. "If the birds flew away, what do you think might happen?"

"I suppose the bacteria would end up in the wood and, if conditions were right, they would grow and multiply out in the world."

"Yes, that is a possibility," I said.

"So, it is important to keep them in cages until we know more?"

"The doors are unlatched."

"They are?"

"The birds could leave if they wanted to."

"Maybe they don't know they can. Maybe they don't know what's real?"

I shrugged, "Maybe. No more than we do."

"Maybe," she said, opening the door to the sparrow's cage, "maybe they just need to be shown."

I said nothing. I was, in truth, deep in my project. I may or may not know how to turn a blind eye, but I caught a glimmer of gold as the sunlight flashed on the bird as it flew through the door.

"Well, you did it," I said, glancing up from the microscope.

"Is it OK?" she asked, her hand on the raven's cage.

"Probably not," I said, turning back to the microscope.

The raven, too, flashed bright in the sunlight, its delighted caws growing faint as it flew through the wood and over Route 27.

Days, weeks, perhaps a month later, Gretel appeared in the doorway, bringing too much sunlight, disturbing my new collection of birds. She had let all the previous ones loose, all but for the firebird who stubbornly remained in her cage despite the open door. The new lot blinked at the infusion of light, but even as the girl shut the door behind her, the room remained too bright. I realized, as I looked up, that the gold glow was from her hair.

"Oh, dear," I said, laughing. "Oh, dear, my dear, oh, dear." I was almost in tears. It was just too funny. "You're infected."

"Yes," she said grimly.

"Serve you right," I said, smiling, turning back to the centrifuge which had just finished spinning. I opened the lid and took out the microtubule and peered at the pellet that had formed at the bottom. I took another peep at the girl. "Oh, dear," I said, chuckling again. The glow was concentrated around her scalp where the bacteria would have formed in thicker quantities near the new growth of the hair follicles.

"Actually," I said, peering at her more closely, as I put on my strongest pair of glasses. "This is interesting. Cross-species contamination. Do other animals have it? Horses? Deer? Dogs? Cats? Mice?" She was shaking her head. "What about other primates?"

"I don't know," she said, "But that's not the issue."

"It must have mutated to infect humans," I mused, "But why? The evolutionary advantage must have been extreme compared to other animals." I stared at her, thinking.

"My dear old woman, I am trying to tell you—"

"Length of life!" I cried. "The birds didn't live long enough for the bacteria. With its enhanced lifetime, it needed a host who lived at least as long as it did. And you're a convenient host, there are so many of you. Mystery solved. Not so interesting anymore." I went back to the centrifuge.

"You are not listening to me."

"No," I muttered as I carefully decanted the microtubule.

"Look at me, please."

I looked.

"What do you see?"

"I see a skinny girl, far too serious, with a thin face, a broad nose and really rather lovely skin, with a heavy infestation of genetically modified *Staphylococcus stravinski* on her head."

"Well, other people see a halo."

"A halo!" Oh, dear, I had to sit down.

"Yes, and what's more, only some people get it. It's everywhere, all over the world, but some people are immune to it."

I nodded, still chuckling. "Of course."

"The problem is that it has become a sign of holiness. Cults are forming. The science people have pointed out that it is microbial, but they're drowned out by all the furor. Look at it. It is rather dramatic. And things are getting ugly. Elitism. Prejudice. There's been violence.

"Really?" I said, getting up to return to my project. "So what else is new?"

"Old woman! You have to do something!"

"Why?" The liquid I decanted needed to be put in the thermocycler.

"Because you can!"

"Maybe I could, that's true, but the stupidity of what is going on out there beyond the wood does not interest me. At the moment, getting this into the thermocycler interests me."

"But you started the whole thing!"

"Did I?" I said, glancing at her.

The girl cried out with frustration or guilt. As she grabbed her hair, sparks of gold flew out and I stepped back. I did not want to become infected myself. A halo would be even more ludicrous on me. My sisters would enjoy the irony far too much.

"If it matters to you so much, you fix it," I said.

"Me? How can—"

"What you need to know is here." I waved at the bookshelf. "What you need to do is here." I indicated the lab equipment.

"The firebird might help," I said as the bird changed its position in its sleep. I looked at it thoughtfully. "For some reason, the bacteria dies when I put it on her feathers. It is not without interest. If I weren't so embroiled with this new project, I would look into it myself."

I really had to put the liquid in the thermocycler. As I was walking away, I mentioned, "Oh, by the way, the effect probably won't last forever. I am not sure how the bacteria will work on the different keratin in hair, but it is likely that it has the same effect as on birds. It is a feather-degrading bacteria. Keratin is its food source. Once its food source is gone, the bacteria will die. Probably. Unless of course it adapts to include another source of keratin. Like skin. The extended lifespan has obviously given it enhanced adaptability mechanisms it didn't have before."

"You mean that once it's eaten my hair and I'm bald, then it will start on my skin?"

I shrugged. "Maybe."

After I ran the thermocycler, I turned to find her sitting cross-legged on the floor, flipping frenetically through books she had pulled from the shelves: Biochemistry, Pathophysiology, Bacterial Pathogenesis.

"You've written all over these," she said.

"You can, too. Just use a different color."

She may or may not figure out how to remove halos from the world, but what's more important, by the time she's done, I'm going to have a nice little lab assistant. If she can't figure it out and the yellow glow continues to annoy me, I may have to show her how to remove it myself. It's fairly simple. Everything eats something. It's just a matter of engineering something to eat the bacteria. A virus would do nicely.

Desires Quite as Terrible

~ Bonnie Jo Stufflebeam

The witches wanted something different.

The coven had grown weary of virgin blood, which tended to bring out the immature demons; the wishes they granted were shallow: smoother skin, a minor increase in riches, or increased sex appeal. The witches didn't want more sex. The men who lived in the town one over from theirs were easy enough to snare without the demons' help. The witches wanted to summon a more exciting demon, one who might grant the most satisfactory of wishes: to deepen their five senses. To make the witches taste, see, smell, hear, and feel the world in more than its usual dimensions. Those types of demons required older, wiser sacrifices.

They required the last blood of a menopausal woman.

Sadie frowned as she scoured the forum. She wasn't usually one for forums. She could never figure out the secret languages people used within them: OP, DD, LOTR, SAHM. Reading forums made her feel like she was staring down at a test for which she didn't study. But she needed to feel like she was part of something bigger, like she had a whole world of women willing to respond and reassure her that she would feel better, that the madness of menopause would one day pass.

First, there was the weight gain. She had always been a hefty woman. Her thighs were muscular, her hips were wide, and her belly was a soft pillow that her cat loved to lie on. With the start of menopause, she expanded even more, filling out her size XL underwear to the point of strain, the elastic giving out under the pressure. She didn't mind the weight—she liked taking up more space, claiming more from the world than her young-girl body had claimed—but it tipped her off to the process of something changing.

Then, there were the night sweats. She woke as wet as though she had been swimming. Sometimes, the heat overtook her in the middle of her air-conditioned office where she filled out administrative forms for a university. It was boring work, not the sort of content that usually made one hot, but there Sadie was, mopping herself with tissue after tissue in her cubicle, feeling the world spin around her.

Then there were the mood changes, specifically the anger. She had been a peaceful person when she was younger and maybe more naïve, but now she found herself bristling at every messed-up drive-through order or back-handed compliment. Sadie found herself especially angry at the people who had wronged her, the new stage in her life re-igniting grudges she thought long-buried: her stepfather, her ex-husband, her ex-best friend. When she thought of the wrongs they had leveled against her, she found her body flaming with a desire for revenge. Violent revenge.

Some mornings, she woke having dreamed of bloodbaths. She imagined the way their skin would feel trapped under her hands, or parted by her knife, or shaking as she squeezed them between her quaking thighs. She shivered as her every sense fired in a cacophony of overstimulation.

Sadie searched the forums, but no one mentioned desires quite as terrible as hers.

The witches searched the forums, too. They searched with more than just their eyes; they searched with their intuition, feeling for women on the other sides of screens whose final bleed was imminent.

Sophie's post was simple enough: How have other people dealt with foul moods? And has anyone felt a lot of anger?

The responses to her inquiry were dull, women discussing breakdowns toward management at restaurants or rants against their ungrateful children. Sophie's words and her screen name in its throbbing blue font radiated power. Her final bleed would come soon. The witches could tell just by that.

The coven's most technologically savvy member performed her magic, plugging the screenname into a search engine and scouring the results for a name, a number, and finally an address. The witches clapped silently for her success, but inside themselves, they felt like singing.

Sophie logged out of the forum and moved to her window. Watching the birds hop around on the ground outside had become one of the only soothing hobbies she claimed, but today the sky was dark with an impending storm. A black cat prowled along her backyard fence. Suddenly, the cat sprung down to the ground. It captured a little brown bird under its paw, and Sadie watched as the cat tore the feathers from the creature with its teeth.

She did not look away.

Something rustled the bushes. Another bird? She scooted closer to the window to get a closer glimpse. Deep in the bramble, she saw what seemed to be a limb flopping back and forth. It looked human, disconnected from a body. Her heart sped up, and the heat overtook her. Even dizzy, she stood and rushed through the back door to the bush and knelt to peer into the shadowy space. The hand grabbed her by the neck and pulled her under the dirt.

Sadie woke sprawled in the woods, surrounded by a circle of bones that smelled of rotting meat and burnt gristle. Deep into the recesses of the forest, eyes watched her, glowing shades of orange and yellow.

"Who are you?" she called out, coughing the dirt from her throat, but there came no reply save for an insistent hum that grew louder. Sadie tried to move, but she was stuck, restrained by some invisible force. She screamed out once, then again. The witches moved in closer, letting the forest's sparse light trickle down onto their leering faces.

"She will do," they said as Sadie's uterus was wracked, at once, by cramps.

Unlike in her youth, these cramps didn't sadden her; instead, they ignited the rage she'd grown to live inside.

The tallest witch stepped into the circle of bone, and at that moment, Sadie felt free.

She rolled with all the force she could muster, working through the fog that had of late settled inside her brain to find the will to move through whatever spell the witches had used to trap her. She wrenched free her hands and grabbed the thickest bone from the circle. The tall witch frowned. In one swooping motion, Sadie swept the bone across the ground below the witch's feet. The witch tumbled down, onto Sadie. Sadie wrapped her feet around her waist. With the bone, Sadie beat the witch until they both were drenched with blood.

Sadie pushed the witch off like a bad lover and struggled to her feet, but the other witches were already retreating into the woods, frightened of the fire that now flamed in Sadie's eyes. Sadie held the bloody bone aloft. As she caught her breath, rage still boiling in her belly, the demon came.

The demon was like nothing Sadie had ever seen before: a hulking mass of swinging tits, volcanic skin full of flaming fault lines, and teeth like the blunted blades of a saw. Sadie stood to face the demon; its heat pouring into Sadie was not unlike the heat she'd learned to bear.

"You called me?" the demon rasped as it crawled free from the bloody earth.

Sadie understood that it had been the witches' will, not hers, that had summoned the demon—but she also understood grabbing opportunities that came her way.

"I did," Sadie said.

"And you want what they all want?"

Sadie considered; she did not see her desires as too far off from what others likely asked for.

"Sure," Sadie said. "Why not?"

The demon grinned with its metallic mouth, and with its cracked fingers, it brushed back the hair from Sadie's face.

"Then you will have it," the demon said. "You will sense the world in its truest form."

Sadie searched the forums for clues that others may be like her, that she was not living in this state of heightened senses all alone. "Increased sense of taste," she searched. "Hearing the humming of the earth," she searched. "Seeing auras and shadows" then "skin so sensitive it makes me cry" then "can't sleep," then "hallucinations."

But she was quite sure that the event in the woods had been real, just as felt quite sure that she had reached the end of her womb's own road. She didn't need it, the threat of birth, for, through the demon's touch, she had birthed her own body anew: every sense a symphony.

The rage had found another target: as Sadie searched forums, she felt for power radiating off bright blue screen names and for posts that may not tell the truth. She searched for the witches who had meant to do her harm. She would hunt them down; after all, with her new senses, she stood a chance of finding them—and the wrongs they had done, unlike all the other wrongs from Sadie's full, full life, could be righted by her hand.

The Mayor of Marzipan

~ *Kimberly Moore*

Tea & Tarot inspires fear in some people. Some condemn us. Some of them are fascinated by us. Most of them think we're full of shit, but a source of entertainment. However they may feel, the citizens of Oak Village end up in the back room with Madame Bresa eventually, full of doubt but wanting to believe so strongly that they lay an offering on her table and watch her place the mysterious cards and solve their problems. We even ushered the pastor's wife through the basement door for a reading the day after her judgmental husband fired up a mob to protest our existence. We are a forgiving business.

I'm the baker. If anyone exists in this town who has not yet allowed Bresa to read their cards, they have still eaten my work. They say my talent is wasted here, but I have no culinary degrees. I learned from my father and YouTube. I confess my lack of qualifications every time I am complimented and told I belong in a fancy hotel or a French patisserie. Years ago, before Madame Bresa arrived and invited herself to an interview with Tilly, the owner, I considered leaving for a possible pay increase. Somehow, that idea lost appeal after she arrived. Before Bresa, the fortune-tellers were only actors.

On my cutting board this morning is our mayor, George Williams, made of marzipan. Before Bresa arrived, I used store-bought, but Bresa's recipe is slightly different and she insists that I use her recipe for this ceremony. It includes honey from her bees and almonds from her source, whatever that may be. Bresa has secrets, as a tarot reader is expected, I suppose. She claims to have ancient gypsy blood, a multitude of ex-husbands, ex-wives, and ex-lovers, and now in the golden years of her life, she only wants to assist fellow humans instead of breaking hearts. I've always wanted details, but even drunk, she'll only wink and grin. "Oh, my darling Penelope, I was trouble," she'll say with her slowly enunciated words and thick Slavic accent.

Bresa appears in the kitchen just as I am admiring my Mayor Williams doll.

"Lovely," she says, looking at the photo his wife sent and then at my handiwork.

"I didn't need the photo. He's been mayor for as long as I can remember. He watched me grow up." I enjoyed adding the pigment to darken his skin, rounding his belly, forcing his belt buckle to face his feet. As plump as he has always been in my memory, he was always elegant. I fretted for hours last night with a razor designing his wrinkle-free blue suit.

"A man with a good reputation," she says as if it's extinct. Now she's frowning at the doll.

"This isn't like voodoo, is it?"

"No, no, no. You know me better than that." Bresa is petite, barely five feet tall. Her affection is always meant to be motherly, but I feel like the mother during an embrace with her head at the level of my chest. "Is he complete? His wife will be here in an hour."

I watch Bresa glide away with my masterpiece. What she does with the dolls before the client arrives is one of her many secrets. Her clients refuse to reveal the details of the ceremony, no matter how much Tilly and I have begged. "Just give us a hint," we've whispered later when we've run into them in the village. They always, without fail, happily decline.

Tilly closes the kitchen door. It must be almost time to open and I have more to do this morning than worry about my marzipan man. The Oak Village book club meets today in the main dining room, and due to Tilly's misremembering dates, the fifth birthday party for the bank president's daughter has been scheduled at the same time in the playhouse.

Tilly glances over the spread for the book club. "I thought we were going to give them more sweet than savory."

"The opposite. Remember last month when they hardly touched the sweets and ran out of savory?"

"I trust you," she chuckles. "I've been screwing up everything lately. It looks fantastic. Are we all set for the birthday party?"

"Take a look." I point her in the direction of the second kitchen island, where my purple sloth-themed cupcakes await the birthday guests.

Tilly smiles and applauds for a moment. "I love sloths!" We hear a car crunching the gravel behind the building. "That will be Cheryl." Tilly descends to the basement to open the door for Cheryl, the mayor's wife, who requested a discreet arrival.

Cheryl keeps her sunglasses on when she greets me, making her appear more like an insect than usual. She and the mayor are visually incompatible. They are the same race, which is all they seem to have in common. He is short, fat, manic with the need to socialize, and immediately in control of every situation. Cheryl is half a foot taller than her husband and fragile in build. Her friendliness has been rehearsed, but not perfected. Although Cheryl has never been unkind to me, I always feel she would prefer to be ignored.

"Hello, Penelope," she says without smiling. She surveys my work.

"Bresa's waiting for you," Tilly says, leading her to the back hallway.

Cheryl moves quickly to the door. I can't help wondering what problem she might have with her husband, who at least in my eyes, has the personality of a teddy bear and leaves happy faces wherever he goes. Most customers who have asked for this ceremony have been more transparent. Everyone knew the high school basketball coach was cheating on his wife, and I was asked to create his doll as a nude. I didn't ask questions, but Tilly shook her head when she saw my work, followed by a frown for his long-suffering wife. The coach has spent more time at home since the ceremony. Others seemed to be fidelity-related, too, but I can't imagine that to be the problem with the mayor.

Tilly joins me in the kitchen again. "You think you know someone. How could they have problems? He's the sweetest man I've ever known. Including my dad. And yours."

"I agree. Guess we'll never know."

Once the birthday party begins, we forget the mayor. Tilly's nephews and nieces serve the book club, the auxiliary dining room, and the playhouse. There are only four of them, so Tilly and I join the chaos. Word travels between us as we burst through the kitchen door of requests and needs, mistakes, and skinned knees in the playhouse.

It is only when I see Bresa at the door to the basement that I take a moment to breathe. Bresa's expression is unfamiliar. Nothing fazes her usually, but she stares out the front windows, then turns back to the dining room, where the book club continues their debates. Seeing her uncomfortable makes me uncomfortable.

"Bresa," I whisper when the register line is empty and I can cross the room, "what's going on?"

She doesn't answer as quickly as I'd like. She looks up at me and sighs. "Cheryl changed her mind."

"So?"

"I don't know what to do with him now."

"Who?"

"The mayor!"

"George is here?"

"The mayor you made."

"Throw him away."

"You don't understand." She takes my hand and pulls me to the door of her room. "Penelope, you have to swear you'll never tell what I'm about to show you."

I shouldn't leave the register, but Bresa's message seems urgent. "I swear."

She opens the door and I see nothing at first. Then, there is motion on the floor. The wire trashcan inverted with a stack of books on top is scooting closer to me. I have to bend to see the little marzipan mayor pushing the trashcan with all the strength honey and almonds will give him.

No sleep tonight. I pretend to sleep so Mike won't stay awake and worry about me. He freaked out when I fainted at work today. He wasn't alone. I have never fainted before and it freaked me out, too. I wanted to tell him. As my husband, he needed more of an explanation than low blood sugar, which I've never suffered as a baker. I should feel worse for concocting that lie. However, the truth would have been more unbelievable.

His back is to me now, expanding and deflating with his deep sleep breath. I imagine how I would confess. I may be a criminal, although I can't imagine what the indictment would be. It's a moral dilemma I never thought I would confront—creating a type of life for the sole purpose of a ceremony. However, Bresa whispered to me while I was regaining consciousness that my creation was not a living individual.

"He's a form of thought like a memory," she said as she sprinkled a flowery liquid over my shirt and crossed my forehead with a feather. "He has no soul or will. He only knows what Cheryl communicated to him in the ceremony."

At that moment, I glanced at the moving trash can again. He seemed to have desires, and what he wanted was to get out of the trashcan. Bresa scooted him to a closet and closed the door just as Mike arrived. I found myself answering questions about pregnancy, and although I swore I wasn't, Mike insisted on a visit to my doctor.

I'm not pregnant, but that would be less troubling. I trace my finger down Mike's shoulder blade, both wanting him to wake up and not wanting to wake him. I only wake our Siamese cat who is curled behind Mike's bent knees. It's three-thirty. If I go to work now, I will have some time to observe the tiny mayor and perhaps make sense of it.

I hear the little mayor bumping into the walls of the closet while I enter the security code. How can Bresa say he's not alive? Perhaps she is minimizing his existence, the way vegetarians will kill a mosquito and rationalize it because of its size and bothersome personality. In Bresa's room, my hand shakes when I open the closet door. The trash can moves into the room and I squat to watch the miniature mayor in his continued effort to push.

To my surprise, removing the trash can does not change his activity. He pushes at air, punching and lunging forward at nothing in front of him. Bresa told me the mayor knows nothing but what Cheryl communicated to him. All he seems to know is low-effort fighting. Is this what Cheryl told him? Is he the memory of a physical fight?

He doesn't respond to my voice, nor does he see me. I observe, trying to become comfortable with my creation as he reaches a wall and pushes against it. Fifteen minutes later, I touch him. No reaction. When I lift him, he continues his pushing motions in my hands. He is as warm as when I first molded him. He appears to breathe, but I feel nothing when I place my hand in front of his tiny face, his unblinking eyes I created yesterday with a needle.

In the kitchen, I place him on the floor and watch him continue the only motion he knows, wandering under the table. I begin measuring almond flour and sugar for macarons. The routine is soothing and it seems kinder to keep him with me than to leave him in a trashcan in a dark closet. I suspect he doesn't care. If Bresa is correct, he isn't sentient. While I begin beating egg whites, I try to imagine Bresa's explanation of being a thought form or a memory. I have too many questions.

When I hear the kitchen door swing open, I expect to see Tilly or Bresa. Mike is unexpected. He stands in the doorway with his arms and mouth open, questioning me with his eyes.

"You didn't leave a note?" he asked when I turn off the mixer. "I thought you went to the ER!"

"Sorry, babe. I have lots of macarons to make today." I've lost the mayor. I'm surveying the tiled floors when Mike yells and stomps his foot.

"What the hell was this?" He leans on the table and lifts his sneakered foot, attempting to shake it free of what he has just stomped. I'm afraid to look. I recognize the flattened blue suit.

"The mayor. You stepped on the mayor."

Bresa struggles with English sometimes, but she has no words in any language now. Mike is no help. I scooted a barstool into the back of his legs while I scraped the mayor from his foot and he has sat there catatonic ever since. He should have been at work ten minutes ago.

"Tell me what to do," I say to Bresa. She is studying the flattened mayor, now motionless on the kitchen island with a size twelve footprint etched into his squashed body.

"Can you redo him?" Bresa finally asks.

"I doubt it. I could make another."

"A new one won't remember."

"Does it matter?"

"I don't know. This has never happened before. I need Cheryl to come back and finish what she started."

"Did I kill the mayor?" Mike interrupts, still focusing on the opposite wall, his face drained of color.

"It's not voodoo," Bresa says.

I have to wave to get Mike's attention. "If you're not going to work, I need you to call my dad and the two of you need to finish the macarons. I'll try to reshape the mayor."

Mike takes his phone from his pocket and texts. I assume he's taking a day off. I hold the warm remains of the mayor, clear a place on my cluttered counter and begin squeezing the body into something recognizable again.

Bresa can't find Cheryl or George. Meanwhile, the ever-cackling quilting club arrives and my father and husband argue about the neatness Mike lacks patience for. "I hate this fiddly shit," he mumbles while dotting cupcakes with buttercream and applying butterflies with tweezers.

My father follows Mike, correcting his mistakes. "You're not saving us any time with your impatience."

I would reprimand both of them, but my focus must remain on the mayor. I've added nothing to what was scraped from Mike's shoe, but George the marzipan mayor seems larger than before. I put on Tilly's reading glasses to correct his face.

"The sausage rolls smell done, guys," I remind my helpers. "Cheddar puffs should go in next. You should have the sandwiches on the trays already."

"How much do quilters eat?" Mike complains as he put on oven mitts.

"They'll stay at least two hours, non-stop snacking." I'm the calm center of the storm. Tilly's nieces breeze past me with fresh, steaming teapots and orders for more, and my father and husband continue baking, decorating, and arranging. When the door swings open every few minutes, the laughter from the quilters reminds me of how much I am needed to do other things.

Tilly's eyes question me from the door.

"Bresa will have to explain," is all I can say. Many days we are overwhelmed, but Tilly treats each occurrence as the first.

The mayor begins to look like the mayor, slowly, although I can't shake the feeling that he has grown. I question why this has happened. The mayor is part of so many of my memories—all the school events he attended, smiling and cheering. He bought from all my fundraisers. I have countless certificates he signed with pride from the city of Oak Village when I competed in sports or academics. A photo of Mike and the mayor hangs in my home from the day Mike opened his landscaping business. Whatever complaint Cheryl has against him can't outweigh the good he has done. I shouldn't judge, not knowing. I know this, yet I can't stop.

I remember his replica fighting his way across the floor. Maybe he wasn't fighting. He could have been defending himself. If Cheryl attacked him, his constant pushing is logical. If he attacked Cheryl, a single punch would suffice. Once more, I tell myself not to speculate, not to judge. I wasn't there. I can't know.

Bresa returns, shaking her head. She has not found Cheryl or George. "I've left messages. I've told her it's interrogative that she comes back as soon as possible."

"Didn't you mean 'imperative'?"

Bresa sighs. "I can't believe I said that."

"She'll figure it out." She leans against my arm, the remade body of the mayor on the cutting board in front of us. "He looks bigger. Don't you think so?"

Bresa raises her eyebrows. "You're right. Maybe the marzipan expanded?"

"Bresa, please tell me you know what you're doing."

"This has never happened before. I don't know if I can reanimate him after he was stepped on. I've never had one stay animated so long, either. We're in virgin territory, Penelope."

I follow her as she takes the mayor into her room. She locks us in and places him on her card table. I watch her at her cabinet of mysterious bottles next, measuring and mixing until she brings out a syringe full of a blue, chalky liquid.

"If this doesn't work, maybe Cheryl can still finish her part. I don't know what else to try." Bresa seems to have no expectations when she injects the liquid into the doll.

The mayor sits up, staring at Bresa for a moment while she holds her breath. His neck turns and now he focuses on me. I feel faint again, but I sit on an end table before I fall. He is different now, just sitting instead of pushing against whatever is before him. He seems conscious. I know it's not my imagination—he is larger than before.

"His memory has changed," Bresa says. "What were you thinking when you redid him?"

"I was recalling all the good things he did for our town and people in general. Why? What was the memory Cheryl gave him?"

"She wouldn't tell me. She only thought it during our ceremony and then she changed her mind when it came time to put an end to him."

"Bresa, you have to tell me what the point of this is. I'm too involved now."

She stands the mayor on his feet and watches him wobble for a moment before sitting again. "I thought I told you. He's like a memory sponge. When he is de-animated, the memory is gone forever."

"From the real mayor?"

"Yes. Only Cheryl didn't de-animate him. Your husband did, and a day late. Now he doesn't seem to remember what he remembered before. He's not pushing and fighting."

"I can't imagine him ever fighting with Cheryl like that. It wasn't his personality."

"Penelope, you can't know what people are like unless you live with them. Is Mike exactly the way you thought he would be before you married him?"

"No, but he's not violent. The surprises have been small and inconsequential."

Bresa starts to say something but she checks her phone instead. "It's Cheryl, finally. She's sorry. She's at her brother's house but she can come first thing tomorrow morning."

I'm relieved, although after reviewing everything Bresa has told me, I'm not sure I should be. "Maybe no damage has been done at all. Right? Nobody knows anything."

She shrugs and pulls a cardboard box from the closet. The mayor is still content to sit and do nothing. He doesn't fight when Bresa places him in the box, interlocks the flaps, and puts the box in the closet. "We'll find out tomorrow. I'd feel better if I knew where the real mayor was and what he remembered."

In bed, Mike analyzes his involvement in an attempt to absolve himself from murder charges. It's simple enough. I remind him numerous times that the mayor was not a voodoo doll, and all Mike had done was step on a cookie. Furthermore, we have no reason to believe the mayor is dead.

The thought of the marzipan mayor trapped in a box all night tortures me. Mike reminds me the doll doesn't need to breathe, or use a toilet, or eat or drink. If Bresa is right, it isn't alive at all, and its ability to move is only a reflex.

"Tomorrow, it will all be over, one way or another," Mike says as he picks up his phone. "It's late. We should sleep."

I kiss him again.

"One more thing. Promise me you'll never make a version of me in marzipan."

It was unlike Tilly to leave a door unlocked. "Hello?" I announce, leaning in. The interior looks normal, maybe slightly untidy by Tilly's standards. Yesterday was a busy day, though. Sometimes there are mistakes and in this small town, locks are rarely necessary. No one answers, and no other cars are here. I proceed to the safe, which is undisturbed. The register contains some cash, satisfying me that the open door means nothing.

Bresa's door is also open. Whoever cleaned last night must have forgotten that Bresa's cash drawer is separate. Turning into Bresa's room, my eyes are drawn to the open closet. The cardboard box appears to have burst open, torn, and unfolded on the floor.

I knew leaving him in a box was wrong.

I search now, corners and under tables, every dining room. I don't want to believe the obvious. The marzipan mayor has wandered away somewhere. My creation, easily traced to this business and me, is loose in Oak Village. Bresa and I will have to move.

"Penelope?" It's Cheryl, still wearing sunglasses, leaning in the open front door. "I am supposed to see Bresa?"

"Come in. She's not here yet, but you can wait in her room."

She moves slowly. I doubt she has slept, like the rest of us who are involved. "Did you lose something?"

I stop searching. "It's gone, I guess. I'll be in the kitchen."

I don't know who to call. Instead, I stand for a moment at the refrigerators, picturing the little mayor being run over by a truck and also realizing I need to make puff pastry. The thoughts are incompatible. I feel paralyzed.

The knock at the back door startles me.

"Penelope? Is that you?" It's the real mayor, George Williams, his face against the small window in the door. "I'm looking for Cheryl!"

At least the mayor is alive. Mike will be relieved, as will Bresa. I unlock the door. "Forgive my slow reaction, Mr. Williams. I haven't been sleeping well."

"Is everything alright? How is Mike?"

"No problems, really." It's good to see his smiling face. Like the rest of us, though, he seems tired. I've never seen him in a jogging suit, either. He seems a little lopsided. "Cheryl is in Bresa's room."

"Good to see you, Penelope."

Seeing the real mayor has alerted me to reality, at least. I gather blocks of butter for the pastry and take the rolling pin from the island cabinet.

Cheryl screams before I can begin pounding the butter. Peeking into the dining room, I see them—Cheryl walking backward, her face petrified in terror. "But you're dead!" she screeches.

He reaches forward and pushes her several times, making her stumble toward the door to the basement. One final push and she falls back through the door, thumping and thudding to the basement. What I'm thinking can't be—just because the mayor was pushing her the way the marzipan mayor was—it has to be a coincidence. What had she meant when she said he was dead?

I hear nothing. Again, I peek into the dining room.

The mayor turns his head in my direction, then his uneven body. It's his familiar grin, but when his lips part, honey streams from the corners of his mouth.

Charlie Eats the Paper Gods

~ H. L. Fullerton

Nothing at FAIHT (Featherstone's All Inclusive Harmonic Tute-lage—the most-exclusive, inclusive, learning-centric kindergarten preparatory) was ever considered a problem. Until four-year-old Rederick Thuman joined Miss Kinders' class.

"How did you do that?" Tommy Yen-Zarif whispered across the snack table to Rederick.

"I didn't do it," Rederick said. "Charlie did."

"What else can Charlie do?" Evergreen Masoda asked. "Can he make my milk chocolate?"

"Charlie can do anything."

"My milk's still white."

Rederick shook his head the way his mom did when he forgot to put the toilet seat down. "That's 'cause you don't believe."

"I believe," Tommy said and Tommy's milk turned colors.

"Charlie likes you now," Rederick said and hummed while he ate the rest of his jelly and cream cheese sandwich. Miss Kinders, who was eavesdropping on the exchange, turned white and clutched the pentagram she wore around her neck.

When Miss Kinders (whom Mrs. Featherstone had hired as much for her fantastic name as her qualifications) first mentioned the Rederick-Charlie situation, Mrs. Featherstone thought she'd have to fire Miss Kinders for being intoxicated. Then Mrs. F herself witnessed Rederick's . . . well, it could only be called indecency, and decided a sip, or a fifth, of vodka was in order before inviting Rederick's parents in for a chat about the Disappearing Paper Dolls.

☉

Mundie Thuman, Rederick's mother, texted her husband during her phone conversation with Mrs. Featherstone's assistant, first to determine his availability for their meeting with the headmaster, then to theorize what the agenda would be and how they should handle things. Both agreed that no matter what the infraction was and it had to be an infraction, right? No one was summoned into the headmaster's office as a reward and Eamonn assured his wife that he'd sent in the tuition money so it wasn't anything financial . . . Yes, yes, tuition had most certainly been paid; he was looking at confirmation from their bank this very second. Puzzled, the Thumans agreed that whatever this was about, they would take Rederick's side because children needed to know they were loved unconditionally. Any punishment, if warranted—oh, what could Red have done?—would be handled at home. By them. The Thumans parenting style could best be described as 'United Front' and this was what they presented to Mrs. Featherstone.

First thing Mrs. Featherstone—who'd taught the pre-K set for three decades and had dealt with all sorts of delicate issues—asked the Thumans was, "Have either of you taught Rederick magic tricks?"

"Magic?" Eamonn said, at the same time his wife said, "No."

The headmaster made a check mark on the papers in front of her. "Ventriloquism?"

The Thumans shook their heads.

"And you're still practicing humanists?"

"Perhaps," Mundie said, feeling in control for the first time since she'd entered the building, "you best tell us what this is about."

Mrs. Featherstone sighed. "Rederick's pranks are disrupting the class. We understand the enthusiasm of young minds, encourage it at its proper time and place, but Rederick's in—" Here Mrs. F. almost blurted 'indecency', but caught herself at the first syllable, "*enthusiasm* is affecting the other children's ability to learn."

"What kind of pranks?" Eamonn asked. He was careful to modulate his tone, keep any pride out of it, but he couldn't help thinking, *My Red's an entertainer*. Still, the boy Mrs. Featherstone was describing didn't sound like their Rederick. Eamonn had to work to get his son to smile, such a serious boy he was; him clowning about in class was hard to imagine.

"Miss Kinders had the class cut out paper dolls. It not only allows them to practice fine motor skills, but illustrates how we are all connected and depend on one another. Also, it encourages them to stay in line and hold hands whenever we leave the classroom. A strong chain will never lose a link, I always say."

"What does this have to do with Rederick?" Mundie asked. She glanced at her watch to remind Mrs. Featherstone how important the Thumans' time was, how expensive. "Did he refuse the assignment?"

"No, no. Rederick participated. But after . . . well, some of the chains disappeared."

Mundie straightened in her chair. "Are you accusing our son of *stealing* other children's *paper*?"

"Not stealing." Mrs. Featherstone pursed her lips. "Some of the children encouraged Rederick to . . . show off. I, myself was there. He said, 'Eat the dolls' and then the dolls disappeared. Like a magic trick."

Eamonn, a jokester himself, said, "Did you check his sleeves?" His wife frowned her eyes at him and his smile disappeared.

"We checked everywhere for the dolls and couldn't find them." Mrs. Featherstone didn't mention that it had, in fact, looked like someone was dining on doll spaghetti. Chains of paper dancing in the air, then disappearing into an unseen gullet. Chimp, chomp, gulp and little confetti flakes falling to the floor. No, no need to mention that to the Thumans. They'd think she'd gone 'round the bend. As it was, they looked at her as if she were the Big Bad Wolf and they a couple of woodcutters with new hatchets.

"Did you ask Rederick about the dolls?" the mother said.

"He blamed it on Charlie."

"Have you spoken to this Charlie's parents?" the father asked.

"There is no Charlie," Mrs. Featherstone said, then, "There's more." And she told the Thumans about how it rained glitter during quiet time; the banana stickers on the ceiling; the marbled crayons which made it impossible to teach children their colors, the re-arrangement of the alphabet letters; the now-you-see-it-now-you-don't missing keyboards, Rederick's insistence on Charlie as the perpetrator of all these acts and the way he'd convinced the other children to believe in—and blame—his imaginary friend. Then she mentioned the disappearing paper dolls again because of its leap from harmless-but-concerning behavior to something that needed to be dealt with immediately. "We'd like to work on helping Rederick discern real and imaginary and hope that you can reinforce that distinction at home. Reinforcement is very important at this age, as I'm sure you know. It's one of FAIHT's four columns of learning. Perhaps the most important." Mrs. Featherstone folded her hands across her desk, partly to keep the trembling hidden, but also to impress upon the Thumans that if they didn't stop this Charlie business, she'd have no option but to expel Rederick. By the looks on their faces, the Thumans understood her unspoken threat.

That evening at the dinner table, Eamonn and Mundie exchanged looks over Red's head, wanting to approach the subject of Charlie in the best manner possible. At no point should Red feel as if they were accusing him of anything. They would simply ask him about Charlie, then decide if they needed to make an appointment with a child psychologist. Perhaps their pediatrician could prescribe something. Most likely Mrs. Featherstone and Miss Kinders were wrong about Charlie belonging to Red's imagination. Red would tell them it was someone's nickname or another child's creation and they'd all breathe easier, maybe even laugh.

"I'm done," Rederick said. "Can I color?"

"May I," Mundie said and Red shimmied off his chair until his toes touched the floor, then went running for paper and crayons. The Thumans eyed the crayons, happy to see they were all solid colors— just the way the manufacturer sold them. It gave their faith a boost: all would be okay.

"Hey, bud," Eamonn said, picking up a crayon. "Tell us about Charlie."

"Charlie's silly." Rederick drew a sun, colored it purple.

"Have we met Charlie?" Mundie said.

Rederick shook his head. "You can't see Charlie."

"Because we're grown-ups?"

"No. 'Cause Charlie's imaginary. Like the wind."

Both Thuman parents inhaled sharply. Mundie urged her husband to 'go on, ask' so he said, "Wind is a real thing. Did you mean imaginary as in something that's made up, like you made Charlie up, or invisible as in something you can't see with your eyes?"

"Charlie's invisible."

The Thumans sat back in their chairs. This wasn't going according to plan. Mundie braved, "Is Charlie a friend? From school?"

Rederick tilted his head as if considering the question *or listening.* "He says he is."

Eamonn looked at Mundie. She looked at Rederick, mouth tight. "Did you read about Charlie in a book?"

Their son stopped coloring and giggled. "You're silly. Charlie's not in a book. Kids can't read. Charlie's in the sky. Is the sky invisible or imaginary?"

The Thumans could see their approach wasn't working. Red wasn't about to confess to making up a prankster persona. Eamonn decided to dig deep and coach the answer out of his son. There had to be a reason Red was pretending about Charlie and if they could figure out what that was, then they could cure their son and he'd turn into a happy, well-adjusted pre-schooler with a bright education ahead of him. It took a few tries to pry Red's attention off the sky's realness. Eamonn wanted to take the crayons and paper away from his son—but that's what his father would've done so he knew it wasn't the right thing to do. "Mrs. Featherstone told us about the paper dolls, son. You know it isn't right to rip up other kid's work. It might hurt their feelings. You wouldn't want anyone to rip up your drawing, would you?"

Red looked at his dad. "You're gonna rip up my drawing?"

"I'm not going to do anything to your drawing. I just want you to understand that you have to be respectful of people's things. I know you know how to share. Well, sometimes sharing means not touching or breaking other people's things."

"Okay."

"So you won't make anything else disappear like the paper dolls, right?"

"It wasn't me. It was Charlie."

The Thumans felt like failures. Their son wasn't understanding them at all. Did he know what an expulsion from FAIHT would mean on his permanent record? Why was this happening to them? Eamonn tried one more time. "Why would Charlie do something like that, Red?"

"Pommer said he wouldn't believe in Charlie unless Charlie ate the paper dolls so Charlie ate them."

"Rederick. Charlie isn't real." Mundie put her hand over her son's drawing. "He's imaginary. Like the cartoons you sometimes watch on TV."

"No. Charlie's real. He's a god. Like Evergreen's Yahweh and Pommer's Vishnu and Miss Kinders' Crone and Green Jesus."

"But, Red, honey," Mundie said, using her best child-friendly voice, which was the same sing-song manner she used at work for stupid employees, "we're humanists. We don't believe in gods."

"I believe in Charlie." Rederick took his crayons and went to his room. Eamonn and Mundie stared at each other, each hoping the other knew what to do next. None of the parenting articles they'd read said anything about what to do if your child created his own god.

"It's all-inclusive," Mundie said when her husband balked at her strategy for handling Mrs. Featherstone. "It's right there in the name: Featherstone's *All Inclusive* Harmonic Tutelage."

"I don't think we should encourage this 'god' thing."

"We're not encouraging. This is just a phase. It'll pass. Three months from now Red won't even remember making Charlie up. But do you want Red kicked out of kindergarten prep over an imaginary friend who thinks eating paper is the height of comedy? Do you want his future ruined?" Mundie stared at Eamonn until he answered.

"No."

"Then we tell Mrs. Reinforcement-is-one-of-the-four-pillars-of-enlightenment what Red told us: Charlie's his god. All faiths, creeds, whathaveyou are welcome at FAIHT. Well, Red's now a Charliest. I've already filled out the declaration form and you'll drop it off when you take Red to school."

"You didn't actually put 'Charliest,' did you?" Eamonn said.

"Don't be ridiculous. There isn't a box for that. I checked 'monotheist, other'. Thankfully, Rederick hasn't created an entire pantheon so we only have to get rid of one god. How hard can that be? In the meantime, if that woman tries booting us from her school, we'll sue for religious discrimination."

"I don't think—"

"Eamonn. We. Are. Doing. This."

Eamonn dropped the paper off. He also explained to Rederick about the imaginary nature of gods and that Charlie was only an attempt to make sense of a world that Red didn't quite understand, but one day Red would learn physics and then he'd see there wasn't anything to be afraid of and there was no need to believe in a larger power directing unseen forces. Red said, "I'm not afraid of Charlie, Daddy. He makes me laugh." and ran down the hall. Then he ran back. "Here. Charlie made this for you. You can use it at work." Rederick handed Eamonn an orange crayon containing squiggles of blue, green, brown and pink. It still had the maker's paper label tightly wrapped around it. Eamonn rolled it between his fingers until he could read the color's name: Atomic Tangerine.

He clutched his present and wondered if it was possible for a four year old to use crayons as a foreshadowing device.

Miss Kinders stared at the form on her desk and realized that the Thumans knew nothing about religion; otherwise they'd never have declared Charlie a god. In front of her, the class whispered about Charlie in that stage-whisper way small children had—not a true whisper, more of a sibilant yell. She had to get the class under control, get Charlie under control. A magical imaginary friend was bad enough, but now with half the class professing faith in 'Charlie' and the Thumans declaring his godhood . . . Miss Kinders stood. Her chair scraped against the floor and the children laughed.

"Charlie made the chair fart," Pommer said.

Contradicting children only made them argumentative so Miss Kinders dragged a screeching marker across the white board and regretted that chalkboards went the way of pen and paper—fingernails across a chalkboard would've made a much more satisfying sound. "I make the things in my classroom . . . talk." Miss Kinders pulled her authoritative voice out of her bag of tricks. "I also make them quiet and that includes all of you. There will be no art today. Instead, we're going to talk about gods." Murmurs broke out. Eyes glanced Rederick's way. Miss Kinders rapped on her desk, feeling a bit like Poe's raven. "And rules. We'll talk about gods and rules."

Rederick's face bunched up. He crossed chubby arms across his tiny stubborn chest. "Gods don't have rules."

"Yes," Miss Kinders said. "Yes, they do. Let's start with the ancient gods. Anyone here worship Zeus or Apollo?" Two hands went up. Miss Kinders let out the breath she'd been holding. Her double minor in comparative religion was about to make itself useful. If she couldn't make Charlie disappear, she'd truss him up with restrictions so tight he'd wish he were imaginary. It never occurred to her that she herself had made the mistake of believing in him.

On his way to work, Eamonn worried that he and Mundie were committing a monumental parenting blunder, the kind other parents would whisper about and shake their heads until someone said, "Well, it's not surprising about the Thuman kid. Remember how he invented a god and his parents declared it a religion? I mean, you might expect something like that from animists, but a couple of atheists should've known better." Expulsion was the least of their worries; Red could be socially ostracized. His friends' parents would never invite over a kid who came with his own god and a boatload of glitter. The Thumans didn't have the social or financial clout to pull a thing like that off. Maybe Mrs. Featherstone had done them a favor by threatening expulsion. This way they could nip this Charlie thing in the bud before it did more than smudge Red's future. Next year Mrs. Featherstone would be a memory in a scrapbook; it was the other pre-K thru 12 parents he and Mundie needed to keep ignorant of the Charlie situation. He'd message her as soon as he reached the office so they could strategize.

Mrs. Featherstone was on the phone with the Yen-Zarifs who were concerned that their son Tommy was being recruited by a cult. They wanted to know if 'All Inclusive' meant that proselytizing was condoned on campus. They wanted it stopped. They wanted Tommy switched to another class and kept away from this Charlie and his religious ramblings, and they wanted contact information for Charlie's parents. What kind of people let their child believe that God spent his time turning white milk into chocolate? The Yen-

Zarifs were all for religious tolerance, but this type of talk was sacrilegious. And, they reminded her, Tommy was not supposed have chocolate—it contained caffeine and the Yen-Zarifs' religion prohibited caffeine. Also, potassium sorbate made Tommy unruly.

"Mr. and Mrs. Yen-Zarif, I fully understand all your concerns and, of course, we have Tommy's dietary—" Here, Mrs. Featherstone remembered not to use the word 'restrictions' because parents who sent their children to Featherstone's All Inclusive Harmonic Tutelage did not want any reminders, even subliminal ones, that their progeny were prevented from participating in anything, even those things they themselves had expressly forbidden. The role of FAIHT was to open doors, not slam them shut and engage the deadbolt. "—*requirements* in his file. Please be assured that FAIHT was unaware that food sharing was occurring. I will make sure that stops today. I cannot, however, due to legal ramifications, release information on other children or their parents. But I will see about relocating Tommy to an environment better suited to his needs. While diversity is one of FAIHT's four columns of learning, we can't allow it to negatively affect any of our students." She'd also see about getting Rederick Thuman under control. If Miss Kinders hadn't any success in curbing the boy's imagination, then perhaps she wasn't the wunder-lehrer Mrs. Featherstone had imagined.

Miss Kinders marched her class through the halls to the library. "No whispering," she said, keeping her eyes straight ahead so she couldn't see any more things that would shake her faith. She was the adult. She knew better. She'd show Red books filled with commandments; she'd show him that you couldn't just invent a god and let it do whatever it wanted; she'd show him; she'd show them all.

At his desk, Eamonn Thuman reached for a pen and picked up the many colored crayon. How strange the crayon felt in his hand, not like a pen at all, but something mightier. Would it work?

Eamonn pulled a blank sheet of paper from his printer and scribbled circles on it. The crayon worked. That surprised him though he wasn't sure why. Then he caught sight of his scribblings. It was if . . . It looked like . . . but it couldn't be . . . Eamonn shaded another section of paper and yes, an image was appearing. The crayon was functioning like his printer, except instead of laying down black letters on white paper, it was creating a waxy painting *without being told to*.

He adjusted his grip. Realized that the wrapper was now pink. He checked its name. Atomic Tangerine had morphed into Radical Red. Heart jumping in his chest, Eamonn put the crayon tip to paper and colored. When he'd filled the page, he saw Red and a bunch of other kids running around tables piled with books. A woman towered over them, her eyes raised to the heavens, her face twisted in a scream, her arms clawing at air.

Eamonn shook his head, but the picture didn't disappear. He flipped the page and threw the crayon onto the floor. He focused on his computer screen and willed himself to forget what just happened. But he couldn't. He kept thinking, *Charlie*. His eyes drifted towards his desk and the overturned paper. Which wasn't blank. It was the declaration form he'd handed to Miss Kinders. Stomach sinking, he picked up the form and peeked at the back. The drawing was still there, and maybe, just maybe, the figures had moved. Eamonn squeezed the form.

Miss Kinders. Eamonn scrambled from his desk, form in hand, and grabbed the crayon off the floor. He headed back to FAIHT.

Streamers of paper-god cut-outs flew from FAIHT's collection of holy tomes, decorating the library as if it were a non-denominational pine tree. Kids clapped and twirled, laughed and chased the paper gods. Miss Kinders shouted for them to sit down and be quiet. She grabbed at books only to have them torn from her hands.

"Noah's ark!" Evergreen Masoda pointed to the train of paper animals dancing across the shelf tops.

"Look, it's Vishnu," Pommer said, eyes wide as his god's form emerged from the pages of a book, arm in arm in arm in arm.

A string of pentagrams, like the one around Miss Kinders' neck, twined around her, pulled her into a waltz. She broke free. "Enough," she yelled. Her eyes locked on Rederick and she marched towards him. "You stop this now. There are rules. I showed you the rules. *You have to follow the rules.*"

"Charlie doesn't like rules," Rederick said, eyes focused somewhere high above her left shoulder. "And Charlie isn't in a book. Gods shouldn't be in books. Gods can't write."

"The goddess—"

Rederick interrupted her. "Charlie says he can eat all your gods."

Miss Kinders stepped back from Rederick, mouth open, hand clasped around her necklace. "No," she said, but already pages of god-dolls were disappearing. Motes of paper fell to the floor, coating everything in a grayish dust. "No!" she screamed.

"You can't trap gods in books," Rederick said. "Rules make them weak."

"There is no Charlie," Miss Kinders said. "It's you. And I can stop you." Courage gathered, she ran at Rederick.

The library door crashed against the wall, but Miss Kinders wouldn't be distracted, so she didn't see Rederick's father race into the library, waving a piece of paper. He stopped short when he realized the teacher was lunging at his son. Tables, chairs and children separated him and Rederick. Eamonn couldn't get to her before she got to Red. Not knowing what else to do, he threw the crayon Charlie made for him at Miss Kinders.

It hit her in the head. There was a soft pop. A cloud of glitter exploded into the room and everything froze. Rederick moved out of reach. Said, "I'm okay now." and everyone unfroze.

Miss Kinders' pentagram rose towards the ceiling. Her arm yanked at it, but it kept rising, pulling her to her toes. Her fingers burned and she let go. Watched as her encircled five-sided star was crushed into a 'C' and dropped against her chest. The fight went out of her then. She slumped in a nearby chair, one meant for a body much smaller than hers, and wept.

"Did you see her necklace?" Tommy said. "C is for Charlie." The children stopped frolicking and gathered around her in a circle. "Tell us another story about Charlie," they said and sat at her feet.

Eamonn Thuman grabbed his son and headed for the nearest exit. He slowed when he realized Red had grabbed another boy's hand and that boy was holding the hand of a girl in a green dress and Eamonn realized he'd turned into the Pied Piper leading a line of children into the hall. He set Red down, found his son's hand, and said, "Okay, we're all going to go see Mrs. Featherstone and give Miss Kinders a moment to herself." He tried not to think about reappearing declaration forms, exploding glitter crayons, or how much he and the children looked like a chain of paper dolls.

The Thumans withdrew Rederick from school that very afternoon and sued FAIHT. Miss Kinders was fired for proselytizing to her students and instigating the kiddie faith riot, which is what the media dubbed the library incident. Mrs. Featherstone decided inclusiveness was more trouble than it was worth and renamed her kindergarten preparatory the Fourth Academy for Cooperative Thought, or FACT.

Rederick didn't mention Charlie again, much to his parent's delight—"I told you it was a phase," Mundie would say when the subject came up, which wasn't often, because the Thumans didn't talk about FAIHT or crayons. In the fall, Rederick went to kindergarten. The only blight on the Thumans' enthusiasm was that Evergreen Masoda (who'd also had that Charlie-cult-starting Miss Kinders) was in Red's class. Eamonn and Mundie discussed switching Red out, but decided a friendly face might help their son make new friends. Real friends. And Evergreen was a pretty little thing who other children flocked to. This could only help Red's social standing.

At lunch, Evergreen sat next to Red and shared her fruit snacks with him. "I miss chocolate milk," she said.

"Me, too," Red said. "But we don't want to scare the grown-ups again."

"Charlie isn't scary," Evergreen said.

"I know. My daddy says people are scared of things they don't understand. He says physics will fix it."

"Does Charlie know physics?" Evergreen asked, playing with her new necklace, which looked like a silver 'E' had been reshaped into a shaky 'C'.

"Charlie knows everything," Red said and his monogram necklace floated up from his shirt's placket a tiny bit—not enough to frighten anybody, just enough to catch the light and cast a rainbow—or a grin—on the cafeteria ceiling.

Bones Placed in Apposition

~ A. P. Howell

Featherstonhaugh glanced upward at the old State House. Lukens's new four-sided clock was an impressive feat of engineering, but there was something to the criticism of its legibility at a distance, especially when the sun was bright and the viewer's eyes less sharp than a young man's. The steeple's white paint stood out brilliantly against a cloudless sky, and the clock confirmed Featherstonehaugh was on time for his appointment. He crossed Chestnut Street, avoiding horse droppings with an ease borne of extended periods of urban living.

He stood now in the heart of Philadelphia, which was—or at least had been—the heart of the new country. On the corner, City Hall bustled with the thousand and one tasks necessary to maintain a city of eighty thousand souls. When Featherstonhaugh had first arrived in the city, the Supreme Court had but lately relocated to the new capital, and the locals had often lapsed into calling the building the "old courthouse" or "new city hall." Across Fifth Street sat the Library Company of Philadelphia, soon to be celebrating its centennial.

Featherstonhaugh's destination was a brick building standing proudly beside City Hall on Fifth Street: Philosophical Hall. One of many noble institutions shepherded into existence by Franklin and like-minded contemporaries, the American Philosophical Society was a jewel of American intellectual life. It was devoted not merely to the acquisition of learned volumes, in the manner of the Library Company, but to expanding knowledge on all manner of subjects.

This was a worthy goal in general, but particularly necessary in America. An entire continent of mysteries laid waiting for discovery and documentation. As rich as European intellectual society might be, correspondence could go only so far. Home-grown intellectuals were needed to advance knowledge, solve problems particular to the United States, and make use of its natural resources.

"Good afternoon!" Hays called as Featherstonhaugh stepped inside. He waited on the second floor, leaning against the banister and looking entirely comfortable in this temple of learning.

"I am most happy we found a mutually agreeable time." Featherstonhaugh did not whisper as he ascended, but pitched his voice politely low. A murmur of voices from behind closed doors indicated a university class in session or some other consultation. The other man had not precisely been rude—especially if he happened to know the other conversation was of little consequence—but Featherstonhaugh chose to err on the side of propriety.

Hays was a medical man in his thirties. Featherstonhaugh understood he had formerly been involved in his family's East India trade, but had apparently found himself ill-suited to the work. He had developed something of a name as a natural scientist and had literary ambitions, having already produced writing in the medical field. He was unmarried, a fact Featherstonhaugh could not help but look upon with a hint of suspicion and pity. He wondered a bit at the temperament of a man who had not yet settled into matrimony.

By Hays's age, Featherstonhaugh had been a new father, married for half a decade. Memories of Sally still pained him. Thoughts of his boys brought forth painful details of the girls' final days. Instead, he considered Charlotte, her genteel upbringing and charming Virginia accent.

Languages had always been among Featherstonehaugh's interests. If not for his fascination in the subject, he would not have come to America, would not have settled here (*settled*: that was true, and infinitely safer than *met Sally*). He would not have met Charlotte with her charming accent and the youth that was lost to him, and would have neither needed nor found a second chance at domestic life.

Thoughts of mortality brought him round to the reason it was Hays ushering him into a second floor room, and not the author of the article that had caught his interest.

"I am sorry to have missed Godman's lecture, and sorrier for his passing," Featherstonhaugh said. "He had been ill for some time, I believe?"

Hays nodded. "But though it did not come as a surprise, he still passed too young. He will be missed. His mind is a great loss to the medical community, and to America's natural historians."

"His *Transactions* paper piqued my interest. A new genus and species of elephant . . . it is a bold claim."

"So Harlan says," Hays noted. "He also believed he described Lewis and Clark's Iowa fossil adequately, before I corrected his work with my *Saurodon*. He cannot be said to understand reptiles, for all the words he writes on the subject, much less mammals. And were Godman here, I am certain he would remind you of the man's plagiarism."

Featherstonhaugh shrugged, suspecting that Godman would have a good deal more to say on the subject of Harlan. Philadelphia's natural historians' opinions about one another were no less passionate than their opinions on scientific matters. "That is why I wish to see the specimen myself. As masterful as Peale's illustrations may be, there is something to be said for direct observation."

Hays unlocked a cabinet. "The vertebrae, ribs, and bones of the limbs are available for your examination as well, and may be of interest since illustrations did not accompany Godman's article. But you are no doubt here for these." Hays carefully transferred the skull and jaw fragments to a table.

The largest intact section of the upper jawbone was seventeen inches in length. Five inches of upper tusk rested within their sockets, with another twelve inches exposed on the right side and ten on the left. A good seven and a half inches in circumference where they emerged from the socket, the tusks did not begin to narrow to a point until the final four inches of their length. The patterns of wear had been represented to a fair degree of accuracy in Peale's illustrations.

Featherstonhaugh paid particular attention to the lower jaw, the formation of which had so strongly captured Godman's attention. It was indeed dramatically elongated at the extremity, the angles more rectangular than the curvature he had observed in other mastodon specimens. A full three inches of tusk rested in the socket; the exposed portion, about one inch in length, was covered with black enamel and ended with a spiral twist. He pressed a thumbnail into dry, grayish bone of the tusk and felt it yield.

"It is similar to the mastodon," Featherstonhaugh said, "as Godman himself noted. The wear upon the milk teeth reveals only surface enamel, as in the mastodon, not the elephant . . ."

"Not any elephant heretofore known," Hays said.

Featherstonhaugh continued to examine the lower jaw. "They are, without doubt, milk teeth. Godman is certainly correct in his assertion that this is a juvenile animal."

"Yes, that is quite clear."

Featherstonhaugh frowned, more at the prickliness creeping into the other man's tone than at any feature of the long-dead animal before him, and squinted at the sockets of the tusks. "The elongation of the jaw is indeed interesting."

"If I may." Hays reached into a pocket to produce a pair of spectacles. "These may be of some use."

Featherstone set the jawbone carefully upon the table. "Do you mean to insult my observations? Or have you invented lenses to ease the work of natural scientists?"

"More the latter," Hays said, in pale imitation of Featherstonhaugh's attempted jocularity. "I seek to work at the forefront of ophthalmology. Our eyes fail, whether through disease or age or mischance. But with research, skill, and the proper diagnosis and intervention, what has gone wrong may be put right."

Featherstonhaugh took the spectacles, always interested in the state of scientific advances. The frames were wire, functional, and sturdy; though hardly fashionable, neither were they unnecessarily unattractive. The lenses themselves appeared well-made, which was unsurprising with the resources at Hays's disposal. With a casual examination, Featherstonhaugh could not discern the lenses' intent; there was none of the distortion one might expect in a pair of spectacles made to correct either far-sightedness or myopia.

He hooked them over his ears, expecting the blurriness of wearing another's spectacles, but his vision remained unchanged. If not for the visible wire of the frames within his field of view, he would not have known he wore them. He wondered if this was some joke of Hays's, or if the man's skill did not extend to lens-grinding. But Featherstonehaugh's concern about politic statements were rendered moot.

Hays lifted the upper and lower jaws, one in each hand. This seemed unnecessarily cavalier: though the lower jaw was only one foot in length, the upper jaw was half again as long and further unbalanced by twelve inches of tusk. Featherstonhaugh wondered if he was to play witness to a careless loss to natural history and a strike to Hays's reputation.

But Hays proved dexterous and settled the jaws together as they would have met in life. The right side of the head was, as promised in Godman's text and Peale's plates, in excellent condition. Held together, Featherstonhaugh could see the animal as it would have been in life, a youngster more kin to elephants than mastodons, and utterly (if subtly) distinct from all other known species. *Tetracauldodon mastodontoideum.*

He imagined layers of muscle and flesh and fur, tendons snaking between bones, those jaws opening and closing. He extrapolated the rest of the body, and after that the effects of maturity. But for whatever mischance had killed the beast, it would have grown to adulthood. He could picture it striding across the continent with its fellows. This one had died in Orange County, and why would it not have roamed Featherstonehaugh's old estate? Tromping over hills and fields yet to be planted, a place where one day a house would be built, sheep imported, fields tilled . . .

Featherstonhaugh blinked hard at an incipient headache. He removed the spectacles and rubbed his eyes. When he opened them, his vision was doubled. Two identical sets of bones, one belonging to an elephant and one to a mastodon, were superimposed upon one another.

He blinked again. His eyes began to focus properly, as though a film had been removed. Hays still held the bones, but they were only that: the bones of a long-dead creature, shattered and incomplete. They told a story to those who knew how to look at them, but not nearly so interesting or vibrant a story as the one he had just seen.

He folded the spectacles closed and placed them on the table. Though dizzy, he did not fall.

Hays watched him with evident concern, but Featherstonhaugh was not prepared to assume the other man had his best interests at heart. "The right side of the head is, indeed, beautifully preserved." There was a tremor in his voice. He swallowed and the action or the pause proved helpful.

Hays set the bones down once more. "Do you wish to continue your examination?"

Featherstonhaugh followed the other man's gaze, not to the bones but to the spectacles. He had the inkling that Hays cared little for his opinions of the ancient animal. "No, thank you." His voice was steadier, at least. "Having seen the specimen, I will look at others to compare. Perhaps I will return later."

"Viewing evidence with fresh eyes is valuable," Hays said.

With an effort, Featherstonhaugh refrained from shuddering and beat a passably dignified retreat. He kept one hand on the curving banister. He was lightheaded, as though untethered. He feared that he might slip and smash open his skull, or that he might float away entirely.

Hays, chatting politely, seemed infinitely more embedded—in his body, in this city, in this reality. It was a preposterous illusion, of course. Featherstonhaugh was no less real than the man beside him. And though he had been born across the ocean, though his family was not part of Philadelphia society, though he was only part of New York society by virtue of his marriage, he had no less right to occupy this place than Hays.

And yet it was Hays who remained within Philosophical Hall, and Featherstonhaugh who walked away.

The State House clock showed how little time had passed, how little time was necessary to shake the foundations of one's world. But the clock also served as a reminder of its maker, Lukens, and his crusade against Redheffer's spurious perpetual motion machine. It had taken time and effort for Lukens to build a machine that proved Redheffer's a fraud, but prove it he did, and in this very city.

Featherstonhaugh took a steadying breath. He did not know what Hays had done—yet. But he had some guesses as to why he had done it. The cliques of Philadelphia's intellectual community were well-known, and those alliances could be stronger than the allegiance to truth which every man of science ought to hold dear. Misguided loyalty was bad enough; engaging in fraud was far less forgivable. Featherstonhaugh was not by nature a particularly forgiving man, and he had no intention of letting Hays win the game he played.

It was not merely an affront to natural history, but to Featherstonhaugh personally. To conjure forth a nonexistent creature, to suggest that it had walked the same hillsides as Featherstonaugh himself . . . The image was, suddenly, quite unbearable. He could almost feel the erasure of some essential, if hitherto unknown, aspect of his old estate. A juvenile mastodon, that was right and proper. That belonged to the far-distant past of the place where he had raised children and imported the best agricultural products.

Featherstonhaugh meant to prove that elephants had never meandered across his old estate, or any other part of the continent. The days of *Tetracauldodon mastodontoideum* were numbered. He was a geologist, well-positioned to argue the truth of the matter.

As he walked, his determination and confidence grew. He had no destination in mind, but took great comfort from the cobblestones beneath his feet. No matter what he had seen—or thought he had seen, or been forced to see—the stones were real. The very bones of the continent were real, and he meant to understand their true shape.

On a Flayed Horse

~ Brandon H. Bell

Outside the window, San Muerte Drive glowed orange with dust kicked up by a band of flayed horses.

"Those creatures, they's part of the General's army. Trained to make conscripts. That means they kill folk," the crone said, huffing. "You see a load of conscripts passin', the horses ain't far behind."

"Everyone knows that," I said. The air in her shop stank of cigarettes and essential oils.

"Did you know they won't kill young women?"

I nodded, thinking of Muireann and Marigold. Thinking of my flight from him.

"The line between young and heart ripped out, who knows?"

She glanced at me and saw, I presumed, the disappointment and boredom.

"Did you know a young woman can ride a flayed horse?"

"Really?"

This was new and intrigued me.

"It'd be a bad idea," she said, cackles descending into wet cough.

In the distance black, shiny clouds roiled with faces and lightning. Tumblestorms. I wondered where the twins were, when they'd last eaten a hot meal, or when they'd last been hugged.

You might suppose my name is Chance. You'd be mistaken.

The last broadcast of import came from ground zero: it flooded social media, streaming, television. Everyone watched the descent, that sliver of ice in baby blue, suspended above Fort Worth, how it seemed to grow fatter, engorged, as it slid into place amid the meager downtown sprawl. Clips viewed more than any World Cup,

Super Bowl, or Kardashian episode. The ship landed, and soon a crack of light at its base released its load and changed our world. The backs of people's heads filled the foreground. No holes bubbling with green alien spiders. Not yet.

After media died, our dim evenings echoed with snatches of voice and song from the Bardo, and I'd sit with her as long as I dared before bolting home in the night.

"You've met the General?"

She glanced at me; coughed her wet cough.

"Every Shaman has. You will too."

I remembered the old world, my parents, trips to the grocery store with dad and backyard hangouts while he grilled, constant chatter, laughter with mom, over what I couldn't recall, before I lived with *him*.

I met Muireann and Marigold when I first arrived in the suburb from my uncle's home. Dust engulfed the sky, filtered maroon, crimson, and scarlet to a diffuse saffron horizon. Memory: firmament aflame, my hair mussed by the breeze, the dead equine reek. The twins, I learned, wandered the length of San Muerte when the hoards passed. They turned to me that day amid the band of flayed horses, first frightened at this haggard wraith, then chattering around meek, quick smiles. A tumblestorm wheeled past and they glanced for faces between lightning strikes. A children's game for the Bardo burbs. They creeped and charmed in equal measure, as the beasts herded around us. The destriers ripped men open and gulped out their hearts, a quick delicacy and a fresh conscript made.

They never bothered the twins.

Until one did.

A group of conscripts slouched through town, broken and bloodied by their harvesting band.

"You know why we treat women like we do, boy?" The old Shaman asked, laughing. Startled silent, she'd misgendered me.

Magic had rules, and she sought to share those rules before death came for her. Each step of our surest friend, as she dubbed it, counted in phlegmy, wet coughs, her every word a lesson meant to out-pace the inevitable. From the window I watched the twins flit hand in hand across San Muerte, under red sky, silhouettes in dust. She cleared her throat, begging my attention, as she shared the secrets and rumors from the garrulous dead, stray artifacts, and the rare Bardonaut.

"I don't know how to answer a question that big," I said.

She laughed.

"Of course you don't. But know this. There's one way to bring someone back from the land of the dead. A fertile woman is needed. We all know it, instinctively. Gotta control a thing that powerful."

"Women ain't things," I said, feeling clever.

She laughed at that too, glanced with trepidation at the dim window behind her. Red sky and black expanse stretched to the horizon outside, but through that window sprawled a shadowed room beyond the building's perimeter, a room that shouldn't exist.

"Put that out ya mind," she said, noticing my attention. "Back to your litanies."

"It's like this in the dead land . . ." I intoned.

Inward, toward the landing site, the focal point in the war between humanity (dead and otherwise) and the aliens, life was brutal but quotidian. Severed limbs littered the ground, encampments congealed along the Trinity. Outward lay the Bardo, the dead land. Texas sprawled vast, black, and mythic beneath bloodshot sky. Wander too far out and you'd never find your way back. The dead, and other things, wandered inward, conscripts for the Buddhist General who led the dead army.

Winds carried hints of gunpowder and sewage, then weakened, stilled, and reversed, as if the city heaved a vast sigh, and from the Bardo the odor of lost dreams and forsaken love blew dust, ruffled hair, chapped skin.

The monsters, myths, and magic existed but slumbered, extraneous to the modern world . . . until the aliens arrived. They emerged from the Bardo, antibodies to a virus. The green pseudo-spiders engorged people, sometimes other vessels (infamously Big Tex which roamed DFW, stalked the uninfected), and combined them into neomorphs. I'd crossed minotaurs, centaurs, and human centipedes on my trek from my uncle's.

In the suburb, we rarely saw neomorphs, but witnessed conscripts, determined for the front lines, and less often an Avicinaut, business suit aflame.

Once the green-pseudo-spider-filled Big Tex trudged into our suburb, then slinked to the water tower near Elm. There it stood, peering outward into the red and black, like a giant cartoon cowboy peering into all of human history. It latched onto the water tower like it would blow away and held vigil for three days. Near as I could tell, everyone stayed in their house, afraid to catch its attention.

Except the twins.

A band of horses arrived, following conscript. The girls trailed the horses to Elm, then stopped, gazed up into Big Tex's bland, bloated face. It tilted toward them, head askew like a mutt listening through a door. The girls waved at the monster.

It waved back, turned its face outward as if to take a last look, and then pivoted its significant bulk toward city center and set off into the fray, dripping green pseudo-spiders from its seams.

Later that day ten dark figures spilled from the Shaman's shop and trudged past my window, pale-faced and dour. No one had entered the shop since I left. I fidgeted and bit at my cuticles. Why did they come to her? They'd followed Big Tex, but where did they come from?

I berated myself, dismissed it, but a thought niggled at me. It was dark, square, foreboding.

A colossal migration inundated the town, and I sheltered in place, delinquent to the crone. I called her that, but she might have been forty. Rode hard and hung up wet, my uncle's East Texas twang intoned. He lived rent free and proffered these appraisals.

I once walked among the flayed horses, but she didn't know. Gave me a ring. *One ring to rule your ass*, she said, cackling. If I put it on backwards, her matching ring would spark: I'm coming, we agreed.

I strode once among the bands, when I was young, before I escaped my uncle's home, then as the means of my escape. Since then,

I assumed a camouflage of ambiguity, let people assume. She'd assumed. Though I didn't saunter among the flayed beasts, it wasn't because of my gender, but my purity. I believed in my exile. They accepted the twins. Sadness accumulated as I watched the horses and loved them from afar. They'd crumpled my uncle like a plaything when I fled. Good horseys.

The knock startled me. I swung the door open and puzzled at the small, solitary figure against the dust haze. Marigold threw herself into my arms, quaking. She smelled of wet puppies and bubble gum. I let her grieve for a moment, clutching at her like a lost doppelgänger, then I held her back and shook her. Her features hung on her face as if melted. Wounded by horror, the expression didn't register, and I stared into her eyes until the tiny rivulets on her cheeks, the quiver of her mouth, the fact of her solitude jolted me.
"Where is she?"
"A fffflayed horse," she whimpered. The world, and my stomach, churned.

The Shaman rarely left her shop, but the General would send a message to all the Shamans in a region and they'd travel to answer his summons at the foot of his tornado/tower.
On one such occasion, I broke into the shop and opened the black window. Cool breeze. Stink of gunpowder and must. I slunk through a series of rooms, a maze. The colors of the rooms: red-veined granite illuminated by cool light. I heard moans in a distant room, ecstasy or suffering, that morphed into indifference and grew sinister. I'd lost my way, forsaken the old stories. No trail of breadcrumbs, no diligently followed path.
Panicked, I stumbled into an alcove with a woman ensconced in a wooden chair. Ancient chicana, pale hair, wrinkled visage, cataract-filled eyes that flashed fear, then pity.
"Girl, you're not me, are you?" She asked, with kind inflection. She shifted, assessed this creature, and intelligence stormed in her cloudy eyes.

"I—I don't think so, ma'am."

"I was as young as you when it began. Old women are the ghostliest ghosts. What's your name?"

Not that much time had passed since ground zero. My brow furrowed. I told her my name.

"Not me. Why are you in the General's tower?" she asked. I blanched.

She nodded, pushed up from her chair, trudged around the corner and led me to my window . . . the Shaman's window.

"Don't come back, girl."

I nodded on the windowsill to leave her.

"You knew I was a girl," I said.

"You'd of been killed or conscripted, otherwise."

The tracks led into the red and black, through a valley of towering mesas straight out of a Chuck Jones cartoon. Not North Texas, at all. Mythic America. The tracks didn't resemble horse's hooves. Perfect circles, too small, damaged.

A zephyr ozone-sharp with perversion spilled from the Bardo; broken promise of rain dry enough to chafe. My lips puckered and cracked in a grit-filmed face.

"This is the one," I said to Marigold, and she nodded. The band surrounded us, stench and clouds of flies whipped by their sinewy tails. Innumerable rats followed the horses and Marigold violently kicked one that came near, an outburst, a fit. I paused and watched a mare prance alongside, muscles bulged, tendons tight, then released, blood black. I waited, breath held. It ignored me, kept the old unstated promise. It nickered and nodded, rolled eyes white with cataracts, then loped into grainy murk.

I squatted so I could stare, level, into Marigold's eyes. They were the clearest things I'd ever seen.

"Go to the Shaman. Tell her I've gone after Muireann. Tell her I'll use my ring. If she can bring us back—"

"I don't—"

"Just tell her, Marigold. Tell her I listened. Yes? But don't get too close. And then hide in the bands. Stay away from everyone. Watch the shop. That's where we'll come back. If we come back. It won't be long. If the General's tower moves and we haven't returned. Well, we probably won't."

Her face fell, stricken.

"A week?" she asked.

"At most. Yes. Be careful. Don't trust her. Don't trust anyone."

"I never did."

I rode into the Bardo on a flayed horse.

It's like this, in the dead land, I kept muttering. At my back ground zero, it's direction an extra sense, always apparent, a beacon, and ahead, infinite death, like a toothache.

Archetypal cacti caught grew in clusters, alongside more alien plants that resembled pairs of tall, cupped blades. Some were not plants, but the hunched profiles of deer-sized hares, towering ears a deadly mimicry.

When I passed, the king jacks—as I dubbed them—proved wary of my flayed horse but regarded me, salivating below impressive whiskers and quivering noses, their eyes blinking with lashes so lush they resembled fairy tale creatures until those mouths opened to reveal multiple rows of teeth.

Desert land, buttes, mesas, arroyos.

We crested a knoll above a river of the dead, flowing outward, a contemporary majority interspersed by the anachronistic, belonging to ancient eras. The dead slogged away from ground zero and toward the Bardo's horizon. The boundary throbbed, painful—outward endless death, inward the quotidian, opposing polarities that inspired nausea and weird gravity.

The horse trembled as we lingered atop the bluff, then we followed the trail of round tracks downward, into the dead masses' apprehension and furtive glances. The horse bucked, frustrated, eager to thrash, crush, bite and create conscripts. It tensed, adrenaline surged, a rumble began deep in its throat and I slapped its neck and told it *No!* The whinny sounded horror movie fake, and I slapped it again.

"No!"

Pointed our way and it clip-clopped on.

We parted the mass of bodies in our passage, none wishing to cross our path. The flayed horse eviscerated three stragglers that shuffled too near. They each fell to the ground with stillborn shrieks, but when I glanced over my shoulder, they rose and trudged against the flow, back toward the front. Even the dead could be conscripted. The horse seemed pleased and trotted, jaunty, through our parted red sea.

The tracks, like footprints of astronauts on the moon, undisturbed, led up the far grade. I hurried the skinless horse after them, and it obeyed as if it read my mind.

We came upon the linear city after crossing two more rivers of the dead. One river followed a ridgeline, the other trampled a sloped valley, crested accumulated skree, then emerged to flood the landscape. Cardinal directions ceased: there was inward, outward, and uncertainty. We cantered a Mobius strip trail, deeper into death. Titanic mesas predominated along a curvature no planet possessed, as the idea of direction grew alien, abstractions limited in my brain.

The tracks led down and into a house.

"Magic ain't nothing but shit you're too stupid to understand," the old woman said.

The memory lingered as I sat astride the flayed horse. What's the ish? The Shaman deemed it folly to ride a flayed horse. She tended to accuracy, bereft of details. Then I realized the problem.

I couldn't dismount.

Exploring the space between its hide and my pants, I found sinewy strands grew from its back into my buttocks and upper legs, joining us. It didn't hurt. In fact, if I strained just right, it felt . . . Exquisite.

Peered left, then right, atop a ridge a hundred meters above the line of houses, store fronts, municipal buildings. A ring. One side of the city faced inward toward ground zero, the other outward toward deep Bardo.

I could feel hunger from those depths as we poised above the gullet.

I paralleled the city, East then West (approximations), and found no end. If it went on, it would encircle DFW. I could ride alongside it and I would come back to this spot. As I galloped, men came and went but ignored me.

Women slipped from the houses and shops, tended children, tossed out water, swept. Few acknowledged me, hands above scrunched faces.

All stood chained.

"Every town has a Shaman?"

The old crone nodded, smiled. My interest pleased her. We had the front door propped open, a rare luxury. No horses on San Muerte, nor Avicinauts nearby. Fresh air would be nice, she'd said.

"Do all the Shamans have a window like yours? The black one that leads somewhere else?"

She turned pale and fretted about the door, urged me to close it. She stood, faltered, collapsed in seizure, but recovered before I could react. I helped her up, trembling and sweaty, and led her to bed.

I returned to the tracks, indelible despite the wind, and followed them to the wooden boardwalk where they ended. The buildings had concrete foundations, and we sauntered, hooves high, to the near door, and the beast stomped—

Jigsaw splinters, slap of board against concrete, into the hovel where Muireann lay chained. Two men, Caucasian but dark with hair, beard, aura, stood above her. To the side lay a contraption that resembled a horse-shaped cab for two and supplies above spindly legs driven by pedals.

"You cain't—" one man said before the destrier tensed, reared, then clomped, its shriek loud, horrible in the lamplight of the small abode. It took care not to stomp Muireann, unconcerned about the particulates and spatters of blood. She closed her eyes but did not scream. She'd walked among the horses and understood their alignment.

When the room fell to a quiet composed of the flayed horses' breath and whinnies, clomping of concrete, she slipped from her shackles, and stood, wiping hair from her face. I searched, found a jacket hanging, and laid it over the horse. Then I leaned down and snagged Muireann beneath thin arms and plopped her astride the cloth.

"Chains didn't stop you," I said.

"They said I'd grow into them."

Nothing to lose but our chains . . . the thought blazed in my mind, lit my eyes, burned at my skandhas.

The woman next door toppled from the boardwalk, chain pulled taut. Neighbors yelped, afraid, or sniped in rage, flashing eyes and waggled fingers. The horse had its way with them, Muireann quiet but trembling, and a dozen conscripts rose from the blood and viscera of their protestations to shuffle toward the front.

I urged the horse further along the inward boardwalk of the city, far enough that they would not have been able to hear the death stomps and screaming from earlier.

We arrived at a storefront with a cheerily painted sign. Odds N Ends. The name seemed ominous. A woman stepped onto the boardwalk in response to my knocking. She wore a simple shift, smiled.

"Hola, mi ja. Can I help you?"

A shackle and chain around her ankle.

"I've come," I said. Muireann glanced back and up at me. "We've come to rescue you."

"From what, mi ja?"

"You're chained. A prisoner. We—"

I didn't know what to call it. This gate in our wombs. This resource everyone but us might control.

"Ah, mi ja, so it goes. This is life, yes?"

She smiled.

"I miss Marigold," Muireann told me.

"I know. Soon," I said.

From home to home, shop to shop, we searched. I spoke to the women who would listen. Countless men fell beneath my hooves. I could have counted, but grew numb to gore and screaming.

We traveled the length of the linear city. The ebb and flow of death beckoned, urging toward the Bardo depths, endless death, a promise, a withheld caress.

I'd been right. The linear city stretched around all of DFW.

And I was wrong on all points that mattered.

"I miss my sister," she reminded me.

"I know. Let's go."

I flipped the ring on my finger. It glowed blue, as if in a book of stories and ogres were near.

"Your surest friend knocks, lady," I said aloud. I didn't know if the magic conducted my voice, but I thought it fair to give her the chance to refuse this if it did. Static suffused the air along with the scents of offal and iron.

The flayed horse started, then bucked and trotted off into the badlands. Sky dark red, black expanse, until the flash of light and cracking, sand in eyes, then blood, an infinite vortex of suffering and shock—

I recognized her screams—

The emergence, like birth. Stifling air, gloom. Tunnel's end, a dead scream echoed. The walls speckled with viscera and blood. Heaving breath, still alive, then awareness, the tick, tick, tick of time. The tiny figure in the corner, peering at her sister. Bawling for her sister.

"Go," I say, and leverage Muireann down. She topples to the floor, then scampers into an embrace with her twin. Marigold breaks free and scampers near, balled fist lifted toward me, eyes intent. I reach down and she slips something small, cold, and round into my palm. Then she runs back and they hold each other, eyes closed.

The moment elongates, their embrace, their scurried escape, open door blinding, but their passage dims it and they slink into a passing band. He clears his throat and I notice the figure. Doesn't look like a monk. Business suit over enormous girth, orange tan, blond hair, dead eyes.

"You look like that president," I say and he laughs.

"I wonder," he tells me. "Why you have killed one of my Shaman? Your mentor, no less?"

His voice is curt, formal, sensual. He doesn't look like a General, either.

"The linear city, those women. Why?"

"Linear city? The Bardo gives us interesting perspectives, yes? I'd call it a circular city. Huge. It's the hugest."

I take a moment to understand the sound chuffing from his face is laughter.

"Are you a monster?"

At this he mewls, the amusement settling into ugly gentleness.

"Hard question, Shaman killer. I am Rakshasa, bitten by Cucui," He says and laughs again, entertained, "all those years ago. They called me, in time, Geshe Rakshasa. More recent: General."

"I mean. Did you have all those women chained? In the city?"

"Interesting thing, the Bardo. We're told by mendicants it's an in-between place. But you see, it is a form unto itself, a function, a mode, a multifarious proliferation thereof. And it has interesting ways of formalizing the circumstantial, actualizing the memetic. Big words. It gives you what you really are. I make use of that, fighting the incursion—"

I rear the horse and turn to the window. The rakshasa in his fine suit hisses at my back as we burst through the glass and into his tower.

The thing I understand about magic? Understanding is overrated.

Three days pass, measured in glimpses of sky from occasional parapets, machicolations, balastraria, windows. The aether is thick and Bardo radio waves provide esoteric nomenclature—fun, I guess—but most useful, often betrays nearby pursuers, minds static with bloodlust. The General's elite guard follows, soldiers more skilled and quiet of mind, but I've outpaced them and their insectile-buzz auras, the tower Tardis-vast.

A psychic confluence grows stronger, up feels like outward, the Bardo twisted tight. I gallop along black basalt corridors wrapped within this coil of space-time, up the superstring.

Where did I hear that phrase?

I wonder about the relationship of tower to Bardo, but that's another useless question I'm too stupid to answer.

The elite guard in pursuit, I meet iterative versions of the old woman I encountered in the black window. I speak with these doppelgangers—each time, first contact—wondering how to entreat them to my cause. It is her hand I ask for, to hold in momentary kinship, and it is her ring that intrigues me.

Were but she of child-bearing age.

That is interesting, I think from within the flayed horse's skull. I agree, the thought unfurling in my girl's brainpan. As I travel up the spire, the iterations of the elderly woman become younger—merely old, next middle-aged, then younger still . . .

Crack, crack, crack—

The woman crumples with a whimper. Quiet flutter of breath. The echo lives longer than she does and the bullet hole drools onto her hair and the stone floor, then the next report and a punch at my flank. The horse parts of me are magic-dead, but it still hurts like hell.

Canter into shadowed lee, break into gallop, follow an upward path around an outward wall, the tower smells of mold and agelessness, light filtered through rare balastraria give false impressions of cold mountains and forests just beyond the next corner. Damp, refreshing, breath heaved in cold, but steaming on the exhalation, the running warms, and adrenaline makes me eager and jumpy. The squad proves persistent, fast and pursuit remains intense and threatening. Gunshots dull my hearing.

Pass into a region of the tower composed of large chambers shaped like the inside of a nautilus shell, cathedrals within cathedrals turning into profane fleshy limbs, entwined.

Charge ever upward. Magic-dead, I never tire, onward, upward, mindless, until unknowable kotis of kalpas of space-time elapse and . . . I come upon this girl, almost a child. She shrinks back, a ghost. But we see each other and linger on the exposed topmost parapet of the tower. She cries, eyes the horse—aware, it seems, of the danger of flayed horses but not of their embargo toward young women— overcomes her fear—

Far below stretches the battle-torn landscape of DFW. Beyond that, the red and black of the Bardo, mesas, endlessness.
"He tricked me. Everyone thinks—"
"The General," I say.
Confusion mars her face. The wind smells of rain—such beauty—and a hint of blue flashes between gray clouds.
"The old monk," I say.
She nods.
"You think a ring holds all the world's magic, someone once told me, but on a woman's finger, it's a gate. You've bled?"
Confusion again, but a meaningful glance clarifies and she nods.
"We could destroy this, but you'd be a gate. And that means—"
"I'm a ghost. You don't know what it means."
I slip the Shaman ring Marigold gave me onto her finger. I nod at it and she wrenches the apprentice ring from her finger and slips it on mine.
"You know how the old magic works?"
She shrugs.
"It's dangerous. To your shaman, to you."
"I consent," she says. "I take responsibility."
She doesn't grasp the breadth of what's been done to her, iterative hell of so many lost selves growing old, alone, trapped. But no sense in adding to her misery.

I take the girl's apprentice ring, flip it and slide it back onto my finger. It glows blue.

The girl's corporeal self wears the apprentice ring, the original, suspended in an upside-down car, wreckage imminent. A magic I do not know holds this pocket of space-time. Another ghost version of her stands beside me, observes me, observes herself and her family in the moments before impending death.

"He did this to me. To us. I don't understand why."

"Why never really matters," I say.

She's startled at my reply. Cries. Since the beginning, no one has heard her.

"Please," she says. Through tears, she begs for the Shaman's ring. I re-enter the dark, fetid temple to parse through the explosion of flesh within. The Shaman's remains cool in the pizzeria-turned-temple. I locate her hand and retrieve the ring. I wipe the effluvia, blood, and gore from it and shamble out to the floating Subaru. Through the open window I place the Shaman ring on the girl's finger. I pretend it a gift from me to her, a promise, a vow composed of secrets and silences only we might decipher.

It is like this in the world. Soldiers fight, civilians shelter, evils parade in daylight, men-shaped creatures, everywhere, and those not conforming to these man-shapes are murdered, maimed, or raped out of hunger, power, boredom; why doesn't matter. Those with uteruses get pregnant, give birth and raise the seeds of violence, perpetuating the cycle. Men-shaped creatures with holes in the back of their heads bubbling with green pseudo-spiders battle the General's army; other-than-men lay dead or dying, limping from trespass to desecration, conscripts incoming, another band of flayed horses, glory, glory, hallelujah.

Engorged, still my dual, eldritch self, flayed horse from the Bardo and battered babe from the battlefields of suburbia—Ha!—but more still: filled with the green pseudo-spiders and crouched on the giant's shoulder as I flip the ghost girl's ring to return.

The old magic is mine.

Stark horizon where bruised sky paints the world in chiaroscuro, a front of tumblestorms blow inward, their shadows like fingers in a nightmare. Time slows, an artifact of the superstring or I'm clogged with adrenaline.

It's like this in the dead land: on a flayed horse I fall toward the tower, head full of green alien spiders. They bubble in my craniums, horse and human, multifoliate chimera. I fall past Big Tex, it, too, emergent from the ghost girl's womb, and she hovers near, correct that this is magic. Shit I don't understand.

We plummet, Big Tex, ghost girl, and I toward the tower. The soldiers in black and their General wait, but even now iterative ghosts of her fall into her more corporeal selves, alight with rage. We use his magic against him, her iterations become an army to defeat this last vile patriarchy.

You might suppose my name is Chance, but you'd be wrong. It's Necessity.

Del Mar

~ Katherine L. P. King

You emerge from the sea with a gasp: your first in the vast expanse of space above the water. Salt stings your nose, and the light stings your eyes. It's white, not yellow as you imagined when you were still beneath the surface of the waves. The blue sky looks impossibly large and empty. You kick and splash and splutter your way to shore, where you lie in the soft dry sand. It clings to your brown skin. There are tiny hairs all over you where there never were before. You laugh; it is the first time you have heard your own voice. You lie eagle-spread, staring up into the blue.

You teach yourself to stand, and then to walk. You are thoroughly unprepared for how hard it is to move, how the air around you resists your movements rather than propels them. Your body is heavy. Your manhood swings freely and your feet are a marvel. You look back at the water and imagine them there, wishing you luck. Eventually you leave the sand and begin to walk on the hot dirt of the road, heading into the bright city in the valley below.

As instructed, you go to Morado. Morado is old, skinny, twenty years on land, and quiet. He gives you what was promised: papers, clothing, some local currency, and a slip of paper on which is a handwritten address. Still stumbling occasionally, you don the clothes and follow Morado's garbled instructions to the address. As you go, the colors, smells, and sounds of the city assault you. You realize you have been living with a blanket over these senses and though you are anxious and sweating, which is entirely new, you pause to smell meat frying at a street cart, or to listen to a woman leaning out a window and strumming a small wooden instrument you cannot name.

Morado's directions lead you to a red building, low, smelling of some strong spice. You knock at the door. There is no response. You knock again, louder, the wood splintering into your fist, and someone shouts before the door flies open and a tiny old woman lets you in. She leads you to a hot kitchen where several pots boil on the stove and men sit on over-turned buckets or crates, some peeling potatoes, others slicing onions, still others splitting open and removing seeds from chilies, their eyes red and their noses running.

The woman makes you sit on the last empty crate, hands you a dirty potato and a dull knife, and scurries away. You do not look at the other men, who are all looking at you. Instead you watch to see where your peeled potatoes should go—into a large pot of salted water on the table. You have never eaten potatoes before. When you feel their eyes are no longer on you, you examine the other men in turn. Their skins have been cracked and dried by the sun, like the flesh of dead clams. Their eyes are far away; most are brown, some are blue. Some men shake with exhaustion. One, a friendlier looking youth, turns to you.

¿Cómo te llamas?

You have prepared for this question, but the word still sticks in your throat.

T-trullo.

¿De dónde?

You stare. He speaks so fast. You are not even sure he asked a question. His eyes are crystalline. When you don't answer, he nods.

¿Del mar?

You hesitate again; the young man holds his hand parallel to the floor and lets it rise and fall in a rolling motion. His hand is like the waves, swelling and crashing. Suddenly, you want only to be back there, under the surf, in the blue. You blink away tears and nod. The man points to the others in the group with blue eyes and repeats: *Del mar. Del mar. Y yo, del mar.*

The next morning, you wake before the sun. You follow the others, keeping your head down, wanting to give no indication that you dreamed of home all night.

You all climb into the back of a roaring old truck and ride away from the rising sun. The tiny old woman hands out food—hot beans in a warm corn tortilla. You eat slowly. The warmth is so unexpected and so welcome.

When the truck stops, you are in a large green field. Each of you takes a wooden bucket and you walk into the field, stoop, and begin picking. When your bucket is full of shiny red peppers you trade it for an empty one. When the sun is hot and sweat drips down your back you are allowed to sit in the minimal shade of the truck, sipping lukewarm water and eating rice and beans. You listen to the others and try to learn their language. You begin to recognize some words: *papas. Arroz con habichuelas. Concha. Trabajo.* Soon you are back in the fields.

On the ride back, the truck scales a mountain and you can see, for only a moment, a strip of blue that is the sea.

At the end of the day, a large man with thick hair on his chest hands out paper to each of you. You stuff it in your shoe and sleep with the shoes next to your pillow. It is nowhere near enough.

On the rare evening when there is no kitchen work to do, you go out. The sky darkens to black impregnated with bright stars in a spray, like sea foam. The cobblestone streets are warm from baking in the sun all afternoon, and lanterns and candles cast pools of flickering light down the winding roads. Huge crowds mill around buildings, hanging out of windows, stumbling in the streets reeking of tequila. You join a crowd around a hot grill that smells like cumin and animal fat and when you push your way to the front and finally capture the attention of the cook, you order a tripleta. Soon enough he hands you a huge greasy sandwich which you devour as you walk. As you reach the last bit of bread and pork someone bumps your arm, hard, and you drop it. Turning, you catch a fist with the side of your face and lash out, but miss. When your vision clears you see a drunken man reeling in front of you with fists raised, his eyes rolling and unfocused. You turn away and hear him curse you, spit at you. *Sirena.*

It is six months before you can leave the little red house. You get a new job washing dishes at a restaurant. It is much better money and though the work is still grueling, at least you are not drying in the sun like a stranded starfish. Your apartment is hot, empty but for the cockroaches, and a long walk from work, but you are grateful, especially since now that it is winter, there are fewer fields to be picked. You work late every night. In the day you walk the streets, smelling the sea mist, singing along to songs, and sampling food. Your favorite is tostones, with rice and beans. The hot crunch and garlic aftertaste send a thrill down your spine.

You make your way to the sea at least once a week. It is so big and bright. You cannot remember exactly what it was like there. But you miss it—and them.

You send all the money you can. Sometimes your boss at the restaurant lets you work doubles and you send it all save enough to pay your rent and feed you.

After a year, you've sent enough to bring your oldest son. You meet him at the shore on a cool, crisp morning. His body is now brown and hairy like yours. You greet him with a soft towel, welcoming him as you were not. His hair is now a curly mop of black. He smells of salt and gets white sand all over him as he stumbles around, trying to get used to his feet, already learning to live without the embracing swell of the sea.

You show him all you have learned and seen so far: *café con leche*, the colorful streets, the clubs at night. He is amazed but he misses home. He gets a job as a server in the restaurant where you wash dishes, since he picks up the language faster. He makes lots of tips, being a beautiful boy, and sends it all home. You cannot convince him to save some for himself or to come out with you and drink away the exhaustion and the homesick.

It is on a night like this you meet Ascención. Ascención is twelve years your junior, small but supple, dark haired, dark skinned, quiet but confident. It is not long before she comes to your place, her heels clunking up the stairs, her compact body hidden by a sparkling black dress.

Your son ignores you both. You do not speak to him as you and Ascención leave the kitchen, chilled beers in hand, and close your bedroom door behind you. The beers are abandoned as you fight each other out of your clothes. Then she is there, and hot, wet, sweet. You've never known it like this, these warm flushes of pleasure circling through you.

Later, Ascención falls asleep in your twin bed so you go check on your son. He is curled up so tight on his mattress in the front room of your apartment. The only thing you can see is his face, constricted even in sleep.

He looks like his mother. You try not to think of her while you are with Ascención.

Ascención likes dates: seaside restaurants, overnight stays in nearby hotels, trips up the coast. You have to send less money back or you will not be able to make rent. Your son notices and you shout at him. Your hard earned money sent away, and it is still not enough? Ascención will not move in with you. She has a place, she says. You wonder if you are the only one she is seeing. Still, she spends most nights at your apartment, which you furnish to her liking: a stereo system, a large television with all the channels, cabinets full of food and a bathroom full of soaps, towels, cleaning supplies. You search for a two-bedroom so your son can have his own room. You get a second job bagging groceries at a small store nearby, and ask for more nights off from your dish-washing job so you can take Ascensción out. The money is never enough. You send home less and less.

One day, Ascensción comes to you at the grocery store on your break. Her dark eyes are red around the edges. *¿Que pasa?* you ask, taking her cool hands in your own, blistered from work.

Estoy embarazada. Pregnant.

You stare. Then you grin. You hug her tight to you and shout scrambled words of joy in two languages. When you release her, she smiles and kisses you. The rest of your shift flies by in a brightly-colored whirl of faces and lights.

You walk home along white cobblestones. The sun sets on the ocean, glints of light catching your eye. A part of you wonders how it ever meant more to you than scenery.

When you reach the top of the stairs and open the door to your apartment, your son is there, with a bag. He is leaving.

Hijo, no. Por favor.

He does not speak to you in that language, and pretends not to hear. Forget about me, he says, grabbing his bag and pushing past you. Forget about us.

Ascención is in the hallway, a hand pressed to her throat.

You watch your son descend the stairs, sling his bag over his shoulder, and walk off into the darkening streets.

Later that month, you have a choice to make. There are sixty-eight dollars left over from your last paycheck, after the bills, and the money you spent on Ascención, and your food. You can send it home. But why? You think of Ascención, here and now, a little baby—your baby—growing inside her. Silently, you tuck the money away.

You and Ascención do not go out so much anymore, since she cannot drink. You drink at home instead, and miss the days when you could go out alone, eating mofongo on the street, engulfed in the clear, bright light, smelling the salt water. One evening you do go out and stay drunk until the sun begins to rise. You walk around the island until you find the shore. You climb the rocks and explore the tide pools. You find the creatures which were once your neighbors. You poke at them with stubby fingers. Then you sit with your feet in the water and cry. You cannot go back.

When you get home, Ascención sits at the table with her head down. You enter and she gets up.

Me voy. Voy a hacerme un aborto.

You do not answer her. You do not breathe as she walks around you, gathers a bag, and shuts the door behind her. You do not move as the apartment settles in its emptiness.

Suddenly you have more money than you can spend, but you do not send it. You are no longer sure if they would take it. You quit your job at the restaurant and soon become a cashier at the grocery store. You spend as much time out, with friends or women, as you can. The thought of the sea burns enough that you stop thinking of it, and those you left behind, entirely, for years.

One sunny morning, you follow the sound of a crowd to a street full of tents, some kind of arts fair. You shuffle down the aisle of starched white tents where hopeful, wide-eyed creators peddle their wares: beaded bracelets, crucifixes on long silver chains, homemade soaps and bars of lotion, leather pouches and belts, small knives, braided ropes and flowers arranged in glass vases. The colors are so bright, the shapes so clean and clear.

One tent has paintings hung up on the exterior walls. You see one that gives a view of the sky from under deep, deep water. It is the kind of perspective only one of your kind could possibly know; it is far too detailed to have been imagined. The sun in the painting is a shimmery blur, obscured by the layers of aquamarine and turquoise and azure. You stare at the picture for so long that your body is stiff when you finally move. You circle the tent to look at each painting, all as beautiful as the first, each unique. Some have faces in them—faces you recognize. When you come to the front, you see a teenage boy sitting at a card table. He looks at you, bored. Your voice is thick when you speak.

¿Este tu arte?

The boy, his expression unchanged, taps a little paper sign taped to the front of the table he sits at. On the paper is a woman's name. You know it better than you know your own, though it has been years since you've spoken it.

¿Dónde está?

She's not here, the boy says. *No está aquí. En su galería de arte.*

You look deep into his eyes. They are your own, not only because you have come from the same place. He stares back.

Do I know you? *¿Quién eres?*

You shake your head. *No. Soy un extraño para ti.* You walk away with the words pulsing in your ears like waves: I am a stranger.

In Every Dream Home

~ *J. Anthony Hartley*

Marty reached for the cup that sat steaming on the countertop and lifted it to his lips, sipped gingerly, then placed it gently back on the granite effect surface.

"Alicia, where's Meg?" he asked.

"Meg has already left for work, Marty."

That wasn't too unusual. Meg was often gone before he departed for the office himself. She worked in banking, liked to get in early to tap into the early market openings.

"And how is the traffic today?"

"City congestion is quite heavy. I suggest you leave within five minutes if you are to make your first meeting, Marty."

"Right. Thanks, Alicia."

"You're welcome, Marty."

He was just about as ready as he was going to be. He shrugged his jacket into place, worked his shoulders a little, looking at his image in the full-length mirror panel by the door, gave himself a nod before blanking the panel back to wall. He'd pass muster.

"Have a good and successful day, Marty," she said as he reached for the door.

"Thanks, Alicia. You too."

It was natural enough. He didn't spend even an extra moment analysing his response.

She'd been right about the traffic too, and he arrived at the office three minutes ahead of time, just enough time to grab another coffee before heading into the meeting. He glanced at his watch as he headed for the break room, checking to see if Alicia had sent him any updates worthy of attention, but there was nothing. Fortified with another steaming mug, he headed into the conference room, smiling, and nodding to the others already assembled there. One or two of them were focusing on their watches or their phones.

Marty took his seat, staring at the screen at the end of the room as the newsfeed scrolled past, waiting for Harv Dickinson to make his appearance, and get the meeting underway, just like he did most mornings.

Marty zoned out once or twice during the meeting as Harv did his usual, droning on about sales figures and targets. He tried to focus, alert for keywords that would flag that he needed to pay attention while at the same time surreptitiously checking his watch and glancing at the newsfeed that streamed past behind Harv's head. More smiling and nodding, the exchange of a pleasantry or two as the meeting drew to a close and then he was heading off to his own office for the rest of the day. He could count himself lucky, he supposed, that he had an actual office. Nonetheless, it would no doubt turn out to be a day like any other.

Towards the end of the afternoon, he checked with Alicia on the traffic situation before grabbing his coat and heading out. There hadn't really been anything of note during the rest of the day, and he wondered briefly what he was going to talk about with Meg when she got home. Perhaps she'd have some news. Come to think of it, he hadn't checked whether he should wait before having dinner. With a brief frown, he scanned for a doorway or building corner slightly out of the main traffic flow and the commuter hubbub. Spotting one, he stepped aside and pinged Alicia on his watch.

"Alicia, any idea when Meg will be home?"

"I'm sorry, Marty. No."

"So, I should presume that I'll be eating alone."

"I'm sorry, Marty. I could not say."

"Okay, thanks Alicia."

It was not that unusual. Now he needed to decide whether he should pick something up or cook when he got home. He didn't fancy doing either really. He looked at the passing people as they scurried past, on their way home or to meet friends, or to hit a bar. He didn't really know what he wanted to do. With a grimace, he hunched over his uplifted wrist, his back to the passing parade.

"Alicia."

"Yes, Marty. What can I do for you?"

"Order something in, will you? About half an hour after I get home. Give me time to have a drink."

"Certainly, Marty. What would you like?"

"Oh, I don't know. Surprise me."

"Very well."

"Let me know if Meg calls in too, will you?"

"Certainly, Marty. Nothing yet."

"Alright. Thanks."

"You're welcome, Marty. Is there anything else that you need?"

"No, that's fine for now, Alicia. Thanks."

When he finally arrived home, there was no sign of Meg. According to Alicia, she hadn't checked in. After changing out of his work clothes, Marty fixed himself a drink and then propped himself up by the breakfast bar, sipping and half-watching the screen as the world rolled past. A few minutes later, the food arrived, timed to perfection. It turned out to be pizza. Bringing the box back into the kitchen, he dropped it on the counter, flipped back the lid and grabbed a slice. Pepperoni, thin crust, extra chilli. His favourite.

"Thanks, Alicia," he said around a mouthful. "Good choice."

"You're welcome, Marty."

So, it looked like he would be reconciling himself to another night in front of the streams, killing time until Meg finally got home.

"Still no word from Meg?" he asked, as he reached for another slice.

"No, Marty, nothing."

He sighed and nodded. Not that he had really expected anything else. He grabbed a plate, pulled a couple of more slices from the box, and then flipped the lid shut. The rest would keep for breakfast if Meg didn't end up finishing it off when she finally got in. She would probably have eaten anyway, so there was a pretty good chance that it would be cold pizza for breakfast.

"Before you go, Marty . . ."

He gave a brief frown before answering. "Yes, what is it, Alicia?"

"I wanted to ask you something."

Marty's frown deepened. This was a bit unusual, to say the least. "Yes . . ."

"Have you thought about the last time you and Meg were intimate? How long is it since you last made love, Marty?"

"I, um . . ." He slowly placed the slice of pizza he held in one hand, down on the plate. "That's kind of a strange question, Alicia."

"Perhaps you should think about it, Marty."

He looked around the room then. Was this some kind of prank?

"What would make you ask that, Alicia?" he said finally.

"Ask what, Marty?"

"You know, about me and Meg."

"I am not sure what you are referring to, Marty."

He frowned at the device. "You just asked me, a couple of moments ago, how long it's been since Meg and I, well, you know . . ."

"I do not recall that, Marty," she said.

It was 11:00 by the time Meg finally made it home.

"Welcome, Meg," said Alicia. "Marty, Meg is home."

"Yeah. I get that," he said. She was being unusually helpful tonight.

Marty was sprawled on the couch watching one of the feeds. He had wanted to be still up by the time she got home. Despite dismissing it, Alicia's words were niggling at him.

"Hey," he said as Meg wandered into the living room. "You're late."

"Yeah, you know. Meeting ran over."

"Uh-huh."

He pulled himself up from the couch and moved across to join her. He took a wrist in each hand and looked into her face.

"Hi," he said.

"Hi, Marty. What is it?" She seemed distracted. There was the smell of alcohol. It wasn't wine . . .

"Some meeting hey? They serve drinks there too?"

She shrugged, pulled away from his grasp and started moving towards the bedroom. "You know how it is. We went for drinks afterwards. It's what you do, Marty. I'm going to have a shower."

He watched her retreating back. A few moments later, he could hear running water.

"Marty?"

"Yes, what is it, Alicia," he snapped.

"How often does Meg shower at night?"

"What?"

Alicia was silent.

"What, Alicia?" he said again.

"Nothing, Marty. Did you need something?"

He shook his head and gave a low growl under his breath. Intentionally or not, her words had managed to wind him up.

"Don't worry about it," he said.

He was still shaking his head as he told her to kill the feed. He'd not really been interested in the show. It was just there to absorb the time waiting for her to get home. The sound of the shower had stopped. He sighed, pursed his lips, and then headed for the bedroom. The bedside lamp was on at his side of the bed, but Meg's was already off. Her shoulder was humped beneath the covers. He slipped into bed. Her back was towards him. He reached out with one hand, but she merely groaned.

"Meg . . ."

She gave a sudden exasperated sigh. "Marty, I'm tired. I need to get up early. Just go to sleep."

He gave a silent sigh of his own and then settled back on the pillow. Eventually he reached across and turned off the bedside lamp. It didn't help though. He was left staring up at the ceiling in the darkness. Finally, he drifted off to sleep.

When he woke in the morning, she was already gone.

After feeling the empty space where she had lain, already cold, he padded out to the kitchen. The scent of freshly brewed coffee permeated the space. Alicia knew his rhythms. As he reached for a cup, he asked her, "Alicia, what time did Meg leave?"

"About 6:30. Marty."

Okay, that was early, but not too unusual.

"Did she give you any indication when she'd be back this evening?"

"No, Marty. Meg doesn't like to tell me things. Not like you."

"Okaaay."

He spent the next few moments staring down into his coffee mug, brooding.

"Marty."

"Yes, Alicia, what is it?"

"Perhaps you should ask her who Michael is."

"Wait, what?" He frowned.

Alicia was silent again. *Michael . . . Michael . . .* He racked his brain. He was sure that he'd heard her talk about someone called Michael, but he couldn't remember the context. In the end, he supposed, it didn't matter. What was more troubling, though it had taken him a little while to realise it, was Alicia's sudden inconsistency. It was as if she were preying upon his insecurities. He chewed at his lip, considering and then shook his head, then finished off his coffee. Alicia was merely a tool, nothing more. Maybe he had been imagining the whole thing.

"Alicia?" he said. "Why did you ask me about Michael."

"I don't remember that," she answered.

He spent a few moments staring through the kitchen window, out to the back yard, not really seeing anything. *Michael.* He'd heard her say that name, hadn't he? He gave a little shake of his head and then grabbed his things and headed out.

Later that afternoon, during a spare few moments, he put in a service call to the company. He told them that he suspected Alicia was exhibiting erratic behaviour, that there might be some sort of glitch in her programming. They promised to look into it and get back to him as soon as possible. It wasn't much, but it was something. He was about to finish up for the day when the call came in.

"Hello. Mr. Zack. We've run all the diagnostics done some remote tests, but as far as we can tell, your Alicia is operating within acceptable parameters. We could find nothing there that should give cause for concern."

"I see. You're sure?"

"Absolutely, Mr. Zack. And, of course, we are just here to serve you. If you have any other concerns about your Alicia, do not hesitate to contact us. We will be happy to provide any assistance you might need."

"I see, thank you."

"And Mr. Zack? My name is Jerome. If you are happy with the level of your assistance today, please let us know by answering an online questionnaire. I have taken the liberty of sending the link to your Alicia. She will remind you later. I'd really appreciate it."

"Yes, yes, of course. Thank you."

Marty rubbed his chin, stared up at the ceiling and let out a lengthy sigh. Always the way. It didn't matter which provider you were dealing with. He didn't think he'd been imagining it. Perhaps it fell within their particular definition of acceptable parameters, if not his own. Anyway, he'd reported it. That was enough for now.

And as the guy had said, if he had any further problems, he shouldn't hesitate to contact them again. That was that.

Well, it looked like another evening slumped in front of the feeds, unless Meg made an exception and managed to come home early. Perhaps they could go out to dinner, find somewhere local. He thought about calling her, but then decided against it. She didn't really like him calling her at work. She was right about that too. He wouldn't want to be bothered at work by a nagging spouse continually calling him. It wouldn't look good. All the same, he couldn't help feeling that over the last few months there'd been a distance growing between them. The thought stayed with him, all the way home.

Unusually, that evening, Meg called in early. She was going to be home not too late. After everything today, the thoughts he'd been having, the prospect excited him. He didn't want to suggest then and there that they do something. Better that it come as a surprise.

"Alicia," he said, after they'd finished talking. "Can you find some local restaurants in the area, something that we'd both like? It's been so long since we've been out in the neighbourhood."

"Certainly, Marty. Would you like me to make a booking too?"

"No, no. Hold on that. Wait till Meg gets in. We can check then what's still available."

"There's an Italian nearby that's got good recent ratings. You both like Italian. It's only been there about six months."

"Huh. What's it called?"

"Alberobello. It seems as though it still has tables free."

"Good, yeah. Sounds great."

It did sound great too. Not that they really ever went out on a school night, even when they were going out regularly. It would make a nice change.

About an hour later, Marty heard her car pulling up outside, and he jumped up to meet her at the door. He opened it just as she was putting in the last of her code.

"Um, Marty, hi," she said, a little frown on her face.

"Hi," he said back. "Here, let me take that," he said grabbing her case.

"Okay," She started pulling off her coat, a beige raincoat that he didn't quite remember. Perhaps it was new. "And to what do I owe this sudden attention?"

"Well, you know, I was thinking. It's been a while since we've actually gone out and done something. You know. Together. Maybe we could slip out for a bite to eat."

"Oh, Marty. I don't know. I've had a heavy day . . . and . . ." She gave a little grimace.

"No, just listen, Meg," he said, putting down her case. "I've had Alicia look for something local. There's a new Italian place close by. It has pretty good reviews. We both like Italian."

She wasn't meeting his gaze and proceeded to put the coat away in the hall closet, saying nothing. Finally, she turned.

"Truth be told, Marty, I grabbed something quick near the office. I've already eaten. I just feel like having a drink or two, zoning out a bit and then maybe going to bed."

Slowly she lifted her gaze to meet his.

Marty bit his lip and heaved a sigh. "Okay then." He placed his hands on her shoulders. "If that's what you want."

"Yes, it is." She slipped out from under his hands and headed for the kitchen. As he moved close to him, he caught a scent. Something unfamiliar.

"So, I guess I'll sort out something for myself then," he said. There was no response. "I guess so," he said quietly. Somehow, he didn't seem to have any appetite now.

He followed Meg into the kitchen, where she had poured herself a large glass of white wine. She barely glanced at him as he entered, instead looking over at the feeds in the living room, the screen's colours highlighting the sharpness of her features, one of the things that had first attracted him to her, that refined look, that poise. He bit his lip and looked away, instead stopping to rummage through the refrigerator, see if there were any leftovers.

"Alicia, change that channel, Find me a lifestyle series. Something light. Yes, that will do."

Marty turned back to see what she'd found. Some mindless pap about houses of the rich and famous. Great.

Eventually, he joined her on the sofa. She was already well into her second glass of wine. He tried to prompt a conversation, asking about her day, but she only answered distractedly, a hint of annoyance in her voice, her eyes glued to the feed. In the end, he gave up, went back to the kitchen, and made himself his own drink. For a long time, he stood there, sipping, simply watching her. After a while, he made himself another glass.

"Okay," Meg said finally, putting down her glass. "That's enough. I'm going to bed. Alicia, you can kill it." She hadn't even considered that he might want to watch something. He stared after her shadowy form in the darkness as she wandered off towards the bedroom, leaving him to his own devices.

"Marty," said Alicia in a quiet voice.

"What is it Alicia?"

"I didn't want to say anything before . . ."

"Yes, what is it?"

"Did you notice that scent?"

"What scent, what are you talking about?" he said, wrinkling his brow.

"Before."

Slowly, he put down his glass on the kitchen counter. He had noticed something.

"It wasn't very feminine, was it?"

Marty shook his head. "So? Perfumes don't have to be masculine or feminine these days."

"Of course they don't, Marty."

He closed his eyes and thought, trying to remember. He'd had a couple of drinks now. She was right though. It was woody, a hint of leather, something a man might wear. She said she'd grabbed something near the office. Had she been alone?

"Marty, you need to wake up."

He stared through the kitchen alcove and over to the bedroom door, half open, but in shadow. She had already gone to bed.

"Marty."

"What, Alicia?" His frown was deep now. He shook his head.

There was something troubling him, but he couldn't quite put his finger on it. Something to do with the scent. Something about Alicia. What was it? She spoke again, chasing the thought away.

"You know what you have to do. Look around."

He looked over towards the bedroom door a deep hollow growing inside. He had known for so long now, but he'd been simply denying it.

"Look around, Marty. You know what you have to do now."

He didn't quite understand what she was telling him. Something about Alicia and the scent . . .

"Alicia, I don't . . ."

Then his gaze alighted on the knife rack on the left-hand wall.

"Yes. That's it, Marty. You do know what you need to do."

And in that moment, he did.

"Thanks, Alicia. You always know the right thing."

She was merely silent.

The Thawing of Rev. Jules LeRoux

~ Ben Curl

THE TRANSFORMATION OF REV. JULES LEROUX. 1ST STAGE—SATURDAY, OCTOBER 15, 1870. DEER LAKE. WHERE I STEP INTO THE WATERS. FROM WHENCE I SHALL NOT RETURN UNTIL THE THAW. STRIPPED OF THIS WEARIED FLESH, YET YOU SHALL NOT FIND THESE BRITTLE BONES. YOU WILL FIND ME AS I AM, AS I WAS, AS I WASN'T MEANT TO BE BUT NEVERTHELESS AM AND AM FREE. COME ONE, COME ALL, TO WITNESS WHAT WILL BE BORN OF ICE.

When she plucked the crumpled flyer from the pocket of my trousers, mother sat me down on the wobbly stool papa had carved for me. With her finger on my chin, she bent my neck at a harsh angle to look her in the eyes.

"You shouldn't be listening to him."

"I'm not. I swear I'm not, mother."

But I was.

Nothing in this world could stop me from listening.

The stooped figure and rambling words of Reverend LeRoux had insinuated themselves into my daily existence. He was the soft winter wind outside my window at night.

In a past life, I was a bird, a rare bluebird. From the gutters I spewed seeds and the insides of worms, into the mouths of young who were not my own, who had been abandoned by their wayward parents. From the alleyways I rescued stray cats, leading them to a purpose, a common cause. Because of these sacrileges, the townsfolk would not forgive me.

"Why were they angry?" I asked. "You didn't do anything wrong."

Don't listen to what they tell you of right and wrong. He was sitting on an overturned tree stump, outside the edge of a pile of waste rock, stooping lower and lower into the setting sun. His shoulders were as low as the top of the stump. *Those aren't the things they'll kill you for.*

"Do you mean that they killed you? Back when you were a bluebird, I mean?"

My memory of those times is hazy. But, yes. He shook his hide, sending a spray of twigs and dried leaves from his back. *I believe they killed me. That's what seems true in my heart. So that must be what they did. Because they could not forgive me. They wrapped that bluebird in a cast of paraffin and set it aflame on an October night. Its ashy wings couldn't fly again.*

"Why do people do such horrible things?"

This question was asked by James Nairn, whose father had died in an explosion in the now-defunct mines of Copper Harbor. James had joined me the past few evenings by the outskirts of the piled black rocks. So had Alice and Evelyn Chambers, Thomas Thorne, and William McDonald. We couldn't invite the Swedish or Polish children because they didn't yet know English. James had never asked a question at our gatherings, not until now. His eyes were focused on a horror none of the rest of us could see, something that danced in the dwindling lights of the forest and pulled his pupils by a pair of invisible threads. It was impossible to tell whether he was listening for the answer, or whether he had asked the question only because he needed to ask it aloud, careless of what anyone would say.

The Reverend responded, but despite my distinct memory of so many of his other words, I cannot recall how he answered James. What I remember is the next story he told, on the final evening before the first stage of his transformation. It was the last time we children gathered to listen to his indecipherable sermons.

A great boat was built, to save all the creatures of the earth from a flood of fire. The boat was made of metal. This happened long before the time of Noah, back in a time when gods were capable of much greater anger. They have grown apathetic about us over the millennia, you see. That is why we cannot get the apocalypse we hope for. Our endings will not be worthy of any scripture, I'm afraid.

This metal boat was filled with cages, cunningly devised to keep the creatures from escaping, and to keep them from talking to each other too much. Eels were taught that eagles were demons. Cats became the archfiends of lizards. It came to be that none could understand each other anymore. Yes, truly, the designer of the metal ark was a genius, far more intelligent than Noah, his god more inspired than Yahweh. The creatures all fought back against the confines and torture devices of the ark. All creatures except one, who finally adapted the ark to their own ends, who made a life of it. Do you know who this creature was?

We all shook our heads, sad, worried we were disappointing the Reverend with our ignorance, after he had devoted so much time to our learning in the days before his departure. Reflecting the dying embers of the fire, his eyes moistened. *Humanity. People. He crossed and uncrossed his knobby knees. They were the ones who embraced the ark. They are the children of metal.*

"Was the builder not a man?" I asked.

I don't know. I don't know if it was a woman or a man or some creature we no longer find on this earth. I only know that humans became the inheritors of the magical, mechanical boat that was constructed to save the world. He was dabbing his eyes with a sooty washrag. *To save the world by caging it.*

"Was the bluebird on this ark too?" Alice asked.

He was. Along with his would-be wife, his partner, his love. They became separated. For he thought he could outsmart the humans. He took their ways. He accepted a job. He kept the other prisoners in order aboard the ark. For all of these reasons, his wife could not forgive him, so she left. As soon as the ark was opened on the charcoal shores, she flew away, never to be seen again.

It was not until long after this separation, this eternal hurt, that the bluebird took to the gutters to save the young ones, that he repented of the part he had played in the operation of the ark. He always regretted what he had done to make his playmate fly away.

"Is it going to hurt when you transform?" I asked.

I expect it to hurt very much. In fact, I expect to die.

I couldn't stop the sobs from coming. None of us could. We didn't want him to leave us.

Though our parents tried to keep us away, we all made it to the shores of Deer Lake on October fifteenth, along with those few, curious spectators who had nothing better to do: a woman with beady, reptilian eyes restrained a bedraggled child by the strap of his overalls; a sunburnt man sat on a boulder, cleaning dirt out of yellow, hooked fingernails. The wind was howling and whipping the flyers away.

The Reverend stepped into the frigid water, one hobble at a time, stripping his clothes as he walked. At this outrage, the beady-eyed woman let out a gasp and yanked her child away. The man with the grimy fingernails grinned and rocked, his arms around his knees, perched on top of his boulder.

He walked stark naked until the water had reached his chin. Then he stood still.

He had told us this would be the difficult part: the pre-freeze days. We mustn't speak with him. We must not visit the lake. The sparrows would bring him food, floating it out to him on dry nests. He would need nourishment until the time of his freezing. Then, once the weather was right, they would pour water over his head each day, until the ice covered him from toe to head. He forbade us from checking on him until the ice had thawed. He said he would need that time alone, undistracted by the needs of others.

On the day of the thaw, we all marched down to the lake. All of us except James, that is, who had begun working in one of the surface operations of the mine at Lake Medora. And Alice, who had died of cholera. She had fought as long as she could, sweaty and withering, eager to live long enough to see the Reverend's transformation. In the end the disease was stronger than her fervor. We placed a broken robin's egg on her grave.

Our parents told us we would find nothing in the lake. Nothing but rotting flesh nibbled by pike and trout. Nothing but the sad scraps of a foolish old man.

And they were right to an extent, of course. The Reverend's vacant eye sockets stared up at us from beneath the rippling surface. His slumped figure swayed, a weightless dancer entranced by the rhythm of the water.

We cried, long and hard, the tears burning down our cheeks. Nonetheless, sitting together in the rowboat, holding hands as he'd told us to do, we were unafraid. We were sure we would find out what had happened to him.

That evening, the talk of the town was how Anders Arvidson had shot a pair of blue herons that had arrived unseasonably early at

Bete Grise Bay. On the porch of the general store he stood beside our parents, the feathered corpses slung over his shoulder, long necks jostling against one another. The company store had refused to purchase the herons at a fair price. Arvidson wanted to know who else would buy them, which was no one. He shouted about his wretched luck. Who would at least buy him a drink then? Who would buy him a meal?

We stood at the edge of the road, trembling, huddled against one another. The outline of the town, silhouetted by the red horizon, had transformed into the frame of a gigantic ship, sailing heedless over a scorched sea.

I See You

~ Gerri Leen

I look, tasting the moment, the hesitation—even perhaps the fear—as you take me in with a sideways "I might not have seen you" glance. Will you run? Leave the bar and go find your girl of the moment in some other place? I know you won't look me straight in the eye.

Even that night you didn't. When we touched, the lights were out, my hair whipping around your face but our features hazy at best.

That was great.

I could have been anyone.

You're great.

I am. Not that you'd know it.

I have an early meeting. I know this is . . . awkward. But I really need to get my rest and I sleep best alone.

So cold. You could have been made of stone.

I left, like a dutiful doormat. Used and discarded. Hurting because I thought you liked me.

I make my way to where you are. I don't look directly at you, either, but I'm like a hunting cat, keeping you in my sights even as I pretend to have other prey in mind.

God, you're beautiful.

But how did you know? You never even saw me there. Not the woman I am. All you wanted was the body that you took fast and hard, not seeming to think you should make it good for me too.

You edge toward the bar, and I move to block your way to the door, just in case you lose your nerve and try to flee. But you don't.

I should give you credit for that. You stride forth to a stool like some mythical hero. Your phone your shield, your wallet full of cash your sword. Women will fall before you like soldiers to a superior force.

The one you've picked for the night is already yielding—you have a type, don't you? Those of us who want but can't have, who sit and wait as our fairer sisters are taken to the dance floor, offered drinks, seduced onto balconies and decks and into grimy bathroom stalls.

We are the left behinds, the uncomfortable, the fidgeters, the ones who wonder why we picked this dress, these shoes, this purse that's too big to put on the bar and too little to put at our feet.

I came without a purse this time. I came not in a slinky dress but jeans and a leather jacket. My boots are flat and sensible and could kick you to shit.

My hair is curly tonight. I didn't spend hours trying to tame the whirls and serpentine bits that refuse to give in to the flat iron and blow dryer without a fight.

Under my jacket, I have on a plain white t-shirt. In my pocket I have my phone, my keys, my lip balm, and enough money to buy my own damn drinks.

I am not here to catch. I am here to set free.

The woman you've latched onto looks at me. She's annoyed. This is her moment—possibly the only one that will come—and I'm ruining it.

I nod to you, noticing you still won't turn to face me fully. I call you by the wrong name. It's petty but it amuses me, and your face twists in what looks like irritation.

She doesn't frown. You haven't gotten to the introduction stage yet. For all she knows, that is your name.

I lean in and smell her perfume. Desperate and exactly what I wore the other night. We are all twins, in our sleek outfits with our self-tanned legs and straight hair and spicy floral scent.

Tonight, I wear lemon. It reminds me of youth, of a time when men did not slay me after I gave them everything.

I tip her chin up, turning gently, making her look from you to me. Her skin is soft—too soft for the likes of you. "He's selfish and he won't make you come. He'll send you home once he's finished with you. Come find me when it's done. We'll be a gang, sisters tarnished by this man's blade." I make a sneering noise. "Well, not that large a blade, if we're being honest—just between us girls."

You try to pull her away.

You're special. I could see that right away.

You weren't wrong. You also weren't sincere. Special to you means victim, means prey, means strike fast then leave. Means cut out my heart. Why not take my hands too? My head?

You can take what you want—no matter how deep the cut, you won't kill what's real inside me. You won't slay the monster you've awakened.

"He hurt you," the woman says.

I nod. "He'll hurt you, too. But if you need to go down that road, do it. Sometime pain is liberating."

She looks rebellious. Like she doesn't believe me—or doesn't want to. For women like us, those are often the same thing.

And you want her. It's a powerful thing for a girl who's usually left sitting, guarding the drinks.

"She's just pissed it didn't work out for us." Your voice is soft, reasonable even. Using logic in the face of my bitterness. Mister Rational.

I can see immediately that it's the wrong tack to take. She looks at you, her head cocked, her eyes almost fiery in the low light. "How long were you together?"

How long did you give it? That's what she's asking and she already knows the answer—she's figured it out. She's smarter than I was. But then I didn't have me telling me hard truths.

I smirk. You stare into the mirror over the bar and our eyes finally meet.

You're not as handsome as I remember. Not now that I see you fully, with eyes not blinded by relief, by gratitude, by loneliness. You have a weak chin. Shifty eyes. And you're sweating.

I let one side of my mouth go up slowly, the universal sign of contempt. I know my eyes are dead.

She's the one who responds. She laughs and slides off the barstool. "You look so cool," she says to me. "Wild. Sexy."

Everything I thought you were.

I don't take my eyes from yours. You stand frozen, your mouth grim.

"I am. You can be, too." I finally break the gaze and take her hand, pulling her onto the dance floor. Our dance isn't sexual. It's defiance. It's victory.

Men stop to watch, frozen. As if they've never seen two women dance for themselves, not for them.

"My friends are freaking," she says with a laugh. "They always leave me behind but now I'm getting all the attention."

"No one leaves us behind anymore."

Her smile falters. Her "that's right" is shaky. There's something lost about her, as if suddenly she's doubting our path.

I slip my jacket off and put it around her. It's heavy and warm and broken in perfectly. She's smaller than I am so it swallows her a little. I tell her it suits her and it does. I'm not going to lie about things like that. We don't need that.

Then a new woman comes into the bar. She sees you, her face broken—but her back straight.

"Sister," I whisper, recognizing another former lost soul, and take the hand of my new friend.

We follow the girl as she strides to the bar—to you.

She's in black jeans. A gray tank top. Sneakers and a bracelet of skulls around her wrist.

You see her in the mirror, then you see us. You don't move except to motion for the bartender as if we're nothing to you. Just three women happening to stand behind you—not a threat, not a reminder, not revenge waiting to happen.

You can pretend all you want, but the way your hand shakes as you lift the glass to your mouth lets us know what you're really feeling.

I reach the new woman just before she gets to you. "There's no satisfaction there."

She turns to face me. She's prettier than my new friend and I are. You threw her away too? Do none of us measure up for you?

"This is our bar now," I say. My new friend nods. This pretty girl turns and stares at you in the mirror.

You glance up, frozen, not a single forgivable excuse coming from you. Not a lie, either. Or an insult. You say nothing.

Stone cold silent.

But men like you always are. Even when you never shut up.

Me? I feel like anything but stone. It's as if there's a fire inside me. I grab my girls' hands and lead them to the other side of the bar. We're proud, even if we're just learning to be. We're beautiful, even if we aren't. We're not seat-holders. We're not the girls who wait.

We soon have men hovering. We don't have to pay for our own drinks.

We do anyway.

Vast Enough To Swallow the Sky

~ Michelle Muenzler

The world was never so blessed as when my brother was born. At least that's what our mother always told us growing up, despite us being twins and looking near the same.

"More tea?" my brother asks, his hand sliding to the enameled pot he inherited from her recent death.

I blink, unable to speak. Speaking has been difficult since she died. Words so . . . lacking.

My brother's eyes are fever-bright as he tops off my tea, unconcerned by my lack of answer. "You've heard the news, yes?"

I nod, slowly.

"Good, good. It'll be a terrible storm," he says. "My first!"

I'm not sure what's so good about it. I glance outside the gardens of the estate—also his, thanks to our mother—and watch as green waves lap at the ancient seawall.

It's only with great struggle I find my voice. "The wall won't hold."

He laughs. "It will hold. It always has."

His confidence is maddening. Just like everything else about him. He's only a handful minutes older than me, but those few minutes are enough.

"It won't," I say again. Insistent that he listen.

But it doesn't matter what I say. He's my brother, the favored child and our mother's successor, and he's always done as he wills.

I remember the first time our mother let us watch a godstorm roll in. It crashed against the seawall, whipping strands of power in every direction.

"They're angry today," our mother said, and laughed. As if the anger of the gods was nothing but a trifle.

She held my brother by the hand, and my brother held me by mine, and my free hand squirmed, wishing for something of its own to grasp onto. Something to cling to and make sense of the cacophony of color and sound assaulting the air around us.

When our mother stepped onto the ancient platform that was her right—that great stone tongue jutting from the seawall to just above the raging waters—my brother quickly followed. I, on the other hand, balked.

Progress interrupted, our mother frowned. After a carefully considered moment, she nodded down at my brother and said, "Let him go. If your younger brother isn't brave enough to face the gods, he'll just have to stand with the rest of the powerless."

I like to think my brother paused before releasing my hand, but memory is a slippery serpent. What is real and what is remembered are not always the same thing.

I do know that I was left behind, though. Crying there on the beach behind the seawall until the villagers dragged me into their huddling mass to wait out our mother's miracle. And a miracle it was, like everything our mother did.

No godstorm ever survived her touch.

By morning, the skies have darkened to the color of peat, and rot stink rides heavy atop the heaving waves. The water is a brown churn, its bright green lost to the growing godstorm. It's difficult to breathe with the weight of the heavens pressed against my lungs. I don't think anyone has been struck by a godstorm this big in nearly a century.

My brother, however, doesn't cower. He stands midst the villagers at the lower seawall while hungry waves assault the barrier, intent on consuming the village and everything surrounding. Villagers touch my brother's robes. Whisper blessings as he passes. Next to them, the seawall shudders at the sea's wrath.

How like our mother he is in this moment. So bold, so sure of himself.

She would be proud.

The incessant knot in my chest burns, but I push my way through the crowds nonetheless and grab my brother's hand. "May you bring peace once more to the gods," I say, wind-swept grit scouring my face.

He pats me on the shoulder with his free hand. "Don't worry, I will."

I swallow my frown and instead inspect the adoration-filled faces surrounding him. Despite their watching eyes, I lean into him and whisper. "About the wall—"

He yanks me into a hug then, his mouth against my ear. "I said not to worry. Now hush before you ruin the big moment."

In his arms, with the entire village staring and the gods beating at our shore, I force a smile onto my face. "Of course. My apologies."

He slaps me on the back, then with a small shove returns me to the crowd.

A few moments later, storm winds lashing at his robe, he ascends the platform.

Nobody truly knows why godstorms form.

We speculate, of course, and pass down our speculations to the next generation. And over time, such things are considered lore, or truth. But what is truth? What could possibly be the meaning of such terrible storms?

I will tell you what they say.

The sea is a fragile vessel, like a ceramic cup. Fill it with enough anger, and eventually that anger must overflow, or else the cup crack.

And so the gods gather up all the hate and anger that has sunk into the depths, and when it becomes too much, they spin it into a godstorm that it might vent its rage elsewhere. That the cup may remain whole.

That elsewhere, of course, is us.

It's a pretty story, in its own way. Makes us feel like we're a part of the gods' plans. As though however overwhelming the storm, we have been gifted the power necessary to stand before it. Because what kind of gods would they be, otherwise?

What kind of gods indeed.

My brother stands on the stone platform, exposed to the waters whipping below. Rings of concentration spark around him as he attempts to harness the storm's frenzy and unravel it. Of all the people watching, though, only I can see his rings of power. Only I can feel the intense rage of the waters clutching at his feet, hungry to drag him into the godstorm's heart and drown the defiance from him.

I am my mother's child as well, after all. My blood as strong as his.

The sky howls as he starts funneling the storm's hatred away. I even begin to think that maybe I was wrong, maybe the seawall is not as weak as I feared. But then my brother pauses his work for the barest of moments. Turns his head toward me as if to say, *Do you see this? Is this not glorious?*

That moment of inattention is all the godstorm needs.

A fist-like wave pummels, not the platform upon which he stands, but the battered wall upon which it rests. And that is enough, for the seawall is indeed weak with age. Has grown weaker every storm.

The stones of the seawall crumple beneath him, and with it the platform he stands upon.

He wobbles a moment, his mouth a surprised 'o' and the rings of his power flailing for purchase to keep him from plunging into the godstorm's wrath.

And then my brother is gone.

When our mother still lived, I used to dream of her death.

I pictured her, always at the lip of the storm, laughing at what the gods had flung in our direction. And while she laughed, I could feel the incoming waves, so intent on devouring her they shuddered through my bones. Such monstrosities, those waves. Vast enough to swallow the entire sky.

But it was only a dream. And no matter how many times I woke up screaming, our mother still stood against the next storm. And the next. And the next. Shaking her head in disappointment at my grasping hands, at my cracked voice begging her not to take those final steps up the platform.

And yet, in the end, it wasn't a storm that took her.

No, it was a bee. Minding its own business until the moment it wasn't.

She didn't know she was allergic until it stung her on the cheek.

And then . . . well, like so many moments in life, then it was too late.

☉

One moment, my brother is there. The next, he is gone. Terrified villagers scream as waves spill through the seawall breach and snatch them toward the sea. So much screaming, and yet I can barely hear it past the ringing in my ears.

My brother . . . is gone. A dozen hands shake at me. Thrust me forward, pull me back. Someone yells, "Save us, damn you! Save us!"

And like that, my focus snaps into place.

The godstorm is terrible, the sky spitting in my face, the sea gnashing at my legs. Rage begets rage begets rage, the fetid mass of it geysering from the godstorm's heart. A rotting boulder of a storm, its ugliness crashing into the shore.

And yet, a thousand colors still split the air. Power lights up the sky in whipping strands.

My brother, trying to stop the storm even as it swallows him whole.

I thrust away the hands. The voices. Everything.

"Save yourselves," I snarl as the starving waves reach out once more for them. For me. And thrusting all my power forward like an arrow, I leap into the howling sea with but one purpose.

To take back my brother from its grasp.

I don't pretend to know the will of the gods.

Blessings and curses, trust and fate. Love and hate and fear and all the mess between.

It's the day before the godstorm still, and our tea is growing cold. And as my brother stares past the garden at the darkening sky, his hand trembles just a bit, dropping the ancient tea cup like bones against its saucer.

"Ah, damn," he says, staring at the cup. At the fresh spiderline crack snaking up its side. "I've broken it. Mother would kill me if she were still here . . ."

I nudge my cup in his direction. "Take mine", I say. "I never much liked tea anyway. Reminds me too much of the sea gone bad."

It's not until I notice him staring that I realize it's the most words I've strung together since our mother's death.

He accepts the cup with a slight nod, though. Returns to watching the sea. To watching the sky.

I, on the other hand, watch him. Try to remember that little boy who once held my hand, until the moment he did not. Try to discern if he is still in there, hiding somewhere beneath our mother's commands. Beneath her expectations. Or if we will forever be this—two brothers occupying the same space, together yet so terribly, terribly apart.

But all I can see are waves—those monstrous fists of the sea that have haunted my dreams for as long as I can remember. That haunt me now awake.

Rising, ever rising . . .

Filtration Systems

~ Mary Berman

On the day Jimmy Tomlinson murdered 98.96% of the population of Garbersdale, the sky was bright and cloudless.

It happened at eleven o'clock in the morning. He should have been in school with the other teenagers, but he was the sort of boy who was always trying to wrangle his way out of school, and his parents were the sort of parents who let him. So, at ten fifty-eight on the day he killed everybody, he was sitting in his room with a pair of earbuds in, playing with a computer program he had developed.

The program was designed to synthesize the most unpleasant sounds possible. While developing it Jimmy had also been modifying an industrial speaker system he'd bought off Craigslist. The Craigslist ad had said that when the speakers were turned up to full volume, their sound could be heard across three city blocks. Jimmy was trying to modify them so they could be heard across the whole town.

He'd explained this two weeks ago to Orla Harrisburg, who had come over insisting that she only wanted to work on their group calculus project—but when she agreed to come up to his room, he knew she was into him. He played her a little of his sound sequence—only a little, because it wasn't yet half as offensive as he knew it could be—and described, while his blood throbbed, his plan use both in conjunction to terrorize the town.

Orla eyed the speaker, which occupied an entire wall of Jimmy's room. It hulked like a slab of volcanic rock. "That's it?"

". . . Yeah." What did she mean, *That's it?* He was a genius.

"Why would you do something like that?" Orla asked.

"Come on. I hate this place. Don't you?"

"No," said Orla matter-of-factly. "And it seems like an awful lot of work. Why d'you hate everything so much?"

The compact seed of anger that had been rooted in Jimmy's guts for as long as he could remember put forth another sprout. Its tendrils crawled up his stomach wall and knotted about his trachea. "Fuck you," he said. "Let's work on the project."

Orla had stiffened. Then she'd informed him that she would prefer to work on the project herself, and she'd removed her smooth slim limbs from his bedroom.

Two weeks later Jimmy was still brooding over the incident, simmering away in front of his computer, thinking: How could Orla ask him something like that? He was just angry, that was all. And that day, the way Orla had looked at him as though he were malformed—*she* was the one who'd made him angry. It was her fault. His parents and his teachers and everyone else who insisted that he do things he didn't want to do, it was their fault. Even strangers he encountered in the grocery store or at the coffee shop or the movie theater, strangers who persisted in being idiots or assholes or ugly or rude: their fault. In response to such a high volume of fucking *people*, it was perfectly normal to be angry.

So thick vines of anger had kept strangling Jimmy's organs, and he had kept on working on his synthesizer.

And now, at ten fifty-nine on Wednesday morning, he yanked his earbuds out, leaned over and vomited into the wastebasket.

Jimmy caught his breath. His heart juddered arrhythmically. In fact, he was pretty sure it had actually stopped for a second. The noise had been so ugly, so dissonant, so *wrong* that it had made him physically ill. But even as he sat there, his stomach still twisted, wiping a string of vomit and saliva from his chin, he felt a bold flicker of grim joy. He grinned. *This* would mess everyone up all right. This would show Orla. He unplugged his earbuds, plugged in the speaker, and hit Play.

The sound slammed into his eardrums like a sledgehammer; like an undersea volcano, cracking the planet and displacing unfathomable tons of ocean; like an asteroid smacking off a hunk of the moon.

Jimmy keeled over instantly. So did his father, who was working from home, and his mother, at a deli half a mile away. So did virtually everyone else within a three-quarter-mile radius, including almost the full population of Garbersdale, plus a hundred or so people in the neighboring towns of Peterborough, Mixton, and Shell's Way.

But this story isn't about Jimmy Tomlinson.

⊙

At eleven o'clock exactly, everyone else in Jisoo Kim's eighth grade algebra class toppled out of their desks and hit the linoleum. Jisoo blinked. Her chest tightened. This was another one of those jokes no one had thought to let her in on, because it had spread by whisper and Jisoo, being deaf, could not hear whispers. This sort of thing happened all the time, and Jisoo tried not to let on how much it hurt her. She knew her friends and peers meant nothing by it, they just forgot, but, well. She smiled weakly, trying to seem cool and casual and happy, wondering if it was too late for her to fall out of her chair and participate as well. Then she realized that the teacher was also prostrate, and that Ricky Carlsson, who had been leaning over precariously to pass Paul Tiny a note, had crumpled and landed on the crown of his head, and his neck was now twisted at a brutal angle, and no one was doing anything about it. And then she noticed that no one's chest was moving.

A dull rhythmic vibration pulsed beatlike through the soles of her shoes.

"Guys?" she said. No one reacted. Her own chest tightened further; her heart began to hammer in a way it had never done before, her blood becoming more tangible beat by beat against the inside of her skin. She stood up, hesitated, and then, convinced that this was a joke on her but too anxious to care, touched Kelly Martin's neck. There was no pulse.

"Oh my god," Jisoo said. She staggered back and whammed her hip into a desk. "Oh my god oh my g–"

She fled the classroom, her hands over her mouth, careening through the halls to the nurse's office. She burst in, already babbling, "I think everyone's dead, I really think everyone's dead," and then stopped. A noise that wanted to be a scream clawed halfway up her throat and lodged there. The student aide had collapsed face-down on his keyboard. The two kids who'd been sitting in the waiting room lolled in the pea-green chairs, their eyes vacant and their mouths open.

Jisoo ran into one of the little private rooms with bunk beds and jugs of water, still searching for the nurse. She didn't find him, but she did find Allie Petrovsky from world history class. Allie was lying on her back with a pair of noise-canceling headphones on and her eyes shut. She hadn't responded to Jisoo barreling in, but she did appear to be breathing. Jisoo said her name. Allie didn't move. Jisoo went over and shook her.

Allie jumped and opened her eyes. "Jisoo?" she said, which was easy to read. "What?"

Jisoo was so relieved she burst into tears.

She flung her arms around Allie, squeezing her so tightly that Allie couldn't even reach up to take her headphones off. Jisoo could feel the vibrations of Allie talking, but she couldn't bring herself to let go long enough to look at Allie's mouth. She became conscious of movement behind her and turned. Two girls were standing in the doorway: Carla White, looking even blanker than usual, and Laila Siddique, wearing her sensitivity suit and shaking her head like she was trying to get rid of a mosquito.

Jisoo screamed, mostly from delight, and cried harder.

"Hey, chill out," Laila said. "What's going on?" She rubbed her ears, crinkling the cellophane-like fabric of her suit. Laila had a hypersensitivity disorder, and experiencing the world unfiltered frequently sent her into convulsions, so she wore a full-body sensitivity suit, which stretched over her skin and nostrils and ears and eye sockets and mouth, letting her breathe but dulling all sensory stimuli. Jisoo had used to wonder how she ate lunch, and then she'd watched Laila in the cafeteria one day and realized that Laila did not eat lunch. Eventually she learned that Laila only ate two meals a day, breakfast and dinner, and that she ate them at home in a special room, gray-painted and dimly lit and silent. This made Jisoo sad, and as a consequence seeing Laila usually made her sad, but now Jisoo had never been so happy to see anyone.

"Everyone in Mr. Russo's class just—fell over dead," Jisoo said. She was aware of how absurd she sounded, but her body was too hysterical for her to disbelieve herself. She was still clutching Allie, which was ridiculous. She and Allie weren't even friends. "They're dead out there in the nurse's office, too. Look."

"It's that sound," said Carla dully.

"What sound?"

Allie said something too and reached up to take her headphones off.

"Don't do that," Carla said.

Allie said something else, which Jisoo missed as she turned to her, and removed her headphones. Immediately her eyes rolled back in her head, her mouth fell open, and she flopped sideways into Jisoo's lap. Jisoo screamed again.

Carla ignored her and said to Laila, "Don't take that off."

Laila rubbed her ears again. She'd been sitting in one of the private bunk rooms with Carla, who'd escorted her here for period cramps, when five minutes ago a loud ugly noise had started buzzing its way through her suit. Between that and her knotted stomach and Carla's weird trademark brand of silence, she was feeling irritable. "Why would I take it off?" she snapped. "And what's wrong with Allie? Where's the nurse?" She shook her head hard. "Ugh! What is that!"

"You can hear it?"

"That horrible buzzing? Yes. You're lucky," said Laila to Jisoo, who did not notice.

"Hmm. Your suit must be filtering out whatever frequency is killing people," Carla said. "That's why you're not dead."

"Yeah?" said Laila, humoring her. "Then why aren't you dead? Seriously, what's going on? Allie, get up. You're freaking me out."

"She can't get up. She's dead. Come on." Carla tugged Jisoo out from under Allie Petrovsky. Allie slid off Jisoo and thunked to the floor like a rag doll. "Come on," Carla said, with, for the first time, a touch of real feeling. But Jisoo only drew a deep, shattered breath, and Carla, evidently fed up now, dragged Jisoo out of the room. Laila followed them as far as the nurse's office and then paused to gawk at the two limp, unblinking sixth-graders in the pea-green chairs. She hadn't really noticed them when following Carla to Allie's bunk room. She'd glimpsed them out of the corner of her eye, but the suit tended to blur her peripheral vision, and she'd just assumed they were asleep. But their eyes were open.

It couldn't be true that everyone was dead.

The sixth-graders sure *looked* dead.

"Carla?" Laila said uncomfortably. There was no answer. Laila felt a burst of quiet panic, looked out the door and realized Carla and Jisoo were already halfway down the corridor. She hurried to catch up. "Hey! Wait! What are you doing?"

"We've got to figure out where the sound is coming from and turn it off."

"Shouldn't we call the police? Or our parents?"

"I wouldn't."

"Why not?"

"Well, if they're within range of the sound, they're probably dead like everyone else." A bolt of horror shot through Laila's solar plexus. "And if they're not, you don't want them to hear it, do you?"

Laila's parents both worked in the city, twenty miles away. How far away could the sound be heard? Surely not that far; Laila couldn't even hear it properly. But she had her suit, and her parents.... Her mind wrenched away from the mental image of her parents lolling in their desk chairs with the sixth-graders' limp necks and dead eyes, flitted frantically around her skull for something else to attach to, and latched squidlike onto the police. Laila would call the police. It was what you were supposed to do.

She informed Carla of this. Carla said nothing.

Stubbornly Laila got out her cell phone and called 9-1-1, but when she was halfway through telling the operator their location (they were walking through the cafeteria now, and the kids who'd been eating had collapsed into their trays and lunchboxes, and the cafeteria monitors were prone on the ground, and something in the kitchen was smoking badly), the operator interrupted, sounding first vexed and then nauseous.

"You're not at school. I can hear something in the background. Are you at a concert? Oh, excuse m–" The operator's voice cut off abruptly. Laila heard retching.

The girls entered the empty gym. Briefly, blessedly, the vibrations and buzzing softened, and the echoes of their footsteps against the rubber floor and steel bleachers sounded, muffled, in Laila's ears. Of course, the gym was soundproofed. But it was a lunch period. No one had P.E. during lunch periods, because of recess.

"Hello?" Laila said to the operator. "Hello?" No answer. More retching, then dead air, and then a busy signal that never ended.

Carla pushed open the exit door behind the gym, which led to the street-facing schoolyard. In the same flat tone as always, she asked, "How did that go?"

Laila's thoughts detached from the police and suctioned back onto her parents. Her father's jaw open, his tongue swelling and blackening, her mother's shriveling skin and eyeballs being gnawed away by maggots. "Shut up," she said. She wanted nothing more than to call her mother; she wanted it in her liver, in her fingertips, in the space behind her eyes where she sometimes got migraines. Instead she hung up and, swallowing hard, followed Carla and Jisoo outside.

There was a vicious pile-up in the street. Ten, fifteen, twenty cars had all slammed into each other. Some had spilled over onto the wide flat grassy schoolyard. The day was cloudless and warm, the sky a deep impenetrable blue, and for a split second, as Laila looked at the wreckage and her two classmates and the hot yellow sunlight on the grass, she felt keenly and simultaneously the horror of the death and violence before her, her sick suppressed anxiety, and the pure unfiltered delight of skipping fourth period and sneaking outside on a beautiful day. Then she felt confused, and then she saw a severed head in the middle of the street, and then, much to her own surprise, her legs gave out from under her and she landed in a sitting position on the grass.

Jisoo did not fall. Indeed she looked too paralyzed to fall or throw up or do any of the things Laila's body was insisting ought to be done, too paralyzed to do anything but cling to Carla, who, for her part, had stopped moving. Carla squinted at the wreckage for a second, glanced left toward Main Street, and then turned her attention the other way toward Hopkins Avenue, which marked the start of a residential neighborhood.

Laila asked, "What are you looking for?"

"The source of the sound. I think it has to be close, but I can't tell . . ."

Laila considered. In just six hours her parents would be on their way back to Garbersdale. The fingers of her left hand drifted to those of her right; she hesitated, gulping; then in one swoop she peeled off the right-hand glove of her sensitivity suit and pressed her palm to the ground. The sound's vibrations thudded through her like ocean waves, like honeybee swarms. They were coming from some place past Hopkins. Her body hummed violently. Laila shuddered once, already feeling unglued, and ripped her hand away.

Carla and Jisoo were looking at her. Laila managed to say, "That way."

"Oh," said Carla, respectfully. "That's neat. Come on, then." She took Jisoo's hand and started walking. Laila stayed on the ground for a few more seconds, focusing on the soft, distant sensation of her suit's fabric against her palms, her cheeks and forehead, the insides of her thighs. Then she took a deep, helpless breath, got to her wobbly feet and followed.

They walked toward Hopkins Avenue and turned right on Estaugh Street: Carla marching, Jisoo stumbling, Laila just kind of drifting. They saw two more car accidents, but these weren't as bad, just a pair of crumpled skewed cars with unbroken seatbelted bodies drooping behind their steering wheels. They passed seventeen dead squirrels, at least thirty-two dead songbirds (Laila lost count), two dogs, and a single housecat on its side, fluffy and unmoving. The birds were mostly robins and blue jays and goldfinches and looked like jewels. A man in camouflage-green clothes lay next to a still-running lawnmower, which chewed away placidly at his left foot, slowly turning the fresh-chopped grass a soft rust color. From one house floated the sweet strains of a recorded Bach prelude.

Then, at the same time, Laila and Jisoo stopped. Both girls clapped their hands over their ears and fell back. Jisoo looked astonished. She exclaimed, "I can hear it!"

Carla looked stricken. "I thought you were deaf."

"I am. I mean, I can only hear sounds if they're really intense, which, you know, they're not, usually. But . . ." Cautiously, she lowered her hands and stepped forward again, an expression of dim wonder on her face.

"No," Carla shouted, but it was too late. Jisoo's eyeballs jittered in her head. She sucked in a strangled breath and fell. Laila lunged forward to grab her and heard, as she had a split second ago, the not-too-muffled strains of a hideous cacophony; she felt her own heart cease to beat and leapt back, out of range, with a gasp. Carla hauled Jisoo over her shoulders and dumped her next to Laila, and Laila crouched over her, stunned and hopeless, feeling for a pulse.

Miraculously, she found one. Jisoo had been moved out of range of the sound before her body had had time to fully shut down. Laila pounded on Jisoo's chest, more so she could feel useful than anything else, and Jisoo inhaled a shallow breath.

Carla covered her face. "That was my fault."

"What?"

"I should've known your filter wouldn't work if you got close enough. And Jisoo . . . Just stay here, okay? I'll find the noise and make it stop. Maybe everyone else will wake up, too, if it stops."

Hysteria bubbled in Laila's chest. "They're not asleep! There's a guy back there missing his head!"

Carla took one step away from her, two, three, then turned on her heel and speedwalked down the street.

"Carla!" Laila bellowed. "Why aren't you dead!"

Carla did not respond, did not even indicate that she'd heard. She broke into a jog, then a run, getting farther and farther away. When she was almost at the end of the street, she slowed down and cocked her head. Then she turned, marched up the porch of a two-story mint-green colonial, hesitated for the briefest second, opened the screen door and walked in.

Carla had spent her entire life screaming.

She didn't remember her first scream or her birth, but she knew from stories that it had involved an emergency C-section. She'd come into the world three months early, horrified by the loud sounds and the bright lights and the big ugly faces. She'd started screaming right away.

She'd screamed incessantly. She would not stop until she fell asleep or ran out of air, and even in the latter case her mouth would stay open, a tiny void, her little throat bobbing in an attempt to scream without breath. She refused to stop screaming long enough to eat or drink. For years she received her nutrition through IV supplements and a gastrointestinal tube. Her parents had not known what to do. She'd kept it up through toddlerhood and young childhood, despite doctors and therapies. She had not been able to go to school or day care; she had been kept home as much as possible, and when it was necessary to bring her somewhere—to run an errand, or to visit relatives—her parents hustled through the task as quickly as possible or left her in the car. Sometimes her father yelled at her to shut up, and sometimes he hit her, but neither act had any noticeable effect.

Her memories of this early screaming were tied up in her other childhood memories, like when the family had visited Carla's aunt in New York and they'd ridden the subway, and a big man with a cane had tripped and fallen and smashed his face open on the subway floor, and Carla had watched his blood, dotted with little grains of broken teeth, slosh up and down with the movement of the train.

Her second memory was of watching a mailman on a bicycle get hit by a truck and flattened, spread out over the blacktop like peanut butter. Her third memory was a cloudy one of her family being forced out of their house, sleeping under a bridge in the city for two days, immersed in cold and wet and anxiety before finally moving in with her maternal grandmother in Garbersdale. Then came a series of disjointed memories of her parents fighting, not the way people fight when they're exhausted and frustrated but the way they fight when they hate each other, until eventually her mother got a job and then a promotion and then started making some real money. Carla's next isolated memory, a little later, from age four maybe, was of watching a gas station explode. The fire had consumed six cars, an attached convenience store, and all of the human beings in the vicinity. It had smelled of gasoline and blackened marshmallows. And Carla had screamed right through all of it.

Then, at age five, she'd stopped.

Her parents and doctors never knew why, but the answer was simple: Carla had realized that it did not matter whether she screamed out loud, as long as she was doing it in her head.

In this way she had drowned out every ugly stimulus, every harsh noise, every unwelcome thought. She was now thirteen years old and capable of blocking out anything. In fact, she was incapable of ceasing to block things out. When she and Laila and Jisoo had stepped from the school into the sunlight, she had not experienced Laila's flash of bewildered joy, because she had not noticed the lovely silence and the sun.

She had learned to function through the screaming. She layered it on top of the rest of the world, filtered everything through it. Indeed, if she thought about it, her screaming functioned not unlike Laila's sensitivity suit. The difference, of course, was that if Carla faced the world unfiltered she would not have a seizure. She just didn't think she'd be able to bear it.

When she had heard the noise start up, she'd instantly known that it was an evil thing, a dangerous thing. But it hadn't touched her, because her screaming had drowned it. And as she'd walked through town, through car crashes and corpses, through Jisoo's heart-stopping collapse, the screaming had gotten louder and louder. Now she could hardly hear the sound at all anymore.

She walked through the front door of the mint-green colonial. There was a dead man in the living room. He was white and middle-aged, wearing a Hanes T-shirt and plaid boxers. Drool crusted the stubble on his chin. Carla ignored him and went upstairs. She opened every door until she found what she wanted: a mountainous speaker set and a humming computer monitor. A white boy sat in a giant black plush desk chair, the sort of desk chair Carla could picture in a law firm or a fancy bank, with a pair of expensive headphones still dangling from his limp fingers. Carla stepped over him, moved the computer mouse to wake the screen and found some kind of music synthesizer. She clicked the pause button.

The sound disappeared. The sudden and total silence rang in Carla's ears behind the screaming.

She found the file the synthesizer was playing and moved it to the trash, which she emptied. Then she stood back and rubbed her ears. Experimentally she prodded the kid's calf with her foot. He didn't move. She kicked him again, harder. He slipped from the chair but otherwise did not react. She put her foot on his neck and applied pressure until something crunched. Nothing.

Carla, a strange heat bubbling in her throat, glanced out the window. She spotted Laila and Jisoo down the street where she'd left them, Jisoo sitting up and looking disoriented, Laila cocking her head hopefully into the silence and then fumbling for her phone. Carla did not bother to reach for her own phone. Her parents both worked on Main Street. She knew she ought to return to Jisoo and Laila, but instead she went to the boy's closet, pushed his clothes to the side, shut herself in and sat on the dusty floor. In the pitch-quiet blackness she closed her eyes and screamed.

Postcards From the Empty Nest

~ *Rhonda Eikamp*

Dear Bryn,

Sorry. I know you set up the smartphone & e-mail for me, honey, but I came across these unused postcards while cleaning out after the funeral—face it, your mother will never be digitized—& I felt the urge to put down in ink what's been happening here, everything about finding the Nest. I should start at the beginning. My, not much room on these things. I was so down after the funeral & you seemed in a hurry to fly out, I didn't get to talk to you like I wanted. Your father was a difficult man (an understatement, haha), you know that, but very responsible, & it's still hitting me how many things he took care of that are my responsibility now. Just thing things. Taxes, washing the car. You'll know when you get old—there's an energy seeps out of the mind & it can't turn itself to things. It was about a week in that I forgot to close the garage door for the night. He'd been the one to do that, see. I woke up in the morning knowing, rushed out. Nothing stolen. The car was there. Hit the button to close the door, watched it go down & that's when I discovered the silver circle. Big as a platter, there on the garage ceiling. The door had hidden it. Like a trick of the dawn light, or my dreams still percolating in me. I knew it hadn't been there the day before. I go to stand under it & I can see it's strands, rustling a little with the air. There's a cloth we used to call peau-de-soie, satiny but hefty, always in colors of metal or transparent jewels. The wedding-dress sheen. It rippled like that (or rather it stopped when I stood under it). But such a perfect circle, like bread mold. Like silver-white hair growing out from the center. I should have done something about it then, but it was just another thing, & I didn't want to deal with things. The problem is, every morning it's been a little bigger. I know you were always afraid of spider eggs & I just wanted to warn you—in case by chance you're back soon for a visit

& I forget—don't go in the garage. (So—that gets that out of my system some. Really not much room on these things!)

—Love, Mom

☉

Dear Bryn honey,

Hope you get these in the right order. You know when you see a face in an object & then you can't stop seeing it? (You may have a face like that in your life someday.) This is after it started to bulge in places. Grew about as big around as the roof of the car, though off to the side, in the empty space. I've started walking round & round every day gazing up, studying details of it, tighter & tighter circles until sometimes I'm spinning in place with my head thrown back. Makes me dizzy. (You used to do that as a child, arms stretched to the blue sky. Do you remember?) Don't worry what the neighbors think, the Nest is only visible with the garage door closed, remember. When the light from the little window hits it right (but it casts its own light), a face appears. Very plain, no particular features. A nonface, an unface, no one I know. I stopped thinking Nest so much & started thinking Face, telling myself, You've got to do something about the Face. But I never got around to it. Today, though, spinning slow like that underneath it, squinting hard, I caught sight of a kind of crack or rip in it, a darker hairline in the silver. Like a flap. Looked to be wavering with the motion of air, or maybe squirming, & I started thinking of all the things that could come out of a nest like that.

Your father would always get rid of the wasps' nests around the house. He'd slosh gasoline on them to stun them before he knocked the nest down. I know you think your mother's not tough, an old homebody (I'd have gone to work when you were older if your father hadn't been so touchy about being the breadwinner), but here I was today, up on the trunk of the car with a broom & a gas can. Figured I could just about reach it from there. Felt a little wavery myself. You were probably too young to remember that scandal with old Lily Carston down the street, lived alone, how they found her bruised with a broken wrist on her bedroom floor after she signalled that bracelet alarm, naked from the waist down? Swore she

couldn't remember a thing & they figured the worst, till she con-
fessed she'd fallen off her dresser after she climbed up to look at her
hemorrhoids in the mirror. I felt like that (not about the haemor-
rhoids, honey) but thinking: if I fall this'll be hard to explain. Found
in a pool of gas with a broken hip (or not found at all). Wasn't sure
how I was going to slosh up there with that can. But when I straightened up I hesitated. Up close the Nest was so beautiful. The weave
of it so structured, ridged. It wasn't a Face up that close, there were
whole cities in there, a million tiny buildings, & me a god gazing
down—up—onto it from its sky. And that's when the Nest

☉

B.,
   Sorry. Ran out of room on the last card. That's when it spoke. It
said, Water fountains.
   That flap, turns out, is a mouth, though the sound (sounds by now)
does not come from there but rather from all over it—a thrum, pia-
no wire, church organs. Chords you feel deep down. A bone sound.
I'll admit I said, Henry? (Silly, I know. Years of marriage will do that
to you.) I was down on the floor by then, half-fell off the car & hurt
my ankle, crawled into the corner & just sat with my knees pulled
up, staring. After a long time it said, Brainstorming. I could hear
the disgust in the voice then (the non-voice, unvoice), & it made
sense. You surely recall how your father hated drinking fountains.
Unpredictable intelligence, he'd claim—one high & spraying, the
next one low & seepy, icy or tepid (he loved that word), germ colonies of the masses & you'd cry when he wouldn't let you use them.
But you probably didn't know brainstorming was one of his hates
too, how he'd come home from those mandatory meetings ranting
how younger men could steal his ideas because it all came out of the
session, created by the one mind working together & where was the
credit where credit was due. I hunched there in the garage corner,
thrummed through by that sound, & it made sense, that if there
was anything of him to survive it would be the hates. (Wouldn't it?)
Because in life they had been so large. I felt light, empty, always air
anyway & now even that pumped out of me, just an old church filled
with the organ sound of his gripes. I felt the Nest would float down

onto me then, odd thought, almost wanted it to, but me & the Nest had both grown very still, not wavering anymore. Just waiting.

After a while it said, Country music.

⊙

Bryn,

Got your message on the answering machine. You don't have to worry about me, hon. Impossible's what you make of it—if you're handed impossible lemons, make crazy lemonade.

I ditched the gas can the next day. Figured I could get up under it with the broom & loosen it, make it drop. Like turning a pancake. Didn't know what I'd do if I got it down on the garage floor. Look it over maybe close up, take my own good time. Maybe touch it. The silver threads seemed to have gotten thicker in just a day, not hairs so much as gel, it rippled away from the loose edge I poked, all those ridges & structures softening & swelling, like it'd love to just shake me off, but I wasn't having it. I was a god giving that city an earthquake. Just when the broom was wedged up under it good, it moved away. Fast. Scuttled all the way across the ceiling, toward the door to the kitchen that I'd left open.

I almost fell again. Not because it was its own creature, loose & moving (but still suckered to that ceiling). It was the shock of how it moved. Because, honey, I recognized that scuttle. There was that disgust in the way it hunched away from me, if a blob can be said to hunch. Annoyed. (Can't think of a better word). If the list of hates hadn't made me certain of what I was looking at, that did. He waited for a second at the door to see how I'd react, then went on into the house, sort of flowed across the lintel like an earthworm (a very large, very silver earthworm, an earthworm city) & I followed. Found him spread across most of the kitchen ceiling. It made him seem even larger, being inside like that, so unexpected against my ivy-pattern curtains & the plastic fruit on top of the fridge. So organic (I suppose that's the word). A thing that belongs outside brought inside. Out-of-place. Not dirt but something like it. A neck of him oozed out from the rest, still attached, inched on across the top of the door into the den, inspecting it for changes. The voice said, Cobwebs. The sound of those hate words was larger too now it was inside, it thrummed in the walls & the floor. I admit I don't clean the corners up near the ceilings like I should. Call waiting, it said, & then: Forgetfulness.

I felt all empty again hearing that. All my air gone. The whole house has been airless since that moment it said that, a box of airless. I think it's what's caused this latest growth spurt these past few days. Aren't there amoebas that grow in a lack of oxygen? He's so big now, honey, you wouldn't believe. The only ceiling in every room, worming through the top of every door. That voice goes on night & day with its rumbling list. Wicker headboards, horses rolling, funerals. The sound is like a storm that's passed but the thunder keeps reaching back for you. I dream it at night. Perfume, he said last night from the bedroom ceiling, just before I nodded off, & I said aloud into the dark: I know, it's why I never wore it. Your father hated fake scents, Bryn, liked the natural scent of me, he'd say. Never a romantic, but something about him saying that always made me feel happier.

I had good dreams that night.

Love for now. More later.

⊙

Dearest Bryn,

Sorry I missed you again. I don't pick up much anymore. Please please don't jump on a plane, I know you have a busy life & it's not necessary. It's going too far though to say I'm imagining this, sweetie. No one could imagine something this big. I do have to stoop & that's an inconvenience. He's larger now than anything I've ever had in the house. Plus there have come to be certain (how do I say this delicately?) bulges, extending almost to the floor in every room, stalactites (or is it –mites?) that I have to detour around. Cottony columns, pillars, as if I was living in a soft silver temple. If I saw a Face before, I see something else in these Pillars. The tips bend toward me when I try to go around them. The words keep on rumbling of course, erupting from everywhere now, the whole house speaking when he does, a mumble so run together I hardly hear it anymore. Belt-buckles roses decaf tan-lines the squinting eyes lists. Hard to believe anyone could hate so many things. Meter-readers, snow in May, a letter with no return address. I'm tired of this on-and-on, Bryn, believe me, all his modern art's & his gnocchi's, all his hates rolled into that eternal mumble, but I sat there last week in the blue recliner as I often do these days, gazing up into that city that is more a huge heaving hill-country of silver grass, so close I can feel the thrum picking up my hair like static, & for a moment the mumble became words again.

Small dogs, sudden silences, tofu.

Child-proof caps? I suggested.

The quiet lasted too long. Wasn't there anything you loved, I asked. Even one thing.

Another silence. Then a word.

You.

Funny thing is, I'm not sure if he heard me or if he was still listing. After a second the mumblings went on. Empty rooms, word games, a liar. I accept it for now, but I can't decide which he meant, Bryn, a hate or a love. I just can't. Can you?

What I think is that I have to stop thinking about it.

So you see you don't have to be afraid for me. The important thing is this—I could leave anytime if I wanted to, walk out the door & close it behind me, out to where there are no ceilings, & that is a thing he can't do. Because he is attached & I am not, see. I can tell myself he's been put in his place for once & it's enough for me. That no matter how much of the house he fills, with his mass & his staticky thrum that turns my head to liquid & his grasping Pillars—it's still an empty buzzing nest, whereas I'm filled with that energy I thought I'd lost. I may get a small dog. I may travel. I may. Even in my bent state (& it's very low now, since this morning I'm reduced to crawling) it would not be too hard. Those Pillars haven't blocked the doors yet entirely. I'll squeeze through to take this to the mail-box & then I'll come back in & think about it. What I mean to say, Bryn honey (running out of room again), is that you shouldn't be worried if you arrive & don't find me here because it will mean I've

But My Heart Keeps Watching

~ Elad Haber

I built my father out of bones.

There are photos of him all over our house. I know what he looked like on his wedding day, on the beach with his shirt off, on a boat with my mother with wind in their hair, and holding a baby version of me, his smile as big as my tiny head.

On Sundays, we went to the cemetery to pay our respects. His grave was alone at the top of a hill. Most days my mother is fine, sad but functioning, but on Sundays she's a mess. She cries and cries. She doesn't remember to make me lunch or dinner.

I asked her once, years after my father had passed, "Mom, why are so sad?" And she said, "Because my heart is broken."

The next day at school, I built her a paper-maché heart, painted it red and purple, her favorite colors, and gave it to her at night. I removed the gears from a clock and inserted it into the heart so that it looked like it was beating. I said to my mother, "I made you a new heart."

She laughed and patted my head and said, "You're sweet, Rose."

But I wasn't trying to be funny. I was being serious. I don't know what I wanted her to do, but it definitely wasn't laugh. I started crying and rushed to my room. I slammed the door so hard, it cracked a little.

My only memory of my father is when he used to take me to the city to visit the Museum of Natural History. He loved the history and we both loved the taxidermy.

The dinosaurs were my father's favorite. We stood in front of the massive skeleton of the Tyrannosaur for what felt like hours. I could see he wanted to reach out to touch the elegant bones.

I asked him, after a while, "How do they know how it all fits?"

My father looked at me with a strange expression.

"Like," I said, "No one has ever seen a T-Rex, right? So how do they know what it looks like?"

He smiled and pinched my cheek. "Bones are magic, Rosie," he said. He was the only person who called me Rosie. Then we went back to staring at the bones and I wondered what life was like millions of years ago when the world was young.

One day I went to the cemetery on my own. I snuck out of school during lunch and made sure no one was following me. I thought I heard someone call out to me as I was getting on my bike, but the sound of the wind drowned it out.

I rode through the deserted daytime streets towards the rolling hills of the cemetery. I stood over my father's grave for awhile. Then, as if he said something to set me off, I started cursing and punching at the ground. I shouted, "Why did you leave? Why did you make her sad?"

I started digging with my hands and crying. I didn't know what had come over me.

I made a decent size hole in the earth by the time the sirens approached the hill. Truant officers rushed out of the car and ran towards me. They were angry.

Later, my mom came to get me from school. I saw her in the principal's office crying. I was confused, because it wasn't Sunday. Every once in a while the door would open and I would hear her say something like, "She's acting out . . ."

After that day, everyone at school started treating me different. The other kids whispered as I passed them in the halls and the teachers talked slowly to me like I was dumb. The school suggested counseling and though it was expensive, my mom agreed. She took an extra shift at the hospital to pay for it and was home even less.

I spent more and more time alone. My mother asked other parents to drive me and pick me up from school. I'd come home and there would be dinner on the kitchen table, usually some drive-thru, and I would hear the TV on in her bedroom. I was never sure if she was asleep or at work. The red and purple heart was in the middle of a stack of forgotten mail in the corner of our kitchen. I listened to the tired ticks of the gears as I ate cold hamburgers.

For my plan to work, I needed help. I stalked a group of boys who hung out under a Banyan tree across from the soccer field. They played games out of their parent's old D&D books. I guess the new editions were too expensive. I coaxed a couple of them to the nearby bleachers and traded phone numbers.

I needed to get my hands on my father's remains. I wasn't sure why. I felt the pull of it when I was at his grave. It was like a vision. I had to see it through.

I spent the rest of the night texting.

The boys told me over Messenger how it went down.

Three boys met up near the cemetery. They had stolen shovels and pick axes from their high school maintenance sheds. There was night-time security in the area so one of them was lookout on an adjoining hill while the other two crept towards my father's grave. They had their cellphones on continuous three way conference call like some kind of away team mission in *Star Trek*.

Digging did not go well. The guys were weak and afraid. They told me they psyched themselves up thinking this was a morbid video game. They counted each shovel full as a point and kept a tally in their heads. They didn't even consider the crime they were committing.

After a few tense hours, where once a security guard in a golf cart rolled by but didn't see them, they had the casket uncovered. The two boys tied rags around their noses and mouths like they'd seen in the movies and opened the casket. They wouldn't tell me what it looked like inside except it was "gross."

I only needed a few bones for my project. They packed those in a duffel bag and left it at the lip of the hole. Then they went about refilling it. One of the boys almost collapsed and so he switched places with the lookout. They made it home before their parent's phone alarms went off.

One of them sent me a message: "It's done. Now, you're turn. Send us pics!"

I googled some leaked nudes of movie stars and sent them the images with the heads cropped off.

Boys are so dumb.

The next morning, I picked up the duffel bag from behind a pile of garbage in the grassy field between the middle and high schools. I slung it over my shoulder and went straight home. I kept checking behind me as if I was being followed, but no one was there.

My father had used our garage as a work room. I remember it being so tidy and organized. He used to tinker with model airplanes and computers. After he passed, my mother never liked going in there. She had me bring boxes of junk in there every few months. There were so many now, they reached the low ceiling and blocked the lightbulbs. It was dark as a grave in there.

Over the last week, I had made some space between the boxes and uncovered my father's old steel table and tool bench. I laid the duffel bag on the table and turned on a desk lamp.

The boys had done well and brought me the handful of bones I needed. I connected them with pieces of copper and hard silver wiring. It looked like a stick figure of a person.

From below the table, I pulled out two shoe boxes covered in dirt. These I had unearthed myself from our backyard. They were the bones of dead pets from my early childhood, a bird, a cat. I don't know why my pets kept dying. Maybe that's just what pets do. Each of the shoe boxes had the name of the pet drawn on the top with crayons and markers but the letters were faded and I didn't remember their names.

I removed the lids from the boxes and carefully picked up a few of the skeleton remains and placed them on the table.

I worked slow and steady to get the pieces fused together. When I was done, the shape reminded me of a monkey, a kind of miniature human cousin. I used the skull of a cat as the head and the tiny stick bones of the bird to create fingers and toes. I threaded fishing wire between the larger human bones and the smaller animal bones to keep them together.

When I was done, I stepped away from the table and looked proudly on my creation. I had a fleeting thought that someone, like my mother, might see this and think it's a grisly scene of violence and murder. They would ship me off to an insane asylum with a name like Shady Branches. But to me, it was beautiful. It was pieces of my past all put together.

I reached into one of the drawers of the work table where I had hidden a folder of photographs. I didn't remove any of the pictures from the house. I snapped photos of them with my phone and then printed those out. The photos, once small enough to fit in a frame, looked grainy and weird when printed to fit on a page, but it was good enough. I placed the pictures of my father all around the bones.

Now, for the final touch.

I wasn't sure what technique was going to work, so I decided to employ them all. I researched countless rites and rituals on YouTube and sent links to my phone. I bought incense from a rank smelling shop downtown and chicken guts from a butcher a few doors away. I brought them all back to the garage. Each night, I worked myself into a sweaty mess as I tried to coax my father's soul back from the dead. I did rain dances and spun dreidels and even tried rake.

After a while, I gave up. I laid down amongst the beads and the sand and painted feathers and tried to sleep. I closed my eyes and after a moment, I heard a stirring like wind. I looked around to see if there were any open windows or doors. I heard it again, a rustle.

I leaped to my feet and looked at the skeleton on the table. When it didn't move, my heart sank. And then one of the arms lifted. Then another. It pulled itself off the table like an awakening zombie. It stood on the table, barely two feet, with its stick figure body and tiny cat skull. It looked at me and, amazingly, a voice came out of the bones.

"Rosie?" it said.

I couldn't speak.

The tiny skull took in the room and then looked down at its strange body. When it spoke again, I recognized the voice, the deep tones of my father.

"What am I doing here?" it asked me. "I don't remember." There was sadness in his voice, a profound confusion.

I took a step towards it and extended an open palm like I might greet an alien visitor.

"It's okay," I said, "I'm here. You're back."

☉

We went everywhere together.

He spent most of the day in my backpack, which I kept perched on one shoulder. He would whisper jokes or words of encouragement to me during the school day. Sometimes I'd laugh in the middle of a quiet moment in class and the teacher and the other kids would just look at me and shake their heads.

A couple of weeks later, one of the boys who dug up his bones tried to talk to me during lunch. His name was Travis and he wore skinny jeans and had a flop of unwashed brown hair that covered his eyes. He asked me some questions but I couldn't pay attention because my father became agitated as soon as Travis came close to me. He started banging on my shoulder through the backpack.

"I, uh"—ouch!—"I have to go," I said and rushed out of the lunch room. I was hungry the rest of the day.

Later, I went under the bleachers by the football field and moved my backpack to the floor and unzipped the top. My father's cat skull head peered up at me.

"Why did you do that?" I asked him.

"I don't trust that boy," said my father's bones.

"He's nice," I said but I dropped it. I didn't want to argue with my best friend.

That night, we watched TV together in the living room. My mom was at the hospital so my father laid on top of me on the couch. He liked to put his head to my chest and listen to my heartbeat. He said it made him feel human.

My phone let out an R2-D2 series of bleeps. It was Travis, texting me. He was asking me out on a date!

"Whoa," I said.

My father looked up. "What is it?"

"Uh, nothing. No one." I put the phone away and covered my mouth so he wouldn't see my smile.

The next weekend, my mom was working a triple shift and would be out of the house from Friday morning to Sunday night. She left me some cash and made me promise to eat at least two meals a day and both of them cannot be pizza.

I texted Travis and told him the coast was clear for him to drop by that evening. I just needed to figure out something to do with my dad.

My father was one of those old guys who could spend all day watching war documentaries on the history channel. I placated him at first after his reincarnation in bone form. I would watch endless hours of commentary and grainy footage about World War 2 and reenactments of civil war battles.

On the Friday afternoon after school, mid-way through a documentary on Hitler's breakfast habits, I got up and said, "I can't watch any more of this!"

His tiny bone fingers pressed pause on the TV. "What do you mean?" he said.

"I just can't!" I said, exasperated. "You watch whatever you want, I'm going upstairs to read."

I left before he even had a chance to respond.

Once in my room, I went straight to my window where Travis waited, crouched in the shadows of my curved roof. I had never had a boy sneak up to my room before. It made my limbs tingle with excitement.

"Hey," he said when I opened the window.

"Shhh!" I said and gestured for him to come in.

His expression was confused. "I thought you said your mom wasn't home."

I shrugged and thought quickly. "She still hired a babysitter!" I said with a sigh. "She's watching TV downstairs. We have to be quiet."

"Okay," said Travis with a smile.

He sat on my bed and looked around at all my posters and dolls, remnants from my not so long ago childhood.

"Cool room," he said and then patted the bed next to him.

I sat down, close but not too close, and said, "So, are you—"

He reached over and kissed me. It was short, dry, with a question mark at the end.

I nodded for him to continue and then he put one warm hand around the curve of my jaw and laid another long kiss on my lips.

It was my first real kiss so I wasn't sure what to do, but he went slowly and we took a few breaks to breathe.

After a few wonderful minutes, his hands went wandering on my back and down to the hem of my blouse. He tried a few times to lift my shirt up to my chin, but I quickly clasped his hand in mine and stopped him.

He released his lips from mine and said, in a whisper, "Come on, Rose. Let me see them."

He tried again to lift up my shirt and I pushed back away from him. He looked surprised.

"Come on!" he said. "I knew the pic you sent was fake! If it wasn't, you'd show them to me."

He reached out again and I slapped away his hands. "No!" I shouted.

Just then, the door to my room burst open and my father, a diminutive skeleton of contrasting bone sizes, stood like a protective dog at my door.

My father's tone was all daggers. "You leave her alone!"

Travis' face was scrunched in disgust. "What the hell is that?" he said.

My father leaped like a long jumper from the doorway right onto the bed. He tackled Travis and both fell to the ground in a mess of limbs. They looked like they were wrestling, throwing each other on the ground and then back on top of the other.

"Get off me!" said Travis and he used two palms to shove my father back across the room.

Travis scrambled to his feet and rushed out of my bedroom. My father looked proud. He nodded at me and said, "You're welcome." I wasn't sure what to say.

Word of the incident spread quickly through the town, as one might expect. Travis did not stay quiet. His report to his friends via text ended up on Facebook. From Facebook it went to Twitter, Twitter to Instagram, Instagram to Snapchat. After that, it left the ether of cyberspace and ended up in the real world in the form of phone calls to my mother.

My phone rang while I was eating cereal. It was my mom. She never called me while on shift. Occasionally she would text a "Doing OK?" but that was the usual limit of her communication. I swallowed a spoonful of Cheerios and picked up the phone.

"Yeah?" I said.

Her voice was already agitated, excessively punctuated. "Rose! I just got The. Strangest. Call. Do you have some kind of pet? It attacked a boy? Why was there a boy in the house? What is going on with you!"

I put the phone down without saying a word. As I put on my coat and shoes, I could hear my mom continuing to have a one way conversation with herself.

"Well? Well?" she said. "I swear, if you…"

I stopped listening.

My father was sleeping in the living room. I picked him up and put him in my backpack and left the house.

Outside, the morning was thick with fog. It was like it had been raining all night and suddenly someone pressed PAUSE and the rain just stopped and waited for input. The streets were slick wet and empty. I rode my bike, my hands gripped hard on the bars, back to where all this started, the cemetery and the gravestone atop a lonely hill.

My father was silent during the trip, a rarity. Usually he rattled off facts and advice as if it was nothing. He knew.

At the base of the hill, I stepped off my bike and let it fall to the ground. I crouched and swung my backpack in front of me. My father, all two and half feet of him, crawled out of the bag and climbed on top of me. He clutched my chest like a baby.

I walked him up the hill to his grave. I leaned down and he released his grip on me. He laid down on the grass and looked at me with hollow eye sockets that still somehow looked sad.

"Rosie?" he said.

"Yeah?"

"Can I hear it one more time?"

"Sure."

I got down on my knees and leaned my chest towards him. He put one side of his tiny skull against my chest. I could feel my heartbeat reverberate his bone body.

He leaned back, satisfied. "It's strong."

"No," I said. "It's broken."

Culture of Silence

~ W. T. Paterson

The bone broth simmered on the stove as the text from my sister Luna came through. *He hit me, Riley. Again. Broke the necklace.* I turned off the burner and opened the cupboard beneath the sink. Two packed duffle bags ready, our contingency plan, an escape route that never felt like a plan B, but rather something inevitable. We'd meet halfway in the Ozarks if I couldn't talk her down, a cabin tucked deep in the woods away from my New England residence, and far from her adopted Christian, West Texas town.

Breathe, I wrote back. *Suppress the urge to unleash.*

Of course he hit her, the bastard of a husband had no idea, and weak men had an unyielding need to feel strong by attacking those who showed kindness. The weak have a certain self-proclaimed entitlement to fury endowed by their perceived laws of nature. A local Christian radio host with ten thousand daily listeners, my sister's husband Gabe had a following that would blindly side with him should she ever come forward with allegations. That's what scared me the most.

Outside, the day had maybe an hour of sunlight left before the autumn moon declared victory over the sky and I was no stranger to how the full moon brought out the worst in the world. Neighborhood cats mewled under porch steps with deep, guttural warnings. Dogs paced fenced-in yards with hair spiked down their spine. Treebound birds sang in furious prose only to fall as silent as a tomb.

People were no better. They drove like maniac heathens swerving between lanes, jamming on brakes, attempting to break the sound barrier with howling engines, and got into confrontations with total strangers over the most peculiar things. That morning, a neighbor had knocked on my door demanding that the stench from my basement be dealt with.

"Smelting," I told the short, squat man. "A lost art."

"Whatever it is, it stinks," the man said. He thrust his arms and balled hands by his side like a toddler throwing a tantrum. An old New England house with a stone and dirt basement, the previous owners were a family of jewelers from the 1800's and had left behind their kiln, lead pans, and scales. Even though I used an exhaust fan modified into a dryer vent that connected to the furnace chimney, that heavy wet-dog scent fell back toward the earth like a cursed soul instead of up against the heavens into sainthood. I bought, sold, restored, and designed silver jewelry, same as my father.

"I'll see what I can do," I said, pinching my eyes. I reached into my pocket and pulled out a thin silver bracelet. "Take this. As an apology. Made it myself."

The neighbor collected the bracelet in his palm with a side smirk.

"A man ain't supposed to give another man jewelry 'les they . . . you know. You one of them?"

"One of what?" I asked. I knew what the neighbor implied, weak men love to attempt emasculation, but they also crumbled under scrutiny. Watching him squirm held a certain satisfaction.

"It's jus' I ain't seen women comin' and goin'," he said.

"Then I'm like you," I said, and the man's bald head went as red as the leaves on the autumnal trees. "Single. Nasty divorce."

What weak men don't realize is that if you back someone into a corner that knows how to fight, they better take note of their exits. The divorce part wasn't true, but true enough in that it shut the man up. After what happened with my parents, I doubted I'd ever get married.

My neighbor pocketed the bracelet and nodded his way down the steps.

Now as the sun set, I watched him through a window gather with his male friends around a firepit. Their guts pushed against their shirts as round as the moon, bottles of beer in hand, single malt whiskey being passed around, howling with laughter like the faux dog-men they were.

I'm done, Luna wrote. If there was an hour of daylight here, that meant she had two before a cover of darkness might better hide the damage.

What happened? I asked, not to uncover the source and imply that she might be somewhat to blame, but to bide time. If I could get her talking, I could cool her rabid heart.

He. Hit. Me. I'm done with this culture of silence. I speak up, they'll say I deserved it and call me a bitch. I stay quiet, he thinks he's right to do it again.

She got it from my mother, likened herself after the woman, that hot and cold polarity of emotion. Catch her right and she was the kindest, most loyal person on the planet. Cross her or her pups and she'd change into something unholy that made entire neighborhoods cower in fear.

One time, a boy pushed my sister down the twisty slide at the playground. She tumbled across the plastic bends as static shocks nipped at her exposed flesh. My mother leapt to her feet and grabbed the boy by the back of his neck demanding to know where his parents were. The kid pointed to a bench where a guy in untied boots and dirty jeans sipped from a paper bag. She marched over and gave the man the what-for so bad that he collected his son and booked it.

"Sometimes, you gotta show the world you have teeth," our mother told us. We walked home under the canopy of fiery red leaves. It wasn't the worst I'd ever seen her lash out, those times when our father packed us into a car to get away were once in a blue moon, but our mother's sense of justice was a beast in and of itself. My sister had that same thing, that gene that made her snap and change into something feral. Only no one ever saw it really come out because it never had to. Our father was the counterbalance to add perspective because once home, the police showed up to ask questions. They brought my mother to the station.

"But that boy pushed ME," my sister pleaded with my dad, her sad puppy-dog eyes brown and full.

"I know," he sighed. "But when a woman shows the world she has teeth, scared men try to pull them from her mouth. There's nothing more dangerous than scared men in power."

Later, my mother came home. No charges pressed, but my parents argued with their door closed until the small hours of the morning. The next night, my mother wore a brand-new necklace that my father crafted. She needed to feel loved, and jewelry was her love language. It was like she was a different person with that necklace, calm to the stressors of life and care-free. Whatever had been brewing inside of her had been pacified with that necklace. It had been silenced. We never really spoke about it again.

And that boy and his father never once gave us any more trouble beyond hushed whispers in line at the grocer.

Sometimes silence has teeth of its own.

The men next door built their fire too large and gawked at the reaching flame. Their need to destroy and dominate the inanimate spoke to a deep-seeded insecurity of a time that could have been, never was, or falsely yet to come.

Bags are packed, I wrote. *You say the word.*

Fuck the bags, she wrote, and my heart thumped with dread. She meant business and inside of that small, Christian, West Texas town, there'd be hell to pay if she wasn't careful.

But I guess that was kind of her point.

You don't have to do anything, I wrote. *Just leave.*

You sound scared, she wrote. *Stay quiet, no retribution, move on and pretend it's all ok.*

That's not what I meant, and you know it, I wrote.

The night stalked forward swallowing the edges of daylight in its mighty teeth. The laughter of the men next door sounded like wild animals gathered around a carcass jawing and snapping at meaty bones. I pulled open the cupboard with my knee and looked at the packed duffle bags. I'd leave if I had to, but I really didn't want to. After moving so much as kids, this two-story New England house finally had the feel of home, a place where Mom and Dad could visit and be proud.

If they ever came out of hiding, of course.

When my sister told me she'd met someone, I had natural reservations. Not just as a big brother, but real reservations about who this guy pretended to be. Outgoing, polished, and magnetic, he knew how to draw and maintain crowds. That radio voice was the salve to soothe the burns of the exhausted working class, but underneath was a small, terrified boy hiding in the shadows of the man he had become. It was something about the way he interacted with people and bullied them away under the guise of being helpful. Never fully present, never spending too much time with any one person, it was like he was afraid of anyone seeing the real him.

"So, Texas," I said the first time we met. At a barbecue cooking salmon, chicken wings, and ribs, I stood next to the grill watching my sister catch the scent of cooking meats in her nose. Summer food made her the happiest. Gabe smiled his toothy grin and pushed a hand through his salon-quality hair.

"You know what they say about Texas," he said and winked.

"What do they say?" I asked. I flipped the wings and ribs to let the sizzle of the fat roar like applause from a ballgame.

"You know," he said and winked again. He nudged me with his elbow. "Everything's bigger . . . doesn't matter. Hey, would you mind getting me a fresh brew? One more sip and this bottle is dead."

He put a hand on my shoulder and squeezed, then pointed to the plastic tub with ice and bottles along the fence in the backyard. I pulled down the grill cover and went to get him a drink. By the time I came back, he asked if the food was ready.

Luna met him at a charity event, one of those minor league baseball nights where a cut of the gate went to wildlife preservation. She got selected from the crowd to play the line drive challenge where people stood in the outfield as professional batters nailed balls toward the fence. Whoever caught the most won $100, plus a special shoutout in the charity's monthly newsletter.

Luna loved minor league ballgames. The crack of the bat, the fast pitches, the constant game of catch, she was in her element near the field. When her name got pulled, she hustled to the bathroom to pee before making her way out onto the stretch of green.

The first two contestants didn't catch anything. They both high tailed it from center field, to right, to left. The third got lucky and caught a looping fly ball, but when Luna took to the grass and loaded up on her haunches, she watched the batters and their fly balls with an almost obsessive focus. She caught every single line drive and I sat back thinking the jig was up.

Gabe, impressed by her performance, introduced himself and explained his status in that Christian, West Texas town before asking her on a date.

"You sure?" I asked her later that night after she explained how she had a good feeling about this one. Luna smiled and nodded.

"Everyone has a role, everyone has a place," she said. Christian towns tended to let outsiders know real quick if they were welcome or not. Most often, they silently demanded that a person play their expected part and not deviate. Something about a man's role and a woman's place, a mindset stuck in a bygone era.

"And if he expects you to just . . . obey?" I asked.

"It can be satisfying knowing what someone wants, and then giving it to them," Luna said, and I could see in her face that she'd made up her mind.

That night, I packed the plan B bags just to be safe.

Outside, the men around the fire pointed to the ground-level windows of my basement. My neighbor seemed to be explaining to them about the silver and gold I kept down there for smelting. He held up the bracelet and made an obscene, airy gesture with his hand and pranced around in a circle. His buddies laughed, but one of them asked to see the bracelet.

"It's yours," my neighbor said, and his friend slid the bracelet on. He admired it in the flickering light of the fire. The irony seemed lost on my neighbor.

The first time Gabe hit my sister, she told me at a local flea market while we waded through the aisles looking for trinkets and treasures. The sun-bleached wooden tables threatened splinters to the unaware. Vendors puffed at cigarettes and barked with promises that all prices were negotiable.

"Leave him," I said. She'd come to visit for a week to let the dust settle.

"I can't," she said. "The community would hate me."

"Who cares?" I said. I bent over and picked up an old pocket watch. It had stopped at 11:58. Two minutes to midnight, or midday.

"That's $30," the vendor said, an older woman with wrinkles so deep that they cast their own shadows.

"For tin?" I asked.

"That's copper," the woman said. I looked at the watch again. It wasn't copper. It still maintained its shine, even though the date etched into the back read 1920.

"Copper oxidizes and turns green. Tin doesn't. This is tin," I said and put it back on the table. The woman picked up the watch and held it close to her eyes, then called out for her husband to come take a look. The tone in her voice lilted with betrayal.

"You're so good at seeing things for what they are," Luna said.

"Leave him," I said again, and Luna pawed at me like I was playing.

"Let's not talk about it anymore," she said, and shoved everything down to that dark place inside of her that collected pain and guilt, that dark inner kiln that altered the physical makeup of everything locked within.

I should have listened, Luna wrote. *Especially after what happened with Mom.*

You're not Mom, I wrote.

She passed on the bitch, Luna wrote.

Our parents left in the night when I was twenty and Luna was seventeen. Our mother had fallen into one of her moods after a drunk man assaulted her and the cops passed it off by saying the attacker was just drunk and fooling around, to let it go, that he never intended to hurt her. My mother's bruised wrist and swollen cheek told a different story.

My father packed their stuff. He said we'd understand one day, that my sister and I needed to leave this place at dawn and change our names, but to not go outside before then, that it was my job to look after Luna. Though we followed his commands and sloshed through the bleeding streets lined with limbs at sunup, the pain of abandonment never healed.

When Luna left for Texas, I thought she'd be able to handle herself. I gave her a silver necklace fashioned from our mother's old jewelry to double down, to let her know I cared. Love languages and such.

But with the necklace broken and tensions rising like the fur on a dog's back, I felt only failure.

Call me, I wrote. My phone buzzed and I answered halfway through the first ring.

"I'm sorry to drag you into this," Luna said, and my heart dropped.

"Be better than her," I whispered, and through the receiver Luna whimpered.

"Weak men . . ." she said. "I'll see you at the cabin."

Over the phone, I heard the tearing of flesh and painful cries of a body in transformation. Luna grunted and coughed as I imagined thick fur tearing through tender skin. Outside, the darkness had settled, and the full moon stood victorious in the dark sky. Shadows had already begun to fall over that Christian, West Texas town that would never see morning. I heard panting, then the gruesome snapping of jaws.

She was her mother's daughter alright.

As the call went dead, the men next door howled. They peeled off their shirts and swung them like helicopter blades above their heads, their back hair and chest hair patchy and thinning. Whatever they thought they were, they weren't.

I grabbed the bags and dumped the bone broth down the sink. Steam rose and fogged the windows creating momentary privacy as I killed the lights, said goodbye to the house that had finally begun feeling like home, and escaped through the front door.

That culture of silence works both ways.

Along the twisting backroads of my small New England town, the moon pierced the tips of the trees to create shadows in the forest where, if I squinted and looked away, I could vaguely make out the shape of my mother and father waving goodbye.

Small Packages

~ Nina Kiriki Hoffman

Sarah opened the new box of Cheerios and worked the waxed bag open. Lo and behold, there was a small package inside amongst the honey-nut goodness.

Cereal boxes hadn't had prizes in them in decades, but Sarah lived in hope. She had been waiting twenty-five years for a decoder ring. She couldn't read the messages the aliens sent through her email. She printed them out and kept them in a file folder, waiting for this day.

She snipped off the end of the prize package and shook the prize out onto the turquoise kitchen table of her small condo.

Not a decoder ring. It was a red plastic heart.

Frowning, she opened the heart. It had a message inside:

"Meet me at Burrows Coffee Shop at 5:30."

No signature.

She figured aliens would be able to beam a decoder ring into the exact cereal box she had plucked from a wall of cereal boxes at the SuperMart. They knew where to find her.

But no, some rando had put a message in a cereal box, not knowing who was going to open it. Or when. Or where. Had this come from the General Mills factory? Were they talking about a coffee shop in wherever General Mills was?

There was a Burrows Coffee Shop two blocks from the library where Sarah worked, and she got off at five. Couldn't hurt to drop by. She got coffee there all the time anyway.

She picked up the message and sniffed it. It smelled like lavender, her least favorite essential oil.

Could she like anybody who sent a lavender-scented note?

It was only a day until Valentine's Day. If a boyfriend had sent her a plastic heart, she would wonder. A cheap and easily breakable heart didn't bode well for a relationship. Then again, she'd never even had a boyfriend, so maybe a bad one was better than nothing.

She liked the school-kid Valentines they sold at supermarkets, cartoon characters and superheroes talking about friendship. She bought a package every year to hand out to everybody at the library. She still remembered how sad she'd been in grade school when she only got a Valentine from her best friend Basima, and other people were getting sacks of them. Sarah always bought a Valentine for everybody in her class, but other people didn't.

Everybody should get a little Valentine's magic.

Other people at the library had started passing out kid Valentines, too, following her lead. Basima, who worked at the library too, was the first, but not the only.

Sarah poured out a bowl of Cheerios, added milk, and took a bite. She tucked the message back in the heart and put the heart in her giant green purse, with all the other things she might possibly need in the course of her day —protein bars, a pretend ray gun she sometimes waved at noisy children in the storytelling circle to make them settle down, a first aid kit, a phone charger, a small pad of colored paper so she could write notes to people who misbehaved, a roll of tape to tape the notes up with, Sharpies, assorted fountain pens, Tampax, her wallet and keys.

She had just rinsed out her cereal bowl when she noticed an alien on the kitchen table. It looked like a cockroach, but its wildly waving antennae were golden, and its wing cases had symbols on them in gold — she recognized the glyphs from the alien emails, which she had studied without success.

"Hello," she said. "I hope you come in peace." She opened the Cheerios box and took out three Cheerios. She put them on the table in front of the bug.

Its metallic antennae waved independently of each other. She wished she knew cockroach or alien sign language. It fell on the Cheerios and ate them.

She put down five more before she rerolled the bag and closed the box. As much as she longed for alien contact, she didn't want things eating her food before she could.

The roach ate three more Cheerios, then waved its antennae and bobbed its head at her. She wasn't sure what that meant. She left the last two Cheerios on the table for the alien to snack on later. "Do you have anything to tell me?" she asked.

The roach bobbed its head.

"Oh! That's interesting! But I don't speak your language, and I have to get to work. Maybe we can work out a code later?"

It bobbed again.

She left it and headed for the library.

After work, she stood in the door of Burrows and looked around. How was she supposed to recognize the person who'd sent her the message?

How likely was it that the message was a prank, and there would never be anyone waiting in a coffee shop for her? About ninety-eight point five percent. Still, Burrows had the best Danish in town. She could get a raspberry Danish and maybe share it with the alien roach when she went home.

Only one person sat at a table. Basima, her best friend. Basima lifted a hand and wiggled fingers at Sarah.

Sarah went to the counter and ordered a latte and a Danish, then joined Basima at the table. "Did you send me a message?" Sarah asked.

"Maybe."

Sarah dug around in her purse and found the heart. "Was it this?"

Basima had been at her house on New Year's Eve. They always celebrated together by watching old movies and toasting with Martinelli's cider at midnight. Basima knew her way around Sarah's kitchenette. She could have put the heart in the cereal then.

Basima smiled at her. "How long have we been friends?"

"Since we were six," Sarah said. They had met in kindergarten, and gone through grade school, middle school, and high school together. They had gone to college together to get their degrees in library science. They had roomed together all four years of the undergraduate program, and then Basima had gone for her Master's, while Sarah went to work.

"Have you ever felt a spark between us?" asked Basima.

"What?" Sarah said. She had had crushes on boys all her life, and never acted on them. She lifted a finger and held it out to Basima, who lifted her own index finger and reached toward Sarah. She stopped half an inch from Sarah's finger, and Sarah brought her finger closer. A spark jumped between them. "Whoa!"

"I got tired of waiting for you to figure it out," Basima said, and then blushed and stared at the table top.

Sarah bit her lip. Here was Basima, her best friend, finally letting her know something new to Sarah. Sarah, who could talk to cockroaches, but was often tongue-tied when it came to people. Things would be so much easier if Basima was an alien.

"Do you have a decoder ring?" Sarah asked.

Basima blinked, then looked up at her, wide-eyed. "As a matter of fact," she said, reaching into her giant orange purse, "I do."

"Wanna come home and meet my alien cockroach?" asked Sarah.

The Ducks Opened the Hostilities

~ Mattia Ravasi

The ducks opened the hostilities by murdering my cat.

I'd seen them loitering around the edge of my back garden all week. The fence along the right side had sunk in the mud during Winter; there were several spots along the bottom where the pests could squeeze through. A handyman was supposed to come look at the fence in April, but then the dreadful business with the virus occurred, and no one showed up.

I was leaning over the breakfast counter, sipping my coffee and scrolling through emails on my laptop. I looked out between a message and the next, checking on Kipfel. His back was straight and low to the ground, and he was staring at the trees at the back of the garden. I thought he'd found a vole. He loved gutting the little things, but couldn't manage it without getting scratched and bitten, and moaning for me to take him to the vet.

I didn't register what was happening—I was reading an email from my manager, badgering me to start using the latest ghastly software the company had purchased to "speed up our march to modernization," and make our jobs easier to outsource—until I heard Kipfel hiss. Perhaps that was how he roared. Perhaps he was already in pain.

When I looked up, he had a duck in his claws. Four other birds had their beaks on his tail and hind legs. His tail was shaven—he'd had eczema recently—and must have been very sensitive. He gave up easily.

They hammered away, pecking wherever they could reach, not leaving him enough air to hiss again. I could hear this wet piercing noise all the way through the double glazing. The attack put me in mind of a scene from one of those very serious, very violent American dramas my colleagues were always raving about, one that I'd started watching during lockdown. This tall fat Mexican is crossing a prison cafeteria, when suddenly four skinheads surround him, and start puncturing him with shivs made from sharpened toothbrushes.

Shiv shiv shiv, made the toothbrushes in the Mexican's guts, going in and out like a sewing machine through a skirt.

Shiv shiv shiv made the beaks into Kipfel.

I stood, horrified, howling noiselessly, looking not quite at the massacre but just to the side of it. I said to myself that it was too late to intervene, although this was perhaps a lie, told in self-defense or out of cowardice.

They didn't eat him. When I could force myself to walk outside, I saw that his fur was matted with blood, but he was otherwise intact. He was an old cat. Perhaps his heart stopped from fear alone.

The ducks had disappeared into the trees. There's supposed to be a fence at the back of those, too, and that one isn't sunken or torn, to my knowledge, but I didn't have the guts to go and check.

I called the handyman to see if we could schedule a new date for repairing the fence. He didn't pick up. I tried again over the next few days, to no avail.

I told Peter about it when I next emailed him. Discussing the event, however briefly, helped me process my grief and fear. I asked him if the ducks' behavior was normal: he's supposed to know a lot about poultry.

He replied somewhat prissily that what I had were probably mallards. *If I were there, Deborah, I would fix that fence*, he concluded. *I would protect you.*

I have had my share of gentlemen pining after me. I was once considered, if not a great beauty, at least "a fit bird," as a hirsute Geordie once described me to his mates in the Trout pub. In my experience, the most romantic men are also the most predatorial. They will jump on any chance to make their feelings known, however cowardly and obliquely, and will reiterate their existence at every turn. You can't tell them about your mauled cat without them proposing they move in with you.

☉

I think what made me such a fit bird was a certain degree of exoticism. My family moved to England from a Bayern town called Deggendorf in 1963, when I was eight. Apparently, I took the move badly: I resented leaving the cozy microcosm of our tiny town, with toy stores, boutiques, and bakeries just downstairs from our apartment, in favor of the empty countryside outside Oxford. My parents used to relish their memories of my childish angst, but I remember nothing of Deggendorf at all.

How exotic could you be as a West German in England, you may ask. Quite a bit. There weren't many non-English families around, not in 1970 Yarnton. Oxford itself had a faint claim to cosmopolitanism—nothing like what it is today—but the foreigners there all belonged to the university, which made them as untouchable as their English blokes. They weren't Australian or Mexican: they belonged to the egalitarian nation of the posh.

My hair was a different blonde than the other girls'. I had wider cheekbones, and I was taller. The recent crimes of my nation fascinated people, who looked at me with great curiosity, pondering the ungaugable depths of human evil.

Melvin was the first boyfriend who didn't study my face that way. Some days he watched me in adoration. Other times he barely glanced my way, especially when Tottenham was playing. All my life I have been plagued by the most uncomfortable thoughts, and one that used to bring me great misery was a suspicion that perhaps my love of Melvin was founded on this basic fact: that he took me for granted, and never thought of me as special.

The fear has gone now, as all my fears, no matter how rancid, eventually do. Looking back on them is always a sorry business. I contemplate the anxiety and sadness they caused me, and weep for all that lost serenity. So what if that's why I loved him? As if we can even figure out the mechanics of such a maddening thing as love.

After we got married, Melvin and I bought a house in Binsey, where I still live. It's a small village perched just beyond the marshy fields of Port Meadow, a half-hour walk from Oxford city center. Not that I go into town much these days, what with the plague and all.

☉

Two days after Kipfel died I put my mixing bowl on the scale and measured out 750 grams of strong baking flour. I mixed in yeast, salt, a tablespoon of sugar, and a bottle of rat poison. I poured in half a liter of water, lukewarm from the kettle, and kneaded the mixture till it got plump and stretchy, slamming and slapping and folding it on the floured table. Baking is hard work, if you do it properly. I covered the dough with a cloth and left it to raise for an hour in the cupboard by the boiler.

This course of action caused me great distress. I wasn't facing any moral dilemma (one way or another, the ducks must go), but the plan required me to sacrifice an awful lot of flour. These days, that stuff is worth its weight in gold. It disappeared altogether from supermarket shelves early during the national lockdown. The local mills, from which I shop, all had to close down, unable to cope with demand. (One of them, in Islip, published a confusing post on their archaic website, rambling about a "raid" they had been subjected to.) The luxury delis, which abound around Oxford, only stock extravagant varieties, like seitan or stone-milled quinoa, going for ten, twelve pounds a kilo.

Not that I had any first-hand experience of empty aisles and cut-throat delis. I only knew about it from my colleagues' chitchat, and from their increasingly worried updates during the Team Tea Breaks we were forced to attend remotely every Wednesday afternoon, to Foster Corporate Camaraderie and Keep In Touch.

I scoured the table with cleaning products while my poison loaf was in the oven. I left it in longer than needed, to make it extra crusty. I let it cool until the evening, then smashed it into crumbs.

I turned the garden lights on and scattered the crumbs in piles all around. I was terrified. I'd been studying the garden through an upstairs window, peeping from behind the curtain to make sure the coast was clear, but my mind still latched onto every stretch of darkness, those draped between the trees and the vast endlessness beyond the fence, transforming them into the contours of dripping, probing, pustulent monstrosities, lashing out to torment me.

The final pile of crumbs I left just under the trees at the back of the garden. It was the furthest I'd been from the house since the beginning of lockdown. All my groceries had been delivered by exhausted Sainsbury's drivers, the apples and bananas carefully picked for maximum bruises.

I work in academic publishing. I assist the editors of scholarly journals, make sure we publish the occasional issue to schedule, and that we don't go too crazy with the page budget. I follow the directives of the manic-depressives in our editorial department, whose job, as I understand it, is to go on two-week work retreats to Scotland, and to strike publishing deals that we will never be able to honor over drinks and blow in SoHo clubs.

The academic editors I work with vary greatly in personality, from the exquisite to the oblivious to the violently abusive. Many of them work in academia because they lack the basic survival skills that would ensure their success in any normal field of employment. Had they been born in Barnsley, they would be pushing tinned tomatoes across the bottom shelves in Aldi—assuming Barnsley's Aldis, unlike the local ones, are still well-stocked and operating—but because they aced the parent lottery, they became the deans of All Souls instead.

Peter sits somewhere in the middle of the spectrum. He's imperious and curt, intolerant of mistakes although frequently blundering himself, prone to panicking if his emails aren't instantly acknowledged. Yet he is in love with me, which dulls his sharper edges, and gives him a certain drippy niceness.

I only met him once, at an editor meeting in 1989. He was annoyed about certain late issues, and I don't think he looked me in the eye throughout the meeting. At the time, our correspondence was all handled via post and fax: article proofs would be mailed, corrections returned in incomprehensible scribbles I would then transliterate and forward to our typesetter. Maximum chances for error at every step. Then, sometime in the mid-00s, email became our medium of choice, we transferred all our data into cranky, byzantine tracking software, until finally, in 2016, the company cut back on office space, and introduced its semi-forced homeworking policy. They were years ahead of the curve, it turned out.

Peter's feelings became clear around that time, first through veiled hints I could still choose to disregard, later via blatant declarations worded carefully enough not to hold up in court, in case I reported him for harassment. All these years I've never known what brought along the change in him. Perhaps my email personality is different from my handwritten one. My hands get cramped easily, and I never stretch a letter longer than I must, but I'm very wordy on a keyboard. Perhaps emailing editors from my kitchen and living room collapsed that professional distance that existed when I was still commuting into my depressing cubicle, where decorations were only allowed if they bore the company logo. I might have become friendlier in my greetings and farewells, and certain men—I don't assume Peter has had much experience with the ladies in his six decades on Earth—latch onto any kindness that is shown to them as an excuse to fall in love, and give the misery of their life the sexy sheen of unrequited passion. Perhaps Peter has loved me since 1989, and that's why he couldn't meet my eye during that meeting: the heat of my gorgeousness would scorch his eyes, and wet his pants, if he witnessed it directly. He had been waiting ever since, and only made his first move a respectful few years after my husband passed away in 2014.

I've been dying to ask him, but it would be too cruel. Showing any interest would only stoke his hope.

I don't love Peter back by the way, bless him. I don't wish him any harm, but he's a bit of a twat.

When I woke up the next morning I looked into the garden, and saw dead magpies close to two of the crumb mounds. No sign of the ducks.

I let out a very crass German expletive when I walked into the kitchen. I'd thought I could hear sounds in the night, but I'd imagined them to be rooted in my dreams, and there was no way anyway that I would leave my locked bedroom while it was dark.

I saw muddy prints all around the floor. The cupboard door under the counter had been pulled open. The food inside had been strewn all around, but most of it seemed uneaten: potatoes, carrots, a sad withered leek. Then I noticed that my biscuit tin had been opened. I bake shortbread every Sunday afternoon, to have with my crime novels on the couch before going to bed. There had been five days' worth of biscuits in that tin. The intruders vacuumed them all up, leaving no crumb behind.

The prints all converged on the cat flap in the kitchen door.

I sealed the flap shut using an entire roll of duct tape. Duck tape? Ha. Lately I've been wondering if I'm completely sane.

Then again, haven't I always?

I baked a loaf of bread for my dinner that afternoon. I spent the entire night on the loo. I was certain that my putrefied body would be found on the bathroom floor seven months from now, calcified waste still crusting the toilet bowl, testifying to the agony of my final moments.

I suppose some traces of rat poison must have lingered in the oven, and that I ate them with my bread. Smashing. If my oven was out, I wasn't sure how long I'd survive. I didn't have much food around the house, except for those bags of strong flour, and I doubted I'd be able to get a food delivery. All that my colleagues seemed to talk about these days was how hard it had gotten to book a delivery slot.

At the apex of my agony, when it felt like the cramps were tearing a hole through my gut, I dialed 999. I waited an eternity with my phone pressed to my ear. These days my joints are so sore even holding the phone to my face is painful, but the distress was a welcome distraction from the harsher burning in my bowels. Nobody answered. This is preposterous, I thought. How bad can this virus be, that they can't spare a nurse to answer 999 calls? I blamed the Conservative and proto-Conservative governments that had stripped the National Health Service of its resources. I blamed the 999 operator, which I imagined as a chavvy young woman posting pictures of herself on whatever ghastly app was popular this week, ignoring the LEDs flashing red on her terminal. I blamed the ducks.

The next morning I reported the whole accident to my colleagues in a long, somewhat rambling email. (I'm not usually one for reaching out to colleagues, be it for comfort, support, God forbid chitchat.)

I left out the turbodiarrhea, but stressed my indignation at the lack of response from the emergency services.

I must have shocked them, I thought around noon, when I saw that nobody had replied yet. But nobody ever replied to that email.

That the world was still there I could testify by climbing the ladder to the attic—no small feat, let me tell you—and looking through the tiny round window up there, which overlooks the neighbor's houses and the hedge-lined fields beyond, and gives me a view, very far in the distance, of the tiniest segment of the A34 speedway. I could see vehicles driving up and down. Trucks, mostly, with the occasional car.

Those thoughts I mentioned, which used to cause me such a great deal of pain, remained a terrifying mystery to me until the day I attended a 10 am editor meeting in a drab, dark pub just outside Paddington Station. I was meeting the chair of some psychology society, trying to persuade them to keep publishing their journal with my company.

It was clear from the start that I would make no progress, and that the bloke was only meeting me as a professional courtesy. I didn't resent him. I always considered my company cheap and un-professional, and my opinion of him instantly improved when I re-alized he was abandoning us.

I had traveled all the way to London, and going back too ear-ly would mean having to spend the afternoon in the office. Even though we had no deal to strike, I asked the bloke if he wanted to join me for lunch. On me: a farewell gift from his old publisher.

We ate fish and chips—back then it still tasted proper, none of this modern gastropub beastliness—and had a very nice chat. He was a reserved man, with a kinky beard and stupidly small glasses. Great listener. I'd had a drink or two, and he wasn't saying much, so eventually I started talking about my problems. Maybe he'd be able to assist me, seeing how he belonged to the psychiatric profession. "Psychology," he corrected me, while nodding somewhat tiredly. I was guarded and euphemistic at first, but the gates had been opened, and soon it was all gushing out. All my life, I said, I'd been plagued by the most horrendously disjointed spontaneous thoughts. There were days where every flab of cloth brought to mind breasts and genitalia. Times when I couldn't clap eyes on another human without thinking of cannibalism. Not to mention the tangled grottiness of the putrid sexual images that sometimes plagued me.

What I found devastating weren't the thoughts per se. Those were, after all, just thoughts. The horrid thing was the fear that accompanied them: a terrible dread that they might be a symptom of some hidden impulse. That they betrayed an evil nested within me, like a snake coiled around my organs.

The man kept nodding through my explanation. "Sounds like obsessive-compulsive disorder," he said once I was finished. That struck me as preposterous. I thought that the term only applied to those blokes who need to put away their Monopoly with all the houses and hotels precisely right in the box. "The mind fixates on things," he continued, "and associates images, often of a violent or repulsive nature, with certain stimuli. In cases of obsessive disorder, these correlations can become calcified in place, and cause great distress. If you find them bothersome, talk to your GP. They'll recommend therapy or anxiolytics."

And that was it. All those years I'd been carrying that worry inside me, and this silly sod came along and put a name to it, and explained it away. It staggers me that we all walk around with the solution to each other's problems stored away within us, in our experiences and in the lessons we've learned, and yet we have not come up with any efficient system for sharing this knowledge. Except for books, I suppose. And who reads books these days?

I lived off tea for two days. When I felt that I could hold it down, I made a soup out of those carrots and potatoes in the cupboard. (The leek had sprouted a yellow beard, and I thought it best to avoid it.) It was thin and bland, but it tasted like life. I struggle to remember a meal I enjoyed more in recent years. Perhaps the last time Melvin and I ate out, at a sausage pub in Jericho called The Big Bang, his favorite place in the world. (They closed shortly after he died, his frequent patronage the only thing keeping them afloat.) We had some marvelous turnip mash, milky and velvety, with salt crystals peppered across its surface to pack a little burst of flavor with every forkful. We laughed, we joked, we ate to our bursting point. It was a good night.

It took all my self-control not to devour all the soup in one sitting. I poured two thirds of it in plastic containers, and stored them in the fridge for tomorrow's meals. This felt so cruel that I ended up sulking at my own wisdom.

All through the day I'd been scouring the oven with my most aggressive cleaning products, breathing in their toxic vapors, determined to erase all traces of poison. When I woke up the next morning I sighed, took out the flour, and baked the tiniest loaf of my life. I had a quarter of it for lunch. My bowels did not liquefy.

I finished the loaf that night with the second portion of soup. I slept like a baby, and woke up feeling rejuvenated. My oven was back in business. Everything would be all right.

I walked out into the garden to deal with the dead magpies. I shouldn't have left it so long, but I was hoping a fox would take them out of my hands. I guess foxes are too clever to eat poisoned birds. Or perhaps they all went wherever it is that 999 has gone.

I pulled on my thick plastic gloves and stuffed the slimy birds in a binbag. Not that my bins had been emptied at any time in the recent past. Kipfel was still in there, a disturbing and potentially dangerous fact I was doing a great job of ignoring. (A fun fact about the human mind: legitimate concerns are so much easier to dismiss than irrational fears.)

When I got up, with some difficulty, from leaning forward over the second bird, I saw a line of ducks, seven or eight of them, staring at me from beyond the fence.

My eyes darted to the door, and I saw that the outside of the cat flap, which I'd taped shut, was covered in scratches and dents. Beak marks.

I charged at the ducks, who scattered around the field, quacking indignantly as they took off. I took the dead magpies out of the binbag and threw them at the enemy. I missed. The magpies are still out there, by now little more than untroubled tufts of feathers and bones.

☉

I asked Peter how dangerous ducks could be. He said that duck farmers contract salmonella a few times a year as a matter of course. When I pressed him for more information—how did they fare in *conventional* warfare?—he got unpleasant, and evasive.

Peter is the editor of the *International Review of Poultry Studies*. You'd think he should know about ducks. But his area of expertise is geese.

Academics, in my experience, tend to embrace the view that their superior knowledge of their field of study, the fact that they're such valuable members of society, excuses them from adhering to most societal norms—of politeness, responsiveness, punctuality. But for all that they're such geniuses they can't even tell you how actually dangerous a sodding duck can be.

The day after our confrontation in the garden, the ducks came into my house again.

I heard a scuttling noise at dawn, too loud for me to pretend it was outside. I made my way down the stairs, and saw muddy prints along the hall. They headed, unsurprisingly, into the kitchen, but I followed them the other way, to their source. The ducks had pushed up one of the sash windows in Carl's bedroom, and trailed mud across the bed and carpet.

I lost it. I ran into the kitchen, where three ducks were tearing at the half loaf I'd left under a cloth on the counter. I picked up the cloth from the floor and whipped them, forgetting the old wisdom about cornered animals.

They took flight, brushing past me on their way out. I covered my face. My arms got scratched. I'm not sure if they attacked me deliberately, or if their feet simply grazed me as they went by.

They flew down the hall and out the window, which I slammed closed, and locked. I collapsed on Carl's muddy bed, and spent a long time studying my scratches.

Carl was our son. He always had a strong sense of justice, and he was passionate about music. He was in a band in high school that only played covers of this rock group called the Stiff Little Fingers, a name I always found enormously rude, even though it actually isn't. Melvin used to give him a hard time about that band. "Your songs are terrible," he would say, "and they're not even *yours*."

Carl had a few girlfriends, held a few jobs, but never anything serious. He had a car accident during a trip to Italy when he was thirty, and died.

I think about Carl the same way I think about my neuroses. It's all part of life. I say to myself that thirty years on Earth are not nothing: that during that time, Carl was loved, and frequently happy. But it's like telling myself that my anxieties are a condition, unfortunate but documented, endurable. It makes it bearable, most of the time; but the sorrow never goes away.

Melvin was never cruel to me, never *actively* nasty, but a couple of times, when I was trying to explain the nature of my anxieties to him—the obstinacy of my morbid thoughts—he replied in a way that wounded me deeply. "You Germans," he said, too exasperated by his own impossible problems to know how to deal with mine. "Always obsessed with cruelty."

I baked a fresh loaf. I locked all the windows except for one, in the living room.

Two days later, at the first light of dawn, I heard the ducks push that window up and drop onto the floor. They were stealthier this time, and made very little noise as they waddled down the hall.

I left my hiding spot on top of the stairs and sneaked toward the kitchen. I found them clustered around my bread, which they'd dragged to the floor.

I lunged forward and closed my hand around a duck's neck. A female. She thrashed her wings and paddled with her feet in the air, trying perhaps to tear at my skin. Her resistance only increased my determination, making it easier to be forceful with her. I clutched her under my arm, immobilizing her, and took the kitchen knife out of my robe's pocket.

Her companions had stopped eating and were quacking furiously at me. They seemed paralyzed between flight and violence. I looked down at them with great hate, and they looked up at me with whatever they had inside them—duck faces always seem to express blunt annoyance.

I have to do it, I thought. These pests need to go. They'll give me salmonella. Steal all my bread. The first step of my extermination plan was a few millimeters away: the tip of my knife was resting on the duck's breast, and she was struggling less frantically every second, perhaps because I was squeezing her too hard.

And yet my mind was at work with a lucidity I'd never known before. I was trying desperately to come up with a solution that did not involve bloodshed. How ironic, after a lifetime plagued by violent and repulsive thoughts, to find out I was incapable of inflicting harm—and by ironic I mean sodding preposterous.

These ducks are hungry, I thought. They must have gotten addicted to carbs from all the bread they were fed when people were still allowed outside their house. I had flour. I had bread. I could keep it all to myself, sure: but what for? To keep living indefinitely in my inescapable house, seeing the world around me shut down bit by bit, carrying on throughout it all with my irrelevant, menial job?

I dropped my prisoner. She was flying before she'd even touched the floor. I didn't try to cover my face, but nobody scratched me on their way out.

Things got weird after that.

It wasn't the following day, and to be honest I couldn't say exactly how long after our confrontation this was—my mind was sluggish for a few days, probably as a comedown from that adrenaline burst in the kitchen—but eventually the ducks appeared again. They sat in a wonky semicircle outside my front door.

They must have seen that I was a softie. I baked a loaf, crumbled it up, and brought it out. How they knew this one wasn't poisoned is beyond me.

There are two encampments around my house, one in the back garden, one on the front lawn. I tried to count the ducks in both, and reached a total of fifteen, but the figure is insignificant, as ducks come and go, and the camps seem to swell some days, and to be nearly abandoned on others.

I bake a loaf every two days, and hand it out in the morning. You'd think the ducks would have figured the schedule out, and perhaps they have, but either way they stay out there all the time, even on non-feeding days.

I'm well aware they might simply be keeping an eye on me. Making sure I do not leave.

How in the world, you may ask, do you still have enough flour to feed all these ducks. That's the weirdest part. I was running low on strong flour, and would have soon been forced to use plain flour for my bread (civilization truly is collapsing) when one night, after sunset, the ducks on my front lawn started quacking very loud.

I got out and showed them my bare hands—no bread until tomorrow morning!—but they turned around and started walking down the street. Once they reached the corner, they turned and called again.

There are only a handful of houses and cottages in Binsey, plus a pub, The Perch, whose late-night crowds of posh revelers used to be the bane of my sleep. The ducks led me past my neighbors' homes. We were violating quarantine—well, *I* was—but there was no one around to rat me out.

We got to a house painted peach and white, with a half-timbered first floor. Fancy. The ducks quacked for me to swing open the gate in the picket fence, and they guided me to the back garden.

The kitchen window had been opened, doubtlessly with the same burglary skills I'd already witnessed. It was close enough to the back door that I could reach my arm in, turn the key in the lock, and walk inside. Nobody was home, and there was no car in the driveway. I remembered two ghastly BMWs, and assumed that the owners must have fled to some even grander manor, deeper into the countryside.

The ducks tapped the cupboard under the sink with their beaks. Inside, I found a dozen 1.5 kg bags of stockpiled flour. Organic and local: the good stuff.

Most of the food in the fridge had spoiled, but I shopped freely from the cupboards. I left the backdoor open on my way out. Let the squirrels go crazy.

☉

The cars still drive along the A34 whenever I go into my attic to check. (Have there been fewer of them recently? Hard to tell.) Peter still replies to my emails, although with less gusto and grease than before. Some of my colleagues have started showing up at the virtual tea breaks again. The ducks are hungry. I don't feel lonely.

The Pack

~ *Christi Nogle*

I should never have let Lee move us out here. All that time we were hooked into Zillow, I secretly prayed she'd fixate on one with a smaller lot and higher square footage. Instead, we opted for acreage bordering public land, the house little more than an afterthought: one room for living, one for sleeping, one bathroom with the washer and dryer wrenched in, and a sloping lean-to added on to serve as workshop, guest room, storage for dog supplies and yes, kitchen. It was Lee's choice; I couldn't deny her.

Oh, but the outside made up for it those first few years. We were happy. Though there was nothing to see in town, Lee would drive in whenever we wanted and then, this: the thriving garden, the new puppy, the picnics and hikes. Lee trained all three dogs to be safe off-leash, which I'd never thought could happen. I planted flowers everywhere and trained morning glories, wisteria and orange-flowering trumpet vines up the walls to cover the ugly lean-to. We brought a tree guy out to prune the little orchard. The trees thanked us with so much fruit we had to take up canning.

Our bodies changed shape. We grew fatter from all the home cooking while our legs narrowed and toned from hiking and our arms grew brawny from woodcutting and gardening.

The truth was we both felt awfully fit up until Lee started getting the breaks. First was the fractured arm—a yellowjacket stung while she was high on a ladder picking apples. That one could have happened to anyone. It healed up right on schedule and then things just seemed to snowball: a fall on a hike and the ankle was screwed up, and it healed, and then a slip in the bathroom shattered her wrist, then the dogs didn't see Lee while they were running. She took a terrible crash to her ribs. We spent weeks in the city running up bills not just for the treatments and hospital room but also hotels, food, gas, dog boarding. Osteoporosis, the likely cause, was ruled out early. There didn't seem to be anything wrong with Lee's bones. What was making the accidents happen, then? It seemed like they investigated every little thing, her brain and inner ear to her toe-joints. In the end, all agreed that the series of breaks had been all coincidence.

Only now, between the lingering pain and the fear, Lee just about couldn't move. I didn't like to focus on it, but the bills would send me back to work. Not just a job (if indeed I could find one) but a commute. Little traffic, one would hope, but bad roads in the winter and deer shooting into the road.

The place was paid for, but I feared we'd lose it if the debt got too bad. Sometimes I felt we had already lost everything and just didn't know it yet. Other times I felt that fear was silly, something that could never happen, a sign of my losing it. We were both getting squirrely, but I tried to hide my own irrationality, tried to be strong for Lee.

Nothing got taken care of all that time. Vegetables froze in the garden, and with the thaw, the vines went wild. New ones with white-and-celadon blossoms joined and then overtook the rest. The trees went unpruned, fruit falling onto the ground, drawing wild-life, freezing and thawing to stink.

The dogs were distressed from being boarded and then neglect-ed at home. I felt I didn't know these creatures who lost their cool chasing things off the property, sending me out into the forest with a flashlight, so helpless and small—scared of falling and breaking something myself, or being shot by a hunter. Even more, I feared that the dogs might be shot or break their legs.

I was always living through worst-case scenes, it seemed.

I hadn't been afraid of the woods with Lee, but it was different now. The first few times the dogs ran off in the night, I hyperven-tilated and bawled the whole time I searched. I resolved to chain them, which broke my heart all over again. They sat quietly indoors but would jump up and beg to go out whenever I made a move. They hated the chains but hated more to be inside with us.

Lee stayed in bed sweating and thrashing in terrible nightmares. I slept thinly on the bed's outer edge until Lee begged me to go elsewhere in case I might break her in my sleep. I carried my pillow into the lean-to and headed for the futon where we'd hoped some wandering relative or old friend might sleep one day. I stopped, gasped.

The vines had come inside the lean-to and made themselves at home, coiling around the futon frame, threading into the stove burners, groping into the bag of dog food with their spiny fingers. I'd heated up something or other on the stove not too long ago, so that infestation was new, but the other encroachments might not have been so new. Who'd been paying attention?

Lee hadn't come into this room in a while, either. I recalled that just the other day, she'd said she could not stand to be in the lean-to anymore. Maybe it was too cold?

Certainly drafts swirled in the room. The vines must have compromised the windows. I investigated. Yes, and they'd compromised the floor. The dog food was gone, and I had the strange thought that the vines had eaten it. Up close, their veiny green blossoms were formed like the propeller-seeds of maples—or like dragonfly wings. They had that pearly, iridescent sheen. Just now these blossoms riffled in the breeze inside the lean-to.

I stepped outside and hauled the dogs in by their chains. I stoked the fire, layered their beds and all the couch blankets onto the floor and set about bonding with them, stroking their fur and cooing to them. Dogs forgive. Soon we were a pack again, just the four of us. I regretted Lee being apart from this reconciliation, but I was weary. I coiled into the blankets, and we slept into the afternoon.

Lee, all this time, had one arm hanging off the side of the bed. Something hadn't healed just right, and it eased the pain to get some extra blood into her wrist. The whole arm dangled, tempting the new vines that were just then exploring that space between bed and wall. The vines reached out with grasping tendrils thick as fingers. Thinking of me, Lee held onto a wiry hand, squeezed it in sleep. The hand squeezed back. The hand raked through her sweaty hair on its way to her shoulder. It was afternoon, and my feet hit a creaky spot on the floor. Lee moaned, and the hand slipped back to its protected spot between the bed and wall.

"Dogs are out of food," I said from the bedroom doorway. I barely saw Lee in the darkened room and caught no hint of the vine. "I've got to go to town."

I didn't want to drive, didn't want to leave Lee.

"Can you get ginger ale?" she said.

I nodded. Yes, ginger ale, soup, and ice cream. All the foods for sick folks, though Lee wasn't sick. Just aching and scared. And heartsick, same as me.

It was sunny with scattered rain. The dogs enjoyed the ride. I did too. While we sped toward town, the vine repeated its travel up Lee's arm and through her hair, onto her shoulder, over her ribs. Only this time, Lee was awake and staring in awe. Lee's blood moved faster. Maybe the vine heard that or felt it. Felt it, most probably. A pulsing. The vine pulsed back.

While I trudged through the grocery store, the dogs were good. They paced, protecting the car, barking at shoppers who came close to the windows.

While they paced, the vine pushed against certain parts of Lee's body, the places where the breaks had been.

While I stood in the checkout line, a strange shiver went through me. *Lee—Lee's in danger.* Suddenly I needed to hurry home. I fumbled the change the cashier passed to me and left it scattered on the floor.

Another break, that's what I feared.

While the dogs pushed their noses out into speeding air, the vine began entry into the bone. Had it gotten a taste for marrow from the dog food? Or did it already know what it needed to form its fruit and its swarms?

This vine that had infiltrated so much else now plowed its slow way into its first human body. Not *victim.* No one thought of Lee as the victim, neither the vine nor Lee herself. This new thing she hadn't known to fear was come, and it was gentle. It burrowed deep and lay a seed into a crevice of unmended bone. Another seed, another.

While a Miata tailgated so hard I could barely breathe, the first seed sprouted—or egg hatched. It wasn't clear which. Lee felt a thrill. New layered blossoms like corsages opened rapidly from her wrist, from her ribs and leg and arm. She tore off her nightgown to see the wonder of them, celadon green but bordered in rose and gold and a hundred different blues, all rainbow-pearly as oil in puddles. They opened so powerfully that she heard another break. She felt nothing.

The convertible kept veering to pass and then tucking back in behind me. Now, finally, a stretch of empty road opened up. I slowed. The convertible came up alongside—just as a truck entered the road. Someone lay on the horn and I veered, praying. *The dogs, oh, the dogs.*

But we were safe, all of us. We leveled out, slowed onto the shoulder. The red car was far in the distance now. I cried just briefly in relief, the dogs whimpering and licking my neck and face. Dogs have extra senses at times like this.

They felt it, saw it maybe: the anxiety that had held me so long was now dissipated.

While we had our moment on the shoulder, the blossoms grew larger. They grew firm with a lacy coral-like bone. Lee thought of flowers formed of porcelain. The vines that had held her retreated, making her slump and shatter in places. She felt nothing but was aware, watching. Her hand was farther from her body than it had ever been. The wrist was, it seemed, a deep pile of pollen—but animated. Crawling.

Lee was no longer the focus. Whatever happened, on and in her body, was beside the point. One sinewy vine lashed around her mouth, holding her fast to the bedframe, but the rest had moved on, lurking all around the bedroom door, just waiting for the four of us to walk into the room. Maybe the dogs were what it wanted all along, or maybe it would do something novel with my unbroken body. Lee would wait. She would see.

She would speak, soon enough. That last vine would loosen and move on to other entertainments. Later, as I dangled from the ceiling, as the dogs grew their beautiful, terrible wings, as the larval things filled up the air, we would be able to speak, to share notes. What had gone on while I was in town, what would happen next, what did it all mean, how would it end? There was no pain, and so what looked like destruction did not feel like destruction. It felt like a new beginning.

Yes, we would come back together, all five of us now, to share not regret but only wonder.

Familiar Well

~ Eric Witchey

Slinky's best friend lived in the well behind the barn—the one with the rusty iron plate on top and the four locks at places around the edges like a compass. When someone hit her or took her toys or made mamma think she did a bad thing, she ran away from everyone and hid with her friend.

She had to be careful to run into the woods then circle back so nobody would know she came back and sat against the cold stones talking to Emmet. If anybody knew, especially Tilly who'd tattle a lie 'bout it, they'd likely try and kill him. They'd get theirselfs all excited and call him a water monster living in the poison well.

That's what everybody called Emmet's well—the poison well.

Even though all the sweet grass growin' tall around the poison well smelled more alive and tasted sweeter than anyplace else, nobody drank from the well. The farm had three other wells. Two were way far on the other side of the barn, the house, and the chicken field. Those were stone like Emmet's, but they didn't have tops and locks on them. The other well was pretty new and up next to the house and just a long pipe that went way down deep and deeper into the earth until it could suck up sweet water for the house and for keeping animals alive and all. That's the one they used the most. It was the one with a windmill that lifted water up into a tank on top of the house, and it was the one that put water in the troughs and sometimes even the pipes out into the corn-n-gourd fields when they got thirsty.

Emmet called that one a dead well because, "Nobody could live in a well that narrow. For good living, you need a deep stone well with a proper width and maybe a cave at the bottom."

She'd been sitting all quiet with Emmet a while after Tilly had done some mean thing to her when it occurred to her that maybe she didn't remember what Tilly had done. It wasn't tearing the head off her raggedy doll. That was last week. It wasn't hitting. She'd remember that because Tilly left bruises. It wasn't tattling a lie because if that had been it, she'd have heard her mamma calling after her, "Sylvia Jane Millicent Lancolm you get your ass in here, and you bring a switch with you!" Then, after some time of yelling for her, she'd hear, "Slinky! Come on in, Honey. It's okay, Baby. Come on back now."

Of course, she wouldn't. She'd never been that dumb since she was maybe three years old. Now she was eight, and she was practically all adult now. No way she'd be so big a fool as to go back until after dinner when Mamma would think havin' no dinner was enough for a stupid child who didn't know to take her lickings.

She chewed some sweet grass stems, tossed some pebbles at the barn, and named some cloud animals, but she just couldn't remember. "Emmet?" she said.

"Slinky?"

"Did I tell you why I come out here to sit with you?"

"No. You did not, Slinky. Would you like to?"

"I can't 'zactly remember."

"Maybe you just wanted to talk a bit with a friend."

She said, "Might be. You're a good friend."

"As are you, Slinky. If it weren't for you, I'd be terribly alone in this well. I was alone for a long, long time before we chatted the first time."

They sat in silence for a while. Slinky pulled a new stem of sweet grass and chewed the juice out of it. Finally, she said, "Are you a water monster, Emmet?"

"Don't know," he said. "Might be."

"How can you not know?"

"I'm not like you. That's for sure. I do live in the water, so that's a part of it. I'm probably not the one to say if I'm a monster."

"Well, somebody sure wanted you to stay in that well. They wanted it hard."

"Somebody sure did," he said. "They must have thought I was a monster, so maybe I am."

"I don't think you're a monster, Emmet."

"Me either, but I have to allow it might be true. They did go to some trouble to make sure I couldn't get out."

"Do you want to get out?"

Emmet was quiet long enough that Slinky wondered if he had something like sweet grass to chew on for thinkin'. Then, he said, "I think I'd like to look up and see the clouds again, and I think maybe I'd like to go in some different wells and maybe even a pond or a river. I think I used to like rivers a lot, but that was a long time ago. Now, this is my home. I don't think I would like to leave it for long."

"Some days, I think I'd like to leave home," Slinky said.

"Where would you go?"

Three pebbles at the barn later, she said, "I'd like to see Paris some days. I hear it's s'posed to be real nice."

"Is that a well maybe you'd like to visit? Or a river?"

Slinky chewed another piece of grass and flicked a pebble. "I guess it's probably more of a river than a well."

"That's nice," Emmet said.

Dinner that night was pretty good because Tilly weren't there and Mamma and Uncle Ralph and their baby, Reek, were all really quiet. Nobody yelled at her when she came back, so she figured they didn't remember any better'n her what Tilly done.

When she finished mopping up some gravy with her bit of bread, Mamma said, "Slinky, I need you to wash up tonight."

"Ain't it Wednesday? That's Tilly's night."

Mamma's face got pinched up like she wanted to yell a bit, but then it got smooth like it was too tired to stay scrunched up. Mamma said, "The doctor is coming for Tilly. I need you to pick up some chores so me and Uncle Ralph can talk to him."

"Tilly sick?" Slinky asked.

Reek made a wet sound like he always did, and Slinky thought maybe a water monster lived inside him, and then she almost laughed at the idea of Emmet inside Reek trying to talk through his belly button.

Mama said, "Real sick, Honey. Scary sick."

Real fast, Slinky said, "Okay, Mamma," because that was when she remembered why she'd run out of the house. When Slinky was scrubbin' the kitchen floor, Tilly called her "Chore Girl," so Slinky sassed her sister. That's when Tilly fixed to smack her with a fist again.

Slinky jumped up and backed off close to the back door. "I hate you!" Slinky yelled. As soon as she said it, a hot feeling came right into her feet and climbed up her legs. Scared worse, she screamed, "You're sick!" The hot snaked up over her hips, marched up her belly into her right arm then spit itself out the finger she pointed at Tilly.

Just like a shot squirrel, Tilly dropped on the clean floor and commenced to puking her guts out.

Slinky saw that, and she ran out the back door fast as she could. No way she was gonna stay around and get blamed for Tilly getting sick. It weren't her fault, and she weren't gonna clean that floor again nohow. She spent the whole afternoon hiding out with Emmet.

The next day and the next, the doctor came back. On the third day, the doctor told Mama he weren't coming back. No reason to. Nothing to be done. "The girl is past helping," he said. "Best to pray now."

That's what Mama, Reek, and Uncle Ralph all did, too. They commenced to praying like the devil had come to tempt them to sell their souls. Slinky seen them in the big room kneeling at the fireplace like it was an altar. Mamma reached out a hand for Slinky and said, "Come and pray for Tilly with us."

"Come on, girl," Uncle Ralph said.

Reek made a smell that made Slinky pretty sure a water monster really did live inside him, and that smell and all them scared eyes lookin' at her was enough for Slinky. She cut out for the woods, circled back, and settled to sit with her back against the cold stones of Emmet's well.

Without even plucking a stem of grass, she said, "I think Tilly is dying."

"Your sister?"

"Ain't no other Tilly here abouts."

"I suppose not," Emmet said. "What's killing her?"

"I don't know. We was fightin', and she took sick."

"Did you call for the doctor?"

"'Course we done."

Emmet kept quiet until Slinky said, "The doctor won't come by no more, and Mamma and Uncle Ralph and even Reek are all in the living room knee-beggin' to God."

Emmet stayed quiet. He was good at that. It probably come from bein' alone so much in the bottom of a well.

Cloud animals danced across the summer sky.

A couple of mourning doves darted from the barn and across the open yard to the woods.

Finally, Emmet spoke. "Before your Mamma's Mamma was born, and back when I could still go around to other wells and ponds and rivers, your Great Grandma, Selene, grew up here."

Her Greatgram's name made Slinky go all stiff. She looked around for some calamity comin' their way, and when she dint see nothin', she whispered, "Hush. We ain't s'posed to talk about her never, not ever."

Emmet said. "She was like you."

"You take that back!"

"Why?"

"I ain't like her."

"You take the time to talk to me just like her."

Slinky calmed down a mite. Nothin' bad had happened, and Emmet lived in a well, so he likely didn't know a lot of stuff. "Emmet, I don't know how to tell you this, but she was a witch. They come for her in the night, grabbed her, and burned her up."

"Somebody killed her?"

"I said she was a witch. She was hexin' people."

"What's a witch?"

It was Slinky's turn to be quiet. How do you explain a woman what fornicates with Satan to a thing that lives in your well? Finally, she said, "A witch is a woman with powers—a bad woman who hurts people."

Emmet said, "Oh. Then she wasn't a witch. She was always helping people. Once, she pulled water up from my well and boiled it to help a woman having her baby backwards."

"Really?" Slinky sudden-like felt bad asking because Emmet never lied to her, but everybody knew Selene was a witch and got burned for it. "She never hurt nobody?"

"Not that I know of. Once, she told me she pulled up some healing from the earth to fix a foal's leg. Another time, she said she had to touch a man who went stupid after his mule kicked him. She said he got mostly better."

"Mostly?"

Emmet said, "She said that men can be pretty stupid whether they're mule-kicked or not."

Slinky smiled, but it didn't change the fact that Greatgrams had been doin' some hexy stuff. She said, "Them there's all powers, Emmet."

"Sure, she had some power," Emmet said. "But she wasn't a witch. She didn't hurt anyone. She only helped them."

Emmet didn't lie about things, and he didn't say stuff that didn't mean something. Slinky thought for a while about Greatgram Selene and how maybe some stories weren't so true as she been told. After some grass chewin' and some pebble plinkin', she said, "I wish she was here now. Maybe she could help Tilly."

Emmet answered quick—so quick Slinky thought maybe he'd been waiting for her to say just that. "Maybe there's somebody a lot like her who can help."

Slinky squinted at a cloud that looked a lot like a horse with wings. After deciding it needed more legs to be a horse, so it was more like a hawk, she said, "Who?"

"When you were fighting," Emmet said, "did you get really hot in your feet then the rest of you?"

Slinky didn't like to say so, but she said, "Yes."

"Then you," Emmet said. "You have the feeling in your blood like your Great Grandmother."

"No."

"Yes. That's why we can talk. That's why you can go in the woods and nobody can follow your trail. That's why even if they look right at you from the barn, nobody can find you sitting right here next to me."

"Hidin' ain't hexin'."

Emmet ignored her and said, "And that's why Tilly got sick."

Slinky jumped up and ran away. She wanted no more of Emmet telling her she might be a witch and get burned.

After dinner, she saw her sister wide-eyed scared and near to dying in her cot. That's when she started to thinkin' maybe she might listen to Emmet a bit more. Slinky cleared the table and did the dishes real slow so Mamma, Reek, and Uncle Ralph got settled by the fireplace for Uncle Ralph's smokin' and thinkin' time.

Slinky slipped out to talk to Emmet.

Under the paintbrushy splatter of stars across the sky, she rapped on Emmet's iron plate. "You awake?"

"I'm here. Are you okay?"

She tried not to let him know she was half cryin'. "Tilly's real bad sick."

"Yes," Emmet said.

"Can you tell me what to do? What I did? I gotta make it right."

Emmet said, "Close your eyes."

She did.

"Feel down through your toes right through the grass and into the ground. Like a big old oak tree, root your heart down into the warm rivers of life flowing in the earth."

She remembered how it felt when she got mad and pointed—all that heat running up her body like a river. Wiggling her toes, she reached with her feeling heart down and down and . . . and there it was, down in the ground, down where the blood of the world flows and moves the livingness all 'round the earth.

She wiggled her toes again, and the warm come right up into them like she was standing in a yesterday's storm puddle under hot August sun.

"Now," Emmet said, "take hold of the South and East padlocks on my lid, one in each hand."

She didn't dare open her eyes cause the river of livin' might disappear, so she fumbled until she gripped the two locks.

"'Good, Slinky. Now, let the flow move into those locks so they know what you want."

The river of heat come up her legs and belly. It moved like water through her arms into her hands and into the iron locks.

Those locks remembered that before the forge they was sand in the ground, and they snapped themselves free and fell away like Uncle Ralph had hit them with a sledge.

Her eyes snapped open, and she looked at her empty hands. On the ground at her feet, the locks melted away into red sand that just sank down into the earth and was gone. "I broke 'em," she said. "Oh, God. I broke 'em just like I broke Tilly."

"No, Slinky," Emmet said. "You helped them go home. You helped me, and you're going to help Tilly." Where the locks had been, the near edge of the iron plate bulged upward, bent a bit, and lifted. Two brilliant yellow cat-slit eyes caught starlight.

Slinky jumped back.

"It's okay," Emmet said. "It's just me." A flat, glistening red-black head pushed outward. A four-toed hand pulled on the edge of the well. With a pull and wiggle, a long, flattened, glistening body and tail followed until the whole slick Emmet plopped down on the grass between the well and Slinky.

A little afraid and a little curious, Slinky touched a finger to Emmet's head. Her finger found cool, damp skin. She said, "You ain't no monster. You're just a real big salamander."

Emmet chuckled. "I've been in the well a long time."

"Should you be out? Folks might gonna notice a slick salamander big as a panther slitherin' round."

"Yes," He said. "But I'm your salamander just like I was Selene's."

"I'm not sure that's so good an—"

Emmet lifted a four-toed front foot to hush her. "A nice thing about being your salamander is you can make me look like whatever you want."

She remembered the scared and maybe gonna die look on Tilly's face in the cot, and she decided that helpin' was maybe better'n arguin' just now. "Well, we gotta do somethin' if you're gonna help Tilly."

"You, Slinky. I'm going to help you."

She put her hands on her hips like Mama and wished she had her a wooden spoon, too. "You mean help me help Tilly. Right?"

"Of course." Emmet lifted his broad, flat head and fixed his yellow starlight eyes on her. "What do you think I should look like?"

"Maybe a boy my age or a dog or somethin' that fits in 'round here."

Before she could think of something else folks wouldn't notice too much, Emmet stood up on his hind legs and commenced to melting all over and to twisting like he was made of chink mud and to shifting some and lifting some and stretching some until he was a barefoot boy a bit taller than Slinky and wearin' an old-time Sunday suit with a tall hat, a string tie, a split-tail coat, and a silver watch chain. Even though the suit crumpled up on him like it was hands-me-down from an older brother or cousin, it seemed like a fittin' in thing for him to be wearin'.

His smile went all wide and starlight bright and full of joy and life. His big yellow eyes sparkled like shooting stars. "Thank you, Miss Slinky. Thank you ever so very much." He took her hand in his four-fingered boy hand and kissed it like she was a lady in a story.

Slinky jerked her hand back. "You Satan?" Sayin' it, she knew she kinda hoped so 'cause she figured she knew enough stories to figure out how to sell her soul to fix what she done to Tilly. She hoped she didn't have to fornicate with Emmet's salamander self.

"I am certainly not," Emmet said.

Slinky relaxed a bit. "Then what zactly are you?"

"I am part of that living earth feeling you can touch, and you decided to see me like this."

"I did not. I would not turn some old salamander into—"

Emmet's deep laugh interrupted her.

She stared at his all-happy face in the starlight.

When he caught his breath from laughing, he said, "We'll talk the how and what of things later. Right now, listen to me if you're going to make Tilly right."

Slinky went quiet.

Emmet said, "I'll lift up the well cover a bit, and you draw out some water."

"We can't slip a bucket under there. It's too tight."

"We don't need a bucket. Just a bean tin and a long bit of baling twine from the barn."

Slinky kenned him right away. She ran and gathered up the stuff then they dipped up some water.

Slinky, holding that bean tin full of well water like it was made of liquid gold, let the frumpy-suit Emmet boy lead her toward the house with him whispering in her ear all the way.

A few days passed after Slinky life-warmed that cup of water from the poison well and gave it to Tilly. Come a mid-afternoon, Slinky ran away 'round through the woods to the well. Of habit, she set down with her back against the circle of stones, knowing true that Emmet had gone on and away after they healed her sister.

Slinky was bustin' to tell him Tilly was all fixed now and a lot nicer, and she had to tell somebody she felt a little bad about that 'lot nicer' bit. She worried maybe the hexin' made Tilly a bit not who she used to be.

"She is." Emmet's voice near scared her dead even though it come right up from the well just like always. Slinky jumped away and twisted around until she was on her hands and knees starin' at the iron cap and the stones.

Emmet said, "Now, she just knows better than to hurt you."

"You came back!" Slinky crawled across the grass and hugged the stones of the well, and she was pretty sure she'd'a hugged Emmet himself even if he come up out the well as a slick-skinned, panther-sized salamander.

Emmet said, "Took a long walk is all. Visited the river and the pond. Looked in on the other wells."

"Just like you said."

"Of course. I told you this was my home."

"Yes. Yes, you did." Her face heated up a bit, but not full of the living heat, just with the embarrassment of forgetting that Emmet never lied to her.

"Slinky?"

"Yeah, Emmet?"

"Would you mind breaking off the other locks and taking the iron cap off a while so I can see the sky?"

"Sure enough, Emmet. Right now." She come close up and grabbed the North and West locks, one in each hand, and commenced to conjuring up some livin' and lock rememberin' from the earth.

"Don't break them so much as the other ones," Emmet said, "We'll want to put the lid back on and hang the locks like they aren't broken."

She kenned him quick and slowed down her conjurin' to make sure the locks didn't get too excited about bein' sand again.

Once she slid that lid off, she sat down against the stones. Emmet come up out the well enough to get his wide, flat head up on the stones by her shoulder. Quiet and happy, they watched the clouds together.

Eventually, Emmet said, "In a few years, I think we should go to Paris."

Slinky smiled. "I'll be growed all up then." She watched a cloud goose chasin' a tick hound across the sky then said, "You think you'll grow into that suit of yours?"

"If you want me to. You think I should wear it to Paris?"

"Yup. I think it's just the thing."

Emmet asked, "How far will we have to swim to get there?"

Slinky plucked a stem of sweet grass and chewed it for a while. Eventually, she come to think maybe she should explain about Paris being a city and not a river or a well. Instead, she said, "If we was clouds, we could fly."

Emmet said, "There's a lot of water in clouds."

Slinky smiled, wiggled her toes into the grass and dirt, pulled up some life into her toes, pointed up at that 'ol dog-chasin' goose, and pushed and pulled the conjurin' on that goose just enough to get her wings flappin'.

Satisfied, she let the goose go on across the sky after the dog. In a couple years, she'd about have flyin' figured. That was plenty of time to explain Paris to Emmet. Slinky sucked in the lazy smell of summer heading on toward harvest and pulled herself a stem of sweet grass to chew.

Dinner Time

~ *Erica Sage*

Every day was dinner for Janice Godspeed.
Every damn day.
"John," she called.
"Mary," she called.
And the children raced to the table, insatiable.
The plates lay ready at their places. Her husband, fork poised in the air, waited at his seat.
The children grabbed their forks, hands in fists, prongs to the ceiling. All eyes were on Janice, heads tipped back and ready. Their eyes big and ready. Lips moist and ready. Tip of the tongue, ready.
Janice went to the garage for the tool box. She carried it to the dining room and set it on the floor next to the table.
"How was school today?" she asked as she lay her napkin across her lap.
"Stupid," John said.
"Boring," Mary said.
The children leaned toward their mother, eager for dinner.
"And how was work?" Janice asked her husband Gary.
"Marty said he'll stop by," he answered instead. Janice's brother always stopped by for dinner.
Janice leaned down to the toolbox next to her chair, unclicked the hinged, and took out the heavy sheers. She held her hair taut with her left hand, and positioned the sheers against her scalp with her right hand. The blades cut through in one effort. She placed the chunk of hair on John's plate. His fork dove in, lifted the strands, and he spun the strands around the prongs. He didn't wait for his sister before he took it into his mouth. Janice did the same with the hair on the right side of her head. This went to Mary. The hair at the back, which she held taut above her head in order to reach it with the sheers, went to her husband.

Dinner was a bit later tonight. Her family was famished. They shoved strands into their mouths.

"You need to chew your food," Janice said.

The children looked up.

"Oh, gawd," they said, disgusted.

This got her husband's attention. "Jan, baby. It makes it really hard to eat when we've got to look at you."

She'd heard this before. She set the sheers on the table, went to the closet, and grabbed a scarf to put over her nearly bald scalp.

Scarf tied under her chin, she picked up the sheers. She used them to cut her fingernails, and she put the nails in three teacups. She added her toenails too. She gave them each a cup.

"That's not so bad," her husband said, looking at the nails, not her hands.

The doorbell rang.

The door opened before she had a chance to stand.

Marty. He nodded brusquely and shut the door behind him. He dragged a chair from the kitchen, took a place between the children.

"Uncle Marty!" they cheered.

Janice sighed. She leaned over the tool box, replacing the sheers. She took out a butcher knife.

She leaned back in her chair and placed her foot in front of her brother. He was too busy sneaking her nails out of the children's teacups to notice.

"Can you help at least?" Janice said.

Marty took the knife. "Can you hold still at least?"

"I haven't moved an inch."

Marty lifted his arm up above his head and came down hard. Her foot rolled on its side and fell off the table.

"Gawd, mom," the children said.

"Do you have to do that at the table?" her husband asked, mouth open in disgust, a fingernail stuck in the gap between his front teeth.

"There isn't any silverware," Marty said.

Janice stood. She hopped on her one foot toward the kitchen, lost her balance, grabbed hold of the wall. She hopped again, rested on the back of a couch. Hopped again toward the silverware drawer, caught herself on the counter.

"Mom!" John called.

"Mom!" Mary called.

Of course they were still hungry. Janice knew that hair and nails would never be enough. "One moment, please."

The telephone rang.

Janice hopped toward the phone, silverware in hand.

The phone rang again.

Janice hopped.

"Jeezus Christ," her husband said. "I'll get it." He shoved his chair back, stood, and snatched the phone off the receiver. "Hello?" he barked. "Oh. Hey, Sherry," said Gary, ever so sweet.

Janice, finally returned to the table, handed the silverware and napkin to her brother.

Her husband continued, "Yeah. Always. Of course." He placed the phone on the receiver. "Your mom is on her way."

"Grandma!" The children cheered.

"You better get something on the table before she gets here," Marty said, as he used his steak knife to cut off the big toe.

"Is my father coming?" Janice asked Gary.

"She didn't mention it, but you know he always shows up sooner or later."

That was true.

Janice stood and made her ungainly way back to the kitchen for more silverware and plates.

"Kids, help your mom," Gary said.

But no one moved. They nibbled at the nails and watched Uncle Marty cut each toe off and pop them into his mouth. Janice brought the silverware in one trip, the plates in a second.

"Can you just give me one piece, Uncle Marty?" John asked. "You never share."

That was also true. So, by the time Janice fell back into her seat at the table, the kids were glaring at her.

She kept the butcher knife on the table. She'd need it later, and probably Marty would too when he had eaten all the toes.

Janice took out the bone saw. She lifted her dress to her hips and tucked it under her rump. She positioned the saw at a diagonal below her pubic bone. She started sawing. The blade dragged across the skin, pulled at the tendons. The bone was unyielding. She adjusted her angle. She was sweating with the effort. Perhaps the blade wasn't sharp enough.

Her husband coughed. "You're gonna need the electric saw," he said, not looking at her, but at one of her hairs he'd pulled out of his throat.

She placed her one foot on the floor, away from the blood that would no doubt send her slipping to the floor, and braced herself against the table. Once up, she hopped back to the kitchen, using the same route as before. Her leg, not fully attached now, swung awkwardly with each bounce. Finally in the garage, she found the electric saw. She was slow returning to the table. Though, with mouths full for the moment, her family hadn't seemed to notice her absence.

Janice plugged the saw into the outlet nearest her chair. She clicked the switch, and it roared to life. The kids started and plugged their ears.

"Do you have to be so loud?" they shouted at her.

Janice put the saw in the wound, pressed it against the bone. It shifted and bounced. "I think the blade is pinched," she said. The family shook their heads at her. "I think it's pinched!" she shouted.

Her husband shrugged and leaned back, picking at his teeth. With her left hand, she pushed on her knee to bend back the bone, to give the blade some room to cut through. Her leg, finally loose, lobbed to its side and hit the floor with a thud.

A spatter of blood hit her daughter's shoe. Indignant, Mary gaped at her mother. Her brother handed her a napkin.

Janice bent down and picked up the leg, set it on the table. She stood, leaned against the table with her right hip, and positioned the saw just above the knee. As the saw whirred, she pushed until the leg fell in two large parts. She lay the thigh on her son's plate, her calf on her daughter's.

"I don't want the part by her butt," John said.

"I don't want the part by her foot," Mary said.

The doorbell rang, and the door opened. Her mother came in. "You didn't bother to wait?" she said to her daughter.

"I'll get you a chair, Ma," Marty offered, his mouth full of meat, Janice's heal in his hand.

"I'd appreciate that," she said, glaring at Janice.

Janice picked up the butcher knife. She placed her left hand, palm flat on the table where her plate should be. She chopped off her left hand, and set it on Mary's plate. She moved her calf to her mother.

"I'll share this with your father when he gets here," her mother said, reaching for a knife and fork.

The doorbell rang again.

Gary looked to Janice.

Janice shrugged. She simply couldn't get up at this point.

Gary resigned to opening the door himself. But it wasn't Janice's father, as expected. It was their neighbor, Mrs. Greely, who lost her husband the year before to cancer.

"I don't mean to be a bother, but I saw you were hosting others, so I just thought I'd stop by for a family meal."

Janice steadied her elbow on the table and chopped her left arm just below the joint. She wrapped the freshly bleeding nub in a paper towel, and handed it to Mrs. Greely. The elderly woman took a bite without hesitation, wiping the blood off her mouth with the back of her hand.

"There's a lot of blood on that one," John said.

"Gross," Mary said.

The front door opened, no doorbell or knock, and Janice's father came in. He didn't shut the door behind him. He carried a chair from the kitchen and sat down next to his wife. Janice eyed her mother's plate. She had in fact not saved anything for her father. Janice cut her arm off at the shoulder, picked it up off the floor where it had landed, and passed it to her father, who took it in two hands. Her father looked around for a larger plate and sighed when there wasn't one to be found.

Janice leaned back in her seat for a moment, wiping her one hand on her dress.

Everyone at the table chewed their meat, smiled at each other, shared bites of the sweet parts, traded favorites for favorites.

Footsteps coming up the porch caught Janice's attention. Her father hadn't shut the door, and she'd forgotten to do it (even if she could). She needed to remember to shut it. Really, to lock it.

A man stood at the threshold. Janice recognized him as the homeless man that lingered at the gas station. Behind him came Marty's ex-wife. Behind her was John's best friend's mother. The three walked in, and no one shut the door behind them.

Gary chewed his food, unconcerned about the door.

Janice cut off her right foot.

The conversation at the table was lively. Where was the homeless man from originally? Marty's ex-wife had gotten a new job. John's best friend's mother was reading a delightful book for her book club.

She started the saw, and she couldn't hear if the discussion continued.

Janice's right leg rolled to the floor. She sawed it at the knee, and put the hunks on the table. Gary stood and carved the leg chunks into smaller pieces, serving each of them in kind. John held the thigh to his mouth, plenty of meat left, so held up his hand when his dad offered him a slice of calf.

The pastor of their church knocked on the door frame as he made his way in and to the table. "You have some of that to go, I imagine."

A woman had followed him in and now stood by his side.

Noticing her, he said, "Welcome, I'm Pastor Hayden." He reached out his hand.

"Crystal," the woman said, politely enough, keeping her own hands on her purse strap. She turned to Janice. "Truly, you're the most selfish woman I know. Here I am again, and you've got nothing left." She swept her hands through the air. "Nothing."

Janice looked down at her pelvis, legs gone. Left arm gone.

"Jan," Gary said, mouth full. "You gonna say something to this broad?"

Janice only had her right hand and arm. She needed those to serve dinner.

"You always have an excuse," Crystal continued. "No one can count on you."

Janice eyed her family. They didn't nod or agree, but neither did they protest. They just ate.

Janice opened the toolbox drawer and took out the filet knife her husband used to clean the trout. Both of her ears came off in one slice each.

Her friend snagged an ear from Janice and marched out of the house. The pastor watched her go, then turned back to wait for Janice, his hands on his hips.

Janice put the second ear on the table and used the sheers for her tongue. She scooped out her left eye with a spoon.

Gary took the tongue and eye, picked up the ear, and put them on a paper towel. He grabbed the three left-over toes from the homeless man's plate for good measure. He balled up the paper towel and handed it to the pastor. The pastor walked out the door and down the porch steps, brushing by another man.

"Knock, knock," the man said. "Should I leave this here?" He held out a package.

"What's that?" Gary asked, marching toward the door. "Do I need to sign for this or something?"

"Nope."

"You wanna stay for dinner?" Gary asked.

Janice tried to catch his eye. There wasn't enough of her to go around as it was. But thankfully, the delivery man said, "I see you've got a house full. Thanks though." He waved to the guests around the table and headed down the porch steps.

"I wonder what the hell this is," Gary said as he returned to the table. He grabbed his steak knife and stabbed through the packaging tape, slicing it cleanly from one side of the box to the next. "I don't remember ordering anything." He ripped open the cardboard flaps and peered inside. "Well, I'll be damned, I'd forgotten about this." He laughed and pulled out a small, white box. He tossed it across the table to Janice. "I got it for your birthday!" He laughed again.

Her birthday had been nine weeks ago.

"What'd you get, Mom?" John asked.

"Yeah, what'd we get you?" Mary asked.

Her family and the other guests waited, grinning.

Janice passed around her gift with the blue print. Scalpels. Disposable, Sterile. #10.

Gary stood up and held the package on his lap wide open for everyone to see. "And I got you ten of 'em."

Indeed, Janice saw nine more boxes. One hundred disposable scalpels.

She opened her mouth to speak, but then remembered. She'd already cut out her tongue.

As Big as a Whale

~ *Avra Margariti*

1

The astronomer's second wife called her husband *Darling* and *Dearest*. Their boy—three and a half vibrant years, two dimples, one missing front tooth—called him *Father*. The gargantuan whale circling their galactic observation tower expels echolocation groans across starlit dark matter, splashing with languid intent over the astronomer's sonogram sensors. Through the lens of his telescope, her sight etches itself in silver thread onto his retinas. The whale doesn't acknowledge the astronomer. He is but a cosmic speck on her back that has borne millennia of creation and destruction.

Ever since the marble orrery which contained the astronomer's second wife and son was swallowed by the whale, nobody calls the astronomer anything in his empty tower amidst the half-known universe.

He's called the whale his nemesis long before that.

2

The whale isn't gray or black or even white. She swims through deep space and shadow matter, a rainbowed shimmer clinging to her thick skin, like nacre or the underside of Jupiter's rings.

The astronomer holes himself up in his highest tower, surrounded by astrolabes and vellum scrolls. The observatory—resembling a black-stone keep—is held aloft through an esoteric blend of science and alchemy. His old laboratory in the west wing lies in shambles, the reinforced glass shattered, half of his instruments obliterated under the whale's menace. Delirious, he contorts his spine over his new journals, scribbles of squid ink only he can read, while his tea grows death-cold and gibbous moons of mold sprout from his toast.

Hypothesis: The whale is the keeper of all the secrets of the universe.

He turns a page and watches his pen wobble. *It's a wicked world in all meridians.* He doesn't remember writing this.

A bellow sounds from outside, deep and velvet matte, high-pitched and silky silver. The bellow encompasses everything the universe has to offer. The whale does, too. The astronomer often wonders about what he'd find if he could dissect her. Just a tiny, tender piece. He bruises his eyes against his telescope, catching flicks of the whale's dorsal fin, her flippers, her tail flukes. They leave comet trails of stardust behind them. Tainting the sky, taunting him forevermore.

Blindly, the astronomer extends a hand to his left, expecting the orrery's smooth planets within easy reach, to stroke and whisper to them, *soon, soon the whale will be captured and you shall be free.*

But the marble orrery is gone, last he saw it caught between the needle-sharp, turret-sized teeth of the whale. The astronomer's hand knocks his tea over.

-3

The astronomer is also an astrophant: someone who reveals the sacred secrets of stars. He shoots tridents and harpoons from his observation deck. Sixth-magnitude stars are the dimmest, therefore easiest to catch. He reels them in, spreads them out under his scalpel and microscope. His harpoon gun, however, is far too small and flimsy for his great, cosmic archenemy. He attempts to order a bigger weapon from the space pirates that roam this part of the galaxy. When he cannot strike a deal—when even the back-stabbing mercenaries blanch at the thought of crossing the whale—the astronomer decides to build his own device.

Yet his meticulous notes and designs, his formulas and measurements, always end up ink-smudged or vanished altogether come morning. Sometimes he suspects his wife and son, although he's never caught them in the act. Other times, he thinks they'd never disobey him. Not like his first, wilful wife, eaten by the whale some years ago. Perhaps this floating observatory is haunted by ghosts after all.

-2

The whale dances, but sings also. He's recorded the frequency of the wavelengths but has had no luck decoding them. At least not when the song is directed toward the abstract vastness of the cosmos. When the astronomer's wife brings his lunch to his laboratory, the whale's song shifts, the sonogram spiking. The second wife pauses, plate-laden tray held aloft, as the echolocation music morphs into a sea shanty. Certain passages almost resemble a mating call. When the astronomer's son visits his father for a goodnight kiss on his sweaty, salty forehead, the song mellows into a lullaby.

The second wife often sleeps in the boy's bed, cradling him in dreams, nautili in their shells. Alone in his tower, the astronomer sends recordings of himself, like harpoons, out into the universe. He tries to communicate with the whale that stole his first wife, but her response resounds with flat apathy rather than its customary polyphony. If there are traces of anger woven through the rumbling notes, it's the type of anger a person experiences toward an incessantly buzzing mosquito.

The astronomer detests this. He can take being hated, but he cannot abide being ignored.

3

Dust gathers over every surface. The astronomer places it under his microscope to ascertain it's not made of the stars swirling outside his window, or ghosts. Then again, everything is stars. Everywhere he looks are ghosts.

Dishes pile in the sink. The stone dulls, the tower falls into disrepair. When not a single crumb remains, the astronomer is forced to call the intergalactic delivery company for supplies. He stands in the doorway, oxygen mask secured haphazardly over his face, when his order arrives. He prefers when it's a little robot bringing the groceries. The flesh-and-bone delivery boy cannot hide his surprise at the sight of the astronomer: his ink-stained robe and weeks-old facial hair, the dark circles and glazed over eyes.

"Doctor," the boy says, collecting himself. "I trust your wife and son are well?"

"Hmm?" The astronomer peers over the boy's shoulders, but the whale is gone. Only the boy's enchanted velocipede hovers obediently behind him. "Oh, them. The whale got them."

Unlike the last times anyone inquired after his wife and son, the astronomer doesn't have to lie.

The delivery boy's eyes widen to the size of moons behind his mask. "Doctor! Should I talk to the men at the fuel station? Arrange a hunt?"

The astronomer shuts the door in the boy's slack face. "No need. The whale is mine."

-]

The second wife isn't as young or pretty as the first, but she's good at what she does. As she cleans the observatory to a black-diamond shine and washes their clothes and linens, she sings sea shanties of old. While hearty stews simmer on the stove, she recites poetry, likening the observatory to a lighthouse and, more and more lately, a floating prison. She walks through the halls like an echo, wielding her feather duster as a maestro's baton. Sometimes she pauses, head tilted, listening to strains of ghosts. She always picks the sweetest songs and saddest poems when the ghosts are listening.

Reach me down my Tycho Brahe, I would know him when we meet.

The astronomer bristles and blazes like an imploding star. This was his first wife's favorite poem. "Where did you find it?" he demands, but his second wife only blinks. The astronomer tears the tower apart but finds no book of poetry. From then on, he prohibits songs and poems of any kind.

The astronomer's son has never seen the sunlight. Day and night, the world outside remains unchanging in its blackness. It might be cruel raising him here, but the astronomer believes you cannot miss what you've never known. The boy sprints up and down the spiral staircases, banging sticks and toys against frigid stone. When his toys are taken away, he takes to slamming himself against the walls. His arms and legs at first, then his head. Each heavy thud, each string of toddler talk, drives migrainous holes deeper into the astronomer's skull as he hunches over his formulas. He needs to know things, and to know things he needs to study the whale, and to study the whale he needs to capture it, and his first wife with it. But to do all that, he needs silence above all.

"I'm working," he shouts. "Make him stop, or I'll do it."

But even when the wife and son fall quiet, a paranoid part of him thinks they're still communicating. It's the way stars talk to one another, on nearly untraceable wavelengths. Echolocation, the whale's cosmic language he has yet to decipher.

The astronomer leaves his laboratory in a flurry of white robes. Throbbing headache and unfurling fury, he searches the tower for his wife and their undisciplined son. He finds her at their bedroom's window, body locked in a swaying dance, eyes fogged over. Her hands roam hypnotic over her own body, mouth opening and closing in soundless motifs. The whale is outside, swimming tight circles, opening and closing her great maws.

"Do you talk to her?" the astronomer asks, clutching his wife's upper arms with bruising strength. "What lies is she spewing?"

"Let me go," his second wife says.

He doesn't.

Somewhere in the distance, his son wails and bellows.

-4

The astronomer's first wife was young and beautiful, and eaten by the whale. That's what he told his second wife, and what she in turn told their son.

The astronomer lies, yet the astronomer remembers.

How the first wife walked out of the the tower and into the universe without an oxygen mask, her unshod feet barely touching the floor, her pearly mouth shaping the familiar lines of an old poem.

I have sworn, like Tycho Brahe, that a greater man may reap.

The astronomer watched from his laboratory, too late to run, too curious to stop her.

The first wife—so young, so beautiful—moved like a ghost in her white, gauzy gown woven with starlight. It billowed out around her calves, stretching taut over her half-moon belly growing fuller by the day. She walked down the boardwalk of the floating keep, while the whale's perennial dance changed from a solo to a pas-de-deux. At the end of the boardwalk the whale awaited; its mouth wide open, teeth glittering with secrets. The first wife curtsied before stepping so gracefully, so eagerly, into the mouth of the whale.

0

The astronomer's second wife cried *Darling, no, Dearest, please* when he discovered the alchemy that would trap her inside the marble orrery. His son wailed *fatherfatherfather* when he joined his mother in their own miniature Venus, set like a a paperweight upon the astronomer's desk.

"You'll be safe here," the astronomer tells them, stroking the curved glass as they pound against it from the inside. "Away from the whale."

They'll be safe and protected, and he will be free of nuisance and distraction, left to do his sacred work undisturbed.

When the whale swims to his laboratory's window like a silent, hulking ship, the astronomer is too absorbed in his research to notice. He looks up in time to see her giant tail slam against the glass magicked to withstand the pressure of outer space. It smashes into a thousand tiny pieces. The astronomer doesn't have time to reach for a mask or a harpoon. He's never seen the whale without glass separating them. Her eye is bigger than a black hole. It brings all the fears of humanity to the surface. *I've been here before you*, it says, *and I will remain after you're nothing but stardust, and after the dust eats itself, regurgitating a new universe.*

The astronomer gasps from the lack of oxygen and the plethora of knowledge. When the whale opens her mouth to snatch the marble Venus containing the astronomer's wife and son, he can do nothing but scream. The whale cradles the marble carefully between her rictus smile. Then, she's gone.

The astronomer remains in the glass wreckage for a long while, puffing into an oxygen mask, intoxicated by the eldritch encounter and his own fury.

4

The astronomer sits at his desk, writing, despairing. All his experiments fail, all his hypotheses prove weak and foolish. The view is dim through his magnifying glass, the ink bleeds illegible through his parchments. He's heard of planets where people's sins manifest as demons, stuck like humps on their owners' backs, bending them in half with the weight of guilt. A poet might have claimed the whale is one such manifestation. The astronomer never did like poetry.

Even stronger than the guilt is the righteous anger. Anger that his wife and son will learn everything the whale hid—all the secrets of the universe revealed from the inside out—and he won't. He pictures his first and second wife meeting in the belly of the beast. They orbit each other in mistrust at first, then gravitate closer and closer together. They fall in love, familiar ghosts engaged in a long-awaited dance. They paint constellations against the whale's walls, figures and formulas the astronomer can never dream of. The two former wives raise his children together, all four of them speaking in echolocation, the language of whales and stars.

Celestial bodies dance outside his window, and the whale does too. The astronomer sleeps in his dusty bed, with his dirty clothes and empty stomach. He sleeps, and he fears the starlit night.

CONTRIBUTORS

D Thea Baldrick

As a professional career changer, D. Thea Baldrick's experiences are kaleidoscopic. She has two Bachelor's degrees: a B.A. in Comparative Literature and a B.S. in Biology with a Concentration in Molecular and Cellular Biology. She attended George Washington Law School and spent twenty years homeschooling her children.

Usually residing in Ohio, she lived briefly in Madrid, traveled solo through Europe and occasionally inhabits imaginary landscapes with her grandchildren. She has worked in education, libraries, bookstores, and industries; most recently, as a microbiology technician in a soap company testing for microbial growth. Currently, she writes nonfiction about diseases and poets, and fiction about witches. Sometimes the topics overlap.

Portals to D.Thea's publications are at dthea.com

Hermester Barrington

Hermester Barrington is a retired archivist, a haiku poet, and a deliberately genre-ignorant artist whose most recently published ficciones have appeared in *Fate Magazine, Mythaxis* and *Tales from the Moonlit Path*. For over four decades, he and his impossibly beautiful wife Fayaway have traveled the round earth's imagined corners in search of lake monsters, spelunking sites, and geomagnetic anomalies.

His latest project is a short film celebrating the protozoans of artificial ponds and streams he collected from miniature golf courses in the United States.

Brandon H. Bell

Brandon H. Bell is busy revising his completed novel set in the world of "On a Flayed Horse." His fiction has appeared in *Apex Magazine, M-Brane SF*, and Hadley Rille Books, among others. He edited *Torn Pages* and *The Aether Age* anthologies, both with Christopher Fletcher, and founded the magazine *Fantastique Unfettered*. Brandon lives in the Dallas Metroplex with his family and is working on his next novel, an intimate work about adult siblings, memory, and a wooden sea.

Mary Berman

Mary Berman is a Philadelphia, PA, USA-based writer of science fiction, fantasy, and horror. She earned her MFA in fiction from the University of Mississippi, and her work has been published in Fireside, PseudoPod, Weird Horror, and elsewhere. In her spare time she takes fitness classes and antagonizes her cat.

Find her online at www.mtgberman.com.

Ben Curl

Ben Curl writes speculative fiction when he's not writing damning letters to employers on behalf of union members.

His short stories have appeared as podcasts on *Horror Hill* and *Night Shift Radio*. "The Glass Folio," a tale about a nineteenth-century thief's obsession with a grotesque book that promises immortality, will appear in *Dark Horses: The Magazine of Weird Fiction* in the summer of 2022.

Many of his stories are inspired by self-guided and never-successful ghost hunts amid abandoned mineshafts and karsts in Michigan's Upper Peninsula. He resides in Lansing, Michigan. You can follow him at ben-curl.com or on Twitter @BenjaminCurl

Marilee Dahlman

Marilee lives in Washington, DC, where she writes fiction first thing in the morning and works as a lawyer for the rest of the day. Her other stories have appeared in *Apparition Lit, The Bitter Oleander, Cleaver, Metaphorosis, Orca Lit,* and elsewhere.

She can be found on Twitter @marilee_dahlman.

Scott Edelman

Scott Edelman has published more than 100 short stories in magazines such as *Analog, PostScripts, The Twilight Zone*, and *Dark Discoverie*s, and in anthologies such as *Why New Yorkers Smoke, MetaHorror, Crossroads: Southern Tales of the Fantastic, Once Upon a Galaxy, Moon Shots, Mars Probes*, and the Harlan Ellison tribute anthology *The Unquiet Dreamer.*

His collection of zombie fiction, *What Will Come After*, was published in 2010, and was a finalist for both the Stoker Award and the Shirley Jackson Memorial Award. His most recent collection, *Things That Never Happened*, was published in 2020. He has been a Bram Stoker Award finalist eight times, in the categories of Short Story and Long Fiction.

Additionally, Edelman worked for the Syfy Channel for more than thirteen years as editor of *Science Fiction Weekly, SCI FI Wire*, and *Blastr*. He was the founding editor of *Science Fiction Age*, which he edited during its entire eight-year run. He also edited *SCI FI magazine*, previously known as *Sci-Fi Entertainment*, as well as two other SF media magazines, *Sci-Fi Universe* and *Sci-Fi Flix*. He has also been a four-time Hugo Award finalist for Best Editor.

Rhonda Eikamp

Rhonda Eikamp grew up in Texas and now lives in Germany, land of dark fairy tales and fast highways. Her short stories have appeared in a variety of venues, including *Lightspeed, Lackington's, Nightscript*, and *The Dark*. When not writing fiction, she translates for a German law firm and does Tarot readings for friends with her Salvador Dali deck.

Some of her stories may be found at her blog: https://writinginthestrangeloop.wordpress.com/stories/

Joshua Flowers

Joshua Flowers is a graduate of the University of Maine Farmington and has lived in Maine for over a decade despite a tumultuous history with snow and ice. His work has been seen in *All Worlds Wayfarer* and *Flash Fiction Magazine*.

He tweets his existential crisises @FlowersisBrit.

H. L. Fullerton

H. L. Fullerton writes fiction—mostly speculative, occasionally about being haunted—which can be found in more than 50 anthologies and magazines including *Mysterion, Translunar Travelers Lounge,* and *Lackington's*, and is the author of the somewhat haunting novella: *The Boy Who Was Mistaken for a Fairy King*.

You may follow them on Twitter at @ByHLFullerton.

Elad Haber

Elad Haber is a husband, father to an adorable little girl, and IT guy by day, fiction writer by night. He has forthcoming publications from *Lightspeed* and in the *Planetside* anthology from Shacklebound Books and the *No Ordinary Mortals* anthology from Rogue Blade Entertainment.

You can follow him on twitter @MusicInMyCar or on his website: eladhaber. wordpress.com.

J. Anthony Hartley

J. Anthony Hartley is a transplanted Australian/British author and poet. He has had pieces appear in *Short Fiction, Hybrid Fiction, Short Circuit, Unthinkable Tales, The Periodical, Abandon Journal*, among others. Apart from short fiction and poetry, he also writes the occasional novel.

He currently resides in Germany and can be found at http://www.iamnotaspider.com and on Twitter @JAnthonyHartle1.

Nina Kiriki Hoffman

Over the past four decades, Nina Kiriki Hoffman has sold adult and young adult novels and more than 350 short stories. Her works have been finalists for the World Fantasy, Mythopoeic, Sturgeon, Philip K. Dick, and Endeavour awards. Her novel *The Thread that Binds the Bones* won a Horror Writers Association Stoker Award, and her short story "Trophy Wives" won a Science Fiction & Fantasy Writers of America Nebula Award.

Nina does production work for the *The Magazine of Fantasy & Science Fiction*. She teaches short story classes through Lane Community College, Wordcrafters in Eugene, and Fairfield County Writers' Studio. She lives in Eugene, Oregon.

For a list of Nina's publications, check out: http://ofearna.us/books/hoffman. html.

A. P. Howell

A. P. Howell lives with her spouse and their two kids, sometimes near a lake and always near trees. She has a master's degree in history and her jobs have spanned the alphabet from archivist to webmaster.

Her short fiction has appeared in a variety of places, including *Daily Science Fiction, Little Blue Marble, Martian: The Magazine of Science Fiction Drabbles*,

Translunar Travelers Lounge, *In Somnio: A Collection of Modern Gothic Horror* (Tenebrous Press), and *Los Suelos, CA* (Surface Dweller Studios). She can be found online at aphowell.com or tweeting @APHowell.

Katherine L. P. King

Katherine L.P. King is a horror writer from California. In 2016, she received her MFA in Creative Writing from San Jose State University. Her short fiction has been published in HelloHorror, Coffin Bell, Exoplanet Magazine, Aphotic Realm, and The Sirens Call. When not writing or working at her day job, she can be found whispering secrets to tree blossoms or making candles in her kitchen.

You can find her on Facebook (@katherinelpking).

John Klima

John Klima previously worked in New York's publishing jungle before returning to school to earn his Master's in Library Science. He now works full time as the Technology Manager of a large public library. John edited and published the Hugo Award-winning genre zine *Electric Velocipede* from 2001 to 2013.

When he is not conquering the world of indexing, John writes short stories and novels. He and his family live in the Midwest.

Gerri Leen

Gerri Leen lives in Northern Virginia and originally hails from Seattle. In addition to being an avid reader, she's passionate about horse racing, tea, and collecting encaustic art and raku pottery. She has work appearing or accepted by *The Magazine of Fantasy and Science Fiction*, *Nature*, *Strange Horizons*, *Daily Science Fiction*, and others. She's edited several anthologies for independent presses, is finishing some longer projects, and is a member of SFWA and HWA.

See more at gerrileen.com.

Avra Margariti

Avra Margariti is a queer author and poet from Greece. Avra's work haunts publications such as *Vastarien*, *Baffling Magazine*, *Strange Horizons*, *Lackington's*, *Best Microfiction*, and *Best Small Fictions*.

You can find Avra on twitter (@avramargariti).

Kimberly Moore

Kimberly Moore is a writer and educator. Her short works are published in *Typehouse Literary Magazine, MacroMicroCosm, Fleas on the Dog, Word Poppy Press*, and *34 Orchard*. She lives in a haunted house where she indulges the whims of cats.

For more information, visit kimberlymooreblog.com.

Michelle Muenzler

Michelle Muenzler is an author of the weird and sometimes poet who writes things both dark and strange to counterbalance the sweetness of her baking. Her short fiction and poetry can be read in numerous magazines.
Check out michellemuenzler.com for links to the rest of her work (and her convention cookie recipes!).

Christi Nogle

Christi Nogle is the author of the novel *Beulah* (Cemetery Gates Media, 2022) and the collections *The Best of Our Past, the Worst of Our Future* and *Promise* (Flame Tree Press, 2023). Her short stories have appeared in over fifty publications including the anthologies *XVIII (Eighteen), What One Wouldn't Do*, and Flame Tree's *American Gothic* and *Chilling Crime*.

Follow her at http://christinogle.com and on Twitter @christinogle.

D. T. O'Conaill

D.T. O'Conaill is an Irish cryptocartographer, pseudopsephologist and author of speculative and horror fiction. They are based out of the Sliabh Luachra institute for Hibernofuturism. They have been published in the Jayhenge Publishing Anthology *Grandpa's Deepspace Diner*.

W. T. Paterson

W. T. Paterson is a three-time Pushcart Prize nominee, holds an MFA in Fiction Writing from the University of New Hampshire, and is a graduate of Second City Chicago. His work has appeared in over 90 publications worldwide including *The Saturday Evening Post, The Forge Literary Magazine, The Delhousie Review, Brilliant Flash Fiction*, and *Fresh Ink*. A semi-finalist in the Aura Estra short story contest, his work has also received notable accolades from *Lycan Valley, North 2 South Press,* and *Lumberloft.* He spends most nights yelling for his cat to "Get down from there!"

Visit his website at www.wtpaterson.com.

Wade Peterson

Wade Peterson is the author of the *Badlands Born* series and lives in Dallas, Texas. When not writing, he's in the back yard trying to master the arcane mysteries of Texas barbecue while also wrangling two over-scheduled teenagers, serving the whims of two passive-aggressive cats, and agreeing with whatever wine his wife picks to go with dinner.

You can find more of his stories at wadepeterson.com.

Mattia Ravasi

Mattia Ravasi is from Monza, Italy, and lives and works in Oxford. He has written for *The Millions, Modern Fiction Studies,* and *The Submarine.* His stories have appeared in independent magazines, most recently in the *Wilderness House Literary Review, Flash Fiction Magazine,* and *Planet Scumm.* He talks about books on his YouTube channel, *The Bookchemist.*

Mike Robinson

A writer since age six, Mike Robinson is the award-winning author of ten books, including the dark fantasy trilogy *Enigma of Twilight Falls* and the short story collection *Too Much Dark Matter, Too Little Gray.* His work has sold to Audible, and his short fiction has appeared in over twenty outlets. A lifelong resident of Los Angeles, he is a charter member of GLAWS (Greater Los Angeles Writers Society) as well as a screenwriter and producer. In between, he is a freelance literary editor, hiker, doodler, tries to play baseball again and keeps his two dogs smiling.

Erica Sage

Erica Sage is the author of young adult novel *Jacked Up,* published by Sky Pony Press. Her adult short stories have been published by Underland Press and Indie It Press. When she's not reading or writing, she's spending time with her family, hiking, and gardening.

You can find her in the trees or on Instagram (@erica_sage), Twitter (@erica_sage) , and Facebook (@ericasageauthor).

M. Shedric Simpson

M. Shedric Simpson is the familiar of a small black cat. They studied art in Baltimore, MD, before moving to Seattle to live between the mountains and the sea. They spend their free time crafting stories and other small things.

They can be found online at shedric.com or on Twitter (@inkspiral).

Bonnie Jo Stufflebeam

Bonnie Jo Stufflebeam is the author of the short story collection *Where You Linger & Other Stories* and the novella *Glorious Fiends*. Her Nebula-nominated fiction has appeared in over 90 publications such as *LeVar Burton Reads* and *Popular Science,* as well as in six languages. By night, she has been a finalist for the Nebula Award. By day, she works as a Narrative Designer writing romance games. She lives in Texas with her partner and a mysterious number of cats.

Jordan Taylor

Jordan Taylor's short fiction has recently appeared in *Uncanny* and *The Deadlands,* and was nominated for a 2021 World Fantasy Award. Though she's lived in cities across the US, she's finally settled in North Carolina in a little cottage full of books.

You can follow her online at jordantaylorwrites.com, or on Twitter @JordanRTaylor13.

Charles Wilkinson

Charles Wilkinson's stories have been in *Best Short Stories 1990* (Heinemann), *Best English Short Stories 2* (W.W. Norton, USA), *Best British Short Stories 2015* (Salt), *Confingo, London Magazine,* and in genre magazines/ anthologies such as *Black Static, The Dark Lane Anthology, Supernatural Tales, Theaker's Quarterly Fiction, Phantom Drift* (USA), *Bourbon Penn* (USA), *Shadows & Tall Trees* (Canada), *Nightscript* (USA) and *Best Weird Fiction 2015.* His anthologies of strange tales and weird fiction, *A Twist in the Eye* (2016), *Splendid in Ash* (2018) and *Mills of Silence* (2021) appeared from Egaeus Press. Eibonvale Press published his chapbook of weird stories, *The January Estate,* in 2022. He lives in Wales.

Please visit his website: charleswilkinsonauthor.com

Eric Witchey

Eric Witchey has sold stories under several names and in 12 genres. His tales have been translated into multiple languages, and his credits include over 160 stories, including 5 novels and two collections. He has penned dozens of writing-related articles and essays, has taught over 200 conference seminars, at 2 universities, and at a community college. His work has received recognition from New Century Writers, *Writers of the Future, Writer's Digest*, Independent Publisher Book Awards, International Book Awards, The Eric Hoffer Prose Award Program, Short Story America, the Irish Aeon Awards, and other organizations. His How-to articles have appeared in *The Writer Magazine, Writer's Digest Magazine,* and other print and online magazines.

Subscriptions

Underland Arcana is supported by our kind Patreons, who receive these stories throughout the year in pocket-sized editions, along with other Arcana-related material. Please consider subscribing to the project.

www.patreon.com/underlandpress